THIS IS MY FIRST MOMENT. I REMEMBER NOTHING BEFORE NOW. THERE IS ONLY ME IN THIS MOMENT—ME AND A NAME:

I AM KARONA. I AM MAGIC.

The goddess of Magic has been born on Dominaria, bringing worship, death, and destruction with her.

Against the Scourge, stands one man, three gods at his shoulder and a mighty sword in his hand.

EXPERIENCE THE MAGIC

ONSLAUGHT CYCLE • BOOK III

SCOURGE

J. Robert King

SCOURGE

©2003 Wizards of the Coast, Inc.

Distributed in the United States by Holtzbrinck Publishing. Distributed in Canada by Fenn Ltd.

Distributed to the hobby, toy, and comic trade in the United States and Canada by regional distributors.

Distributed worldwide by Wizards of the Coast, Inc. and regional distributors.

Printed in the U.S.A.

Cover art by Ron Spears
First Printing: May 2003
Library of Congress Catalog Card Number: 2002114090

9 8 7 6 5 4 3 2 1

US ISBN: 0-7869-2956-1
UK ISBN: 0-7869-2957-X
620-17883-001-EN

U.S., CANADA,   EUROPEAN HEADQUARTERS
ASIA, PACIFIC, & LATIN AMERICA   Wizards of the Coast, Belgium
Wizards of the Coast, Inc.   T Hosfveld 6d
P.O. Box 707   1702 Groot-Bijgaarden
Renton, WA 98057-0707   Belgium
+1-800-324-6496   +322 467 3360

Visit our web site at www.wizards.com

I AM KARONA

THIS IS MY FIRST MOMENT. I REMEMBER NOTHING BEFORE NOW. THERE IS ONLY ME IN THIS MOMENT—ME AND A NAME:

I AM KARONA. I AM MAGIC.

I HANG IN THE AIR, AND I NEED NO WINGS TO HOLD ME HERE. MY LEGS DANGLE BELOW ME BUT STAND ON NOTHING. I SHINE. LIGHT BLEEDS FROM EVERY PORE OF MY SKIN. IT GUSHES FROM MY MOUTH AS I SPEAK AND POURS FROM MY EYES AS I GAZE AT THE GREAT DOME BELOW ME.

A TEMPLE. PERHAPS I AM ITS GODDESS.

THE DOME IS WIDE AND LOW, AND IT RISES OUT OF A VAST, PAVED PLAZA. ON ALL SIDES TOWER THE BUILDINGS OF A MIGHTY CITY. PERHAPS THIS IS MY CITY, FILLED WITH MY PEOPLE.

OH, BUT LOOK AT THEM—BROKEN AND BLEEDING, SOME PANTING AND OTHERS NOT MOVING AT ALL. THEY LOOK LIKE TRASH FLUNG INTO CORNERS. WHAT A MESS OF CLOTH AND BLOOD AND FLESH! THE PEOPLE OF THIS CITY ARE DYING OR DEAD.

DID I COME TO SAVE THEM OR TO SLAY THEM?

SOME FOLK LIVE. THERE IS A WOMAN WHO CRAWLS TOWARD A MAN IN TWO PIECES. PERHAPS SHE WILL PUT HIM BACK TOGETHER. ANOTHER MAN DRAGS HIMSELF, TRAILING RED SINEW AND WHITE BONE. WHERE IS HE GOING? HE CLAWS TOWARD ME. ALL THE LIVE ONES DO.

WHAT DO THEY WANT? I TREMBLE TO IMAGINE. DO THEY SEEK REVENGE FOR WHAT I HAVE DONE TO THEM OR PETITION FOR WHAT I MAY DO?

SOME LIE WITH FACES CRADLED IN HANDS, KNEES TUCKED BENEATH THEM. THEY ARE BOWING TO ME. OTHERS REACH IMPLORING HANDS MY WAY OR GAZE IN LONGING TOWARD MY LIGHT. THEIR SHADOWS ARE HUGE BEHIND THEM, LIKE PITS THEY HAVE CRAWLED OUT OF.

WHETHER I AM A GODDESS OR NOT, WHETHER I AM *THEIR* GODDESS OR NOT, I CALL TO THEM: *I AM KARONA.*

THEY WEEP TO HEAR MY VOICE. HEADS STRAIN FORWARD ON BODIES CRUSHED BEYOND HOPE. EYES STARE SO THAT THEIR LAST VISION MIGHT BE OF ME. THEIR ANGUISH RIPS ME APART, BUT THEY CRY MY NAME AS IF IT WERE HOPE.

KARONA? WHO IS KARONA? I MEAN TO SAY IT TO MYSELF ALONE, BUT I WILL NEVER BE ALONE. *WHO IS KARONA?*

THEY WAIL AND SHRIEK IN LOVE OR HATE, BUT NONE CAN ANSWER ME. THEY KNOW MY NAME BUT DO NOT KNOW WHO I AM. I CANNOT BEAR THEIR SCREAMS.

I MUST BE MY OWN ANSWER. THEY WANT ME TO SAVE THEM OR DESTROY THEM, BUT FIRST I MUST SAVE MYSELF. I MUST KNOW WHO I AM.

THE STONE TEMPLE AND THE ROCK PLAZA AND THE RING OF TOWERS SHIFT BENEATH ME. I AM MOVING MERELY BECAUSE I WISH IT. I FLEE THEIR SCREAMS.

THEY FOLLOW, ALL THE LOUDER. THE FACES OF THE PEOPLE, ONCE LIT BY MY GLORY, GROW DARK. THE SHADOWS FROM WHICH THEY HAD CRAWLED SLIDE UP TO OVERCOME THEM. I AM TORN BY THEIR AGONY AND BY MY OWN.

I SOAR WESTWARD INTO THE BRIGHT FACE OF THE SUN AND WONDER IF I AM ANOTHER SUN, BANISHED TO THE WORLD FOR SOME GREAT SIN. OR PERHAPS I HAVE COME TO END SOME GREAT SIN.

I WILL KNOW SOON ENOUGH. I AM KARONA.

CHAPTER 1

AT HER COMING

Stonebrow wept. His hind legs were broken, and he was stranded in the gutted side of a great tower. The giant centaur had been flung there by the blast that had made Karona.

Stonebrow had been very near the center of the explosion. He had carried Kamahl to the height of the domed temple to strike the blow that killed Phage, Akroma, and Zagorka . . . and created Karona. The resulting firestorm had hurled Stonebrow across the temple plaza and into one of the curving towers of Averru. The impact had broken him.

But Stonebrow did not weep for himself. His tears were for her.

So pure a light should not fall on his brokenness and filth. So beautiful a face should not trouble over his hopelessness. He was utterly unworthy of her, yet he desired her beyond all reason. All the world wanted her. Every eye drank her light, every mouth sang her praise. Though it would kill him, Stonebrow must reach her.

Setting massive fingers in the mortar cracks of the floor, Stonebrow dragged himself nearer the edge of the tower. How he would get down, he could not know, but only to be closer to her—even a finger's width . . .

She was going. She faded like a shooting star, irretrievable above the rooftops.

Stonebrow wailed, and his voice joined the thousand more that rose from the plaza to chase her across the sky. Their ecstasy faded with her. It was as if they had witnessed the last shining of the sun, and now there would be only cold darkness forever.

Stonebrow wept.

* * * * *

In a sandy desert, Kamahl walked toward that beaming presence. He had never seen such beauty. A great spirit had come to Otaria, and Kamahl staggered toward her. She was the lodestone of souls, and Kamahl ached to be with her.

What an old thing he was—lean and tall, his skin bearing a green patina. Cuts crisscrossed his body, the terrible price of bringing that great light into the world. It had hurled him from the City of Averru and out into the desert. Now he wished only to return. His gray-black dreadlocks trailed curtains of dust in the air behind him, but he didn't care what lay behind, only what lay before.

She was there, this marvelous one. The sun had set long ago, but the desert glowed like midday, all because of her.

It didn't matter how old and empty Kamahl felt. It only mattered that she would fill him up and make him new.

* * * * *

The deathwurm slid thickly through the shattered wall of the palace, oozed across a broad courtyard, and plunged into Locus Lake. Its massive head, as large as a house, struck first, hurling midnight water to either side. The front half of the league-long beast coiled across the waves even as its midsection slid, scale by scale, from the boot box that had been its home.

This was the deathwurm of Nivea. It held her soul beside its saclike heart, and in turn, she held it from head to tail. A scent drew it along, a glorious scent that resonated through its rubbery hide and into its black heart. Nivea! It smelled her flesh, an intoxicating scent mixed with the odor of great power.

A new life had come into being, and Nivea was part of it. The deathwurm could not resist its call.

The wurm's head reached the sandy shore before its tail even emerged from the box. No true tail, it was a torn, bleeding stump, shaped by the beast's own tooth marks and half-dissolved in its own digestive fluids. With a gory snap of its stump, the death-wurm slithered across the lake and onto land. It threw loops of its body in wide arcs to carry it forward. Trees fell where its coils struck. Faster than any other land-bound beast, the wurm hurdled through the Greenglades Forest and out across the Nightmare Lands. In a scant hour, it had crossed what took armies days to march. All the while, it homed in on that scent.

Abruptly, the black monster riled to a stop. It had reached the edge of the Nightmare Lands, the edge of all Topos, and it recoiled. It feared to leave the fatherland. Ixidor, within, forbade it to go.

The wurm reared up, its muzzle rising a quarter mile into the air, and it bellowed in dread despair. Perhaps the beautiful being would hear and come. Perhaps she would be drawn to it and fly close enough that its mouth might snap out and eat her. Until then, though, the wurm could only wait on the edge of Topos and trumpet its longing.

* * * * *

"Ow!" Waistcoat said, yanking his foot from a root tangle.

"Yikes!" agreed Sash as he pulled a burr out of his sole.

Neither man was very familiar with having feet, let alone balancing on only one, and they barged into each other.

"Hey!"

They fell, arms flailing and mouths wailing before faces and bellies struck the knobby ground. Pain screamed through them. They curled up on their backs like a pair of pill bugs. Slowly, the agony eased, and the ex-unmen opened their eyes. In a cloud of dust, they stared up at the bright-green canopy of Greenglades Forest.

"What a rip these bodies are!" Waistcoat complained.

Sash snorted. "They seem to sense only pain."

"Yeah," Waistcoat agreed, "and they hurt too."

The two men slowly climbed to their feet. They brushed dust from their bruises and coughed it out of their lungs.

"How come these feet are so damned soft?" Waistcoat wondered. "I thought they were supposed to be for walking on!"

Sash prodded a large blister on one foot. "Most people wear shoes. Now we know why."

With a sullen nod, Waistcoat continued down the trail. "Would've been nice to've know before we left the palace. We could've scrounged shoes somewheres. Wasn't there a boot-box . . . ?"

Sash followed, climbing gingerly over a fallen log. "Remember when all we could think of was having bodies? If we had just known how shoddy they are. The feet are just the start. These eyes—useless at night. And who can sleep inside of skin? It itches and throbs and rips and leaks. Everything leaks. Skin, eyes, nose, mouth—"

"Have you noticed this thing hanging down here?"

"Oh, come off it, Waistcoat. You knew about that thing."

"Yeah, but having one's different. Shriveled, wrinkled, floppy, fuzzy, worthless little hose. Heaven help you if you get it caught in a tree stump!"

"Well, that's why folks wear trousers."

"Still, it'd've been nice to've known," Waistcoat said. "Being a roach was so much better."

The two ex-unmen struggled onward over ankle-deep mud, past a hive of yellow jackets, through a thicket of thorns, and down a deer trail full of fierce little rocks.

"And why mosquitoes?" Sash asked viciously.

"Why mosquitoes? Why leeches! Lake Locus is a leech paradise—"

"Look!" Sash interrupted, pointing past a stand of trees. "The edge of the forest." The light beyond the trees was bright and welcoming. "Maybe she'll be just past the trees, waiting!" Sash's feet quickened on the trail.

Waistcoat started to run. "Whatever, I'm ready to be out of this blasted forest!"

Side by side they pelted, ignoring the pain in their feet. Only luck kept them from falling flat out. Sash pulled ahead, his long legs bounding over the rocks. Waistcoat waddled behind, making up for height with vigor. The two ex-unmen streaked between the trees and out onto a wide, flat place—the Nightmare Lands. They skidded to a halt.

Leathery ground stretched from their feet away to the horizon. Here and there, wide round stones plugged the pits that once riddled this place. The Nightmare Lands glowed brightly with dawn, but there was no sign of the beautiful creature they sought. Only a deathwurm lay there like a black wall, lifeless.

"Awww. Who'd've thought? Full of deathwurm, but no light anywhere. Where'd she go?" Waistcoat wondered.

Sash shielded his eyes against the morning sun and squinted toward the horizon. "These eyes don't work at dawn either."

"Dammit, we should've stayed in the palace."

Sash slowly shook his head. "She's out there, still, just a long way off. A long walk."

Waistcoat hissed. "These feet haven't got a long walk in them." He flopped down on the ground, sitting with his face in his hands. "What's the use? Umbra died so we could live, but life is pointless."

"Not pointless," said Sash, slowly shaking his head. "Full of points. And every last one is sticking into my skin!" He huffed awhile.

"What'er you doing?"

"Trying not to cry."

"Does it work?"

"I don't know. I'm new." Looking toward the southwest, Sash seemed to rally. "Life's hard, Waistcoat. We know that much now. It's a struggle from start to finish, but there's got to be a reason for it, or why would so many people put up with it? It's got to have a point. Take this walk, for instance. We do this, and we'll be in the presence of ultimate light."

Instead of answering, Waistcoat picked at the ground. He scraped at one of the sharp rocks that poked toothlike from the soil. Digging around it, he pulled the thing free.

"What're you doing?"

"Making life easier." Waistcoat turned the sharp edge of the rock down onto the leatherlike ground. Pressing, he cut deeply into the soil and carved a wide oval around one foot. Then, beside the oval he sliced two long parallel lines that met at either end. Setting down the rock, he picked at the end of the lines and peeled up a strip, just like a leather strap. He tugged also at the oval until it came up in a thick, round sheet. Folding the oval around his foot, he tied it into place with the long strip. "Shoes."

Sash stared in amazement as Waistcoat pounded the leathery slipper on the ground. The pudgy fellow then started to cut a second one. Sash searched for his own stone.

"You brilliant fellow. Now you're using your head!"

"Not my head. My feet."

Together, the two ex-unmen fashioned shoes for themselves. When they were done, they stood and set out across the Nightmare Lands, toward the place where the great woman had disappeared.

"Do you think we should make some pants for ourselves, too?" Sash wondered.

"Nah. It's a warm day."

"Good thinking," Sash replied.

Newly shod but otherwise nude, the ex-unmen strode along the deathwurm corpse and across the Nightmare Lands.

* * * * *

Braids had spent the better part of two days watching the frantic little devil grow from infancy to adolescence. Actually, it had been the worse part of two days, and Kuberr was no longer so little. He seemed about thirteen—taller than Braids, though gangly, with shocks of thick black hair and smoldering eyes. He had enviable energy, a tremendous resistance to injury, and an endurance that had driven him straight through to the wee hours of the second morning.

Kuberr also had the mood swings of youth.

"Why?" he sang out, his shoulders drooping and his face dropping. "Why did she have to come?"

Braids remained on the silken couch, the one piece of furniture Kuberr had not toppled or soiled. She didn't answer Kuberr. He preferred monologues to dialogues.

"What's the good of being the greatest sorcerer of all time if Mother's gonna hog all the magic?" Kuberr's head dipped even lower, as if he would fold himself in half.

By "greatest sorcerer of all time," Kuberr meant himself. The boy had shown phenomenal power, though his tricks were decidedly juvenile. With a touch, he had turned the walls of his audience chamber black. With a wink, he had made every chair in the coliseum—including the stands themselves—emit a flatulent noise whenever anyone sat down. A wave of his hand had garbed all the Cabal retainers in giant squirrel costumes. Kuberr had even remolded a stone doorstop into what looked like a pile of dog droppings. These were idle spells, mischief magic.

What could this greatest sorcerer do once he actually tried?

"Aren't you even going to comfort me, Aunt Braids?" asked the petulant little god. "Here I am crying on the floor, and there you are lying on the couch." His voice cracked with puberty, and that meant other things lower down were cracking too.

"You're tired," Braids said gustily. "You need sleep. We all need sleep."

"You're not going to sleep there," Kuberr said, rising. He stalked slowly toward Braids, his eyes intent. "That's Mother's couch."

"That's why I've been guarding it. She'd kill us both if I let you destroy it."

Kuberr shook his head, eyes blazing. "You still don't get it. Mother isn't coming back."

Braids sat up wearily, ready in case the boy should try to jump her. "This whole time you've been complaining that she *is* coming back."

"I'm talking two mothers here," Kuberr said. "Karona is the one who came back. Phage, never will."

"What are you talking about?"

"Phage is dead," Kuberr hissed. He wore a look that was either glee or grief. "My other mother took Phage's body—hers and Akroma's and Zagorka's. She took their forms and became a living thing."

"Phage is dead?" echoed Braids incredulously. She trembled, numb. "I can't believe it."

Kuberr slid down to sit beside her. "Her job was simple—make enough war that I could grow to manhood. Do I look like a man? She failed, then she gave her body to Karona."

"She's gone . . . ?"

"No," snorted Kuberr, standing up again. "She's here—here in Otaria. Someday she'll be here in my coliseum. My spells are nothing next to hers."

Blankly, Braids watched the pacing young man. "What will you do?"

A sanguine smile spread across his face. "Put on a great show, even as we die. That's what we do around here, isn't it? Make death into a great show?"

He climbed toward his throne, crossed behind it to a floor-to-ceiling curtain, and ripped it aside. It revealed the coliseum, empty and silent at midnight. The games were the backdrop of the throne, so that anyone who looked on the ruler of the Cabal looked also on the blood-sports he ruled.

"It's time we made this coliseum the center of Otaria. At least then I'll die as king of the world."

He gazed out on the black coliseum. His eyes sketched out figures, and they became apparitions—two men fighting on the sands, tigers circling them and lunging on their chains, fans roaring for blood, coins passing from hand to hand, power pouring into the Cabal's coffers.

"King of the world."

* * * * *

The wurm was so intent on the scent of Nivea, it didn't even notice the two naked morons until they had sauntered well beyond striking distance.

* * * * *

Kamahl had been walking for two days when she came to him. It was as if she sought him out, but how could she? Beautiful, powerful, pure, could she possibly desire one such as he?

The Glorious One hung in midair above the desert. Sand filled the world below, and sky filled the world above, and at their intersection was she. Her wide-swept arms spread into the very clouds, and her robes trailed down like rays of sunlight. Her eyes were twin lamps in her face, and they poured their light on Kamahl.

As if beneath a great burden, he went to one knee, and his other knee came down beside the first. He fell to his belly and hid his face from that wondrous presence.

"WHY DO YOU BOW TO ME?"

Kamahl said nothing. Could she truly speak to him?

"WHY DON'T YOU ANSWER?"

That question tore his breath away. When at last he could respond, his voice was a whisper. "Forgive me."

"WHO ARE YOU THAT YOU DO NOT REPLY?"

"I am Kamahl. I am not worthy to reply."

"WHO IS KAMAHL?"

His heart pounded in exquisite pain. There were many answers to her question. Kamahl is the champion of Krosan. Kamahl is the brother of Phage. He is the slayer of Laquatus, the slayer of Chainer, the Pardic gladiator. None of those answers were true, though, and she deserved the truth.

"I don't know who I am."

She was silent, and Kamahl wished she would incinerate him. He wanted his body to burn away and his soul to join her light.

"WHO AM I, THAT YOU BOW TO ME?"

Again his mind flooded with thoughts: You are life. You are beauty and meaning, everything I long for. "I don't know who you are, but you are greater than I."

"I AM KARONA. I AM GREATER THAN KAMAHL."

She hung there awhile, the air buzzing with her presence.

"WE ARE ALIKE, YOU AND I, KAMAHL. SIT WITH ME."

He lay on his face, unsure what to do. How could he rise before her, but how could he disobey? Kamahl drew his legs up beneath him and pushed his torso upright. He sat on his heels and watched as she descended.

Her feet touched the sand, and it was purified by them. The hem of her robe pooled on the crude ground. She sank farther, to her knees, and sat across from Kamahl. Perfect hands came to rest on her legs. She held her back straight and her head up. Light poured from her eyes and nose and lips. It was as if her face were merely a beautiful mask on a creature of absolute brilliance.

They sat, facing each other. The sun might have run its race once or a dozen times—Kamahl saw no light but her. Here was true bliss, simply to sit before her and drink in her presence.

Then something disquieting came, a rumble as of thunder.

"What is it, wondrous Karona?"

"IT IS THE WORLD. THE WORLD IS COMING."

He saw them now, beyond her, a dark and spreading stain on the horizon. The thunder came from thousands of feet pounding the desert.

"Why do they come?"

"THEY COME AS YOU CAME, KAMAHL."

In their rabid multitude, these people yearned for her, just as he did. They would do anything to reach her. Here was his own desire multiplied a thousandfold. Kamahl bowed his head and sank toward his face.

"NO, KAMAHL. SIT UP. YOU MUST SEE THIS. YOU MUST SEE WHAT THEY DO."

He straightened and looked first at the Glorious One then at the bloodthirsty tide of Kamahls. They swept in to encompass the world.

CHAPTER 2

OUR ANSWERS LIE

The throng roared as it converged. Centaurs and cavalry galloped in the lead, ahead of a mob of mantises. Behind them came elves, fleet and dogged, and avens in double-time phalanxes, with humans and goblins at their heels. At the rear marched dwarfs and a vast amorphous crowd of stragglers. Without food or water, tents or medical supplies, this crowd of ten thousand had followed Karona onto the desert. Despite their diversity, they were one in desire.

Every eye was trained on Karona. Every mouth gaped an idiot's grin.

They were just like Kamahl. Without sword or even staff, he shifted to stand and fight off this army.

"No. Do not raise a hand. Sit still and watch. Who is Karona? Who is Kamahl? Our answers lie in what they do."

Kamahl tucked his knees and sat still. It was agony to kneel while an army arrived in full charge, but to look at Karona made even agony bearable. Surely she was the greatest good that had ever come to Dominaria.

With a sound like sudden hail, hooves pounded the ground. Horses churned the sand as they stomped to a halt. Riders leaped from horseback and dived toward Karona. They buried their faces in the dust, and their hands grasped the hem of her robes. Not to be outdone, the centaurs bounded in among them—sometimes atop them—to fall before her and cry out their desire. One beast man cantered up the back of a prostrate man, breaking his spine. The centaur went to his knees and crushed the man utterly. On a bleeding prayer mat, he made his tearful entreaties to Karona.

Kamahl stared, appalled at the trampling death. Others were dying. Body by body, the wall of flesh built up around Karona.

At a run, the elves approached. Arrows leaped from their bows and thudded into the meaty backs of the centaurs. Some points burst through hearts and out the chest wall, and those victims fell immediately. Other centaurs could only roar, three or four shafts pinning them. Still, they did not rise to do battle but only cried out to Karona, their hands imploring. The arrows had stopped, but the shooters arrived, swords flashing. Elves wielded their blades like machetes, cutting through the thicket of centaurs. They dragged the dead forms back and ambled like spiders over them. Bowing low, elves reached bloody hands to grasp Karona's robe.

"Do you see, Kamahl? Do you see what they do to reach me?"

Kamahl nodded. "Tribal war."

"Who am I, that they should kill each other to touch me?"

Kamahl stared in dumb dread.

"Who are you, that you watch them kill each other?"

His head shook slowly.

"Our answers are here."

Karona rose from the ground, slipping up from the terrible throng.

They clung on, her robes lifting their hands. Some of the hands were dead already, and others were red with the blood of victims. Sanguine eyes followed Karona, and mouths poured prayers to her. She ascended. Her robes stretched, but the people could not anchor her to the ground. Effortlessly, she drifted higher. Many folk lost their grip, leaving red handprints on her glorious robes. Her radiance boiled the blood dry and bleached it to nothing. Two elves held on a moment more before they dropped onto the heads of the crowd.

Folk bashed them aside, determined not to lose sight of Karona. The desperate mob bunched up beneath her. A few hundred had reached the spot where she was, and thousands more approached, their faces raised. Hope and terror mixed on their expressions: Where is she going? How can she leave? A cry of despair poured out of the throng.

Kamahl stood. He was one of them now. His desires were theirs, and he would run with them, would trample anyone who stood in the way—do whatever it took to sit with her and gaze into her eyes.

The crowd turned on him. They grasped his weary arms and stared into his bleary eyes. Their shouts tumbled atop each other:

"What did she say?"

"Where is she going?"

"What does she want?"

"How can we catch her?"

Their bloody hands stained his arms. Kamahl pried the fierce fingers loose. "I don't know. . . . I don't know. . . . I don't know . . . !"

They spat and growled. Someone reached in with a knife.

"Look, there! She's vanishing!" Kamahl cried, pointing over their heads.

The people turned and saw Karona's fading figure in the blue heavens. They abandoned their victim and rushed after her.

Kamahl stood, panting. They had almost killed him, thinking he would deny them her presence. It was absurd. How could he deny anyone the light of Karona? As the mob moved off, Kamahl took a step in their wake. He was one of them, would kill or be killed in pursuing her. Another step, and Kamahl began to run.

He would not be left behind.

Scourge

* * * * *

I LOOK DOWN ON THE RAGING CREATURES. THEY FILL THE DESERT TO THE HORIZONS AND RUN TO REACH ME. THEY LOOK LIKE A CHURNING SEA, WATERS YEARNING UP INTO THE WIND ONLY TO BE WHIPPED INTO WHITE WAVES.

I AM THE WIND. I LEAVE A WAKE BEHIND ME AND RAISE BILLOWS BEFORE ME. MY MERE PASSAGE STIRS THE FOLK, AND THEIR SPIRITS RISE LIKE MIST.

PERHAPS THAT IS ALL I AM, WIND OVER WATER. I INSPIRE THE PEOPLE TO SHUCK THEIR BODIES AND BECOME SPIRITUAL BEINGS, AS WIND TURNS WATER TO VAPOR. MERELY BY BEING AMONG THEM, I TRANSFORM THEM. I SHOULD NOT FLEE THESE FOLK, BUT SHOULD FLY AMONG THEM AND MAKE THEM NEW.

I AM METAMORPHOSIS.

SPREADING MY ARMS, I DIP DOWN TOWARD THE RUNNING FOLK. *COME TO ME, MY PEOPLE, AND BE TRANSFORMED! COME WITH PHYSICAL BODIES, AND I WILL GIVE YOU SPIRITUAL BODIES.* MY FEET DESCEND AMONG THEM, MOVING TOO QUICKLY TO BE GRASPED. CURVING, I FLY IN A TIGHT ARC SO THAT ALL THE FOLK IN THE CENTER CAN TOUCH ME. IN A SPIRAL, I STIR MYSELF AMONG THEM. *COME TO ME AND BE MADE NEW!*

THE MULTITUDE RUSHES IN. THOSE NEAREST TOUCH ME. THOSE FARTHER OUT FIGHT FOR THEIR CHANCE. THEY SWARM, BODIES PILED ATOP BODIES. BENEATH THE CRUSH, PEOPLE BURST LIKE GRAPES. ANY MOMENT NOW, THEIR SPIRITS WILL RISE, SURROUND ME, AND DANCE IN JOY.

THESE SACRIFICES WILL BE MY ANGEL CHOIR.

BEHIND ME, A RED TRAIL CURVES TOWARD THE CENTER. BODIES LIE LIKE FLOWERS AFTER RAIN. SOON THEIR SPIRITS WILL RISE, AND I WILL SEE THE WHITE HOST OF THEM IN THE AIR.

THE BODIES ONLY LIE, STEPPING STONES FOR THE MOB.

SURELY THEIR SPIRITS WILL JOIN MINE. THEY CANNOT BE DYING IN VAIN. THERE MUST BE MEANING IN THESE DEATHS.

I SOAR UP FROM THE CROWD. THE DREAD IN MY BELLY IS THICK AND BLACK. THE SPIRITS ARE NOT RISING AND WILL NEVER RISE. THESE ARE PHYSICAL CREATURES AND NOTHING MORE. I CANNOT TRANSFORM THEM.

I AM NOT METAMORPHOSIS, BUT MURDER. MASS MURDER.

BETTER THAT THESE DEATHS BE MEANINGLESS, ABSURD, THAN THAT THEY MEAN THIS. BEAUTIFUL, BRILLIANT, BENEVOLENT—I AM NOT MURDER. IF FOLK KILL IN MY NAME, *THEY* ARE MURDER.

I FLY, BEAMING, ABOVE THE VIOLENT THRONG. I CALL AGAIN, BUT NOT IN WELCOME.

NEVER IN MY NAME SHALL YOU KILL. NEVER TO REACH ME SHALL YOU CLIMB ATOP THE BODY OF ANOTHER. ANYONE WHO SLAYS IN MY PRESENCE WILL DIE BY MY HAND!

THE RUMBLE OF FEET GIVES WAY TO THE THUD OF KNEES. THE MORTAL CROWD FALLS BEFORE ME, HEADS BOWED AND EARS ATTENTIVE.

I AM PLEASED. THEY NEEDED LAWS, THESE CREATURES. THAT WAS WHY THEY KILLED. THEY HAD NOT KNOWN THAT MURDER IS FORBIDDEN. ONCE THEY HAVE LAWS, THEY CAN SAFELY APPROACH ME.

I AM THE LAWGIVER.

I WILL COME DOWN AMONG YOU, BUT REMEMBER MY LAW AND ITS PENALTY, LEST YOU DIE.

THE PEOPLE LIFT THEIR EYES AND SMILE.

I EASE DOWN TOWARD CLEAR GROUND. ONE FOOT SETTLES ON THE WORLD, THEN THE OTHER, AND I PEER OUT AMONG MY PEOPLE. IT SEEMS ALL OF THEM ARE DEAD, LYING ON THEIR FACES.

I AM TROUBLED.

STAND UP.

SILENTLY, THE PEOPLE STAND. THEY ARE LIKE STATUES, DEAD THINGS. HOW TIMOROUS THESE MORTAL THINGS ARE.

ONE AT A TIME, APPROACH ME, BEGINNING WITH YOU.

A GOLDEN-HAIRED ELF WOMAN STEPS FORWARD. SHE WEARS THE LIVERY OF A KROSAN WARRIOR, BUT HER DEMEANOR IS ANYTHING BUT WARLIKE. SHE BOWS DEEPLY ON THE WAY TO LYING PROSTRATE.

I CATCH HER ARM AND LIFT HER. *WHO ARE YOU?*

SHE SAYS SHE IS OSWALLYN OF THE ARBOR WING OF THE DEFEND-ERS OF KROSAN.

WHO AM I?

HER PEERLESS FACE CLOUDS, AND SHE SAYS SHE DOESN'T KNOW.

WHY DO YOU SEEK ME?

SHE SAYS SHE DOESN'T KNOW.

OH, PITIABLE CREATURE, TO DESIRE WHAT YOU DO NOT KNOW.

BE BLESSED, OSWALLYN.

SHE DROPS TO HER KNEE AND BOWS HER HEAD.

I LOOK TO THE FACES THAT SURROUNDED US. *WHO IS NEXT?*

THE MULTITUDE ROARS AND RUSHES TOGETHER. OSWALLYN IS SWEPT UNDER THEIR SUDDEN SURGE, KILLED BY THE FEET OF AN OLD MAN, AN AVEN WARRIOR, AND TWO GOBLINS.

OH, PITIABLE ME. . . .

I STRIKE THE MAN'S NOSE, DRIVING IT INTO HIS BRAIN. I CRACK THE AVEN'S NECK. I KICK IN THE HEAD OF ONE OF THE GOBLINS, AND THE OTHER FALLS TO ITS KNEES.

THOSE NEAREST THE KILLING RECOIL IN HORROR. THOSE FARTHER OUT PRESS TOWARD ME. THE REMAINING GOBLIN SHRIEKS FOR FOR-GIVENESS. IT WRINGS ITS HANDS.

HOW CAN I FORGIVE? I PROMISED DEATH FOR DEATH.

THE PEOPLE PLEAD FOR AMNESTY. AM I AMNESTY? THE WORD MEANS TO FORGET, AND IF EVER I KNEW WHO I AM, I HAVE FORGOTTEN.

THE SHRIEKS OF MORE DYING FOLK COME WHERE THE CROWDS RUN TOGETHER.

I AM NOT AMNESTY. I AM JUSTICE.

I CRACK THE GOBLIN'S HEAD, AND HE TOO IS GONE.

I HATE TO BE JUSTICE, BLOODTHIRSTY AND BRUTAL. IT WILL SOON BE UNBEARABLE. DOZENS ARE DYING BENEATH THE FEET OF HUN-DREDS. JUSTICE WOULD HAVE TO SLAY THEM ALL.

I LEAP AWAY FROM THE KILLING GROUND. THE PEOPLE CLAW AT ME, CLING TO MY ROBES, FRANTICALLY TRY TO CLIMB. I SOAR TOWARD THE

SKY. LIKE LEAVES, THE PEOPLE FALL, BEAUTIFUL AND FLUTTERING, ONTO THE HEADS OF THEIR COMRADES. I ASCEND.

FALSE NAMES RING THROUGH MY MIND: ANSWER, METAMOR-PHOSIS, MURDER, MASS MURDER, LAW, AMNESTY, JUSTICE. I AM ALL OF THESE AND NONE OF THESE. I AM TOO POWERFUL TO BE IN THE PRESENCE OF THOUSANDS.

I WILL FADE FROM THEM AND HIDE AMONG THE STARS.

* * * * *

At the edge of the raging throng, Kamahl stood alone, aghast.

She was killing them. With utter impunity, she was killing them.

Yes, Kamahl had run with the others, trying to reach her. He had been one with them in desire. Anyone in his way would have been trampled. Life and death had seemed like nothing in the light of her glory.

No more.

She smiled as she killed them. Creatures crashed together in her wake, and their bodies were borne under by the mad press. Dozens died, and Karona sailed on.

Who is Karona? Who is Kamahl? Our answers lie in what they do.

Karona was not the greatest good in Dominaria, but the greatest evil.

She floated above the churning throng and decried them as killers. She told them she would kill them herself. Justice, she called it, but Kamahl had a different name. Descending again, Karona slew a man and an aven and two pleading goblins.

Our answers lie in what they do.

Karona was the Destroyer.

Kamahl turned his back on the horrid scene and trudged away across the desert. For two days, he had walked toward her light. Karona was a candle amid moths, and they flew into her flame and died and died. Unless someone stopped her, she would destroy all of Otaria, all of Dominaria.

Who is Kamahl?

"Kamahl is the one who will stop you," he said through clenched teeth. "Kamahl is the Destroyer's destroyer."

Certainly, he could not kill her with his bare hands. He needed a weapon, a great weapon. Back in Krosan, there was an underground labyrinth called the Spirit Well. It wound down a mile into the ground. At its base was a huge, black lake with a stone island, and on that island lay a colossal corpse. The body of Laquatus had grown with grotesque life, swelling around Kamahl's sword.

The Mirari sword.

"I'll draw the sword and destroy the Destroyer," Kamahl vowed quietly. His oath was drowned out by screams behind him.

Kamahl glanced back.

Hundreds were dying on the desert sands as Karona, beaming like a star, rose into the hateful heavens.

CHAPTER 3

EYE OF THE NUMEN

*L*ying on his side, Stonebrow yanked open the giant double doors of the Gilded Mage pub. They had grown strangely when the building itself had become a great tower. The doors now were huge, as tall as trees, and sucker branches extended from the transfigured wood. Stonebrow spared them little attention. He needed a drink.

By main strength, the giant centaur had lowered himself down the gutted side of the tower. When he reached the street level, his broken hind legs twisted, and he blacked out. He awakened in a lane that flowed with the living and undead. All marched after Karona. Stonebrow would not. She was gone now—he could sense her absence—and pain and hunger had pierced his desire for her. He lurched, a stone at a time, along cobbles littered with bodies. Most folk steered around Stonebrow's huge carcass, but more than a few climbed right over him, their eyes trained on glory. Now, at last, Stonebrow had reached the Gilded Mage, and he made his way straight to the taps.

He was thirsty, for one. It had been two days since he had had anything to drink or eat. He needed strength for what he was about to do—strength and a little numbness. Dragging himself among tables that had transformed into gigantic versions of themselves, he reached the bar. Strong spirits were stocked on shelves below the bar, and ale and wine in casks behind it. The casks had grown by a factor of ten, and Stonebrow hoped the beer within had as well. He crawled behind the bar, leaned his head back, and opened a tap in his mouth.

The flood of that golden stuff was like bliss. Stonebrow let the foam pour from the edges of his mouth while the ale gushed down his throat. It seemed to flow right through him, down to his broken hind legs. All across his hide, tiny droplets of sweat emerged. He had been hot and exhausted, but he was cooling down now.

Once he had a bellyful of ale, he grabbed an elephantine bottle of spirits and crawled to the back wall, which was lined with a bank of arched windows. Stonebrow grasped an enormous curtain and yanked it down, bringing the wooden rod with it. Thrice more he dragged the things down. Here were strong wooden poles for splints and gauzy fabric for tying them together. First, though, would come the spirits.

Stonebrow bit the cork and dragged it from the rum. He took two long swallows before turning to examine his legs. His left cannon was broken twice, and in one place the bone jutted from the skin. His right thigh was broken just above the gaskin. Though the first break was compound, it was this deeper contusion beneath all that muscle that would be harder to set. Gritting his teeth, Stonebrow upended the bottle over his legs.

It was the second time he blacked out. When he awoke, his legs shivered with cold and pain, and the abrasions burned. How long had he been asleep? The Gilded Mage was dark, and starlight shone in the windows, ten stories up. It would have to be enough.

Stonebrow lifted the curtain rods and, one by one, snapped them in half. He positioned four of the poles around his left leg and tore strips from the curtain. Washing his hands in the last of the spirits, Stonebrow grabbed his left cannon and dragged the bone back inside the flesh. Working slowly, he fitted end to end. It was agonizing work, but soon the jagged breaks had lined up.

With strips of curtain, he cinched the splint around his left gaskin. Moving down the leg, he tightened the splint until the bones could not move.

With a pained sigh, he began work on his right leg. His hands probed through a swollen thigh muscle, rubbing the sinews to relax them. Only then could he straighten the break. The bone ends ached terribly as they ground into place. With a hiss, Stonebrow set the splints around his thigh and tied them. He fell back, panting.

His legs felt awful—stinging, throbbing, and bound up. Still, it was time to test the splints. Grabbing a window sill, Stonebrow shoved himself upright. His forelegs were strong and unharmed, and they lifted him up from the floor. His hind legs rose stiffly, trembling. The pain was sharp but not unbearable. For the first time in perhaps days, he could stand. A centaur who could not stand was no centaur. Now, he would see if he could walk.

A set of stairs beyond the bar led to the pantry. If Stonebrow was going to eat, he would have to navigate those stairs. His stomach growled its encouragement. With a shuffling step, he moved away from the window. Leaning forward brought most of his weight onto his forelegs, and he ventured out among the tables. His hind legs shuffled behind him, scraping along the stone floor. Gingerly, Stonebrow picked his way among the chairs and reached the steps to the pantry. Leaning heavily on the rail, he navigated one stair at a time. Cool darkness filled the lower level, a salve to his trembling muscles. Ahead stood a ragged but stout door. It was huge, like all else in the Gilded Mage.

Stonebrow grasped the ring handle and swung the door slowly open. The air within was wet and charged with the earthy scent of giant tubers: potatoes, carrots, and radishes. There would also be salt pork and jerked beef, pickled fish, and sacks of dried beans. None of it was cooked, but it would be a feast, all the same. Stonebrow staggered into the dark space, reaching out to grab what he could. He gorged himself—a handful of beef strips, a raw potato, a cheese wheel with wax cover, a half-dozen radishes, a jarful of herring . . .

As the chunks slid down his gullet and filled his belly, he slowly awoke. It was not that he had been dreaming all this while but that he had been driven by his basest needs—thirst, healing, hunger. As these desires were sated, one by one, the higher mind began to rouse. Standing there, reeking of spirits and blood and covered with the remnants of food, Stonebrow realized where he was and what was happening. He alone in all of Averru stood and ate and drank. The rest of the world went after Karona.

Stonebrow paused, a bunch of carrots hanging in his hand. Other wounded folk had crawled after her, dying on the way, but Stonebrow had hauled himself the other way.

"I chose my own life over hers. What does that make me?"

"Alive," came an unexpected voice behind him.

Trapped and wounded, Stonebrow pivoted slowly about to see who it was. In the darkness, he could make out only three sets of glassy shoulders and vaguely luminous red eyes.

They were Glyphs, the ruby warriors of Averru. These crystalline men had taken shape within the large petraglyphs that had covered the Corian Escarpment. Glyphs were living words, and together they formed a great spell that had transformed the city and brought war to it. Only two days before, Stonebrow had shattered a phalanx of Glyphs. He couldn't do so now, cornered and wounded as he was.

"Yes, I'm alive."

"And you do not follow Karona?" the Glyph asked.

"I have not," he replied guardedly.

The glassy man seemed to nod. "Averru calls you. He is gathering all folk such as you to his temple."

"Averru? The city calls me?"

"The ruler calls you."

"He has the same name as his city?"

"Yes."

"What does he want?"

"Averru seeks allies, defenders. He will treat you well if you join him to protect the city."

"Against whom?"

"Against Karona."

A sudden weary weight took hold of Stonebrow. He had been fighting for his own life for two days and had almost failed to win. He could hardly imagine fighting for anyone else. "This isn't my battle."

The Glyph's weird eyes stared steadily at Stonebrow. "It is a fight for all of us. It is a fight for the whole world."

Stonebrow shook his bedeviled head. "I don't understand any of this. I came here to kill Akroma and Phage, to stop a war. Now, there is this Karona, and war will be everywhere."

"You do not understand now, but come to the eye of Averru and you will," replied the Glyph. "You helped create Karona. Perhaps you might help destroy her."

Stonebrow snorted. "If Averru wants the help of a crippled, starved, half-drunk centaur, I will not refuse him." He shuffled forward, his hind legs aching. "Lead the way."

It took the rest of the night for Stonebrow and his three Glyph escorts to shuffle back to the high, holy place. Along the way, Stonebrow noted signs of his previous passing—the trail of blood, the dislodged paving stones, the red patch where he must have lost consciousness. Other blood trails showed that the Glyphs had been diligent in clearing away the dead.

As Stonebrow and his escort stepped up onto the temple plaza, the sun emerged in the skyline behind them. Swollen, it hung between two buildings and gushed red light over the temple of Averru. Stonebrow's giant shadow reached across the plaza to the temple, but the Glyphs cast no shadows. Their rubious bodies refracted light throughout the plaza. It shone on other stragglers on their way to the temple—perhaps two hundred of them. All were wounded and thus had been unable to follow Karona.

"It's quite an army your master builds," Stonebrow rumbled, ambling toward the dome. "You'll need more crutches than swords."

"He is not just our master. We are his words, his thoughts. We are part of him. Through us he speaks. Through us he listens."

A chill prickled up Stonebrow's spine, but he tried to dismiss it with a joke. "He hears everything we say?"

"He has been listening."

Stonebrow's chill only deepened, and he stepped more rapidly across the plaza. On this level ground, the going was easier. He approached the great eastward arch of the temple and bent his neck to enter.

Inside, the space was cavernous and dark, filled with watery voices. Stonebrow halted, blinking and waiting for his eyes to adjust. He didn't want to step on anyone or, for that matter, risk a fall. The Glyphs with him gently clutched the fur of his flank and guided him forward. The floor dipped downward, an inverted dome beneath the vault above. At the lowest point of the bowl stood a red crystalline sculpture that was shaped like Averru City itself. It occupied what appeared to be a great pupil, a dark hole in the lowest part of the sphere. The iris of the eye was formed by stone seats and viewing stands that ringed the sculpture. Already hundreds of folk filled them. Stairs of various sizes cut from the center up to the edge of the orb.

This temple had been designed to host all manner of species. It was as if Averru had known it would come down to this.

The Glyphs steered Stonebrow down a set of wide and shallow stairs. They led him to a viewing stand.

"You should be fine here," the lead Glyph told him. "If you need anything more, simply speak, and it will be provided."

"Nothing now," Stonebrow replied.

"Simply speak. Averru knows all that happens within his eye." With that, the three Glyphs slipped away.

Stonebrow stared out across the temple and the other creatures who hobbled into the place. What were any of them doing here? What could a lame goblin or a wing-cropped aven do against a goddess? These were immortal battles, not mortal ones. The problem was that if these weary mortals did not rally to fight, no one would, and Karona would rule them all.

As the last of the stragglers made their way into the great ring, the Glyphs gathered. Some stationed themselves evenly along the upper walk. Others descended the stairways and converged on that great crystalline statue of Averru City. As they reached it, the Glyphs set their hands on it. Glass fused with glass, and the ruby men were drawn inward. Their bodies merged with the sculpture, which grew. Light began to glow within the stones. Brighter, redder it shone, and ruby facets sent beams throughout the temple.

Patterns projected on the walls and ceiling. The dome seemed to vanish: All across it appeared the skyline of the City of Averru.

Stonebrow drew deep and steady breaths and felt a sense of peace.

The sculpture shifted, slowly transforming. It no longer seemed hard like ruby, but soft like an anemone. The vision that poured from it changed as well. Instead of red towers curving against a black sky, human armies took shape.

They fought together against some great menace in the sky. Spears flew and swords jabbed. Men fell and cities burned. Above it all flew five terrible dragons. Their wings touched tip to tip and encompassed the world. In the wake of their flight streamed flocks of lesser serpents, which rained down on the humans.

Into Stonebrow's mind—into every mind in that place—a voice spoke: *When the world was young, it was clutched in Primeval claws.*

The serpents amalgamated into a great talon that gripped the dome and raked the human figures below.

At best, the mortal races were slaves. At worst they were food. But a mighty king rose among the mortals, King Themeus, who sent his greatest sorcerers to bind the Primevals and free the world. First bound was Rhammidarigaaz, who fell to the sorcerer Averru. He gained all the magical might of the bound dragon and became the first and greatest of the numena. After him were bound Crosis, who fell to Kuberr, and Dromar, who fell to Lowallyn. They gained the sorceries of the vanquished and thus became the second and third of the numena.

The claw split into five dragons. One, then a second, then a third descended from the dome and dived into a man, who swelled to loom over his corner of the space.

Averru saw the new danger: The Primevals tyrannized the world because they held all magic among them. Should there be a fourth and fifth numen, the five sorcerers would be tyrants anew. So he and Kuberr and Lowallyn, for the good of all the world, joined to slay the fourth and fifth sorcerers. Thereby they ended tyranny and began the age of mortals.

The figures of the three numena loomed large, but their reach did not extend throughout the globe.

For a thousand years, they ruled the world. Averru dominated the mountain at the center of Dominaria, and from his chambers he woke fires that rivaled the sun. Kuberr dominated the everglade lowlands to one side, and his fetor fed the fires of his brother. Lowallyn dominated the seas on the other side, and his creatures sported beneath the light of Averru.

The dome filled with dancing flames and darting creatures.

Averru was the first and greatest of the brothers, and he saved the others countless times from disaster. After a thousand years, their lives neared an end, and this would be disaster not just for the numena, but for the world they had freed. Averru thus devised a great spell. It would give him a new body, incorruptible and ageless, by which he might remain and keep all the world safe forever.

He chiseled the spell into his mountain home, and when the time was right, these petraglyphs themselves would emerge and combine into a titan that would be Averru.

The inside of the temple was riddled with runes.

His brother-sorcerers were jealous. They wanted new bodies as well. They worked their lesser magics and failed utterly. Kuberr could only take over the body of an infant in the womb, could only gain strength and power through human sacrifice, could only live out the normal span of life, growing and learning as any mere mortal. Lowallyn could do even less, manipulating the mind of one who had gone mad and thus living vicariously through him. They knew their spells would leave them puny and helpless, unable to stand against the ruby titan of Averru. And so, they came to make war upon their sorcerer-brother. They came to claim his magic as their own.

Again, the crystalline sculpture took the form of Averru City. Armies marched on it, one from either side. It could well have been a rendering of the battle that had just gripped the city, but it was without doubt a war of antiquity. The two armies drove toward the temple in the high, holy place. The invaders carried swords and chisels, both.

Kuberr and Lowallyn came, intent on stealing the great spell of Averru. Whatever part of the city they captured, they chiseled out the name of Averru and carved in their own. They so fouled the spell that it gave physical form to none of them, but to another being.

All the other figures dropped away, and in their midst appeared a glorious being with the form of a woman and the brilliance of the sun.

Karona. Here was the tyrant that Averru had feared, a creature who held all magical might. There was but one way to destroy her, and that was to destroy himself and the other two numena.

A great explosion shook the dome above, and Karona and all else were gone.

There were no bodies for the numena. They who had freed the world, who had ruled it in justice and honor for a thousand years, were scattered upon the wind. They lingered, weak and silent, for thousands of years. Slowly, they gathered power, gained mortal servants, and revitalized their ancient magic. They were determined to live again. So too was Karona.

Even as three human figures slowly grew around the perimeter of the dome, the sunlike figure of Karona did so as well.

We must find a way to slay her as of old. We must destroy Karona or be destroyed by her.

Stonebrow released a shuddering breath, and then Averru spoke directly to him. *Join me, General Stonebrow, and I will heal you. You who helped make her must help unmake her.*

CHAPTER 4

THIN SKINS

That night on the rocky badlands, there came a piteous sound halfway between the wail of a baby and the yowl of a cat in heat. Everything that lived among those boulders heard the caterwauling, and two separate packs of predators circled the source of the noise. None, though, had the courage to attack.

What would make such a racket? If humans did, surely they were setting a trap—or were complete imbeciles.

"Good grief! Now I'm shivering *and* burning up!" Sash bellowed to the starry heavens. "What do you want from us!"

Beside him, Waistcoat crouched, his mouth hanging open and hiccup sounds coming occasionally. " 'Member when I . . . made food shoot outta my mouth . . . ?"

"Yeah."

"Well, my mouth's shooting again . . . but . . . nothing's coming up."

"Of course not," hissed Sash. He hugged himself, trying to warm up but shied from his own painful touch. "You've got nothing in your belly to hurl. We've had nothing to eat or drink for days!"

Waistcoat clenched his eyes, swallowed hard, and forced himself to stand upright. He set his trembling arm on a nearby boulder and hissed. "Know what it's like?"

"What? The dry heaves?"

"No, all this. Having bodies. You know what it's like?" Waist-coat said philosophically. "It's like being turned into a giant cheese."

"Oh, no! Sunburn, starvation, dehydration, and now insanity!"

"See, everybody wants to be a big cheese, but then you become a big cheese, and now you're in for it! It's tough being cheese. If you get ate, that's the best thing. Otherwise you melt, dry out, get hard, crumble, turn moldy, get gnawed by rats then just plain rot."

Sash suddenly had the dry heaves. He clutched his knees and panted, each breath growing louder until he finally crowed, "I'm going to die! I'm lost in a wasteland—no food, no water, no shelter—and my only companion is a giant cheese!"

"Bodies suck," put in Waistcoat quietly. "Suck and blow."

"No rest! Every inch of our skin is burned! We can't even sit down! Oh, why didn't we make clothes? Why didn't we stay in Topos? We're going to die!"

"We're at low ebb," agreed Waistcoat.

Sash lifted his fists toward the stars and shouted, "Is this the best you can do! Trap and kill a couple of morons—obliterate a pair of week-old men? We may be in agony, but we're still alive!"

"We can still complain!" shouted Waistcoat.

"We'll survive then you'll see! You're only making a pair of monsters! We'll do terrible things! We'll assassinate kings! Burn towns!"

"Tip cows!"

"Incite riots! Print pamphlets!"

"Steal fish!"

Sash wailed and dropped his hands to his sides, wincing at the touch of skin to skin. "Oh, what's the point? We don't even make good metaphysical rebels." He tried to sit, but his knees wouldn't bend. "Not that there are any gods to rebel against."

"No gods? You sure?" Waistcoat asked.

"Yeah. I read a book in Eroshia. It said Dominaria has no true gods. Some people think there are gods, but they're really just sorcerers or planeswalkers, nature spirits, ghosts—"

"Guys with really good costumes."

"No gods."

Waistcoat shook his head sadly. "We're cheese without a cheese maker."

"Not even cheese, my friend," Sash said. He delivered a light but excruciating pat on Waistcoat's back. "Without a cheese maker, we're just moldy milk."

"How's there milk if there ain't any gods?"

"All you need for milk is breasts. There *are* breasts."

Waistcoat nodded. "Thank the gods—or the stars. Or something." He glanced up at the gleaming heavens. "Uh, Sash."

"Uh . . . what?"

"If there aren't any gods, what's that thing there? That ball of light?"

Sash craned his neck. "Probably a psychotic delusion. I bet this whole journey is a delusion. You're bonked out of your skull."

"The light's getting bigger," Waistcoat said. "Beautifuler. I think it's a god."

Sash lifted a hand to shield his eyes from the radiance. "Haven't you listened to a word? There are no gods! That's just a gas ball."

"She's a pretty gas ball."

The feminine outline was unmistakable now, with arms held wide.

"I read about this too. Meteors, they call them. Flaming rocks. They fall down from the sky and hit people."

"There's no end to trouble," replied Waistcoat. He looked away from the angelic figure. "Here we're hoping for a goddess but instead get a flaming rock. Should we dive away?"

"What's the point?" Sash said shielding his eyes.

The sands and boulders shone as with midday. A beaming figure wafted gently down to hover just above their heads. White robes rose to a belt like a golden cord. She had a strong and shapely torso, and her arms were slender and graceful. Glory poured in broad waves from her eyes as she stared at the two naked, sunburned, parched, and starving men.

"Just our luck," growled Waistcoat. "A flaming rock that won't strike ground." Keeping his eyes averted, he waved at the figure. "Would you mind turning it down? We're kind of burned here."

The figure spoke, her voice like a pipe organ.

"TURN WHAT DOWN?"

Sash answered vitriolically: "The light! The heat! The blasted humming! What do you think?"

"I DON'T KNOW HOW TO TURN IT DOWN. I'M NEW."

"How new?" Waistcoat asked.

"THREE DAYS."

Waistcoat whistled. "That *is* new. We're one week."

"Three days is old for a flaming rock," snarled Sash. "One week is new for a human."

"I AM NOT A FLAMING ROCK. I AM KARONA."

Waistcoat gazed at her stupidly. "What's a Karona?"

She only shook her head.

"I'll tell you what a Karona is," Sash said. "A Karona is a bright, chatty fireball who may think she is a god but isn't."

Karona arched an eyebrow appraisingly and looked to Waistcoat. "IS THAT WHAT YOU THINK?"

He smiled sheepishly. "Mostly. I think you're pretty too."

"THAT WILL HAVE TO BE MY ANSWER: A BRIGHT, PRETTY, CHATTY FIREBALL WHO THINKS SHE IS A GOD BUT ISN'T." She crossed her arms over her chest. "I MAY NOT BE HUMAN, BUT NEITHER ARE YOU."

"What?" blustered Sash.

"We're cheesy."

"IF YOU WERE HUMAN, YOU WOULD BE BOWING TO ME AND CLAMBERING OVER EACH OTHER TO REACH ME. YOU'D BE KILLING EACH OTHER. . . . AND YOU'D WEAR CLOTHES."

"Don't we know it!" Waistcoat said. "Humans're always running around wearing clothes and eating stuff and drinking stuff and living in things. We haven't gotten to do any of that. You're right. We're not very human."

"We're dying, is what he is saying," Sash put in angrily.

A troubled look came across her beautiful face, and the angelic creature lowered herself to light on the ground beside them. "DYING?"

Sash nodded once emphatically. "That's the other thing humans do, only usually they put it off for seventy years. Looks like we'll be dying tonight or tomorrow."

"WHY?"

"Dehydration," Sash said.

"And nothing to drink, either."

The woman frowned but was only the more beautiful. Her countenance darkened.

"You see that?" Waistcoat blurted, pointing at her.

"WHAT?"

"You turned it down," Waistcoat said with a laugh. "You can turn it down! How'd you do it?"

A shy smile came to the angel's face, intensifying the light. Sash and Waistcoat shied back, their hands lifted before their eyes. Karona scowled, and the radiance dimmed to nearly nothing.

"I CAN DIM IT. CONFUSION, SADNESS—THEY BLOCK THE FLOW OF POWER. HAPPINESS MUST STRENGTHEN IT."

"Let's try to keep things grim," Sash said.

"I AM LEARNING. THE LIGHT IS ONLY AN EXPRESSION OF EMOTION. I CAN SMILE THOUGH I AM SAD AND CAN GLOW THEN TOO. I CAN WEEP THOUGH I AM GLAD AND CAN KEEP MY FACE DARK. I'M LEARNING, AND YOU'RE TEACHING ME. I'VE LEARNED MORE FROM YOU TWO THAN FROM MULTITUDES."

"We'll help till we die," Waistcoat offered.

Karona reached out toward them. The ex-unmen flinched from her touch, but she was too quick. One arm wrapped around Sash's chest, and the other grasped Waistcoat. Her touch at first seared their sunburned skin, and they trembled in her embrace. She didn't release them, though, and the sensation moved past pain into deep, enervating bliss. She levitated away from the boulder field and toward the spangled heavens.

Sash and Waistcoat felt the gritty ground drop from beneath their leather-wrapped feet. Nothing mattered now. The pain was gone and with it the thirst and hunger, the fear and mortal dread. Her touch made right all that had been wrong.

As the three souls rose above the badlands, Karona's light jabbed down among the stones, revealing a pack of wild dogs and a pride of lionesses. They rose from their crouches and stared at their escaping dinner.

"You saved our lives," Sash said in wonderment.

"NOT YET. YOU ARE STILL DEHYDRATED."

"I'm not thirsty a bit," objected Waistcoat.

"YOU NEED WATER. I CAN TAKE AWAY PAIN AND DESIRE, BUT I CANNOT REMOVE NEED."

She soared above the badlands, her light rolling across the great stones. Twin beams shone from her eyes, searching the ground.

"What are you looking for?" Waistcoat asked.

"I CROSSED A CREEK SOME TIME BACK. THE WATER WILL BE FRESH AND COOL."

The men's faces lit with a quiet awe. They had resigned themselves to suffering and death, and now here they had comfort and life. It was no small gift, especially from a flaming rock.

"Do you know what I think you are, Karona?" asked Sash quietly.

"A god," broke in Waistcoat. "You and me both."

"No, not a god," Sash barked, and his comrade ducked his head in shame.

"WHAT, THEN?"

"A friend," Sash replied. "Our first. Quite likely our only."

Karona glided along above the rubble field, her nimbus of power suddenly swelling to nearly reach the horizon. "YES. THAT ANSWER FITS AS WELL AS ANY. 'SHE THINKS SHE IS A GOD BUT REALLY IS JUST A FRIEND.' BUT HOW CAN I BE YOUR FRIEND IF I DO NOT KNOW YOUR NAMES?"

"I am Sash, and I'm pleased to meet you, Karona."

"I'm Waistcoat. My nickname is Puddle. His is Stick."

"SASH AND WAISTCOAT, STICK AND PUDDLE. WE THREE ARE THE SAME—NEW AND NEEDY. THE WORLD IS UNKIND TO CREATURES LIKE US. IT MAKES SENSE THAT WE WOULD BAND TOGETHER. BUT HERE IS WHERE WE MUST PART."

She opened her arms, and the two ex-unmen were falling. Side by side, Sash and Waistcoat plunged. Their radiant new friend hung above them, shrinking as they dropped. Out of light they fell toward darkness. The bliss of her touch vanished, and a wash of emotions hit them: first terror and then pain. The agony of the full-body sunburn was compounded by desperate thirst and ravenous hunger. This was their true state, racked with desire and pain. The last emotion was the worst—betrayal. Even their friendship had been a delusion.

The badlands rushed up to strike them, and all those passions were gone.

Sash and Waistcoat crashed down into a deep, black, cool river. Their aching feet plunged through, and the waters swallowed them. The fire of their flesh was quenched. The gritty agony of the past days washed away. They opened their mouths to laugh, and water poured in. They swallowed and swallowed in ecstasy.

* * * * *

I HANG IN THE DESERT NIGHT AND WATCH MY NEW FRIENDS. THEY ARE DIFFERENT FROM ALL THE REST: HONEST, SANE, REASONABLE. THEY ALONE UNDERSTAND. THEY ALONE DO NOT WORSHIP.

They have water, and they sport and splash in joy.

I am drawn to them and glide down toward the river. It is the only source of life in this dry place. It has saved my friends, and they have saved me. I will keep them, learn from them, and become what I must be.

The two men slap the surface and gurgle greetings.

How do you like the water?

Sash nonsensically cries out for air.

No, the water! How do you like the water?

Waistcoat shouts that he is drowning.

A moment more, and they vanish from the surface. Their naked forms slide away with the current.

I swoop down, extending my hands into the black waters. The touch of the river is cold. My friends sink away from my grasp. I follow, plunging into the chill flow. It stings my face and slaps my belly and lays hold of my whole body and thrusts me along. I swim into dark channels, my eyes bleeding light across the bed. Something bumps my fingertips, and I latch on, only to find a knob of stone. Deeper, I grope the sandy bed, but my friends are not here. The waters laugh and moan.

Two thin white columns burst into being ahead: bubbles.

I hurl myself through the waters. Flesh comes into my hands. I grab two wrists and hope I have both men. Kicking my feet, I drive myself up from the waters. My head breaks the surface, then shoulders, and last a pair of drowned and naked men. They drink in air as eagerly as they had water.

* * * * *

Karona soared up from the river, carrying Sash and Waistcoat like half-drowned kittens.

"I thought we could swim!" roared Waistcoat.

Sash shot water from his nose. "We *can* swim, just not at night with a current after starving."

"We're learning lots!" enthused Waistcoat.

Sash nodded. "Let's just hope the lessons get less lethal."

Karona labored up the steep bank to a large boulder. She set the two men down on the rock, where they slumped, panting.

"YOU'VE HAD WATER, AND YOU NOW HAVE AIR. YOU'LL SURVIVE, YES?"

Without looking at her, Waistcoat shook his head grimly.

Sash explained. "In a few hours, the sun will come up. Our skin already is as brittle as paper. We need shelter and after that food. Then there's rest."

"And dancing," Waistcoat said. "Cards. Stories. All that stuff."

"He means amusements—something to do. Otherwise, we go crazy."

"BEING HUMAN TAKES A LOT."

"You're telling us," Waistcoat said. "What about you? Seems it would take lots of work to be a g—um, well, a Karona."

The gleam in her eyes dimmed, leaving them in almost total darkness. "YES."

Waistcoat shrugged. "Well—that's what friends are for, after all. You help us, and we help you."

"ALL RIGHT. WHERE DO WE START? WHERE CAN YOU FIND WHAT YOU NEED?"

"A city," Sash said.

Starry-eyed, Waistcoat said, "Eroshia."

CHAPTER 5

GATES OF THE UNDERWORLD

*O*nce, Kamahl had sat at the height of the Gorgon Mount. Now he stood at its depths.

Before him yawned an enormous cavern, toothy like the gullet of a great monster. Stalactites proliferated across the ceiling, and stalagmites made a jagged forest below. In places, twisted columns of rock stretched from floor to vault, the sinews of this ravenous mouth. Giant bats hung in quivering black masses above, and their guano made poisonous sloughs beneath them.

Kamahl shook his head and laughed bitterly. "I must be a fool." He glanced back over his shoulder.

The Krosan Forest extended behind him, wide and bright beneath the sun. Yes, rot riddled the overgrown boughs, but still it was better than a brimstone-stinking cavern into the bowels of evil. Kamahl could still turn back. He could forget about Krosan, forget about Karona, maybe ship for some other continent . . . but he had spent too much time in forgetting. It was time to remember.

"Remembering and dismembering," Kamahl snorted as he started forward.

Ever since he had turned away from Karona, Kamahl had rediscovered his sense of humor. It was the natural result of absurdity: The fate of the world rested in the hands of an ex-barbarian, ex-gladiator, ex-druid, ex-monk, ragged, shaggy, weary old man. He was even barefoot, unarmored, his clothes hanging in tatters. He had no weapon, no staff, no magic. Nothing remained to him except his will.

"A will. I should have thought of that."

Kamahl stepped gingerly among the stalagmites. The last time he passed into the Spirit Well, it had been a vertical descent. The cavern, like everything else in Krosan, had devolved. It had slid down the hill, and Kamahl had slid with it. He passed from daylight into shadow among the fangs of the cave. The air turned chill, and the stones robbed heat from his hand. His breath was a gray ghost on the air. There would be real ghosts here, the spirits of a massacred forest: Nantuko specters, centaur shades, elf poltergeists . . .

"Keening banshees with bad breath—"

"Ye've got the breath bit right," growled a familiar voice, "but I didn't keen in life and ain't gonna start in death."

Kamahl glanced toward the sound—a dark niche along one convoluted wall of the cavern. There, he saw a faint figure, stout and stolid, as if the spirit of a boulder haunted the crevice where it once had stood. "You can't bar my way. I'm determined to enter."

"Ha! Bar yer way? That's rich. I've stood here for nigh on two years, waiting for ye to come. I'm not wanting to bar yer way. I mean to prod ye along."

"Balthor Rockfist," Kamahl sighed in sudden recognition. He smiled a small smile. "I thought you were dead—twice."

"I was. Choked on a chicken leg, so to speak." The rugged figure of the dwarf came clearer: a wide mane of hair and beard, a grizzled visage, a stout body, and the shade of a battle-axe. The ghost drifted down from the niche, set foot on the rocky ground, and stood there with powerful fists on his hips. "Died right here, same day ye killed Laquatus."

Kamahl's face grew as gray as the ghost's. "Yes. That was a bad day. You, Seton, Jeska—I lost many comrades that day."

"Well, ye've just gotten one back."

Kamahl stared incredulously at the dwarf's ghost. "Why?"

" 'Cause at last you're going down after yer sword and for the right reasons."

"Why would you care?"

Balthor shook his head. "Yer forgetting that before it was your sword, it was yer pappy's and your grandpappy's—that's to say Matoc's, a friend of mine. I'm the one who forged it for him, and from no simple lump of steel—"

"From Thran metal," whispered Kamahl.

"Yup. From the very staff of Urza, I made it. I loosed it on the world, and I'm gonna see it through to do what it was meant to do."

Kamahl huffed, turning the irate sound into a laugh.

"What?" asked the ghost indignantly.

"I'm being haunted."

"Laugh it up. It's true. Yer my project until ye do right by my sword. Let's put it this way: Last time ye wielded that thing, ye killed hundreds of yer own kin—members of me own tribe. I figure ye can use help to avoid the temptation this time."

Kamahl stared soberly at the rocky ground. "Yes. You're right about that. I'd be happy to have you along."

"Nobody else'll see or hear me, mind," Balthor said, "so ye might be cautious how ye answer when with others."

Kamahl nodded. "So, you're really nothing but a figment of my imagination?"

Balthor shook his head. "Ye ain't got enough imagination to conjure me. I'm real enough. Now, let's get a move on. There's a little matter of a sword."

Taking the ghost at his word, Kamahl forged ahead among the stalagmites.

Balthor had an easier time of it, drifting through the air behind him. "Ye should know that I can't help ye physically, only spiritually. I can't affect flesh, only souls."

"What do you mean? You can't chop a monster, only spook it?"

"Aye, I can terrify. I could scare ye to death, Kamahl—curse ye, ward ye, banish ye from this place. That's why ye're needing me. There're powers in this mount that'd do ye in. Without me, ye'd not pass."

Kamahl pursed his lips. "So, I fight the monsters, and you fight the spirits?"

"Right."

The cave grew darker, colder, its throat diving rapidly into the belly of the ground. The slope led onto sharp sections of stalagmite and, here and there, fell away entirely into deep pits. Kamahl carefully threaded his way between these bottomless chasms. "I should've brought a rope." Staring into the profound darkness ahead, he added, "I should've brought a lantern."

"And an army," offered Balthor, hovering easily beside one shoulder, "but ye've brought me, and I'm near as good."

Kamahl slid onto his belly to ease himself down a particularly steep section of stone. "Yeah, instead of a rope, I've got a thread of conversation."

"Aw, this forest life's made ye soft. Come, now, mountain man. Shimmy down. I'll glide on ahead to light yer way."

The ghost soared overhead while Kamahl wrapped his arms around a water-smoothed column and eased himself downward. The air below was so still and cool it felt as if he were submerging himself in water. He descended the column, his feet and fingers numbed by its cold. The pillar led down through a narrow shaft and into an inky chamber. By the echo, Kamahl could tell that the cavern was very large. He dropped down onto soft ground covered in knee-high grass. A huge, low growl came, seemingly everywhere.

"Where's that light you promised?" Kamahl hissed as he crouched, ready for attack.

"Me own eyes're the light," Balthor spat.

"Well, then, illuminate!"

"It's a cave bear. A big one."

Kamahl nodded, remembering the huge, hackled beasts from the Pardic Mountains. "What do I do? Raise my arms and try to scare it off or lie down and play dead?"

Balthor replied urgently, "Ye're not getting how big this thing is—"

"Just tell me!"

"Ye're standing on it!"

Kamahl leaped for the stone column just ahead of a paw the size of his body. Two upper claws—arm-length things—caught his legs. Kamahl tumbled backward over the paw and fell, headfirst, onto the belly of the great bear.

It bellowed.

Kamahl scrambled to his feet and hurled himself again. The paw swung back, and furry knuckles flung Kamahl up the beast's body.

"How about some help?" Kamahl shouted.

Balthor glided through the air alongside his tumbling comrade. "I'm terrifying and mortifying, but it's just making the beast madder."

"Thanks!"

"I should warn ye, it's got three heads—"

"Three heads!"

"—And you're flying right toward 'em."

Kamahl struck the enormous bear's chest, rolled twice, and halted in the threefold path of hot, roaring breath. A moment more and this thing would bite him in thirds. Roaring, Kamahl ran into the central stream of breath. He imagined awaking to find a rat running toward his mouth and hoped the beast would have the same instinct as he. An enormous bruin gasp hissed through the central head's teeth just as they slammed shut. Kamahl leaped up onto the thing's nose, took a step between the eyes, and jumped over the head. His legs and arms spun, flailing through the air as Kamahl dropped. Surely the floor would be only a giant-bear's-width down. His feet struck a little too soon, and Kamahl curled into a roll.

"Learning from the master!" Balthor called out.

Kamahl was too battered and terrified to reply. He rolled to a stop, scrambled up, and began to run full-out away from the three-headed bear.

"What's ahead?"

"A dead end."

"Not the best . . . choice of words . . ." Kamahl responded as he staggered to a stop. Behind him, he could hear the great beast rolling over and rising to pursue. He clutched his knees and panted. "So, what now?"

Balthor's ghost looked particularly white as he stared at the unseen beast. "I'd skedaddle."

"Where?"

"The only exit's behind it," Balthor said.

"Can't you do something?" Kamahl hissed, trying not to let the beast hear the fear in his voice. "If you can mortify and terrify, can't you stultify or stupefy?"

"Ye think this is a word game?"

The cave shook with the footfalls of the enormous monster, and its tripartite breath swarmed over Kamahl. It gave him an idea. "Terrify it again."

"It'll be all the more vicious."

"Don't terrify it of me. Terrify it of itself. Turn each head against the other two! Do it!" Kamahl shouted.

Air whirled above his head, and Kamahl leaped to one side. He still was not quick enough. A giant paw landed on his legs and dragged him to the ground, pinning him. Scythelike claws arched just above him. The bear pressed its massively callused pad down on Kamahl. It would crush his legs then have all the time in the world to kill him.

Through lungs constricted with pain, Kamahl cried, "Balthor! This is it! Now or never!"

The pressure on Kamahl's legs intensified, and blood swelled his upper body. He felt as if he were going to pop. Claws sank down, cutting long, shallow lines across Kamahl's back and shoulders. He bellowed.

The three-headed bear shrieked in outrage and fear. Its claws flashed up, releasing Kamahl. Black air swirled for a moment, then came the sound of a paw striking a huge muzzle. The offended head roared furiously and returned the blow with its other paw. Claws cracked against the fangs of another head, and the bear fight had truly begun.

"It worked," Kamahl muttered excitedly. He could see none of it, but the very fact that he still lived and could stagger away meant that the bear must have been fighting itself. "Thanks, Balthor."

A voice very near Kamahl's ear said, "I could always pick a fight. Come on. Follow me voice. Stay low. Duck when I say duck."

Nodding fervently, Kamahl ran in a stooped posture. "How did you . . . terrify . . . the heads against each other?"

Balthor replied, "Monsters aren't afeared of much. I made each head think the other was stealing its mate. Nothing's more terrifying than cuckoldery. Duck!"

White pain exploded in Kamahl's mind. He crumpled, rubbing the top of his head. "You might say 'duck' sooner."

"Duck."

Kamahl did. Above his head, wind whistled as a giant claw swept by.

"Hands and knees, boy! Crawl ahead to the cliff and over it."

"What?" Kamahl said. "I really hit my head. . . ."

"I said, 'Crawl over the cliff.' "

"There's got to be another way," Kamahl said, wincing as a large hunk of fur wafted down to settle on his back.

The dwarf's voice was quiet but intense. "Aye, ye could feel yer way to the other side of the chamber, crawl through a maze of tiny paths into a nest of elf-wights, fight past 'em to the cave of the giant scorpions, run across their backs and out the other side, jump peak to peak over the magma sea, and finally reach Lake Laquatus. Or ye could crawl over that cliff."

A dying wail began high above, growing louder and higher in pitch. The three-headed bear plunged toward Kamahl, forcing a great wind out over that cliff. It was either die on this spot, or die at the bottom. At least he would have a few more seconds. . . .

"You'd better be right about this," snarled Kamahl, scuttling forward on hands and knees.

The smooth stone beneath his hands gave way to emptiness, and he tumbled over the edge. His knees kissed the ground one final time before he pitched off the brink. Head over heels, he plunged through cold air. A profound boom sounded above him, the body of the three-headed bear striking stone, then there was only the rising roar of air as he plummeted, and Kamahl's own outraged shout:

"Balthooooor!"

"What?" came the terse reply, as if the ghost floated right beside his ear.

Kamahl instinctually lashed out to grab the man, but his hands came up empty. "You got me into this mess! What now?"

"Now? Why, now, ye drop."

"For how long?"

"Till ye hit."

Kamahl yelled once again until his lungs were empty, took a deep breath, and said, "How far is it to the bottom?"

"Ye've got another minute. Ye might as well save yer breath. Yer gonna need it."

Kamahl wished he could hit the spirit. "What do you mean, I'm going to need it?"

The dwarf's ghostly face was barely visible in the rushing air, but he looked unconcerned. "Lake Laquatus is deep and cold. It'll steal yer breath, and ye'll likely plunge about sixty feet when ye hit." He sniffed. "Oh, and point yer toes, or they'll snap off."

"Point my toes or they'll . . . When!"

"Three . . . two . . . one . . ."

Kamahl made his body into an auger, feet jabbing straight down, hands clamped to hips, and face clenched against the impact. It came. The blow felt as if he'd struck rock. His knees and hips bent involuntarily, and his legs folded. Shins smacked the water, and knees and buttocks crashed next, opening a well of air into that iron-hard lake. His back bent forward, throwing his head toward his knees and driving the last, saving breath from his lungs. Enveloped in air, Kamahl plunged dry into the chill flood. With an almighty clap, the waters closed over his head, then all air was gone.

Which way, Balthor? he tried to ask but was underwater and out of breath.

Even so, the dwarf ghost appeared and hitched a thumb, gesturing for him to swim.

Kamahl nodded and tried to stroke, but his limbs felt boneless and stinging. He waggled like a jellyfish. He tilted his head back, looking for the promised air. There was only darkness and the encouraging if frantic thumb of Balthor. Despite his claims that he could not affect the physical world, Balthor clamped his hands on Kamahl's arms and lifted him toward the surface.

He broke through, hurling water from his long gray hair. Kamahl took a grateful gasp of air, allowing his body to go limp as Balthor held him up. After a few more deep breaths, Kamahl laughed.

Balthor hovered, arms crossed, above the churning water. He glared balefully.

"If you're . . . up there, Balthor," Kamahl gasped, "who's got hold . . . of my arms . . . ?"

"Those'd be eels."

Kamahl gave a shriek, reaching his arms around to grab the muscular beasts. One hand found a leathery body and clamped on. Kamahl squeezed. The creature wriggled but did not release its bite on his triceps. "Pernicious little—" Kamahl cursed. "I'll show you how to bite!" Hauling the tail of the thing up, he bit into the eel's back. Cold and foul-tasting blood filled his mouth.

The eel shrieked, let go, and thrashed away, trailing its gore.

"Now its your turn!" Kamahl grabbed the second eel, yanked its body up before his mouth, and bared his teeth.

"Wait, it's a lightning eel!"

Kamahl bit, and everything lit up—teeth, skull, hand, eel, the chopping waves, the stony island nearby. Kamahl tried to let the beast go, but a terrible buzz filled his mouth, and his muscles didn't seem to work. The shocking thing flipped back and forth in his mouth and, leaving a sparking chunk of flesh between his teeth, managed to tumble loose. Kamahl floated there, stunned, the eel-skin in his teeth sending acrid wisps of smoke into his nose.

Balthor looked sympathetic and spread his hands. "Sorry."

Kamahl spat. "Let me guess. Eels have no souls."

"Right," the dwarf replied, "and there're thousands more where they came from. Better swim. Fast."

Kamahl did, striking toward the rocky island he had glimpsed. Something glowed on the top of that land mass—a silvery light. The Mirari sword. It called to Kamahl. Once he held that thing in his hand again, all this would have been worth it. Stroking with alternate arms, Kamahl made good time through the eel-infested waters.

He reached the island. Rough and rankled stones lined the shore, and Kamahl climbed them only to find an enormous, fetid corpse.

The carcass of Laquatus had lain here on this island for two years, run through with the Mirari sword. Like the rest of the forest, like the Gorgon Mount itself, this dead body had grown. It now was larger than a giant, its flesh putrefying even as it swelled.

Kamahl had climbed out near the ear of the monster, and he looked up the scaly shoulder to the hill that was its chest. There jutted the hilt of the Mirari sword, topped by the Mirari. That gleaming silver orb had haunted the continent of Otaria, and it still haunted Kamahl. Even after the three-headed bear, the plunge through darkness, and the lake of eels, Kamahl could think only of wielding that sword again.

"There 'tis," Balthor said reverently. "The Thran-metal sword I forged from Urza's own staff. I gave it to yer grandpappy Matoc, and he to his son, and he to ye; the sword by which ye won the Mirari and slew yer own kin; the blade that impaled Laquatus and began the growth of Krosan; the very weapon that'll save Dominaria. There 'tis, Kamahl. Ye must draw it now, and I must see it drawn."

Setting his jaw, Kamahl climbed the rotting shoulder of the great colossus. He stood there a moment, feeling the cold slackness beneath his feet. Then with certain steps he marched up the monster's chest and reached the place where the sword stood. It jutted from a deep well of flesh through the heart of the corpse.

The Mirari flashed and gleamed like a scrying crystal.

Kamahl wrapped his hand about the hilt, felt the aching cry of the blade, and pulled. In one long, steady draw, he dragged the sword up from the flesh that had held it. The blade cleared the final rib. It rang, a glad sound, and Kamahl lifted it high into the air. He released a joyous bellow. It was as though a missing limb had been returned to him. Now, all would be right again.

A deep voice rumbled, "Hurrrrghhaa."

Kamahl pivoted, looking at the ghost of Balthor.

Balthor only shrugged.

The rolling growl came again, louder: "Hhhurrrraaaghhhaaa!"
Dread sweeping through him, Kamahl looked down.
The eye of Laquatus opened and stared straight at him.

CHAPTER 6

PROPHET SHARING

*E*lionoway sat on his favorite stone beside a sparkling stream and beneath a gloaming sky. He drew a long puff on his pipe and let the smoke sail away on the wind. The elf sighed. This would be his only moment of peace today—if today was like yesterday and the day before and the day before. Soon, the sun would rise, the other refugees would emerge from their makeshift tents, and the caterwauling would begin.

"There he is!" came a gruff voice, and Elionoway glanced up the rocky hillside to see a knot of refugees among the tents. They jabbed fingers in his direction, and the clutch of them set off down the slope to begin their complaint.

Releasing a blue trail of smoke, Elionoway murmured, "Even before the sun, they rise." He shook his head and waited for their arrival.

Of course they had reason to complain. Every last one of them wanted to go toward the glorious light above Sanctum—the city they had fled. Only Elionoway sensed the danger. To him, that light and a return to the god-haunted ruins of Sanctum meant only death. By virtue of his race, age, and elocution, he had become ad hoc leader of this troop of lemmings and had assigned himself the difficult duty of keeping them from plunging into the sea.

"Well, what about it, Leader?" asked a middle-aged woman at the head of the approaching refugees. "You said she was coming here, the light-bringer wanted us to wait here. It's been three days! Where is she?" The folk behind her nodded their agreement.

Elionoway blinked at the red-orange east and said, "She's been busy. You'd be surprised what your average god can do in three days."

The woman grabbed her dirty brown hair in two fists and said, "Ach! More stalling! You're not even looking the right way! She was in the west, in Sanctum. You're looking east!"

"How else can I watch the sunrise?" Elionoway asked placidly.

The woman gave a small shriek of frustration, and a few hairs came away with her fists. A man behind her broke in—a mousy man whose hands seemed to wish for a hat that he might roll in his grip. "It's just, we're not wanting to ship to Eroshia. Not now. Not when the lady's out west."

"She's not in Sanctum anymore," Elionoway pointed out. "Not for days. No point in marching back to where she isn't."

"Well, begging pardon, but she doesn't seem to be here, either, so why wait around?" the man replied. "I mean, I know you said she was coming, but, well, we ain't quite sure on that anymore."

Elionoway released a long, smoky breath. "Then figure out where she is and go, but I'd not counsel leaving this stream, these glades, this defensible spot to go wandering after mirages."

That seemed a satisfactory answer. At least it shut the people up. They muttered among themselves but then turned and marched right back up the hill toward the camp.

Elionoway was left in peace. That's when he knew something was terribly wrong. He turned to the west, which was brighter than the sunrise. Somehow, the night had become day. Worse yet, this misplaced sun sang.

"Damn."

Averting his eyes, Elionoway slid off the rock. He wanted so to look toward her again, lose himself in her presence, but this was a destroying radiance. Elionoway peered intently at the narrow bowl of his bone pipe. He pounded out the old plug of tobacco, which fell smoldering to the rocky ground. All the while, the light drew nearer, its rays more rapacious and its song more enticing. With deliberate motions, Elionoway drew a pouch of tobacco from his pocket, put a pinch in the pipe, tamped it down, drew out his tinder box, lit the pipe, and took a couple of experimental puffs.

There was no escaping it. This all-consuming light was on its way. Elionoway must be with his people when it arrived, or the lemmings would run to their deaths.

Ducking his head against the beaming presence, Elionoway climbed the hillside. He glanced toward the makeshift camp—a hundred refugees beneath bed-sheet tents and lean-tos made of scrub. Amid the hovels lay the folk themselves, prostrate. What other posture could a mere mortal take in the presence of such power?

This posture, Elionoway thought as he strode to the hilltop and planted his feet. The stance of a fighter ready to fight. At last, he dared to look toward her again.

She was magnificent. Hanging in midair above the ramshackle camp was a wondrous woman. Her eyes shone like twin stars, and white raiment hung from her shoulders, cinched at her waist, and trailed past her floating feet. Indescribably beautiful, the woman's light washed out the world.

The refugees of Sanctum lifted their heads and gazed in amazement at her. They seemed flowers surprised by a midnight sun. Their faces opened to behold her radiance. She was too radiant, though, and the people wilted. One by one, they slowly collapsed to their faces, their bodies bent and trembling.

Elionoway almost drooped like all the others, but he distracted himself by looking at the strange pets in the woman's arms.

One creature was slim and tall, the other stout and short, and both were nude except for crude boots. Their skin was the color of cooked lobster, and they mewled like a pair of kittens.

"A piss-poor city, really," whined the fat one.

"They'll have food, though," the tall one replied. "And clothes. Something!"

"Ask them! Ask them!"

Elionoway had never seen these two before, but he recognized their voices from somewhere. They had been the attendants of another great lady—Phage—but hadn't they been . . . roaches?

The angelic figure spoke, her voice great like wind through a wood. "I AM KARONA. THESE ARE MY FRIENDS, SASH AND WAISTCOAT. LISTEN TO THEM, AND OBEY." She was moving again, wafting downward.

The folk lying nearby gave out little squeals of dread and delight. It was unclear whether they feared to die at her touch or hoped to be raised to glory.

Karona set the two naked, sunburned men on their feet. When she released them, the men began weeping. They turned toward her, begging for her embrace. She rose out of their reach with the firm insistence of a parent doing what is right for her children.

"LEST YOU ALL DIE, I WILL DEPART," she told them. Her beaming eyes turned on the two men, and she said gently, "I WILL RETURN FOR YOU."

With that, she soared straight up, faster than a falcon could stoop from the sky. Despite her terrible speed, the heavenly light that poured from her did not quickly fade. At last, she seemed but a star in the firmament, though no other star shone in the morning.

Elionoway had stayed standing the whole time, a feat he complimented himself on.

Awash in the sun's light, the other refugees stirred. As they did, they whispered of Karona, the things she had said, and the two men she had left behind.

"These are her servants," one woman hissed, pointing to the naked fellows. "Prophets of the goddess."

Elionoway said, "She called them her friends, not her prophets."

"No, she said, 'Friends, behold my prophets.' "

"We are her friends, and these are her prophets," the mousy man added. "She warned us to listen to them and obey, lest we all die."

His wife elaborated, "She said she'd return for us. She plans to live with us here!"

"Or take us to her realm."

"What is it like, where she comes from?"

"Will we be the first people there?"

"Has she taken others? Are we the only friends of the goddess?"

"Ask the prophets!"

"Listen to them and obey!"

"Listen, friends, lest we all die!"

The crowd had risen from their bellies to their knees. With hands clenched and eyes pleading, they looked to the so-called prophets, Sash and Waistcoat.

Elionoway snorted. Not so long ago, these two dolts had been insects, and they seemed to have gotten no brighter in the last few months. It was time to set things straight.

"Yes, let's listen to these men. Tell them, Sash and Waistcoat. Tell them what the lady said. Did she call you prophets or friends? Is she coming back for all of us, or just for you? Tell us, please."

Naked and nonplussed, the erstwhile roaches only stared stupidly back.

* * * * *

Waistcoat gave the elf a thoughtful look. He didn't want the man to know that he didn't know the answer to his questions. Leave it to Sash. He always had a smart answer for everything.

"Well, ah, you see," Sash began, quivering, "those are interesting questions. What did she say? That's the question of the ages. After all, we . . . um . . . speak not just with our mouths, but also with our eyes and our hearts. What did she say with her mouth and her eyes and her heart? That's how complicated this issue is. Did she say with her mouth that we were prophets or friends? What is a prophet but the friend of a god? And are you all friends? Well, to know Karona is, as you all demonstrate so clearly, to love her, and what state but love more typifies friendship? So, in answer . . . um—I have to relieve myself."

Like a red streak, Sash dashed suddenly away and around a boulder. Even as he went, he shouted, "Waistcoat can take it up from here."

Nice job, dolt, Waistcoat thought. Sash had spent about a hundred words to say nothing at all. Faces turned toward Waistcoat, hungry for knowledge. They looked as if they might eat him alive. Who was really the hungry one? Waistcoat hadn't eaten in, well—ever.

"You want to know what the lady said? Huh?" Waistcoat asked.

The folk nodded vigorously. The middle-aged elf said, "Yes. Tell them what she really said, Waistcoat."

"She said 'listen,' " Waistcoat replied firmly. "She didn't say 'jabber.' She didn't say 'jaw.' She said 'listen'—and, for that matter, 'obey.' All right then, here's the first thing you gotta listen to. I got a bad sunburn, and it's getting sunny again, and I notice that out of everybody here, who's got no clothes except the guy with the bad sunburn? So, here's the first 'obey' thing. Give me your clothes."

* * * * *

Sash finished up behind the boulder and came trotting back toward the camp. He hoped that Waistcoat hadn't botched things too terribly in his absence. Sash had begun a delicate proof, and Waistcoat probably didn't even know what a proof was except in regard to whiskey.

It took only a glance to confirm Sash's greatest fears.

Waistcoat was climbing into his fifth tunic while naked folk tossed him clothes. Only one middle-aged elf and Waistcoat himself were clothed.

"What's going on here?" Sash demanded.

"Clothes!" Waistcoat proclaimed in his stupid way.

"I know they are clothes, but what are you doing with them?" Sash asked.

Beneath all his layers, Waistcoat had broken out in a sweat. "They protect against the sun and look good on me. Also, they don't want 'em anymore."

"We want to be naked, like the prophets of the goddess," one man shouted.

A woman offered, "We listened, and we obeyed. Please do not kill us."

Waistcoat said, "I think they look good naked. Hey! How come these pants are shrinking? Something's happening, Sash!"

"Go behind the rock and see," Sash ordered. "I'll straighten this thing out."

Waistcoat plodded away toward the boulder.

Sash shook his head. A sorry sight, these poor creatures reduced to nudity at the whim of a moron. "Take your clothes. All of you. Put them back on. You've shown your devotion to Karona, and you will not die. There you go. Well done. Meanwhile, I'll just take one of these bed sheets here and . . ." He lifted a makeshift tent from the rocks that held down its corners, tore a hole in the center, and draped it over himself. "There. Now, if someone could make another of these garments for my friend, the rest of you can have your clothes back as well."

"Anything to serve you! To serve you is to serve Karona! What else do you need, mighty Sash?"

"Well, we're really hungry. We've not eaten a thing since . . . since we saw the light of Karona," Sash said.

"We will fast too, until she returns to us!"

"The finest we have, we give you!" a woman cried, pulling a loaf of flat bread from a satchel in her tent.

A man produced a small bag of figs. "*All* that we have, we give!"

A torrent of people, clothed, naked, and half-dressed, approached to lay their simple rations in a semicircle before Sash. He felt like a common rat, stooping and sniffing, snatching morsels in his greedy hands and gnawing them, but his hunger was too great to wait. He had gobbled down a bundle of jerked beef and drunk a skin of wine before Waistcoat returned. The fat prophet bent to wolf down whatever he could get his mouth around.

Sash was soon sated and sat back on his heels. He looked casually at his comrade, disgust and admiration mixing on his features. "So, how did things turn out behind the boulder?"

"Amazing," the portly man said. "I had no idea."

"They've made you a robe like mine. Take off the clothes."

"Give me a couple minutes."

Sash turned his attention back toward the throng. They had silently waited, watching every move of the two "prophets."

The elf spoke up. "I remember a couple of giant roaches who used to eat exactly the same way."

Elionoway, realized Sash. This could be it. If the people found out that they were not really prophets, that they were just a couple guys lucky enough to have made friends with Karona, they could be stripped and stoned. Still, what could Sash say? He had been identified.

"Ah, yes, Elionoway. I remember you too."

The elf approached among the kneeling folk. "Do you? Well, perhaps then you'll be so good as to tell us who you were and who you really are."

Sash lowered his head, mind racing. What could he say? He had to say something. He was, after all, a prophet, and the people were hanging on his every word. Sash couldn't trust his mind to work it through, so he just trusted his tongue and started speaking. "We used to be giant roaches in the service of Phage of the Cabal."

The kneeling folk visibly recoiled, and Elionoway wore a triumphant grin. A woman said, "But you're not giant roaches now."

"No," Sash said, and suddenly he knew how he would save them both, "because of Karona. We were nothing before she touched us. Now, we are men, truly human, and we would serve her to the end of our days."

"Oh, we too!" chorused a number of the people there. "Just tell us how!"

"How can we please her?"

"What does she want?"

"What does she forbid?"

"How can we bring her back?"

"We wish only to go with her, to her realm. Oh, tell us of the place where she will take us!"

Sash's glib tongue had gotten him in this far. He would trust it to deliver him utterly. "Oh, so many questions! Fine questions too. Did you know that Karona values questions highly? It is good to question. She herself questions all things. Indeed, she may answer your questions with questions, and so shall I."

Elionoway smacked his forehead.

"You asked, among other things, what does Karona forbid? I respond simply, what would you forbid?"

"Murder," volunteered Waistcoat, his eyes staring at the ground as though he saw a massacre happening between his feet. He glanced rapidly up, and said, "Sorry."

Sash nodded. "The prophet Waistcoat is showing you the will of Karona. She despises murder, as do you. Many have murdered each other in her name, in her very presence, and she has slain those guilty of such acts. What does she forbid? Murder, for one. What else would you forbid?"

"Rape," volunteered a middle-aged woman.

Sash nodded. "Right. Rape. Excellent. What else?"

"Public nudity," someone called out.

Waistcoat looked up from the clothes he had finally shed, let out a little squeal, and turned two shades darker red. He snatched up the bed sheet someone had provided and wriggled into it.

"Is it so bad to be naked in public?"

"Yes," said the crowd without hesitation.

"All right," Sash responded. "See? We're learning the mind of Karona now. What else would you forbid?"

"Sunburns," Waistcoat said vehemently.

The people laughed.

Even Sash chuckled. "The prophet Waistcoat has done it again. With a single word, he has shown us that even by creating laws of morality, we cannot remove all the suffering in the world. Sunburns cannot be eliminated through moral law. Neither can disease or death, starvation, injury, or despair. We can do what is right and shun what is wrong and still suffer. We can help those who need help and laugh whenever there is nothing else we can do, but still, there will be suffering."

Into the grave silence that followed, Elionoway said quietly, "Then what does Karona offer us? We knew not to murder or rape or run naked before she came to us. We knew there would be suffering. We are, after all, refugees of a ruined city. What does Karona offer these poor wanderers aside from a faceful of dirt and a backache from bowing?"

"I'll tell you what, Smarty," interrupted Waistcoat. "She lets us see something beautiful. That don't sound like much when you're hungry or sick or lost or frightened. It don't stop you from feeling all that stuff, but it does make it seem like it's all for something instead of for nothing." He had begun his speech with bluster and ended it uncertainly, his voice retreating behind his lips and going silent.

The crowd hushed in assent.

In the silence Sash said, "You asked how we could get her to return sooner. I say Karona will return in her own time. You asked what she wants. I say only this: She wants us to be fed and clothed, healthy and happy."

"Our food and shelter are in short supply," a man said. "We cannot remain here long."

Sash's face fell. "Well, food is critical. We can't wait. Karona will catch up to us. We should continue on to a place where there is plenty of food, where we can be comfortable."

"Where?" they asked eagerly.

Waistcoat spread his hands. "We were heading to Eroshia."

* * * * *

Elionoway couldn't believe it. For three days, he'd tried to get these folks to head for Eroshia. Now, after a few words from a former cockroach, the whole camp scurried off to pack.

CHAPTER 7

THE LAQUATUS COLOSSUS

*U*h, Balthor?"

"Yes."

"The colossus is moving."

"Yer right."

"I could use some help."

"Sorry. It's got no spirit."

"Great. Suggestions?"

"Try killing it."

A huge moan filled the air to Kamahl's right. He leaped backward, and what could only have been an enormous hand rushed through the darkness just before him, stunning his nose and toes and slamming into the giant's chest. A putrid tremor shook the whole pectoral mound, and Kamahl went to one knee. Still clutching the Mirari sword, he scuttled backward.

"Other suggestions?"

"Run!"

Kamahl dived off of the colossus's belly. In midair, he realized this was the second gigantic torso he had escaped in the last hour. Kicking, Kamahl tried to get his feet beneath him. Whether he'd be landing on the rocks or in the eel-infested waters, he'd rather not arrive headfirst. One foot came down on solid ground, and he huffed a grateful sigh, but the other foot set down on nothing. Kamahl flipped sideways, swinging the Mirari sword up to protect his head. He splashed into the chill lake, plunging deep. Muscular somethings swam past him, and above him came a crack like thunder.

The huge hand smacked down on the water. It drove deep, opening a well that laid bare the rocky bed of the lake. Kamahl dived again. Gigantic fingernails scraped his ankles as he escaped into the dark waters. The colossus's fist closed on nothing.

Kamahl swam. He held the Mirari sword beneath him, the handle near his face and the tip near his feet, and waved it back and forth. The blade acted as a great fin, propelling him through the deeps.

Another explosion of sound came behind him, and a third and forth. The colossus was catching up. With the next grab, Kamahl would be caught.

The sword shone on a school of lightning eels, which swam in a tight bunch around the Mirari. Kamahl rolled over, bringing the sword up above him. The eels followed its glow, as he had hoped. A huge hand appeared above the surface, smashed through it, and reached down to Kamahl. He released the sword and dropped away. Colossal fingers closed on the blade and yanked it up.

Surfacing, Kamahl flung his hair back and took a great gasp.

"Ye lost the sword!" Balthor railed.

"No, I didn't."

The giant squeezed its fist. Terrific sparks shot between its fingers, and lightning charges arced and crawled across its knuckles. The hand reflexively opened, and chunks of eel fell along with the sword.

Kamahl watched the weapon fall, swimming toward its point of impact. It cut through the waves and rushed downward. Kamahl followed it down. He cared nothing for the huge monster above him but only for the sword. Colder, deeper, more terrible—the lake seemed to have no bottom. With a double kick of his feet, Kamahl at last grasped the pommel. He swung the blade beneath him and used it again as a fin.

At least if there is no bottom, Kamahl thought, the colossus can't wade across.

A vast concussion behind him put the lie to that thought. The colossus didn't have to walk. It was a merman, after all. It could swim.

Kamahl surfaced to gasp a breath. He glanced back but could not see the enraged corpse. Still, it churned the lake. Waves of four or five fathoms hurled Kamahl like a cork. Their foamy tops gleamed gray in the sword's light, and just above them hung what looked like dwarf boots.

"What now, Balthor?"

"Give me the sword!" the dwarf yelled.

"What?"

"Give me the sword, ye daft man!"

"It's metal! You can't affect it."

"It's more spirit than metal," said Balthor, swooping down in a great trough then soaring up above the next breaker. He reached out his ghostly hand. "Give it!"

Kamahl's mind raced. He hadn't come so far, endured so much, only to give up the blade. "What're you going to do? Terrify it?"

"Now!" the dwarf bellowed, lunging to seize the hilt.

Above him, invisible to the dwarf but all too clear to Kamahl, descended the massive hand of Laquatus. Kamahl relinquished the blade to Balthor, and the dwarf ghost hauled the spirit-blade up and away. Balthor slid from beneath the rotten palm, though it came down full-force on Kamahl.

He flattened in the water and went limp, letting his body flow with the liquid. The giant hand rammed him deep into the lake, and Kamahl was dragged among its fingers like seaweed. He could only hope the colossus would fixate on the sword and forget the man in its grip. Water squeezed his temples and ears, and his skull whined as if it would break. The hand rose, flinging him away. Kamahl tumbled in the choppy tide, forgotten.

The colossus swam toward the far shore, following the sword. It retreated up a long, long shaft high above.

Balthor! That thief. All along, he only wanted his sword. Clearly, he could not draw it himself from the heart of the colossus. He needed a mortal to do that, but now Balthor needed no one. Kamahl had been betrayed. In the space of a few moments, his ally had become his enemy.

Such was the way of the Mirari sword.

Gritting his teeth, Kamahl swam toward the scaly back of the colossus. It rushed through the waters like a pod of whales, numerous spinal fins jutting from the surface. Kamahl stroked to one such fin and latched on. Darkly, he imagined himself as just another clinging eel. Water ran in regular rivers down the thing's swimming back. In a scant minute, the colossus crossed the vast lake. It clambered up the far side. Webbed feet skidded on the stones, its back tilted to vertical, and Kamahl clung on. The giant zombie craned its neck to see the light of the Mirari disappearing above.

Kamahl's face stung with the betrayal. He would ride the monster in pursuit of Balthor, wrench the Mirari sword from him, and use it to slice that thieving ghost in two.

The colossus slapped its feet along the shore until it reached the shaft where Balthor ascended. It began to climb. Suckers on fingers and toes stuck to the smooth stone, and putrid muscles slid beneath a skin of scales. The zombie did not need to breathe, but the gases of decay shuddered out of its body as it ascended the rock face.

Struggling to avoid the noxious fumes, Kamahl climbed the spinal fins. Torrents of air poured down the shoulders of the monster, and above it the light of the Mirari glimmered faintly. It looked as if Balthor had stopped to hover a mile or so overhead.

Had he reached a dead end? Was the chamber blocked by the bear-guardian's corpse?

The colossus climbed higher. Its massive hands rammed into voids in the cliff face, and it groaned with terrible longing. The things that lived on those ledges gave their own groans and scampered out along the giant's arms. Spiders as big as panthers sank their hairy stingers into the merman's flesh. They pumped their black poison beneath the pallid skin. Still, the colossus climbed, and so the spiders swarmed out across it. They rounded the giant's shoulders and converged on Kamahl.

"And me without a sword," he snarled.

A glance upward showed the very blade he sought hanging in the air above Laquatus's head. Balthor was indeed trapped at the top of the shaft. Kamahl launched himself up fins as if up a ladder. Spider stingers reached for him, but he scaled the giant's neck and climbed the back of its head. Kamahl leaped, reaching to snatch the sword from his ghostly comrade.

Too late. The colossus grabbed it first. Its hand enveloped the blade, and Balthor could not hold on. With a putrescent huff of laughter, Laquatus held the glowing weapon up before its face. It slowly opened its hand to gaze on the beloved thing.

Gripping a forehead scale with his left hand, Kamahl dropped down on the colossal nose, leaned out, and snatched the Mirari sword with his right hand. In pure glee, he bounded off the giant's snout and back onto its pate just before a suckered hand crashed into its face. Kamahl crouched to keep his feet on the shaking skull. The colossus was enraged, and huge spiders crawled up all around its head.

Still, Kamahl couldn't remember being so happy. He spun, swinging the sword in a wide arc that cut through three spiders and sent their halves flying. A backhand swing skewered a fourth. With his bare foot, Kamahl kicked a fifth loose. It was just like old times—King of the Mountain, killing all who opposed him.

That jarred him.

"This way!" hissed Balthor, gesturing across the shaft to a passageway.

"Why should I trust you!" Kamahl shouted as he killed another spider.

"Because he'll smash ye otherwise."

The moaning air warned of an imminent strike to the head. Kamahl took two running steps and launched himself across the emptiness. It wasn't empty for long, filled with the flailing hands of the colossus. One digit knocked Kamahl down the shaft, but another flung him up again. He swung his arm out and barely caught an edge of stone in one hand. Roaring, he hauled his sword arm onto the ledge and pulled himself up afterward. Kamahl staggered to his feet and ran full-force into a root tangle. He fell back onto the ledge.

"Now I know why you gave up the sword," Kamahl growled.

He leaped to his feet and swung the weapon as if it were an axe. The edge bit into the roots and sank deep. He chucked the blade loose and swung it again, the opposite direction. This was going to take an eternity. Kamahl yanked on the pommel, and the blade ripped from the tangle, flinging him to the floor. That accident saved him.

The fist of Laquatus sailed overhead and punched through the roots. They shattered in a hail of splinters. The colossus dragged its arm back, intent on grabbing Kamahl.

He vaulted over the wrist, sword still in hand, and charged past the snarl of roots.

Close on his heels floated Balthor.

Kamahl snarled at him. It was galling to be followed by the ghostly figure, and doubly so given that Balthor wasn't even breaking a sweat.

"Get away from me, traitor."

"What? Ye'd call me that after all I've done!"

"Done!" huffed Kamahl as he skipped ahead of the reaching hand of the colossus. "You mean . . . steal my sword and leave me . . . in a pit with a monster!"

"I mean save the sword and get ye out of the pit," barked Balthor. "And it ain't *yer* sword. It ain't mine, neither. That sword belongs to the ages."

Kamahl dashed through a stony arch and entered another large chamber, its ceiling and far walls invisible in the darkness. He skidded to a halt, clutched his knees, and panted. "You can forget about . . . getting it back. It's mine!"

The ghost lifted his hands and edged nearer. "Easy, now."

With a roar, Kamahl swung the sword through the spot where Balthor had been, though now he was gone. "It can destroy you!" Kamahl raged, looking around the cavern. His voice echoed from the distant walls. "I know it can! It's a spiritual weapon, and it can destroy spirits."

Balthor reappeared a stone's throw away, standing with arms crossed and lips pursed. From the corridor down which they had run came the sounds of stone cracking under terrible pressure. Balthor ignored it. His voice sounded like that of an angry dog.

"See, this is why ye need me, Kamahl."

"Why! To steal my sword when the colossus comes?"

"No. To keep the sword from stealing yer soul. Look at ye! I bet ye'd slay ye're own tribe—me own tribe—to keep that thing."

"You'd better believe . . ." Kamahl began, but suddenly he seemed to hear his own words. He stared at the blade, the Mirari glowing at its end. Once the orb had been insatiable, but Kamahl had filled it with the darkness of his own soul. Now the orb was pouring that darkness back into him. "You're right." He held out the weapon. "You take it."

Balthor slowly shook his head. "No. You keep it, but remember the danger."

In the passageway, rock shattered. Dust and cracked stone billowed over them.

"Let's get going," Kamahl said, struggling to see the ceiling. "How do we get out of here?"

"It'll follow ye," Balthor said flatly. "It's digging though solid rock to get to ye. Don't be thinking it'll be enough just to climb out of this hole. It'll chase ye across Otaria—"

"Unless I kill it now."

Balthor nodded gravely. "The sword created it. The sword can destroy it."

"How?"

The old dwarf said flatly, "I don't know."

The floor of the cavern shook as if the colossus were moving beneath it. Kamahl backed up toward the near wall, holding the Mirari sword in a double-hand grip before him.

"We'll know soon enough."

A crack began near his feet and jagged like lightning out into the dark center of the cavern. Another fissure opened nearby. The manifold crackle and boom told of countless more seams opening. Kamahl edged backward, but a section of floor behind him broke free and tumbled into the darkness.

"Balthor, if you've got any suggestions—"

The floor burst open. Great triangles of rock cracked loose and stood on end. They tilted and fell away to reveal the gargantuan corpse, tattered in places to the bone. It reared its scabrous skull and roared. The horrid sound geysered up on putrid breath and shook the cavern.

Kamahl backed against the wall. If not for the jagged ledge where he stood, he would plunge into that darkness. He couldn't escape, couldn't hide, could only stand there with the Mirari sword jutting before him.

It was the very item the colossus had swum and climbed and caved to grasp. Its dead eyes—sagging sacs in its face—fixed on the gleaming weapon, and hands that had been reduced to gigantic pincers of bone reached for it.

Kamahl set his feet and summoned memories of the mountain barbarian he used to be. He sent power sizzling into the blade. It grew red-hot, gleaming in his grip. As the trembling finger bones grew near, Kamahl lashed out.

Thran-metal struck bone and sheered straight through. The fingers of the colossus rang like wooden blocks as they cascaded into the darkness.

Kamahl stood, the fires of mana stoked within him. He smiled, knowing the idiotic beast could no longer grasp the thing it most desired.

The colossus was not quite so idiotic. It clenched its other fist and smashed it into the rock wall above Kamahl. Stone shattered and fell in a brutal cascade on the man. Kamahl collapsed under pelting rocks, and the rushing weight of stone buried him. They cut, bruised, and then crushed him beneath their pile. The sword alone remained beyond, hanging loosely in a nerveless grip. The Thran-metal cooled from its mana-fury.

Kamahl tried to drop the blade, fling it down into the Abyss—anything but let the colossus have it again. He could not move his hand.

The stumps of Laquatus's finger bones fastened on the blade and dragged it loose. In triumph, the colossus lifted the weapon. It was a century old, fashioned from a staff that was nine millennia old. This sword was the source of the colossus's great growth. For a sheath, it had the very heart of Laquatus, and as long as it remained there, the giant would live and grow forever.

"No!" gasped Kamahl, willing his stunned legs and arms to move. "No!"

With almost delicate movements, the massive corpse turned the sword in its hand, set the blade tip on the crevice in its chest, and slid it through its very heart. Only the Mirari remained outside the chest wall, the rest scabbarded in rotten muscle. Power scintillated from the weapon out through the colossus. Its putrid flesh seemed to swell.

Kamahl had ceased to struggle beneath the rock pile. It was not physical war that would win this battle, but spiritual.

"Balthor," he whispered as if in prayer, "guide and channel the mana I draw." Kamahl did not hear the ghost or see him but sensed that he understood.

Extending the hand that had lost the sword, Kamahl closed his eyes and tapped memories of the mountains, of jagged peaks and sun-baked stones, of giant bears and sure-footed goats. He drew upon a lifetime of memories, pouring them through his hand as though he still held the sword. Instead of flowing into its blade, the magic shot through the air—and through the spirit that hovered there.

If Balthor could not shunt the power, Kamahl would bake himself alive.

Kamahl remembered the trail of death he carved with that sword—the fury, the blood. He remembered the betrayal on his sister's face, the red wound that bloomed across her center, the gory glory of barbarian bloodshed.

The power was going somewhere. It did not remain in Kamahl.

He opened his eyes to see the Mirari beaming like a red sun. The blade too must have glowed, for black smoke poured from the hole in the colossus's chest. Next moment, the flesh itself ignited. Pockets of volatile gas exploded, lighting more pockets farther out. The gigantic corpse flared in concentric shells away from the sword. The heart of the monster blasted away, and when the flames reached its foul lungs, it erupted. A terrific blast dismantled its torso, its legs, its head. Pulverized flesh roared out in a putrid corona, sizzling to nothing before it could strike the walls of the cavern.

The blast had etched a blind circle in Kamahl's eyes, but still he did not look away. He wanted to see where the Mirari sword fell so he could climb down to retrieve it.

It did not fall but hung in the air, slowly dimming. At last, all the red force was gone from it, and only its silvery sheen remained.

Kamahl stared unbelieving at it, long enough to see a ghostly figure clutching the blade and walking toward him across the air.

"Come, Kamahl," Balthor said. "Let's get ye out of there. Ye've a sword to wield and a world to save."

CHAPTER 8

THE POWER OF PRESENCE

At thirteen, Kuberr was whip-thin in his black jumpsuit. His ebon cape flapped behind him like the wings of a raven. He stood atop the central column of the coliseum, his favorite perch, for here he could see everyone, and they could see him. They could hear him, too, thanks to Braids's spell.

She stood nearby on the capital and wore a sour smile.

Kuberr lifted his hands toward the multitude, though his eyes peered even beyond the coliseum, to the swamps and the wide world. "Thank you, friends, for joining me today," he cried. His voice was boyish and pure, but an adult malice hid in his words. "After the atrocities of my father, you had every right to abandon the games. He had used this great coliseum for evil. I will use it for good."

Cheers bloomed across the stands, initiated by strategically placed Cabal agents.

"Yes, there is much to account for. My father slew a hundred thousand souls in the seats where you sit. Some folk whisper that I will do the same. Never! To you today, another hundred thousand, I apologize. To the hundred thousand tomorrow, and the next day— I will apologize to each for a year. For every life my father took, I will make penance a hundredfold."

The crowd applauded.

"More—you paid no fee to enter. No one ever again will pay to enter."

That brought real adulation from the crowd.

"This is your coliseum. No one will be turned away. As my father made this a place of death, I will make it a place of life. Here you will come to cheer, to laugh, to weep, to be entertained, to be educated. Here you will come for jobs and for justice. Every city and village in Otaria has an arena. All aspire to be the coliseum. Through those little arenas and this great coliseum, we will bring the continent together."

A standing ovation answered his words.

"You know of Karona the Scourge. Where she goes, people kill each other. Where she appears, war follows. While she lives, we all are imperiled. Only by joining together can we stand against her. But who will rally us? The Northern Order? Their laws strangle them. The believers in Ixidor? They are in schism. The Pardic peoples? Barbarians only fight for themselves. Krosan? It rots. If this continent is to be saved, we will save it. From village to town to city, we are there. Playing, teaching, adjudicating, we will not leave you abandoned. The Cabal is Otaria. We will keep you safe and glad all your days!"

The cry from the throng was deafening, enhanced by Braids's own spell.

"But enough talk. On to the games!" As the great cheer quieted, Kuberr flung one hand out toward the eastern edge of the arena. "Behold, a familiar figure. Yes! It would seem my own mother, so recently and tragically lost. Let us hear a cheer for our hero!"

As the crowd poured out its ovation, from a doorway emerged a woman in black silks. A red thunderbolt was stitched across her midsection. She was not Phage but played her part, and the folk loved her.

Turning to the west, Kuberr gestured again. "There, the slayer of my mother, the progenitor of the Scourge, behold Akroma!"

Boos and hisses heralded the woman who emerged. Artifact-wings had been grafted to her shoulders, and her legs were painted to look like the hind legs of a jaguar.

"We all know of their final battle at the height of Sanctum, now called Averru City. The women led great armies. They fought each other and in the end were slain by Kamahl." Kuberr pointed to the sidelines, where waited a barbarian with dreadlocks and a great black axe. "In this reenactment, both women bear a warding against heat. It will last for five minutes. Both also will be magically set aflame, an enchantment that will last for ten minutes. The winner gets doused. The loser gets burned alive. If neither wins, Kamahl here will put both out of their misery. Now, let the games begin!"

As the crowd roared, Braids waved away her magical amplifications. She crossed to her young charge, shaking her head. "Cheap theatrics. These aren't real fights. There's no skill in this."

The young man lifted his black brows and sneered serenely. "There's plenty of skill—my skill. Besides, the fights were never about fighting. They were always about power. Through them, Dominaria will be mine."

Braids crossed her arms and donned a smug smile. "Until Karona takes it from you. Why don't you raise an army to bring her down?"

Kuberr's expression darkened, and he stared northward over the swamps. "You don't understand Mother. If we send an army, the men only become her followers. You can't fight her. You can only hope she doesn't come to visit."

"What if she does?"

Kuberr snorted, and his cocksure grin returned. "Then you'd better be ready for a damned good show."

* * * * *

"Would you look at that!" Waistcoat said, shielding his eyes against the afternoon glare. The trail to Eroshia had been long and laborious, and the prophets and their fledgling nation were exhausted. Just ahead, the road took one final curve and arrived at the great stone gates of Eroshia. They looked like heaven. The two towers on either side were crowded with guards, and more folk filled the battlements. "That's what you call a royal reception!"

Sash, who hobbled gingerly beside Waistcoat, griped, "If you'd open your eyes, you'd see that those folk are armed and angry. The portcullises are full of bloodhounds."

"Oh," said Waistcoat, spinning around. "Back to Sanctum!"

Sash grabbed the shoulder of his robe and hauled him around. "Too late. They'd only run us down. Besides, I'd rather die at the gates than walk another hundred steps."

"B-but those're the dogs that hunted us for a month, and those're the guards!"

"They hunted unmen," Sash pointed out. "We're not unmen. We've got bodies now. We smell completely different."

"We do?"

"*You* do. Who would have thought bathing was so necessary? Sure, you hear about baths, but you don't understand until you need one yourself." He looked down at Waistcoat. "You need one. There are rules against pigs running loose in the streets."

Waistcoat rubbed his hands together. "Oh, Eroshia! Remember the women, the food?"

"Yes, and we didn't even have tongues," Sash said wistfully. "Let me do the talking. This is a delicate situation, and your brand of sledgehammer diplomacy would be disastrous."

Waistcoat scowled.

"Smile," hissed Sash through an unconvincing grin. "Now that you've got a face, people can read it."

Baring their teeth in cat smiles, the two prophets of Karona led their weary band of refugees to the forbidding gates of Eroshia.

There they stopped, and the people muttered to each other like sheep before the slaughterhouse gates.

Sash called out, "Hail, great folk of Eroshia. We seek entrance."

"The city's closed," a guard shouted brusquely.

"What?" Sash responded. "It's not even dark."

"We've no room for paupers. We use our streets for carriages, not for beds."

Sash flushed, embarrassment and anger battling on his face. "You do not seem to know who we are. We are the friends of Karona, her prophets. We come in her name, and when we are among you, she will come to your fair city too."

"Akroma's dead," the guard replied.

"Not *Akroma!*" Sash barked. "Karona!"

"We don't want any. Go away."

Sash shook furiously but couldn't come up with another word.

Waistcoat helped out. "We wanna see Governor Dereg."

"What for?"

"It's about his stolen harpsichord."

Sash hissed, "You imbecile!"

The guard spoke to a young boy, who ran along the wall to the stairs, dashed down them, and tore off through the city. Meanwhile, the guard turned back to the group of refugees. "How do you know about the stolen harpsichord?"

"We're prophets," Waistcoat said grandly. "We know everything."

Slapping a hand over his partner's mouth, Sash pulled him aside.

Elionoway spoke up. "They call themselves Prophet Sash and Prophet Waistcoat."

The guard's eyes grew so large they looked like boiled eggs. "Duke Sash and Lord Waistcoat?"

Sash shouted, "Actually, no. They're cousins. Bad seeds. They're the ones mixed up in this whole harpsichord debacle, not us."

"Yeah," added Waistcoat, spreading his bedsheet robe. "Where would I stash a harpsichord? I got flesh now."

A terrific commotion on the wall announced the arrival of Governor Dereg. The man was tall and distinguished, with a salt-and-pepper mustache that jutted across either cheek.

"What's this! Duke Sash and Lord Waistcoat?"

"No, Governor," Sash said hastily. "Cousin Sash—I mean, Prophets Sash and Waistcoat, cousins of the ne'er-do-wells that, well, came into possession of your harpsichord."

"At least we didn't leave it by the river," Waistcoat said.

"Ahem. He means we didn't have anything to do with it."

"Where is it?" the governor demanded, his face flaming.

"Broke in the badlands," Waistcoat blurted.

"Don't tell him that!"

The governor said something. A hundred bows along the wall drew taut, their strings whining for permission to release. Steel arrowheads gleamed like teeth in a very wide smile. Sharper still were the eyes of Governor Dereg, who shouted to the refugee throng, "Stay still, all of you, or the 'prophets' will die."

A cry of outrage and disbelief came from the refugees.

Careful not to move, Sash hissed tightly, "In the name of Karona, stay still!"

That hushed the group, though words such as "infidel" and "blasphemer" leaped back and forth through the crowd like notes passed among children. Meanwhile, the two prophets stayed frozen.

While the archers remained in place, the portcullises rattled up in their frames, and grim-looking soldiers marched out, pikes to the fore. Dogs came with them, straining on leather leashes. Slobbery, jowly beasts, they used the prophet's robes like handkerchiefs.

Sash stood stock still despite an intimate search by a wet nose. "I think we've just found something else Karona would disapprove of."

Waistcoat smiled tightly. "I'm trying to decide whether I like it."

The touch of the dogs was gentle compared to the clank of irons around wrists and ankles. Rust rubbed orange on their skin, and the heavy chains dragged nastily at them. Still, even these were preferable to pike points between the shoulder blades.

"Get marching, Your Worship." A guard jabbed Sash.

"Your Worship," Waistcoat repeated pleasantly. "That must be your church name." His smile ended as he was prodded forward.

"Your church name must be 'Pew,'" Sash shot back. He trotted toward the gate, keeping just ahead of the pike point.

Waistcoat's chains jangled as he jogged up beside him. "Church has lots of dirty words—seminary, epistle, rectory . . ."

Sash laughed. "How about narthex, apse, and groin vault?"

Both of the prophets chuckled grimly as they passed beneath the portcullis arch.

"Why're we laughing? We're going to die!" Waistcoat said.

"It's one of those stupid body things," Sash replied bitterly. "Like when you cry because you're laughing so hard."

"Or like how it feels good to pick a scab."

"Yeah."

The conversation was cut short by the sudden clatter and roar of two portcullises descending. They boomed into their wells. Only Sash and Waistcoat were within the city. All the other refugees were locked out.

From the wall, Governor Dereg shouted, "Go away. Eroshia doesn't want you."

There came the sound of fine-leather soles on the rough stairs that led to the street. The governor emerged between his prisoners and joined the escort.

He was winded, but an avid glow lit his eyes. For a few strides, Dereg only studied the two men. Like any good politician, he was gathering his words, wrapping them like a gift. This particular gift contained a bomb.

"In all my time at the helm of this great city, never have I run afoul of such bilge rats as you two. Oh, yes, you dress up in clothes, you give yourselves names, but whenever you speak, I hear that unmistakable squeaking. I smell the plague on your breath."

"Nice town you have here," Waistcoat ventured. It was true: Well-kept row houses lined the streets, lanterns on wrought iron poles lit the cobbles, music rolled from open windows, carriages cruised by with not a horse in sight. "Very few droppings."

Dereg's pretended calm had vanished. "I know who you are! Charlatans. I recognize your voices."

Waistcoat replied, "Who, us?"

"You ate my harpsichord," Dereg growled. He jabbed a finger at Sash. "And you ate my bush."

"I'm not that sort!" Sash objected.

"You may have these poor rubes fooled, but now you're dealing with the educated ruler of a prosperous city. Eroshia is a land of plenty because of me. You fooled me once, but now who is the fool?"

"YES," came a voice above their heads, quiet but huge, serene and powerful. "WHO IS THE FOOL?"

Dereg looked up, and his eyes lit with a golden glow. The ends of his mustache drooped beside a plunging jaw. No longer did anger flare in his face. Now there was only worship. He fell to his knees, and a smile spread across his lips.

Waistcoat looked up to see Karona hovering there, a stone's throw above their heads. "Oh, hi," he observed.

She beamed, bright and strange.

"Just in time, Lady," said Sash. He held up his manacled hands and shook the chains.

Her eyes flared, and the iron links cracked like glass. They fell away from the two prophets. Shackles crashed on the paving stones and melted to nothing.

Dereg dropped into a prostrate bow, bedding his proud mustache in the grit.

Karona slowly descended. She reached the level of Eroshia's skyway—a cable-car conveyor driven by magic. No longer. As Karona slid down near it, the mana lines that drove the mechanism zapped loose. They arced from their conduits through the air and jolted into her. Her glow only increased. Meanwhile, the carts suspended above the city swung to a stop, citizens stranded in their fanciful machines. They didn't seem to mind. Their eyes were fixed on Karona, their faces wearing the same expression of awe as the governor's.

Karona drifted lower. In a ring around her the street lights faded, sputtered, and went out. Those nearest her reignited, brighter than ever. They blazed until they popped, spraying the street with shattered glass. Her presence affected other magical things. An enchanted lock on a clockmaker's shop burst. Magical music boxes in a nearby window blared. A sword smith's enspelled weapons jittered to the ground and melted. A usurer's window, apparently warded, burst into the street. Gardens that bore small growth enchantments twisted into tangled monstrosities. Any mana around Karona was drawn into her, and it flooded back out into nearby magic.

The people of Eroshia were oblivious. They did not care that their thatched roofs turned to shaggy hillocks, that their artifact jewelry burst and cut them with shrapnel. They paid no heed to the crash of sorcerous conveyances or the mad flight of clockwork engines through the air. All eyes fixed upon Karona as the eyes of drowning people fix on the surface. When she drew near enough, they could bear to look no longer, and they lay on their faces.

Only two men seemed immune, two men in makeshift robes. They wore insipid smiles as they watched their glorious friend set foot on the ground.

"So, how've you been?" Waistcoat asked.

"IT'S LONELY AND COLD IN THE SKY. I'VE COME DOWN A FEW TIMES WHERE NO ONE IS, AND IT IS LONELY THERE TOO. EVENTUALLY, PEOPLE ARRIVE, BUT THEN THEY KILL EACH OTHER."

"Poor girl," said Waistcoat. "We got sore feet."

Sash spread his hands, indicating the street, the shops, the prostrate people. "Well, this is Eroshia. What do you think?"

Karona looked around, wonder in her eyes. "IT IS BEAUTIFUL."

"I am the ruler," came the muffled voice of Governor Dereg, though he did not look up. "The city is yours. You may stay with me."

Karona stared down at his back and seemed to consider. "DO YOU HAVE FOOD WHERE YOU STAY?"

"Yes. Of course. Whatever you wish."

"MY FRIENDS MUST EAT OR THEY WILL DIE. THEY ALSO MUST DRINK. DO YOU HAVE DRINKS?"

"Yes. Of every variety."

"SHELTER, PROTECTION, ENTERTAINMENT . . . DID YOUR BODIES HAVE OTHER NEEDS?"

"There's one other big one," Waistcoat said.

"We'll make a list," suggested Sash.

"Anything," Governor Dereg said. "Only promise you will remain with us and never leave."

Sash shook his head. "Karona makes no promises—I think that's a good policy, don't you?"

She nodded thoughtfully.

"Stay as long as you can. We want to be with you, to please you," Dereg said.

"I'LL STAY UNTIL SUNSET, LEST YOU KILL EACH OTHER, BUT I'LL RETURN AT TIMES TO BE WITH YOU."

The man at last dared to look at her. Worship filled his eyes.

"LET THE OTHER REFUGEES IN, AND FIND HOMES FOR THEM—FOOD AND ALL THE REST. ORDER YOUR PEOPLE TO STAND AND CHEER AS THEY COME. THIS SHOULD BE A DAY OF JOY. THIS IS THE DAY WHEN KARONA COMES TO EROSHIA."

"Yes," Dereg said, nodding excitedly. Tears streamed down his face. "It is a day of great joy!"

CHAPTER 9

THE OLD TERRIBLE REMORSE

*T*hey made an unlikely pair: Kamahl was tall and bronze-skinned, and Balthor was short with no skin at all. Kamahl bore new mantis armor, a heavy pack, and the massive Mirari sword. Balthor floated at his side, weightless. The only similarity between the men was their long gray hair and beards and the fact that both grumbled ceaselessly.

"Why so much sand?" Kamahl wondered as he tromped across another dune. The Krosan Forest had swallowed a hundred miles of desert—so had Topos and the swamp lands of the coliseum—yet all this sand remained.

"It gets into everything. I can feel the grit in my gums."

"Sometimes I like being a ghost," Balthor said.

Kamahl's eyes narrowed as he peered toward the sere horizon. "What's the point of a place like this? Useless to people, to plants, to animals . . ."

"The vultures're sure happy," Balthor said laconically. He glanced skyward, where small black forms circled. "And it ain't useless. Without this here sand spit, Krosan, Topos, and the lands of the Cabal'd all abut the Corian Escarpment. There'd be war."

"There *is* war." Kamahl said. He reached up to his left shoulder and slid his hand around the hilt of the sword. The touch was both invigorating and soothing. The Mirari rested like a great pearl against the heel of his hand. "Sometimes I think the only way to end war is decimate all who would make it."

The ghost-dwarf lifted an eyebrow. "Is that ye talking, or the Mirari sword?"

"It's easy for you," Kamahl said, still holding the hilt. "You're dead. Your battles are over."

"Are they, now?" Balthor nodded in exaggeration. "Sure. That's why I waited for two years for ye to draw the sword and now am drifting above a desolate sand spit with a hairy vagrant, traveling to a Nightmare Land made by a madman who'd been eaten by a big wurm. Yeah, sounds like me battles're over."

Kamahl drew the sword. It shone before him, brilliant in the ravening sun. It was no simple sword but an imposing presence, as if a third mind had just joined the debate.

"You know about Ixidor, don't you?" Kamahl asked, his eyes tracing the brutal edge of the sword.

"I know he's nearly a god, or was before getting swallowed."

"A god, perhaps, but more likely a devil."

"What makes ye say that?"

"Ixidor could create anything, but what did he create? An angel of death. He made Akroma to kill my sister. Just as I was trying to save Jeska, Ixidor was trying to kill her. Well, he succeeded at last. Now we have this . . . thing. This Karona." Kamahl shook his head viciously. "All this destruction began with Ixidor."

"Or with ye," Balthor said quietly. "Yer the reason yer sister became what she became. Yer the one who slew her with yer axe."

Kamahl continued walking, eyes fixed on the Mirari sword as if Balthor hadn't spoken. "He deserved to be swallowed by a deathwurm."

"Ye need him, lad. This one sword, great as it is, cannot bring down Karona. Ye need Ixidor."

Kamahl slowly shook his head. "I have a new plan. I'm not

going to free Ixidor. I'll kill the wurm that ate him, and if Ixidor is still alive within, I'll kill him as well. Then I'll take his lands."

"Ye don't need his lands. Ye need him."

"I need no one!" raged Kamahl, ramming the Mirari sword at Balthor's gut.

The ghost vanished, reappearing beyond the reach of the blade. "Ah, lad, I'm ashamed of ye. The sword has mastered ye again."

Kamahl's eyes flared, his brows canting downward. "With that blade, I destroyed the Laquatus colossus. You yourself were the mana channel through which I poured my rage. I am the master of this sword!"

"Oh, aye. Nothing can stand against ye when ye bear that sword. Whole nations have fallen at your feet."

"Indeed."

"Yer own nation, for one. Not even yer sister could oppose ye. Ye still see her, don't ye, lying wounded? Ye did that, or the sword through ye. Finish her off, Kamahl. Kill her as ye should've done the first time."

At last, the great barbarian paused in his tracks. He stood still, the Mirari sword jutting up before him. His eyes, which once gleamed avariciously with the blade's light, now were crowded with bodies and blood. It seemed as if flames burned in his pupils, and the smoke darkened his brows.

"You're right. The sword is using me. I must master it before I go into battle."

Balthor wore a grudging smile. "Yet another purpose for all this sand."

Kamahl snorted a laugh. He inverted the blade, set its tip on the dune, and shoved it downward. "Try to make something grow there," Kamahl said. He released his grip and backed away across the sandy peak. He shucked his backpack and laid it aside.

With a deep breath, Kamahl stepped to the top of the dune. He stood straight, feet directly beneath him and hands at his side.

Closing his eyes, he shut out the wide desert, the hovering dwarf, and even the weapon. There had to be only Kamahl in this moment. His heartbeats slowed, and his breathing stopped.

From utter stillness, Kamahl began to move. With weight centered over one leg, he spread the other out in a slow stride. He shifted to balance above both feet, body straight and arms poised before him. Again he shifted, bringing his fists overhead and sweeping down for a powerful double-strike.

These were the battle forms taught to all young barbarians before they were entrusted with a weapon. Kamahl was starting over at the beginning.

His foot moved in a slow, sweeping kick, designed to clear the field before a fight even begins. Planting his forward foot, he brought the other up for a second kick then executed a backhand punch.

Kamahl opened his eyes. He had gained full awareness of his own movement and now needed to account for the movements of his foe: the Mirari sword. It stood in the sand nearby. Silvery light crawled across the orb. Kamahl gauged the distance and launched himself in a dive and roll. He rose to his feet, well within his opponent's guard, caught hold of the hilt, and ripped the blade out of the ground.

The Mirari sword grabbed him as well. It poured its voracious want into him. Vitality and power filled his flesh—and promise.

You can rule the world, Kamahl. Slay Karona and rule it.

Kamahl clenched his teeth. He turned toward Balthor's ghost, floating on the sands nearby. The dwarf's grim expression provided clarity.

Kamahl shrugged off the sword's seduction and pivoted into the next form. He thrust the weapon out before him and swung it through arcs on either side of his body. The maneuver was meant to scare off lesser foes and challenge those who remained. Kamahl lunged, the precise motion of his first kill. His mind's eye sketched out the impaled body, the blood. Kamahl knew he should have felt regret. Instead, he felt joy.

The Mirari sword was the truest foe he had ever faced.

He imagined more foes, saw them dismantled like straw men. No. Straw doesn't bleed. These men bled wine, intoxicating, and their flesh was rare steak.

Kamahl flashed a look to Balthor. The dwarf's expression was gloomy.

The Mirari sword was winning.

Even as he entered the next form, Kamahl wondered if he could ever stop, or if the blade would dance him to death on the desert sands.

* * * * *

General Stonebrow and his personal patrol stood at the height of Averru City. They were stationed atop a broad red tower that gave the best view toward the desert. Nothing moved in that corner of the world. Stonebrow was glad.

"All right, first shift, you are released for mealtime," Stonebrow said quietly.

Two of his watchers—elves out of Krosan—glanced at him. Their eyes gleamed with the light of the desert. Tapping their shift mates—three humans, four dwarfs, and a normal-sized centaur— the elves motioned them to follow. On their way out, the first shift roused the second from their mats. Groggily, the new eyes opened, and their owners scrambled to posts.

It was tedious work, watching land and sky every moment of every day. Still, one day, doom would come. Karona had last been spotted two nights before, perhaps twenty miles out over the desert. She descended to land, remained motionless a long while, and rose again. Scouts reported dead bodies in a ring around the spot.

J. Robert King

Stonebrow brooded on that. Wherever she went, folk were maddened. Only the Glyphs seemed immune, but they were immune to most desires.

"Anything new, General?" asked a Glyph. It had approached silently behind him, its bubbling voice the first indication of its presence.

Stonebrow waved the ruby creature up beside him and peered into its implacable eyes.

"Nothing new," Stonebrow reported. "We're beginning the dinner rotation."

The Glyph nodded. "Much time is lost in these 'meals.' Perhaps feeding could occur once per day."

"No," Stonebrow said flatly. He had been placed in charge of all organic soldiers, not simply this personal platoon. Morale had been abysmal. Three meals a day provided their only real breaks.

"No?" the Glyph echoed.

Stonebrow shivered. He never knew whether a Glyph spoke only for itself or for Averru—until it was too late. Bowing his head, Stonebrow turned toward the Glyph. "Forgive me, Lord Averru. Mortal flesh and mortal minds have their limits. These troops are already at those limits."

The Glyph did not return his gaze, peering out at the widespread sands. It seemed to be looking at something in the north. "Six hours of sleep is the minimum required to keep the watchers sharp?"

"Yes, my lord," Stonebrow answered.

"Weak stuff, mortal flesh and mortal minds."

Stonebrow drew a deep breath. "Permission to speak freely, great Averru."

"I would expect no less, Stonebrow. You are a confidante. You are part of the spell and of the incarnation and the solution. You must always speak freely."

Steeling his courage, the giant centaur said, "You fight so ferociously for life, but you aren't alive. Life is eating, sleeping, desiring. . . .

These things can make mortal flesh weak but also strong—very strong. You worked great magic to bring yourself back from death, but it will take greater magic to bring you back to life."

At last, the Glyph turned from the northern sky and looked at Stonebrow. "This is why you are a confidante. You are right. Desire is the greatest spell. I must relearn it if I am to live." It gestured to the desert. "But first, someone battles on the sands."

Stonebrow stepped to the tower wall and opened his eyes wide, gazing onto the beaming desert. A flash of light came, and another—fitful and sharp-edged.

"Is it Karona?"

"No," the Glyph said. Its whole being was a huge lens, and it could see minute things at great distances. "Not Karona, but her maker—Kamahl."

Stonebrow strained to see but could not. He hardly dared hope. "What flashes?"

"His great sword with its blade of Thran-metal."

A laugh began deep in the centaur's throat and rolled out across the tower tops. "Forgive me." He pointed to the flashing light. "That man is a friend of mine—a mentor: a confidante. I thought he was dead, but I should've known better. He has more desire than an army. He's a force to be reckoned with."

"He is more than a friend of yours, and more than a force to be reckoned with," the Glyph replied.

"What do you mean?"

"Even as Karona hurled him from the city, I chose him. I set him a task, a series of great feats that will prove his worth. He has accomplished the first labor—retrieving that sword. To do so, he had to face down and destroy another great evil that he had made— an undead colossus. Two labors completed, and now he works a third. He battles for control of the sword, and he battles himself."

Stonebrow stared bleakly toward those minute flashes of light. "That's the one foe he should fear most."

"Indeed, it is a fight to the death." The Glyph watched intently. "But if he prevails, he will be the guide of the numena. He will bring me my two greatest weapons. With them, I will destroy Karona."

Stonebrow could only clutch the battlements and wish for better eyes.

* * * * *

Kamahl whirled again, no longer propelling the sword but being propelled by it. He had become its puppet, jittering mindlessly with its every move. At any time, he could let go, but that was the last thing he wished.

The sword swept through a grand arc beginning at his left heel and rising over his right shoulder to end at his left toe. It spun vertically on either side, his head darting back and forth to avoid decapitation. These strokes slowly flattened until the sword cut huge butterfly wings around him.

He had reached the three thousandth kata in the Pardic ritual of arms, moves designed to slay foes by the score. With this sword, they would die by the hundreds. Even so, the maneuvers were almost as dangerous to the warrior making them as to his foes.

Kamahl did not care. In his mind's eye, he had returned to the mountains and their ferocity. He was killing his own tribe again. Their bodies made the peaks only higher. It was a dance of death, slaying anyone who came near, and killing the swordsman himself.

Subtly, the battle shifted. Bloodlust drained away, replaced by a more desperate humor. He eviscerated a man, and the sight of his spilling life terrified Kamahl. He decapitated a woman and felt utter dread for what he had done. The sword in his hand no longer seemed glorious but depraved. On he fought, lest the savages overwhelm him, but his heart had gone out of the fight. Death brought terror.

Kamahl shook his head, and sweat flung from him. No. He could kill no more. He let the sword droop in his grip, and his enemies climbed over him and flung him to the ground. They would crush him and suffocate him, but he didn't care.

"At last ye lie still a moment," came a familiar voice through the din. "I feared ye'd kill yourself with all that flailing."

"Balthor," groaned Kamahl, still clinging to the sword. The imagined enemies slowly faded into the sky. "I can't do it anymore. I can't kill. I've mastered the sword."

"No, Kamahl. *I* mastered it. 'Twas I who made ye feel terror at each kill—ghostly powers and all. I had to stop ye somehow. No, lad, ye've failed."

Kamahl lifted his head to see the ghost standing nearby, hands on his hips. "But I no longer feel the compulsion."

"That's because of me. If I were to take away yer terrors, ye'd kill yerself with that thing. No. Ye can't master it, so ye can't bear it."

"That's not your decision, dwarf," Kamahl growled.

Balthor wore a sad smile. "Oh, 'tis. All I need to do is make you terrified of the sword. Ye'll drop it and run, and ye'll never kill with it again—"

Kamahl lashed out.

Balthor was too slow.

The blade sliced through the ghost, unmaking him. Balthor cried out in terror and betrayal as the Mirari sword emerged from his far side. Then he vanished forever.

Terrible remorse gripped Kamahl. He had slain the ghost just as he had slain Jeska. It was the selfsame stroke that had begun all this madness. Balthor was gone, and the old bloodlust was returning like a red tide.

The sands around him transformed into barbarian warriors. They rose, taking shape from the dust and stalking him with glee. Kamahl too rose. The fight would begin again, and this time it would end only in Kamahl's death.

"Oh, Balthor!" That death was not an illusion, and the dwarf would never be again.

Kamahl clasped hold of grief, the one thing that could end fury. He clung to it as tightly as he held the Mirari sword. While sharp-toothed enemies converged on him, Kamahl withdrew once again into himself. His mind sank down through the maelstrom of rage to find the calm center.

He reached it: the perfect forest, the spot of utter stillness. Amid endless ivy and eternal trees, he at last stood on solid ground. Now he could master the sword.

Foes fell on him. They bludgeoned him with maces, and he felt every gouge. They chopped him with axes, and his body became a red fountain. Pikes impaled him, and scourges flayed him, torches burned him and garrotes strangled him. He endured every torment and never once struck back. He didn't even realize when he fell.

The barbarian hordes faded, and the agony of their attacks as well.

Kamahl found himself lying on his back in the desert. The Mirari sword was still clutched in his hand. It no longer could tempt him. By drawing on the perfect forest within him, he had gained control over his fury.

He had mastered the Mirari sword.

As he lay there, Kamahl realized how silent the desert had become. "Oh, Balthor."

CHAPTER 10

IDENTITY

*T*he governor was saying something. Sash couldn't hear, what with the lute and flute nearby. Dereg's posture didn't help, either. He was bowed on hands and knees, and he talked into the thick red carpet. His muffled voice had to rise up nine steps to reach the prophets' dais and competed with the crackle of pastries, the gurgle of wines, and the laughter of warm-bodied ladies lying on either side of Sash. All in all, it was very distracting.

Waistcoat said, "Huh?"

Dereg said something else.

"*Huh?*"

The governor lifted his head, dragging the ends of his mustaches off the prickly carpet. ". . . permission . . . approach . . . hear—"

"It's no use," Sash said. "Why don't you approach so we can hear?"

Dereg gave a longsuffering smile, nodded, and stood. "Thank you, Your Worship." He climbed the stair, knelt, and said, "I ask only if Your Worships might know when Our Glorious Lady will return."

Sash's mouth was full of wine, and Waistcoat leaped in. "Well, she'll be . . . she'll, well, uh . . . she'll be . . . getting here as soon as she arrives—"

"You moron!" Sash shoved a large wedge of cheese into Waistcoat's mouth. "Karona's time is her own. We are but dancers and she the music. We await her song."

Dereg frowned. "Precisely. The dancers must know when the music will start. Is it curtain in five minutes, or will rehearsals begin next week?"

"Rehearsals?" Waistcoat said. "Naw. Go ahead and dance, Guvner." He snapped his fingers and grinned.

"You must understand my position, Your Holinesses. I'm delighted to have you as guests of my private residence, offering you larders and cellars, serving staff, my bed—"

"Ah, and the prophecies you have heard, the wonders you've learned—"

"But after a month, the barrels are running dry, the coffers—my resources are depleted. I've offered you the best of my house, but what will happen when Our Glorious Lady comes and I have nothing to offer *her*?"

"We'll vouch for you," Waistcoat said, winking.

"As to your prophecies—in frequency and specificity, they are wanting."

"What?" Waistcoat asked. "What are they wanting?"

"Frequency and specificity," Dereg replied. He fished a rumpled piece of paper from his pocket, flattened it, and said, "I've written down all your prophecies. I'd like to read them."

Sash nodded. "Go on. I'd like to hear this."

Clearing his throat, the governor read: " 'Karona wants us to be happy.' "

"An excellent start," Sash said.

"I have an asterisk here by the word 'us,' which indicates that you meant you two—the prophets—not anyone else."

"He's good with details," said Waistcoat.

"The prophecies and teachings continue: 'Doughnuts are Karona's favorite, especially these here with the sprinkles.' "

Waistcoat beamed. "That was one of my prophecies!"

" 'In the eyes of beauty, we see Karona. Especially brown eyes. Brunettes are good, and the tall ones.' "

"You're purposely misquoting us," Sash objected.

"Aw, I don't know," Waistcoat said. "I *do* like the tall ones."

Governor Dereg dropped his hands, the paper crackling in agitated fingers. "I have questions. Lots of legitimate questions." He swept his arms out, indicating the other folk gathered in the opulent room—suppliants, servants, nobles, dignitaries, musicians, and children. "We *all* have questions. We want to know where she comes from and where she goes, how she lives and how we might live with her. We want to know how to serve her, what she wants from us, how we can become like her. We have so many questions, and these aren't the answers."

"You sound dissatisfied," Sash ventured.

"We're desperate! When, Holy Prophets? When will Karona return to us?"

The chandeliers above the great chamber winked and flashed, then went dark. The musicians plucked their last notes. They stared up at the ceiling, past royal banners and hammer beams, to the great glass skylight. It shone with midday sun and something more. Within that golden glow was a column of purer light, rarer and more intense. It cast down a narrow shaft of radiance that pooled on the floor and widened slowly.

She was coming. Karona was coming.

The chandeliers suddenly blazed again. Every crystal gleamed, and the silver traceries sparkled like mirrors. The room glowed with incredible light. Gems at the center of each chandelier shivered. One by one, the lights began to burst. Glass shards flew out, hailing across the floor. The folk below might have screamed and fallen to the ground, covering their faces and heads, but they were already lying prostrate.

Everyone lay in worship except Sash and Waistcoat. They stood on the dais, arms crossed over their chests.

Waistcoat said, "About bloody time."

The last chandelier exploded, and the only light came from above. The rays of Karona's presence spread through the room as her feet neared the glass. There was a crash and a musical jingling. Shards tumbled in a glittering swarm beneath the descending woman.

"Karona," murmured Governor Dereg.

Her robes gleamed as alabaster. Her hands spread in white beauty beside her hips. She slid through the skylight. Her face appeared—glorious and ageless, with lantern eyes and a sad but beautiful mouth.

The people wept for joy. They had endured a month of servitude to the two who held her power, but in this single instant, it was all worth it.

She descended from among the rafters. Her eyes swept the room, beams racing across the backs of folk lying there. Without touching foot to ground, Karona soared across the chamber. Hands reached toward her from the floor, but none could touch her. She glided over the bowing figure of Governor Dereg and rose easily up the stairs to the dais. There she paused, hanging before her prophets.

"YOU ARE WELL?"

"Dandy," said Waistcoat, spreading his arms. "Look at this robe. Pure silk!"

Sash added, "Governor Dereg treats us well."

Karona's eyes faded to a mere glow. "YOU ARE FED? GIVEN DRINK? YOU HAVE PLACES TO SLEEP?"

"And people to sleep with," Waistcoat added happily.

"And your sunburns?"

"Healed," Sash replied. "I'm beginning to look like my round friend, and he's beginning to look like a pig."

Waistcoat laughed but then shot Sash a murderous look.

"How are you, Great Lady?"

"NOT WELL. I'VE WANDERED THE WORLD SEEKING FRIENDS SUCH AS YOU, BUT THERE ARE NONE. ONLY MURDEROUS HORDES. I THOUGHT THE OCEAN WOULD BE A SAFE PLACE TO GO, BUT MERFOLK FLOCKED IN FROM HUNDREDS OF MILES, AND SHIPS CONVERGED TOO. THERE'S A SEARING DESERT WHERE I HAD RESPITE. THERE'S ALSO AN ICE PLACE, AND THE PENGUINS AND I HUDDLED SIDE BY SIDE. THEY'RE POOR COMPANY."

"Well, you came to the right place," said Waistcoat. "We're always glad to see you, and these folks here, well, they're pretty nearly dying to see you."

Karona whirled, her eyes flashing across the others in the room. They had begun to crawl toward her, over each other. Nobles and dignitaries seemed no more than maggots.

"NOT KILLING EACH OTHER . . . YET."

"They're full of questions," Sash said. "Where do you go, what do you do, what do you want them to do—?"

"What's your favorite ice cream?"

Karona seemed to wilt. "WHAT SHALL I TELL THEM? I DON'T GO ANYWHERE IN PARTICULAR, DON'T DO ANYTHING—AND I DON'T KNOW WHAT I SHOULD DO, LET ALONE WHAT THEY SHOULD DO."

"Her answers are as dumb as ours—"

Sash whispered, "Answer with another question. That always stymies them."

Drawing a deep and fortifying breath, Karona turned slowly around. Her gaze moved across the groveling host. They inched nearer, and between fingers or from behind tresses of hair, they watched her. Nearest was Governor Dereg. Karona rose slightly higher.

"COME NO CLOSER OR I WILL FLEE. REMAIN WHERE YOU ARE!"

The threat worked. Fingers stopped their scooting and clenched in dread beside bowed heads.

"NO MORE KNEELING. STAND, OR I WILL LEAVE."

There was a moment of disbelieving silence. Karona soared up toward the skylight, and the people jumped to their feet, crying, "Please! Don't go!"

"You can't leave us! What'll we do?"

"We'll die without you!"

Karona paused, hovering in the center of the room. "CLEAR A SPACE IN THE CENTER. MOVE ASIDE, SO I MAY SET DOWN."

The crowd retracted like a dilating pupil, and Karona lighted among them. Her feet touched ground, and an excited murmur moved among the people. They strained toward her, some clawing the empty air. It made for a frightening scene, but it was better than genocide.

"YOU HAVE QUESTIONS."

Together the crowd shouted. Serving maids yelled beside duchesses and cooks beside counts.

"SILENCE!"

The chamber became suddenly still.

"I WON'T ANSWER YOUR QUESTIONS UNTIL YOU ANSWER MINE. WHO AM I?"

The stunned silence that followed gave way to a single whisper: "Karona!"

"BUT WHO IS KARONA? WHO AM I?"

No one met her gaze. Their eyes were trained on the woolen rug.

"I know!" said a young voice. The crowd shifted, revealing a maidservant with a dust rag in her fist. A butler grabbed her collar and growled a warning.

"LET HER GO!" Karona commanded, and the butler released the girl and fell to his face. Karona stepped toward the girl. "WHO AM I?"

The maidservant remained rooted in place. She began to weep. "I don't know! I don't know!"

"YES, YOU DO," Karona said. She wrapped her arm around the girl.

All fear rushed out of the child. With eyes wide and clear, she said, "You're the bride of the Sun. That's what pa says. He says that's why you chase the Sun around the sky. He says that's why everything gets burned up when you come and stand on the world."

Karona nodded, staring into the eyes of the child. "THE BRIDE OF THE SUN." She kissed the girl's cheek.

The child swooned, falling atop the butler—her pa.

Karona stepped on around the circle. "WHO AM I?"

Before her, folk melted back, but one young nobleman stood firm. In a trembling voice, he said, "You're the spirit of the great ship *Weatherlight*. She flew the skies and became a living being. She sacrificed herself to save the world. You are her spirit, and you fly above us to save us."

She approached him, wrapped him in her arms, and kissed his forehead. "THE SPIRIT OF *WEATHERLIGHT*." He went limp, and she laid him gently on the carpet before continuing about the circle. "WHO AM I?"

An old woman leaned on her cane and, with a mixture of humor and determination, said, "I know you, Karona—or should I say Gertrude? You couldn't leave me even in death. For fifty years, you said I wasn't good enough for your son, and now I gotta listen for eternity. Well, good luck to you, Gertrude. I'll bow and scrape like everybody else, but you won't get me to give up Max."

"I'M NOT YOUR MOTHER-IN-LAW."

"That's exactly what you'd say. And don't try to kiss me."

With a solemn nod, Karona continued around the room. "WHO AM I?"

"You're the anti-Phage," said one man from the crowd. "When Kamahl killed her, she split and turned inside out, and you're her opposite."

"THE ANTI-PHAGE. . . . WHO AM I?"

Elionoway, a middle-aged elf with a bone pipe in his hand, said, "You're the great goddess Offkirch, whose regard is bounty and whose wrath is privation."

"OFFKIRCH." Karona paced toward the dais. "WHO AM I?"

This time it was Governor Dereg who stood resolute, his mustaches twitching beneath worshipful eyes. "You're none of these, though you're nearly the spirit of *Weatherlight*. Within that great ship's engine was an enormous Thran crystal, and in that Thran crystal was the Realm of Serra, and in that realm was the angelic planeswalker herself. You are she. You are Serra!"

"SERRA," repeated Karona as she mounted the stairs.

Dereg crumpled to his knees behind her, tears brimming in his eyes.

Karona approached her prophets. "WHO AM I?"

"I, well, I . . ." began Sash. He crossed his arms over his chest. "Well, you're Our Glorious Lady, aren't you? And that's just for starters. You're also the Beautiful One, and you're the Shining Light. And, well, you're the Marvelous Presence. There are so many names for you, it's probably easier to answer who you aren't than who you are. Ha. What do you think of that?"

"ANSWER A QUESTION WITH A QUESTION." She turned toward Waistcoat.

"What's the big mystery?" Waistcoat said. "You said it yourself once: I am Magic. That's who you are: Magic."

* * * * *

YES, I HAD SAID IT ONCE. IT HAD MEANT NOTHING THEN, BUT IT MEANS EVERYTHING NOW.

I AM MAGIC. I AM THE LIVING EMBODIMENT OF SORCERIES AND MANA, OF DIVINE POWER AND THE MORTAL APPREHENSION OF IT.

I GRASP WAISTCOAT'S PUDGY HEAD AND KISS HIM ON THE LIPS. I TURN AND FLOAT ON AIR: *I AM MAGIC!*

THEY LIE ON THEIR FACES—THE SERVANT GIRL AND HER FATHER, THE YOUNG NOBLE, THE OLD WOMAN, THE ELF, GOVERNOR DEREG—ALL.

I STRIDE ABOVE THEM. *I AM MAGIC.* IT EXPLAINS EVERYTHING. IT TELLS WHY EVERYONE DESIRES ME, WHY I AM LIFE AND DEATH TO THEM, WHY MY VERY BEING DRAINS MANA AROUND ME. AT LAST, I KNOW WHO I AM.

THEY CRY AFTER ME. THEY DON'T WANT ME TO LEAVE.

I WON'T LEAVE. EROSHIA IS MY NEW HOME. I GO TO WALK HER STREETS AND SEE ALL THAT IS WITHIN HER.

I ASCEND OUT OF THE ROOM, SLIDING THROUGH THE SHATTERED SKYLIGHT AND TAKING MY LIGHT WITH ME.

* * * * *

The chamber went dark, and the people lost sight of their Glorious Lady. They let out a piteous moan and charged for the door. Many cut their feet on glass, which covered the floor. Others trampled those too slow to rise or too quick to fall. Runners reached the doors and crowded there, desperate to escape.

Governor Dereg watched them. He had been in the back of the throng, on the dais stairs. She had rejected his answer, breezing by without so much as a nod, let alone a kiss, and he had felt destroyed. Now he watched his country folk fight their way out of his ravaged great hall, leaving wreckage and bodies in their wake.

Everything would be destroyed. If Karona paraded through Eroshia, the whole city from the wall to the seaside would be annihilated.

Dereg rose, sickened. Even so, he could not help himself. He had to follow. He had to touch her and cling to her. He strode after the rest of the mob, cutting his feet on glass.

CHAPTER 11

THAT OLD SERPENT

Kamahl bypassed the Corian Escarpment and the City of Averru. Through deserts and boulder fields he went, his eyes trained on the Nightmare Lands.

As severe as his outward journey had been, his inward one was worse.

Kamahl had regained the Mirari sword, his ancestral inheritance. He had battled it and almost been overcome. In his madness, he had even destroyed the ghost of Balthor. If not for that atrocity, he would have remained forever in the sword's fury. Instead, he had found the strength to save himself—but lose a friend. It was an all-too-familiar scenario. Kamahl had done the same with Chainer, with Jeska, with Krosan.

It was time to save someone else, a most unlikely someone: his old foe Ixidor.

Kamahl's teeth clenched behind cracked lips, and his eyes slitted against the glare of the Nightmare Lands. The dust of his journey made a fine grit across his skin, almost obscuring his tattoos. At his shoulder rode the Mirari sword. He would draw it only when needful and would kill with it only when necessary.

Soon, it would be. The land ahead showed the fresh trail of a death-wurm. Congealed lines of blood marked the path. Kamahl strode nearer. The trail wove among the stone stoppers and crossed itself many times. The beast sought something, and it was nearby.

The sword was needful. Kamahl set down his heavy pack and reluctantly drew the blade. It sang as it came free of its shoulder harness. The pommel scintillated with power, both energizing and enervating his hands. The blood in his arms began to boil with fury. Before the wave of battle lust could surge through his whole being, though, he sought the perfect forest within him. Green serenity joined red fury, and they filled his body.

Kamahl stalked along the freshest trail. It led across the Nightmare Lands and into a woodland of giant trees—Greenglades. The death-wurm would be within. Kamahl smiled tightly. Perhaps the wurm thought it would be safe in forest cover, but not from Kamahl. Green mana radiated from that place, and it strengthened him.

Something plunged down out of the forest wall. It seemed a tree, leaves roaring in the air. The foliage scattered, revealing a blue-black column covered with long scars. The deathwurm stuck like a lunging cobra.

In a single motion, Kamahl tucked the Mirari sword across his waist and rolled. Head over heels, he spun three times before the wurm hit.

Boom! The ground leaped, and the air thundered. Kamahl rolled a fourth time and clambered to his feet. He had forgotten how enormous a deathwurm was.

Amid clouds of dust lay a rubbery wall of muscle. It curved for a quarter mile into the Nightmare Lands. Almost three more miles of the thing lurked in the forest. The beast coiled its neck, and a head the size of a house rose to obscure the sun. Tiny eyes peered violently from a rumpled cranium. The mouth opened, and translucent teeth splayed. Grave-smelling breath billowed from the foul throat.

Ixidor was in there, and Kamahl would get him.

The wurm lunged. Its curved teeth reached for him.

Kamahl held his ground, the Mirari sword foremost. The thing's mouth slammed down, and Kamahl ducked within. He drove his blade up through the monster's pallet. Thran-metal ripped through flesh and cartilage into enormous sinus cavities. He shoved farther, seeking the brain. Blood poured down around the blade.

The wurm's teeth clamped closed, and the darkness was complete. Great waves of power dragged at him, the peristalsis of death. The wurm was trying to swallow him. Only the sword lodged in its pallet kept Kamahl from being ripped away. He clung on, but the waves grew only stronger. The deathwurm lifted its head, trying to throw him loose. Kamahl could not kill the thing here and could not cling to the sword forever.

With a roar, he set his boots on the pallet of the beast and yanked. Metal raked free of the dark cleft. Kamahl spun over, driving the blade through the flesh of the monster's lower jaw. It jutted out, opening a triangle of daylight. Driving his boots off the pallet, Kamahl lunged. He followed his sword through the gap. Severed muscles pinched him, but his hands and elbows cleared the way. Flexing his arms, he pried his chest and waist out of the dark gash. He wriggled, and his hips and legs slipped loose.

Kamahl was free. He tumbled through the air, and the wurm snapped at him as he fell. Slick boots crashed down on leathery ground, and Kamahl rolled again. The huge head impacted just where he had been. Kamahl clambered up and ran.

The wurm surged behind him, its breath turning the air cold. It was too quick. It would catch him, its mouth gaping again.

Snarling, Kamahl pivoted and lunged. The Mirari sword sank into the wurm's muzzle. He vaulted over it onto the thing's scabrous head. It roared, its fangy mouth descending on the man. Kamahl ripped the sword free and plunged it between the thing's eyes. The tip bit into rumpled flesh. The brain would be just beneath.

The wurm recoiled, stealing Kamahl's momentum. Another twitch, and its head smashed into him. It lurched a third time, and

Kamahl and the sword came loose. He flew toward the boles of the great forest. The blade spun like a cat's tail, and he got his feet beneath him.

With a brutal crunch, Kamahl smashed into a tree trunk a hundred feet above the ground. The whole front side of his body stung, and his nerves jangled. His free hand scraped along the bark, struggling for a grip but failing. Down the bole he went. Suddenly there were ivy leaves, and that meant vines. Kamahl's hand probed beneath the thrashing leaves and found a sinewy growth. His fingers tightened, and he lurched to a halt.

He was barely in time. One loop of the wurm crashed into the tree just where he would have been. The impact bent the massive trunk, then the tree recoiled and hurled Kamahl like shot from a sling.

He drew his legs together, flipped over, and dived downward. Beneath him swung the Mirari sword, heavy but sleek. It stabbed down to pierce the deathwurm, trapped among the trees. As he fell toward it, Kamahl summoned mana from the forest, the undergrowth, the fecund ground. He channeled the power through him. Green might and red fury amalgamated and poured into the sword.

The blade lanced down, punching through the wurm's back. It cleft a plate, sliced the skin beneath, and cut through muscle. Power shunted into the beast. Tracers of green mana splashed among flames of red.

Kamahl landed, his boots astride the sword hilt. He wrenched the sword to widen the wound and set his toes in the rubbery flesh. Like a mule pulling a plow, Kamahl dragged the sword through the beast's body. The cut lengthened to two feet then four, a cartilaginous rib giving way with a wet snap. Sepulchral air spewed up. With two more strides, he had carved an eight-foot wound.

It was a fifteen-thousand-foot wurm.

A shadow passed over Kamahl, and he glanced up. The enormous head of the beast crashed down through the canopy.

Hauling hard on the sword, Kamahl ripped it free and leaped away. He had no chance to get his feet beneath him. He landed on one shoulder and his upper back, but the explosion of pain was almost worth the sight he saw.

The deathwurm's head pounded down atop its own back. Translucent teeth bit into its flesh and tore a great hole out of it. The eight-foot gash became a ten-foot pit, opening wide the alimentary tract of the beast.

Kamahl staggered to his feet. His blood-slick hand tightened on the sword hilt. He drove himself through the undergrowth and swung the sword laterally. It embedded like a stair tread in the convoluted flesh. He jumped, setting one foot on the blade, and leaped higher. While his right hand yanked the sword from the beast, his left grasped the gory edge of the hole. Gastric juice stung his fingers, but he pulled himself up to the ragged wound. In moments, he was within the muscular tube.

The creature nosed at the gap. Its teeth snapped in the hole, and its face burrowed into the wound.

Kamahl retreated up the monster's gut, moving toward its head, a third of a mile away. Let it tear itself apart. Let it suffer the agony of its victims. He rammed the sword into the intestinal wall and cut as he walked. This time the beast couldn't reach him. It would have to kill itself to kill him.

That awful head slammed down on the meaty tube. Teeth perforated the wall in a wide circle around Kamahl. He tried to leap away, but his sword was fouled. The wurm's jaws closed. Flesh folded over Kamahl. The acids of the tube encased him, and all air was gone. The wurm bit through, taking a chunk out of its own flesh and catching Kamahl in the process.

He felt the whirl of motion and knew that the wurm reeled into the air. Folded in that pocket of skin, Kamahl had no leverage with his blade. The gobbet bounced as the teeth took a new hold, piercing closer to his body. Another bounce, and one of the fierce points jabbed through his left ankle.

There was no sense waiting. When the flesh pocket jerked the next time, Kamahl rammed his sword out the edge of the flap. He sat up, thrusting the steel upright. Its tip embedded in the wounded upper pallet of the monster. Roaring, he rammed the hilt of the sword down into the lower jaw. His intention had been to prop the ravenous mouth open. The pommel inevitably jutted through the cut he had made earlier. As the wurm clenched its jaw, Kamahl's feet slipped through the slice. The beast's own bite propelled him out the gash. At least he held onto the Mirari sword.

Plunging in a putrid shower, Kamahl shook his head, acid spraying from his hair and beard. He wiped it from his eyes and only then saw how high he was. Twenty feet below him lay the upper canopy of the great wood.

It would have been safer in the mouth of the beast.

Kamahl needed both hands if he would have any hope of catching himself. He swung the Mirari sword up over his shoulder, planting it in its sheath. He then kicked and flailed to catch the first big branch. It rushed up beneath him, and Kamahl reached for it with all four limbs. He slid by, just short. Another drop yawned before the next branch. It was obscured beneath a wide bundle of leaves, so he extended arms and legs and fell, spread-eagled, onto the leaf cluster.

From throat to groin, the bough caught him. His body folded up on either side of it. Despite the blinding pain, he grabbed on. Leaves thrashed his face, and sticks crackled under his arms, but he kept his balance. He was no longer falling, and soon he would be able to breathe again.

Beneath him, the wurm lifted its great, knobby head. The two wounds in its side were already closing. Its other lacerations had closed entirely.

Kamahl cursed. He couldn't kill this thing by degrees. He would need one great, violent stroke, or it would heal. How could he strike such a blow?

The monster's mouth opened in a wide and drooling grin. It gathered itself to strike the branch.

Kamahl climbed to his feet. The motion would trigger the strike. Drawing the Mirari sword, he ran to the end of the bough and out onto empty air.

The muzzle of the wurm lunged to snap him up.

Kamahl set one foot on the lower jaw, leaped above the open mouth, and set the other foot on the upper jaw. He brought the Mirari sword arcing down to skewer the beast between the eyes. The blade flashed in those vicious orbs, and the wurm recoiled. It dropped away beneath Kamahl, and he tumbled through the air.

There were no trees nearby now. He would plunge to the third canopy, and by then his speed would be great enough to kill him.

Kamahl closed his eyes and thought of Krosan. Autumn skies filled with whirling seedpods, carrying their precious cargoes from the mother tree. Kamahl drew their verdant power into him and channeled it into the whipping sword. It cut the air and carried him gently downward.

He summoned different mana—the war fires of the Auror tribe. A huge pile of wood burned brilliantly beneath the night sky. It poured sparks upward like new stars. Kamahl was one of those stars, and he drew the power of the fire into him, through him, into the Mirari sword.

The brilliance of the blade pried his eyes open. It shone above, below, and all around. He swung the sword through each of the combat forms, as he had done on the desert but with blinding speed. The dance of the sword carried him up through the air, above the forest, above the wurm. When man and blade and power were one, they could even fly.

The wurm followed his path through the sky, preparing to snatch him from the air.

Within his metal nimbus, Kamahl smiled. Why wait for the wurm to strike? With a simple turn of his sword, he dived on the beast. He spun the sword through its final kata and rammed it beneath him. The blade bit into the wurm's face, between its eyes, through its flesh, and into the monster's brain.

It bellowed, white dread rolling across its eyes. The wound was serious but not lethal. Not yet. Kamahl leaped on the blade, intent on driving it in with his full bulk.

The wurm ducked suddenly and pulled away from Kamahl. The hilt of the Mirari sword yanked from his grip. He roared. His hands snatched at the pommel but grasped only air. Sword and wurm both plunged beneath him. Kamahl kicked, falling.

He had failed. He had maimed the wurm but not killed it and had lost his sword in the process.

The impaled serpent rushed up beneath him. Its mouth was a pit, and he fell in. Teeth clamped closed, and gullet muscles laid hold and swallowed.

Swordless and helpless, Kamahl slid down the throat of the beast.

CHAPTER 12

THE TURN OF THE WURM

Drenched in saliva, Kamahl slid down the throat of the death-wurm. Glands poured mucous on him. All of it was preparation for the grinding gizzard.

Kamahl had come to slay the beast and bring Ixidor up from its belly. Instead, he would join Ixidor. Without the Mirari sword, Kamahl was nothing.

Or was he? The sword belonged to him, not he to the sword. He commanded it. Even here, in the gullet of the beast, he commanded it.

Kamahl tapped the life of the forest, the fire of the mountain. Mana brimmed in his doomed skin. Feeling along the inner wall of the digestive tract, he sensed a long, cool lump—a nerve. The ganglion would lead to the brain, to Kamahl's sword. He rammed his hand into the muscles, grasped the nerve, and poured the green-red mana into it. Energy flashed and snapped. It ignited the conduit and raced up the monster's throat. Kamahl felt its surging path. It suffused the brain and touched the Mirari sword.

Come to me.

The blade punched deeper into the skull of the beast, drawn by Kamahl's magic. It severed the nexus between the hemispheres. The serpent squirmed, knowing that it was dying.

Come to me.

The Mirari sword sank through the skull. Even the pommel slid into the cut. Once inside the bone, the crossbars spun on their axis, pithing the brain of the monster. The sword dug like an auger through the creature's flesh. It drilled through the back of the cranium and into the soft flesh of its neck, all the while heading for Kamahl.

Come to me.

Peristalsis ceased. The wurm convulsed too spastically to swallow. Its organelles churned out thicker floods of fluid. A rumble began in the wall of the throat, the Mirari sword burrowing through. With rotary violence, it chewed its way into the canal. The sword cleared the muscle wall and dropped into the chamber.

Kamahl slithered forward, grabbed the hilt, and drove the thing down through wet muscle. A deep slice opened a shaft of air, and he gasped a breath through it. Then he pried furiously, widening the cut until he could crawl through. With sword in hand, he squeezed out the cut and dropped to the ground—mercifully near. Amid thick brush he landed, between the convulsing coils of the dying wurm.

For a moment, Kamahl could do little more than lie there, his heart pounding in his throat and the Mirari sword clenched in his hand. He breathed the fresh air. Rolling, he wiped slime on the undergrowth and stood.

A quarter mile away, the head of the monster bashed itself among giant trees. It hadn't the sense or the strength to strike him now, so Kamahl chopped his sword into its belly and used the blade as a foothold. He leaped higher and embedded the blade again, pulling himself up the rubbery hide. Reaching the wurm's back, he planted the tip of the sword and leaned on the hilt.

Like a mountain climber at a summit, Kamahl surveyed his conquest. He peered forward along the body. The serpent wound like a river among the trees. Its scales and skin rippled with each thrust of the monster's head. He looked behind him. Another quarter mile away, the body of the beast widened. If this creature were like an earthworm, that fat band would hold its heart. That would finish it off.

Idly lifting the sword, Kamahl loped toward the swollen band where the monster's heart must be. The flesh beneath his boots dented spongily. Approaching the mound, Kamahl brought the blade screaming down. It cut into the muscle wall. The wurm twitched but couldn't turn on him. He dragging the sword in a long, curved line across the great mound, and the skin hissed as air escaped. Muscle severed with dry snaps. The sword cut into a cavity and formed a round hole. Soon a flap of flesh and bone came loose. Kamahl kicked the wedge open and shied back as rank air poured out of the wound. He dropped down into the hole.

Beside him was a flailing organ the size of an elephant—one of the serpent's lungs. Brachia topped it, and arteries twisted in a complex network through it. The huge digestive tract ran here as well. It crossed between the lungs, as large around as a hallway. Where, though, was the heart?

"On the other side," Kamahl told himself grimly.

The fastest way to reach it was to hack through the digestive tract. Sliding the hilt of the Mirari back along his right hip, he drove the blade like a battering ram into the tough tube. The sword punched through. Muscles puckered, tugging the hole wider. Kamahl carved a large cross on the flesh and stepped through it into the belly of the monster.

The inside was dark except for the light that lanced through the hole. It cast Kamahl's shadow against the far wall of the tract. When he shifted, though, his shadow moved aside to show a woman.

She floated in fluid within a transparent sac of skin. She seemed pickled. Her flesh was perfect and smooth but dead. Her hair hovered in a golden mane around her. White robes gleamed, and jewelry. Strangest of all, her eyes gazed out, tiny sparks of light in their depths.

"Nivea," Kamahl whispered. He approached, letting his sword hang loose at his side.

He had seen the inside of a deathwurm before, had glimpsed the partially decomposed bodies imbedded in the gut. This was different. This woman was not being digested but preserved. The skin around her guarded against stomach acids, and she resided just beside the monster's heart. Her body wasn't even fleshly—too beautiful for that—but plasmatic, like a ghost's. She had been trapped in this bolus ever since her death.

Kamahl's eyes hardened. He hoisted his sword.

"You've been captive long enough." He set his blade tip on the membrane that encased her. "Now, you will be free."

A banshee keen resounded through the chamber.

Kamahl reeled back from the woman, though her mouth was shut. He whirled, sword ready to skewer this new threat.

A spidery figure ambled toward him, stopping short of his sword. Its flesh was gray and emaciated, and its face clenched in a scream of agony. It had two legs and one arm, and in its hand it held convulsing hunks of meat. It hurled them at Kamahl.

As the clods flew, they transformed. Torn sinews became wings of skin. Hunks of muscle turned into small bodies with blood-red fangs.

Kamahl swung the Mirari, splitting the first horrid bat in midair. In follow-through he deflected the second creature. The blade rang, the creature shrieked, and bats splashed into the acid puddles.

"Away!" railed the spidery thing. "Away from her!"

It ripped another handful of flesh from the wall and threw it. In midair, the chunk became a snapping rat, its fangs dripping foam.

Kamahl dispatched the poor creature. "Ixidor!" Kamahl gasped. "What's become of you?"

Ixidor wailed, his eyes brimming with terror beneath bleached-out brows. "Don't touch her! You cannot touch her."

Kamahl didn't move away from the watery sac but spread his hand toward it. "This isn't her, Ixidor, only her ghost."

"Her spirit!" Ixidor advanced. "Keep away!"

"She shouldn't be trapped here," Kamahl said. "You must let her move on, to go where spirits go."

Ixidor clenched his teeth in a weather-worn grimace. "What if they go nowhere?"

"She must go."

"Move away! You'll kill the wurm and kill her!" Ixidor lunged at Kamahl.

The barbarian swung his blade but not at Ixidor. The sword tip pierced the bag of waters, and they gushed out across the two men. They grappled each other, Ixidor's hands like talons. He screamed. Even as he clawed Kamahl, the ghostly figure of Nivea poured out of the riven sac. She separated from the waters that had held her, drifted across the tortured ceiling of the wurm's gut, and fled away.

Ixidor wailed, released Kamahl, and plunged toward the hole. "Nivea! Come back! Don't leave me!" He splashed through acid puddles and staggered out of the gash. Sunlight broke across his skin, the color and consistency of wet paper. He squinted against the light and wept. "Where are you? Where have you gone!" His gaze raked the sky, but he couldn't see her. "Gone! Gone!" He turned, clambering back through the hole.

"Oh, no, you don't," said Kamahl, who had been heading out of it. He grappled Ixidor. "Out we go. You can't live in there any longer. Nivea is gone, and the wurm is dead."

Scrawny hands punched his back. "I can die in there!"

Kamahl shook his head. "I've worked too hard to allow that."

"Release me! I'm not your slave."

"I saved your life," Kamahl snarled. The man scratched him ferociously, and Kamahl crushed him in the grip of one arm. "You belong to me. Hold still, or I'll kill you myself!" With that, he bent his head and shoved back the square flaps of flesh. He emerged, wet and weary, into the world.

Together, they tumbled out of the dead beast. These two men had once wielded more power than anyone in Otaria. Now, they were wet, sick, exhausted nothings.

Kamahl clutched his unwilling accomplice and laughed darkly. "You might have thought things were bad in there, but they're even worse out here."

Ixidor responded only with an inarticulate moan.

Shaking his head, Kamahl said, "If we're the saviors of the world, Dominaria is doomed."

* * * * *

Braids stood at the rail and stared in exasperation at her legion. Six thousand souls—some of them still in their original bodies—stood arrayed across the sands of the coliseum. They were an impressive force, but compared to the hundred thousand that filled the stands, they were only a handful.

"Behold, the soul-reapers!" called young Kuberr from atop the central column of the coliseum. "They march northeast across a whole continent to capture this glorious new wonder—Karona!"

The stands erupted. Everyone had heard of the goddess birthed at the City of Averru, and they all wished to see her—especially if Kuberr could make her fight.

"The fops in the East think they can keep her captive, but when they see our troops, they'll lie down and wet their petticoats."

Hoots poured from the crowd.

"They're trying to turn her into a puffball, but she's a fighter. Everywhere she goes, battles break out, and she leaves hundreds of bodies in her wake. She's our girl!"

While the audience roared, Braids only shook her head. She had spent a month arguing with Kuberr that he must prepare his defenses, that he must gather an army to repel Karona. At last he relented and charged her with raising the force. Another month had passed, and now he was ordering his "defenders" to march to war. It was insanity—and not the sort that Braids enjoyed.

"Cheer them as they march!" cried Kuberr. "These bold warriors will bring back the world's greatest entertainment! They will bring Karona to you in chains!"

Braids shook her head. Karona in chains. Yes, maybe this was her sort of madness after all. She leaped down from the stands, raising her hand high, to the adulation of the crowd.

"Yes, greet Aunt Braids. You know her as a dementia summoner, a friend of Phage, the voice of the coliseum. Soon, though, you will know her as Angel Bane!"

She had to laugh at that! Yes, Braids Angel Bane. Her laugh turned into a shriek. The first person to call her Babs would end up with a fist through the face.

CHAPTER 13

POINTS OF VIEW

Waistcoat sat with Karona in the governor's estate. The goddess and her prophets often gathered at this window seat beside the only bank of glass not shattered by the mob. The windows overlooked a walled garden, whose flower beds had been taken over by entrenchments and patrols. Occasional rocks still hurtled up over the wall, but they fell short of the window.

Here Sash and Waistcoat took dictation—writing down Karona's wisdom. Sash rendered the words in florid script and Waistcoat in lovely doodles. Today, instead of scribbling, Waistcoat studied the Glorious One's face.

"You been awful quiet, Lady. What's up?"

How can I speak when I am so sad? she sent to him. Karona had learned to place thoughts in the minds of her prophets.

"Aw, don't let the mob get you down," he said, shrugging. "So you wrecked some stuff. It was an accident. If folks rioted every time I wrecked some stuff . . ." His voice trailed away, lost in that dread speculation.

On her first day, Karona had toured the city, unaware of the devastation in her wake. Hundreds were trampled, and thousands were wounded. Magic wards ignited fires, and magic items exploded and killed their wielders. From the plains gate to the sea, Eroshia was laid to waste. Karona had been so intoxicated by the realization of her identity, she had not even perceived what devastation she had caused.

"Anyway, they're not rioting 'cause they hate you but 'cause they love you," Waistcoat said. "They all want to get in here just to see you."

THEY LOVE ME SO MUCH IT SEEMS LIKE HATE.

"Well, that's better than what I got. They hate me so much it seems like . . . hate. You've got no reason to feel sad."

I'M THINKING ABOUT THE CHILD. . . .

"Oh." Waistcoat stared at his hands and wished he had something to doodle on. "You *almost* brought him back."

ALMOST WASN'T ENOUGH.

One victim of Karona's parade had been a little boy, trampled. Governor Dereg had approached her with the dead child. She had tried to resurrect him—after all, what was life but a magic spark, and what was Karona but living magic? She took the child in her arms, cradled him, and sang. The people watched. She laid her hand on his forehead and willed the boy's spirit into his being. He did not stir. She directed her own life-force into his body, and he began to reawaken.

The people cheered.

HIS EYES WERE DEAD. HIS SKIN WAS WHITE, AND NO BLOOD MOVED THROUGH HIM. THAT WASN'T LIFE.

She had sung again, no longer a song to awaken him from death but a lullaby to let him slowly and sweetly succumb. Karona had healed hundreds, had blessed thousands, but in her wake, she had left only despair and destruction.

I AM MAGIC, THE DESTROYER.

"I know what you need," Waistcoat said, levering himself up off the window seat. He waddled out toward the feast table, his fine robe ringing with several pounds of inlaid gold. He spent a few moments among the plates and cups and returned. "Have a chicken leg. There are plenty."

Karona shook her head. She had never eaten or drunk. *LET THE CHICKENS KEEP THEIR LEGS.*

"Aw, come on. You're in the catbird's seat."

WHAT IS A CATBIRD?

"Well," he hemmed, "it's a cat that, you see, looks just like a bird, and the—uh—catbird's seat is a perch the catbird builds that's big enough to hold a whole bunch of birds. See? He just sits on that perch, and all the birds say—hey, let's go sit with him. They fly down and—bam!—he eats 'em."

Karona blinked, staring at him. *AND I AM THIS DECEPTIVE AND PREDATORY CAT?*

Waistcoat lowered his head. "I guess I'm in the doghouse. Um, see . . . that's a house for a dog—"

I KNOW.

Outside the window, Governor Dereg strode through the garden. His head was bent as if beneath a heavy rain. He approached a wooden platform where guards crouched behind barriers. Someone beyond the wall must have glimpsed him, because a rotten pear lofted over to graze his shoulder. The governor ignored it. He had suffered worse indignities. Cupping hands around his mouth, he shouting instructions to the guards on the wall. A turnip bounded off his chest, and an egg splattered his face.

"Ha! Ha! There's something to laugh about!" Waistcoat said, pointing with a gnawed chicken leg. "Old Dereg got that one right on the konk!"

The door to the chamber barked open, and Dereg strode in, bedecked with dripping egg. He was a haunted man. Over the last month, he had grown gaunt, his mustaches matted, his eyes a dull gray. Still, as he approached, a light of desire entered his gaze. He knelt to Karona.

"Glorious Lady," Dereg said in a rattled tone. "There is trouble."

Waistcoat held out a greasy hand and adopted a cultured tone.

"The Lady is indisposed to worry about egg-throwers or egg throwees, which, the latter, are you, sir."

The governor replied to Waistcoat, though his eyes never left Karona. "They aren't the trouble I'm speaking of."

Waistcoat sniffed. "You haven't spoke of nothing much yet."

"An army approaches, in the west," Dereg said feverishly. "They march at double-time. Our scouts could barely outrun them. Word has just arrived, and it's said they'll be camping on the Vonian Fields by sunset." He stopped as if he had run out of words.

"Army shmarmy," Waistcoat replied.

"I WILL NOT FIGHT THEM—"

"Of course not, Great One," Dereg shot back. "I don't want you anywhere near them. Brutes."

Waistcoat said, "What the hell kind of army dares attack Her Gloriosity?"

Dereg gave him a blank look. "We don't know—"

"But brutes," supplied Waistcoat.

"Precisely."

"Well, take care of it, then," said Waistcoat.

Dereg flushed, his ears turning bright red. "I will. While I am gone, my lady, don't leave. It isn't safe."

"FOR ME, OR FOR THE PEOPLE?"

"For you, of course. The people be damned." Dereg looked grieved the moment he spoke those words. "This is your home. You said it yourself. It's not time to leave your home. Only if news comes of my death—then you could flee away. If they would kill me, they would kill you."

"Oh, poor pity for Dereg," said Waistcoat around a hunk of chicken. "You might be killed?"

"I go to parley with a hostile, unknown army. Yes. I might be killed."

"TAKE MY PROPHETS WITH YOU."

"What?" chorused Sash and Waistcoat.

"He said we might be killed!"

"SOMEONE MUST SPEAK FOR ME—"

"Great Lady, I hoped *I* might—"

"TAKE THEM."

"Of course," Dereg replied, backing away as he bowed. "Of course."

* * * * *

Dereg couldn't believe her aloof cruelty. He worshiped her. He prayed to her when she was not with him and lay prostrate before her when she was. True, everyone in Eroshia did that much, but Dereg's love was deeper. He had given his very home to her and watched her destroy it. She destroyed him as well: no good-bye, no hesitation at the prospect of his death. . . . To her, Dereg was just another mortal fool.

Speaking of which: He whistled between his fingers as if calling dogs. "Waistcoat, Sash—come with me."

Waistcoat followed, trotting. Across the room, Sash looked up from a barrel he had been draining and made his sloshing way over.

"It'd serve you well—hck—to give more respect to Our Glorious Lady's two hand-chosen pr-proph-hck—proph—"

"Profligates?"

"Right. No, wait—"

"Prophylactics?"

"What?"

Governor Dereg nodded. "Whatever you are, you're hand-chosen by the Glorious One to accompany me." He strode through the front door of his estate and out into the carriageway.

It was a circular drive leading to the garden wall and its double-bolted gates. A stable hand stood there beside the governor's bay gelding, saddled and ready.

Dereg swung up into the saddle. "Bring two more horses. Saddled."

"Which ones?" the young man asked.

"Nags, hacks—whatever you've got," the governor replied.

"This is the sort of—hck—indignity I was objecting to," Sash said.

"You, sir, are a drunken nuisance," Dereg said. "The only reason I don't ride off without you is that Karona ordered me to take you. Still, she didn't say, 'Take them and like it,' so I feel no compunction against hating it."

Waistcoat laughed. "He said constipation!"

"I did not!"

"You—hck—did."

The stable boy returned, leading a swayback mare and a donkey with colic. "Are these hack enough for you, Guvner?"

Dereg smiled, a good feeling after so much grief. "You're a good lad."

"Wait a minute!" Waistcoat said.

"We don't have a minute. Mount up. The gate will open for only a moment, and if you're not right behind me, you're not going. It'll be your fault, not mine," Dereg said. He prodded the gelding with his heels, and it clomped down the cobbles toward the gate.

The two prophets looked at the swayback beast, traded a glance, and leaped for the donkey.

Waistcoat snarled. "Get your hand off my ass!"

"I'm not that drunk," growled Sash as he fell to the dirt.

The donkey wailed like a baby as it carried Waistcoat away. Sash bounded up, ran to the mare, and slung his leg over it. Though the horse was full-sized, Sash's toes almost touched the ground. He tried to kick the thing into motion, but his heels met underneath it. In frustration, he smacked the creature's rump, and it ran, bounding as if its bent back were a spring. Sash and his steed quickly overtook Waistcoat's beast and pulled up behind Dereg.

The governor shouted as his horse reached a gallop. "Open the gates and kill anyone who charges through!"

One guard hurriedly slid the bolts while the other pointed his pike at Dereg.

"Everyone except us, idiot!"

The gates swung open, revealing the black mass of citizens beyond. Some tried to verge into the gap. The first fell to a pike. The second saw the galloping horses and hurled himself back. The rest scattered before the onslaught of hooves.

Dereg's gelding charged through the midst of them as through a black river. Humanity splashed on both sides. Behind him came the two prophets on their broken-down steeds. No sooner had the haunches of the donkey cleared the gates than they slammed shut. The longer strands of the tail caught and ripped loose, making the already wailing donkey cry like a paid mourner. The ass clattered furiously down the street, passing mare and gelding both.

Standing in his saddle, Dereg shouted, "Make way for the governor."

Folk on the road ahead parted—only to see a fat, berobed fool aback a foaming ass. Dereg ground his teeth together. Oh, what anguish! He kicked his steed, driving it on past the panting imbecile.

"You're a good rider," shouted a voice on his other side. "Almost as good as me!" Sash had pulled up alongside him, the mare's belly nearly bouncing from the ground with each stride. " 'Course, I'm drunk."

Neck and neck, the three men rode toward the plains gate. Despite his best efforts, Dereg could not pass the prophets.

They neared the wall and the double portcullis. Beyond stretched the Vonian Fields and the western road. Despite the approaching army, the dry grasses seemed to beckon. Here was a place untouched by Karona—clean, simple, and sane.

Dereg slowed his steed to a canter and shouted, "Open the gates, in the name of the governor!"

"And Sash!"

"And me!"

The trio slowed to a walk, waiting while the winch crews raised the massive portcullises. Dereg rode up to the guardhouse at one side and called within, "Bring me a parley flag. Mount it on a staff."

A young man stumbled out of the guardhouse. "You're going out there, Governor?"

"I would speak to the army commander."

"You mean commanders," the guard replied, dragging a lance from the corner and yanking a flag of parley from under his arm. He strapped it to the lance. "There are three armies."

"What?"

"Three camps. Three armies."

Dereg could feel his face redden. He shouted into the garrison station. "Someone in there had better be fetching me a spyglass."

Another guard stomped out, this one middle-aged and blustery. He tromped over to the gelding, handed Dereg a brass cylinder, said, "Sir," and returned to the station. The smell of onions and liverwurst remained behind him.

Dereg rode his horse to the arched gates. Both portcullises had been lifted now. Raising the spyglass, Dereg peered out to the southwest.

Beyond the shaggy shoulders of the Vonian Fields, a black mass moved. Dereg adjusted the tube, bringing it into focus. The heads of the creatures seemed no bigger than the heads of wheat in the foreground, but there was no mistaking it. This was an army. A standard jutting near its head identified it as a Cabal force. Dereg swore and spat. He scanned the western horizon and saw another standard with another army—the red emblem of the Pardic barbarians. Dereg let out a long groan. What could be worse? Another army marched from the north, flying the gray and white phoenix of the resurrected Northern Order.

The governor growled, snapping the tube closed and handing it to the young guard. "It's black and white and red all over."

"I know!" Waistcoat shouted. "A skunk with diaper rash!"

Without another word, Dereg grabbed the lance, lowered its tip, and rode through the gate.

"Oh, and be careful, Governor," the young man said. "That black group's got a mean general."

"Nobody could match my mean spirit just now," he growled over his shoulder.

"Oh, *she* could. Nobody's meaner than General Braids."

* * * * *

Braids loved this assignment. After marching a legion across half a continent, she felt invigorated. Fresh air made her violent.

"Yah!" she cried, standing in the saddle and flailing the beast's butt. It didn't hurt the creature, for it was already dead. This horse had been slain and raised as a zombie to serve Phage, but now that she was gone, it belonged to Braids. She had named it Trigger Mortis, and it ran at full gallop beneath her. Braids clutched the reins in one hand and the crop in the other. No carnival performer could have done better.

She grinned to goad the other two leaders.

Across the grasslands clomped a Northern Order lieutenant on a white horse. He rode solemnly and soberly, not deigning to look at the unseemly display. Farther on, an official from Eroshia met with a barbarian chieftain, who whirled at the clamor and drew his great sword.

No sense of humor. Typical. This was just a parley. Did everyone have to be so damned serious?

Braids charged up to the hill where the barbarian and the Eroshian diplomat stood. She reined in Trigger Mortis and leaped from his back.

The barbarian kept his sword trained on her. "Where is your flag of parley?"

"My earrings," replied Braids, flipping her hair to show the small white triangles that hung from her earlobes.

The chieftain's scowl deepened. "You can't wear a flag of parley on your ears."

"Maybe *you* can't," Braids said. "They'd clash with your scalp tattoo. By the way, there are treatments for baldness."

The man's eyes seemed to boil, and he brandished his sword. "There are treatments for impudence!"

"Tsk, tsk, tsk," said the Northern Order lieutenant as he rode placidly up. He was lean and pale, with a nose so big he could have passed as an aven. "Waving a sword while holding a flag of parley . . ."

The chieftain trembled but sheathed the blade.

"Thanks, Whitey," said Braids.

The lieutenant said nothing, though his nostrils flared as though he smelled a bad odor.

"Enough of this," said the fourth person there, a haggard man in a stained jacket, his hair standing on end. "Let's get down to business."

Braids grinned. "Are you the mayor or a beggar?"

"Governor," corrected the man with a cough, and his eyes flashed. "And I am not a beggar. Forgive my appearance. I am Governor Dereg."

"Who're they?" asked Braids, pointing at a pair of white sheets who bounced aback two ragged beasts. "Are they the beggars?"

Dereg tried to suppress a smile, and Braids decided she liked him. "Those are Sash and Waistcoat, prophets of Karona."

"Prophets, eh?" Braids asked. "When I knew them, they were nobodies."

"Let me save everyone some time," the governor said. "I know why you are here, and I don't blame you for coming. I understand exactly what draws you—"

"Why are we wasting time?" broke in the chieftain, shoving past Dereg. "The prophets of Karona are right here." He held welcoming arms toward the two robed men as they rode up. "O Great Prophets, where is she? Only tell us, and we will attack. We will kill this sop, raze Eroshia, and slaughter everyone in it."

"Where is who?" asked the fat prophet.

"Karona?"

"Right there," Waistcoat said, pointing at the city. "Who'd you say you'd kill to get at her?"

"This man, her captor!" the chief answered, indicating Governor Dereg.

Waistcoat shook his head. "Aw, he's not a bad guy."

"We will kill anyone who stands between us and the Magic One. She arose from mountain magic, and she belongs to us. No man will remain alive, no wall will remain untoppled—"

"No sheep will remain unraped," elaborated Braids. "Yeah, yeah, we know how your mountain threats go. You can't have her. Karona belongs to the Cabal."

Every mouth on that hilltop gaped. "What?"

"She's the biggest attraction since the Phyrexian invasion. We missed out on that one, but we're getting in on the ground floor here. She comes back to the coliseum with us, or all of you die." Braids brushed her hands against each other. That had gone well.

"Absurd," sneered the Order lieutenant. His voice was so nasal, it shook the hairs inside his voluminous nostrils. "These miscreants gaze on a glorious being in white and see only war and blood sport. Surrender Karona to the Northern Order and be sure she will be honored and revered. Her every law will become the law of the Order, and the Order will become her enforcers throughout Otaria."

Waistcoat murmured. "Actually, she's not so big on laws."

Governor Dereg shoved his way back into the conversation. "None of you know what you're talking about. We didn't choose

Karona. She chose us. She's not our captive. We are her captives. She has taken our city as her home, and we couldn't be happier, but I have no power to surrender her to you or anyone.

"This means war!" bellowed the chief.

Dereg shouted back, "You would dare attack the City of Karona!"

The delegates all fell to shamed silence. It did sound ludicrous when put that way.

"For that matter, how dare you try to twist her to your purposes! She's not about war or entertainment or law."

"Then what's she about?" Braids asked. "Why is she here?"

Dereg shrugged, holding out empty hands.

Sash muttered. "It's just one of those things."

"You see!" the chieftain said. "From the prophet's own mouth. Her purpose is just *one* of the things we've said."

"No!" Dereg responded. "Not *one* of *those* things, just 'one of those *things*.' "

"Ask the prophet," replied the Order lieutenant. "What did you mean?"

Sash took a calming breath and slurred something.

"He said serendipity," Dereg replied. "It's just serendipity."

"No," the Order lieutenant responded. "He said, 'Serran deputy.' Karona is a servant of the angel Serra!"

The chief growled. "He said, 'Surer than pity!' She is here for war!"

Dereg turned to Braids, "What did you think he said?"

With a laugh, she replied, " 'Sharing pooty.' She's an entertainer."

"What did you say?" the others chorused.

Sash leaned back in consideration, his eyes awash with drink. He opened his mouth and fell spectacularly from the horse. Landing on his face beside the horse's hooves, he began to snore.

The chief roared. "War!"

"Law!"

"Let me entertain you. . . ."

Dereg flung his hands into the air and shook his head. "Fine. Hear whatever you want. Camp. Study war. You're all disobeying Karona. She will hate you for it, but do what you must in her name."

"Thanks, Guv," said Braids.

Dereg mounted his horse, turned it in a tight circle, and charged away.

Waistcoat watched him go. Clambering down from his donkey, he lifted Sash across the swayback and led both beasts back toward the castle walls.

Braids shrugged and smiled. "Well, folks, let the entertainment begin."

CHAPTER 14

PURITY RIVER

Kamahl stared at this pathetic thing that he had delivered, as helpless and squalling as a newborn.

Ixidor lay gasping in the grit. He had been a creature of wet darkness, sustained by the monster that had held him. Now he was changing to something else. Emaciated and trembling, wracked with misery, he cried. His skin was wet paper. Gastric juice had bleached his hair white, and even his eyes had lost much of their color.

"You destroyed her," he gasped, not looking up at Kamahl, who sat nearby. "She's gone forever."

Kamahl shook his head slowly. "I released her to go wherever spirits go."

"They go nowhere," Ixidor said.

"Perhaps." He coughed. The fumes that issued from the dead beast were noxious.

Ixidor clutched his white hair and rocked sadly. "You don't know. You didn't know Nivea."

"I knew Akroma," Kamahl replied. "She had the face of Nivea."

Ixidor lifted white-blue eyes toward the trees. He seemed to see the vengeful angel. "Do you know why I called her Akroma?"

Kamahl also stared into space. "No."

"Akroma means 'without color.' She was like white paint—colorless. Nivea was like white light—full of color. Do you see?"

"I don't know about paint," Kamahl said.

Ixidor laughed condescendingly. "Akroma was a painting; Nivea was the real thing. Now do you understand?"

Kamahl snorted but otherwise didn't answer.

Ixidor knelt, clutching his face. His brow touched the ground, and he laid his hand beside his head. He would have seemed dead if not for his shallow breaths.

Kamahl got up, went to him, and prodded his shoulder. "Ixidor, it's time to go."

"One more fight. Just one more, and we can get out of this place."

"What fight?" Kamahl asked.

"A new gladiator named Phage. Just a little girl, and she fights with her bare hands. Once we beat her, it'll be riches and ease for the rest of our lives. We'll move to our undreamed land—you and I."

"I'm not Nivea."

"Of course not. She led me to you, across the dunes. You bade me kneel and cup the sand in my hands and drink, and I did. I drank sand, but you turned it to water in my mouth, Lowallyn, Lord of Streams. I drank, and the water took possession of me, and you took possession, Lowallyn."

Kamahl let out a long sigh. "Delirium."

Ixidor sat up, his eyes wide beneath a smudged brow. "No. Delirium is veering out of the furrow. This isn't delirium. It's possession. The furrows I follow have been cut a thousand times in this ground. I'm walking the exact steps as one before."

Kamahl ground his teeth. "Damn you! Get your mind out of the beast and into the here and now!"

"Lowallyn knew of lost love, and he used Nivea to lure me. He knew of desolation and madness, of water in the wilderness. He was in the water that filled me, and he became me—"

"That's it," Kamahl said. He reached down and grabbed Ixidor, hoisting him to his shoulder.

"Let go of me!" Ixidor shouted, his fist thumping the barbarian's back.

"Keep your hands off my sword." Kamahl said. "I've had enough mumbo-jumbo. You're not just mad, you're filthy. Maybe I can't cure madness, but I can cure filth."

Marching along the serpent's flank, he headed for the edge of the forest, toward the original oasis of Topos.

"I said let me go!"

Kamahl sternly shook his head. "You need a bath. We both do."

Ixidor laughed—a mad, gleeful laugh. He began to sing:

"There's a place that I know where the blue waters roll,
 and they carry your cares to the sea.
All who come down to wade in the current's cold rage,
 find possession that makes them more free.
If you seek you will find that new life can be thine
 just by giving yourself to the wave.
For our master's strong hand carves out glorious lands,
 and it raises new life from the grave."

"Shut up," said Kamahl as he stepped around the muzzle of the dead wurm.

The great Ixidor had fallen far indeed, Kamahl thought. Once he had wielded awesome power, and it had amplified all of his traits, the best and the worst. Half the world considered him a god and the other half a demon. Now, stripped of his power, Ixidor was just a sad, strange fellow. Kamahl would have put up with his singing, but he needed to concentrate.

Holding out his sword arm, Kamahl took a deep breath. His eyes traced the peculiar foliage of this forest, imprinting on his mind the shape of leaves and blossoms, stems and vines. Beetles walked in red-backed parade up a nearby bough then buzzed into the air. They jagged past a spider that rolled its latest kill in its web. A caterpillar chewed a great green leaf, a bird zipped down to eat the caterpillar, and a bobcat leaped out to snatch the bird. It took only a moment to understand the forest—a listening, looking moment—and its green power flowed into him. Mana salved his wounds and renewed his strength. At last, Kamahl released the breath. He felt all the weary pain of battle pour out of him while the glad joy poured in.

"I made this forest, you know," Ixidor said quietly. "I saw it in my mind before it ever was. I painted it with my own blood, before I had canvas or easel."

"It's beautiful," Kamahl said, even then reaching the end of the wood. It bordered on a river, which flowed between shelves of red shale. "Here is water."

Ixidor's voice was weary. "Not here. The bed is sharp. This river is my blood too."

"We must wash."

"Continue on," Ixidor said, his voice quiet. "Follow the river until it widens, where it crosses the sands. The banks are smooth and solid there, and the oasis will give us shade. That's where all of this began."

"We'll wash here."

"No." His tone was firm now, commanding. "The oasis is the place of beginnings. You can wash yourself in any thimble of spit, but if you want a new beginning, go to the Purity River."

Kamahl thought for a moment then nodded. He knelt down, setting Ixidor on his feet—bare and pallid feet. The skin was still pruny from the wet place he had been. Kamahl looked the man up and down, a wreck in slime and wrinkles. "I think you can walk now."

Ixidor shifted as if the sand irritated his soles. "I can, but will I?"

"The madness is gone."

"Only receded, friend. It comes in tides, raised by the great moon that circles me. The madness ebbs now, but soon it will return, and in a riptide." As if to drive home his point, Ixidor said, "I might run off."

"I'll catch you," Kamahl replied. He turned and started to walk.

Ixidor took a step and winced. He shifted his weight onto his forward foot and set the other one gingerly on the ground. It was as if the sand were shards of glass. Even so, he walked. The man might have become wretched, but wretchedness was not his true nature. Kamahl kept up a steady pace, and Ixidor matched him.

"I never truly understood my creative power," he said. "At first I thought my muse had given me the power. Next I thought madness had, sending image magic over the edge. The death of Nivea was impossible, so if it could happen, anything could. Now I know it wasn't these things. It was Lowallyn."

The river wound on beside them, its deep channel widening as it neared a palm grove. It was still a good hike, and Kamahl was willing to listen.

"Who is Lowallyn?"

Ixidor stopped and stared in amazement at him. "You haven't heard of Lowallyn?"

"No."

"He's lord of waters. He brought hidden streams from the desert. Lowallyn is one of the numena of old. He wrestled the world from draconian tyranny. Haven't you heard of the Primevals?"

"Of course."

"Lowallyn brought them down."

Kamahl scratched his scalp. "No . . . King Themeus did."

"Lowallyn was one of the king's sorcerers, but he became greater than Themeus. Lowallyn and his brothers, Kuberr and Averru, inherited the magical might of the Primevals. With their power, they defeated Themeus and split up the world between them. They became the three rulers of Dominaria."

Kamahl shook his head.

"What?"

"You're talking about rulers who've been dead for a thousand years—"

"Twenty thousand—"

"Fine. Twenty thousand." Kamahl studied Ixidor as the man strode up behind him. "You look old, but not that old."

Ixidor didn't return his gaze, instead striding purposefully along the water. "A creature like Lowallyn doesn't bow to death. A creature like him finds a way back."

"You didn't bow to death either. Look at you—more than a year in the belly of that monster, and here you stand."

"That's because Lowallyn is in me. He's taken possession of me. When I drank that sand, I drank him in. I died, and he took over. He created everything you see. This is ancient artifice, more powerful that Urza's tinkering, than Yawgmoth's phyresis. Not since the days of Lowallyn has such magic been upon Dominaria— not until these days. Kuberr came back too, in the child of Phage and the First. Averru's body is the city that bears his name. We'll rule the world again."

The man's voice had mesmerized Kamahl. It had gotten into his head and become his own inner voice. Kamahl's perspective shifted, and suddenly it seemed the world was mad instead of Ixidor.

The oasis where it all began spread out before Kamahl. The river plunged into a wide green place overhung by giant palms. Trees swayed with desert winds and with the leaping motion of monkeys. Beneath spreading boughs bloomed orchids, wild brush, and long grass. Creatures rustled in the low plants, and tan shoulders of sand rose above blue and inviting waters. A nearby berm of clay showed where someone had dug with bare hands, as if sculpting.

"You created this place out of sand and clay? Out of nothing?"

Ixidor's eyes gleamed like mirrors, reflecting the oasis. "Not out of nothing, and not I. Lowallyn created this place out of desperation and dream. They are everything, and they are one and the same.

"There's a place that I know where the pure waters roll
    in their torrents of passion and pain.
Go immerse yourself there and be washed in your fears.
    Desperation and dream are the same."

Kamahl stood on the clay bank and felt dizzy. How could he keep his balance when he saw the world through Ixidor's eyes? From the outside Ixidor was a crazy buffoon, but from the inside he was a tragic genius. Heart pounding in his chest, Kamahl could barely stand.

Ixidor descended the slope, his bare feet pressing into the clay. He stepped into the winding flow, and the first gush of water laved the pasty slime from his skin. A white trail ran from his legs and stretched through the water, as if his ghost were washing away. Deeper the man went, and the water seemed to restore him. Ixidor drew in the blue mana of that chill river. It cleaned him and strengthened him, scintillating along the gaunt lines of his body. He immersed his shoulders and head, and for a moment he was only a gray outline below the water.

Dizzily, Kamahl watched. Would the man simply fade away?

Ixidor rose for a breath and dived again. He lingered in the river's cold arms, then surfaced, breathed, and submerged once more. He emerged a final time and walked slowly up out of the water.

No longer did he seem craven, but slim and statuesque. All the severity was gone from him, and only the clean lines of bone and muscle showed. He let his hand trail in waves, and it dragged a broad wake. A snap of his fingers changed the wake into a cloak. He lifted it to his shoulders, pulled it around his chest, and cinched it about his waist. The garment had solidified but not into fabric. It seemed made of water, its surface glimmering and rippling.

He had gone down into the river a wretch and had risen a king.

Kamahl kicked off his boots and descended the clay bank. His broad, powerful feet made deep wells beside the shallow tracks of Ixidor. He had saved Ixidor, and now Ixidor was saving him. The man's power was more than charisma. Simply by being in his presence, Kamahl thought what he thought, wished what he wished, hoped as he hoped. Kamahl stepped into the cleansing flood.

The water was alive. It tingled around his feet and scrubbed his ankles. Currents coursed about his legs as he walked toward the center of that stream. Waves ran along the healed scar on his stomach. The water enveloped chest, shoulders, and head. Kamahl held his breath and went under. The oasis vanished, and there was only that omnipresent stream—and a mind in that stream.

It was Lowallyn, *Now you understand. Now you believe. I am the great and ancient power of blue mana, and Ixidor is my incarnation. You will walk in the presence of a veritable god.*

Kamahl surfaced, taking a breath. Still, the draw of that mind was too great to resist. He slipped again beneath the waves.

I could inundate your mind as well, but I will not. I need but one incarnation. You will be a guide, and a guide must have his own mind.

How agonizingly beautiful that voice was. Kamahl wanted to remain beneath the waters and hear it forever, but mortals need breath, and he came up to breathe. One last time, he submerged.

Go, now, Kamahl. Lead Ixidor where I must go. I have been lost in death, and I need a guide. Guide me. Take me to my brothers, Kuberr and Averru. Only together can we defeat Karona the Scourge. Go, now, Kamahl.

Kamahl's mind boiled with questions, but he dared not defy that voice. Striding on the river's torrid bed, Kamahl rose out of the water.

It streamed from him. He climbed up the clay bank, his hair and beard pouring tears on the ground. He stepped back into his boots.

"Now you know who I am, and I know who you are," Ixidor said, his eyes giving off a watery glow. "I am the god-bearer, and you are my guide. Where do we go, guide?"

Kamahl's voice felt sluggish, reluctant to rise. "We go to join your brothers, Kuberr and Averru. We will need them to defeat Karona the Scourge."

"Karona!" Ixidor said, mouth dropping open. "Mother."

Kamahl could only nod, stunned.

"Last time Karona came, she didn't know who she was or what she could do," Ixidor said. "We can only hope she's ignorant of it again this time. She's a fetal goddess, Kamahl. Every day she becomes stronger. Soon, she'll be invincible."

"You and your brothers can stop her," Kamahl said.

Ixidor's teeth set in a grimace. "Yes. We stopped her last time, but she destroyed us. It took twenty thousand years for us to return. Someone else will have to stop her this time."

Kamahl shuddered, bedeviled. "Wait. You're supposedly a god, this Lowallyn, god of secret streams—"

"Lord of hidden waters—"

"Shut up!" Kamahl shouted, fingers clutching his hair. "Give me a moment! You're the god who made me the guide—I can't make sense of any of this!—and now you want me to guide you to your brothers, so you can destroy the Destroyer, except that instead you want to run away? What?"

Ixidor wore a serene expression and spoke as if to a child. "*Lowallyn* wants you to destroy the Destroyer. *I'm* not *Lowallyn*. I'm his *avatar*—*Ixidor*. Gods don't have bodies. I—" he thumped his chest—"*I* have a body. *Lowallyn* doesn't have a survival instinct. I *do*. I want to get as far from Karona as I can."

Blood rose in Kamahl's face. "If she'll destroy Dominaria, what's the use in running?"

"I am all powerful. I don't have to remain in Dominaria. I can live anywhere."

Kamahl swept out his arm, wrapped Ixidor in it, and hoisted him to his shoulder. "All powerful! Hmph! You're not a god. You're a measly little avatar. Lowallyn could escape my arm, but not Ixidor! No!" Kamahl laughed maniacally, shocked at the words that rolled out of him. "You're my captive, and I'm your guide."

"Put me down! It's no use. Where are you going?"

"I'm going to get my pack. There's a tent in it, and food and water. We'll need them to cross the desert," Kamahl growled as he strode along the river.

"I don't need those things. I'm a god."

"Not yet, you aren't, and the shackles I have in my pack will prove it."

"Shackles!"

"I'll wear one cuff, and you'll wear the other." Kamahl gritted his teeth. "We'll be companions all the way to the coliseum."

In a fury, Ixidor ripped hunks of fur from Kamahl's wolf skin cloak and transformed the stuff into rats in his hand. They fell to the ground and skittered around Kamahl's boots.

Kamahl kicked them away. "Rats. Is that the best you can do? Once we're outside of Topos, you won't even have this power."

"My brothers and I will have all power!"

Shaking his head grimly, Kamahl said, "I only hope you're right."

CHAPTER 15

CAPABILITY

A t dawn, Braids emerged from her command tent to stare down over the Vonian Fields. Armies stretched from the wall of Eroshia to the western horizon. She smiled.

Elf, dwarf, goblin, Nantuko, centaur, aven, and minotaur each had brought large contingents. Merfolk and cephalids closed off the shoreline. Four separate human armies came from the great nations of the continent, and another five intermixed all races—the Akroman Crusaders and the Stonebraughan Enforcers, the Krosan Militia, the so-called Army of Liberty, and the Cabal.

Braids whistled, and from the runner's tent nearby a young man emerged at full gallop. As he ran, he hiked his messenger coat up onto his shoulders and stuffed the winnings of a card game into his pockets. Braids encouraged her troops to gamble, but she also encouraged them to answer summons promptly.

Finger-combing his black hair, the messenger rushed up, skidded to a halt, and bowed his head to Braids. "The Cabal is here."

"The Cabal is everywhere," she replied, handing him a sealed scroll. "Take this to the Corian outpost, and hand it off to another runner. It's top-secret and must be delivered to Kuberr as quickly as possible."

"Begging pardon," the boy said as he stowed the scroll in his robe, "but the other armies have captured any runners we've sent. I'll do my damnedest, but I might be captured as well."

"Do your damnedest," Braids said curtly. She nodded to him and watched him run down from the camp toward the nearby ford.

Today's "secret message," like the last three, was an elaborate lie. It detailed the vast secret network of sapping tunnels Braids had magically carved out beneath the walls of Eroshia. It exaggerated the size and armaments of her forces, told of reserve troops ready to sweep down and attack the flanks and rear of any who did not join her in treaty, discussed various magic items certain to assure the Cabal quick and complete control of Karona once she was captured. Lies, all of it. Braids had delighted in devising these fictions, knowing her foes would capture the runners and read the scrolls.

Already, the lies had borne fruit. Eight of the armies had declared alliances with the Cabal. That gave her a nominal majority among the besieging armies. Among the allies was a dwarf contingent that had tipped its hand about its own sapping projects—all much more modest than Braids's.

The folks she could not win over with lies she won over with games. Braids allowed all the armies passage across the ford, though she lined the way with a gauntlet of games and attractions. Even the humans and minotaurs who had foresworn alliance were addicts of Braids's entertainments. There was little to do during an extended siege, and entertainment became the armies' most precious commodity. Braids became its supplier.

A horrible caterwauling began near the city wall. "Time for morning vespers," Braids muttered.

Two factions of Ixidoreans lined up on opposite sides of the city. Stonebraughans worshiped Karona as the slayer of Akroma, but Akromans worshiped Karona as the transfiguration of Akroma. Both groups lifted songs of longing into the air. The opposing keys clashed, and the priests sang all the louder, determined to be heard by their beloved.

Braids laughed. Religion was another racket the Cabal ought to investigate. There was plenty of profit in it. Once the Cabal had Karona in hand, perhaps they would start their own religion.

"Another month, and I'll have these armies right where I want them," Braids told herself as she retired again to her tent, "and I'll take Karona too."

* * * * *

Within the burned-out and barricaded governor's mansion, Sash cringed as the wailing of priests filled the air. "We might as well be serenaded by tomcats," he murmured. Even when the damned priests weren't singing, the din of the mob was maddening. Sash covered his ears, trying to shut out the noise.

He had been doing a lot of shutting out lately. Flesh had its limits, even for pleasure. Too much music, too much food, too much wine, too much cavorting . . . Oh, he'd enjoyed the wild, reeling glory of it for the first month or so, but now Sash felt as burned out as this great room.

In wine-stained silks, he staggered across the ruined chamber. After the third murder in her presence, Karona had banished all but Sash, Waistcoat, and Governor Dereg. Not even servants or cooks were allowed in. The place, therefore, was never cleaned. Meals came under the doors. The goddess, her prophets, and her host had become prisoners of luxury.

Sash headed for the window seat where Karona spent her days. Governor Dereg lay nearby, caught in a paroxysm of longing. He had wasted away, unwilling to leave Karona's presence even to eat or bathe. The poor man could only worship her—and snipe at her prophets.

Sash neared them. "Can't you do something about all that racket?"

The man's eyes looked like peeled onions. "What do you suggest? They're praising Our Glorious Lady. Should I tell them to cease? Or perhaps I should order all my people out onto the plains to kill the folk there. Would the wails of the dying be kinder to your ears?"

"How dare you!" Sash snarled. "You speak to a chosen prophet of Karona!"

"Then *you* fix it!"

"*I* don't have the power to—"

"*She* has the power! She has all power! In her, you have all power! You fix it!"

Waistcoat hurried over, eager to listen to the argument.

Karona rose from the window seat. She was beautiful even in this burned-out place. She had neither eaten, slept, nor bathed and yet looked new-formed out of the mind of eternity. Her robes hung in elegant folds from her shoulders and waist, and her feet lifted gently from the ground.

Governor Dereg went prostrate.

Sash only stared, but Waistcoat waddled up to say, "What's up?"

Hanging above them, Karona said, "I HAVE ALL POWER." The idea seemed new to her. "I CAN DO ANYTHING. . . ."

With a shrug, Waistcoat said, "Well, uh, so far it's just float, glow, burn things, make people kill each other . . . like that."

"But if you *are* magic personified," Sash said, picking up the thread, "you should be able to do anything. Literally."

From his place on the floor, Governor Dereg added, "Oh, oh, oh."

"COME ALONG, BOYS." She wrapped arms around her two prophets and lifted them into the air. "LET'S SEE WHAT I CAN DO." She drifted up among the rafters and toward the smashed skylight.

In their grimy robes, the two friends of Karona did not even kick. They had become accustomed to this sort of travel, like kittens lifted by the scruffs of their necks.

Waistcoat said, "Do you think she could stand on one hand?"

"Idiot. She can fly. Of course she can stand on one hand."

"Can she drink a beer in one gulp?"

"She doesn't drink anything, least of all beer, moron."

Waistcoat shook his head irritably. "If she can't drink a beer in one gulp, she can't do everything. Even I can drink a beer in one gulp."

"And you're a dolt!"

"Right—*hey!*"

Placidly, Karona drifted through the riven skylight. The argument of her prophets blended with the clamor of the world outside.

Below, Governor Dereg scrambled up from his belly and stared plaintively after them. " 'Come along, boys'? I'm a boy! Oh, Karona, *I'm* a boy!"

* * * * *

Braids was lying on her cot when a discordant roar began outside. It was a cloudburst of sound from every mouth under heaven. It could mean only one thing:

"Karona!"

Braids leaped up from her cot and dashed out the tent flaps.

Two suns hung in the sky. One was gold and brilliant, but it had no life to it. The other was white and beautiful, and she made even Braids cry out in desire. In a moan of hope, the gathered nations called to the new sun: "Karona!"

She floated above the rooftops of Eroshia and cast down a silver gleam. Her eyes swept across the Vonian Fields as if to greet everyone gathered there.

"Troops, form up!" Braids called. They had worked out a precise plan for such a moment—titanium nets shot from great ballistae, a swarm of undead avens to tear her down, enchanted shackles on a sledge of steel.

"Form up!"

Her shout was drowned by the great, aching call of the crowd.

Karona soared over the wall and cast its near side in bright relief.

Even the guards on the wall worshiped, their knees kissing stone and their hands caressing air. All the people lay down before her.

Even Braids. Her best-laid plans dissolved in the face of Karoma. How could she ever imagine possessing the Glorious Lady? Braids only wanted to be possessed by her.

Over the armies Karona drifted, converting tents into luminaires. Among them lay warriors from every nation, hoping she would set down nearby and open her arms. Oh, to be incinerated by that woman!

Karona slid past overhead, her arms already filled with her two prophets. They seemed to speak benedictions over the armies:

"—not that *I* could walk on hot coals, but could she?"

"She can fly! She doesn't have to walk on hot coals."

"I know she don't have to, but *can* she?"

"Idiot!"

"Moron!"

Karona and her prophets suddenly rushed away, a fireball across the heavens.

The ecstatic cry faded to disbelieving silence. Armies that had spent months staring east now stared west into empty wastelands. Empty. Karona had become a tiny star above the Shadow Mountains; then she was gone entirely, lost in the sky.

The silence ended. Elf and dwarf, human and Nantuko—they scrambled up and set off after her. Armies abandoned their trenches, their tents, their commanders, and ran after Karona.

"Come back!" Braids shouted. "Form up! We will march after her, but all as one! Come back." Kuberr had been right. Any army sent against Karona became an army for her.

Braids returned to her tent for a water skin, dried rations, and a sword. She collected them all and marched out after the Glorious One.

* * * * *

Arguing, Sash and Waistcoat hung in Karona's arms. She soared above a high valley of the Shadow Mountains. Drifting down to a broad basin, she set down. It was a dry, rounded spot, with rock ledges sheltering one side and the clawlike summits of two mountains behind them.

Karona released her two friends, and they fell over, clutching numb legs and rolling among creosote bushes.

"Only a freak could touch her tongue to her nose!"

"*I* say if she can't do it, she's not impotent."

"*Omni*potent!" shouted Sash, scrambling to his feet. His fury was only accentuated by the creosote leaves jutting like fire from his hair.

"That's what I said. Omnimportant!"

LET US FIND OUT WHAT *I* CAN DO.

Waistcoat stuck out his tongue, and Sash mashed it up into the man's nose. "See? A freak!"

Stepping lightly across the air, Karona crossed to the center of the clearing. Her flesh gleamed, exuding light in pearlescent pulses. *I CAN SHINE, OF COURSE. I CAN DRAW MANA, CAN HEAL, CAN FLY—*

"Inspire love," Sash said wistfully.

"And murder," added Waistcoat.

Karona lifted one hand and held it out toward a nearby mesquite tree. Her fingers spread and crooked, and a wave of motion swept from her shoulder down to her fingertips. It stopped there, failing in the still air. Karona gazed in disappointment at her hand. *APPARENTLY I CAN'T DO THAT.*

"Do what?" asked Sash.

CAST LIGHTNING.

Waistcoat goggled. "You can't? I thought for sure you could. Everybody can cast lightning."

"Try it again," Sash said.

Karona trained her eyes on the scrubby tree and gave her wrist a small twist. Blue-white energy leaped from her fingertips, ripped through the air, and mantled the tree. It shook then burst into flame. Karona withdrew her hand, and the lightning surge ceased. The wood burned, sending up a column of smoke.

"Smells nice," said Waistcoat.

While the tree blazed magnificently behind her, Karona stared at her fingertips. *WHY COULDN'T I DO IT BEFORE?*

"Yeah," agreed Waistcoat.

Karona pivoted, lunging and opening her mouth in a silent snarl. Nothing emerged from her bared teeth.

Sash stroked his chin. "What are you doing?"

"Seems like nothing."

TRYING TO BREATHE FIRE.

"Heck, yeah, you can breathe fire," Waistcoat said.

Karona took a deep breath, clenched her fists, and loosed a great gout of flame. She should have turned away from her prophets.

Sash and Waistcoat ran, flaming, across the valley. "Yawwww! Put us out!"

Karona waved her hand before her, wiping away the fire as if it were merely lines on a chalkboard. In the distance, the two prophets ran a few more paces before they realized they were no longer burning.

Smoldering, Waistcoat trudged back toward her. "This time it doesn't smell so good."

I CAN CAST LIGHTNING, BREATHE FLAME, PUT OUT FIRES—

"Anything we say," Waistcoat blurted.

The angel's eyes grew wide. *YES. ANYTHING YOU SAY. I COULDN'T DO IT WHEN I FIRST TRIED, BUT AS SOON AS YOU SAID THAT I COULD— AS SOON AS YOU BELIEVED—*

"Makes sense," Sash said. "If you're magic incarnate, you can do anything we think you can do. You're limited only by the mortal minds that perceive you."

OTHERWISE, I CAN DO ANYTHING.

"Turn the sky purple," suggested Waistcoat.

The angel lifted her eyes to the firmament, bright blue above her. She swept her hand in a long, graceful arch. Beyond her fingertips, the very air transformed. It rippled, refracting light to new bands of the spectrum. The sky slowly went from blue to purple.

"Hee!" said Waistcoat, slapping his knee. "What about pigs?"

PIGS?

"Make me some pigs—some big, monster pigs. Cow-sized."

Karona shrugged, flicking her fingers. Among the scrub brush, pink things swelled into being. Peglike legs held up huge bodies, and snouts prodding among the roots.

"Pigs? Ha!" Sash cried derisively. "She can do anything, and you have her make pigs!"

"Make them fly!"

With a wink from Karona, the pigs grew white wings from their shoulders. They flapped like startled pigeons and rose into the air. A few, frightened to be off the ground, relieved themselves.

"Oh, that a moron should command such power!" Sash bemoaned. To Karona, he said, "Why not create a river there?"

Her eyes followed the path of Sash's finger, and a mighty cascade flowed from the claw peaks down through the valley to a waterfall on the far side.

"Make it burn," Waistcoat said.

Fire whooshed atop of the river, spreading from a thin thread at the mountaintop to a wide wall of flame nearby.

Sash shook his head in irritation. "How about making these mean little bushes into lovely, large trees?"

With a word, it was done, a great forest beside the flaming river.

"And make them chocolate."

The green heads of those trees turned brown and began to melt. The rich scent of chocolate filled the air, even as the hundred-foot boles began to sink, sag, and topple.

"Oh, you're an aggravation!"

"Let's have the Glimmer Moon back," Waistcoat said. "Everybody talks about how nice it was."

It was there.

"Now blow it up."

The moon flared. Radiance stabbed out from the heart of it, piercing the spherical framework in a thousand places. Metallic panels burst and tumbled out all around the great moon. Hunks of superstructure burned.

"Nice," Waistcoat said. "What about giant, six-legged jackrabbits that you can ride? Everybody wishes we had those. . . ."

CHAPTER 16

OVER THE CLIFF

Chained wrist to wrist, Kamahl and Ixidor stared at the wall of fire. It rolled down from the heights of the Shadow Mountains and cut across the ground in front of them.

"We can't go around," Kamahl said, his mind racing. "Can you fly?"

Ixidor shook his head slowly. "I'm a creator, not a bird."

"Can you create something to get us over it? A bridge?"

Shrugging, Ixidor said, "Certainly. Let's go back and get my paints."

"It comes from up there."

Kamahl set out, and Ixidor could only follow. He had been sullen since the shackles had gone on. The two men toiled up the rocky trail beside the burning river. Soot covered the ground, and scrub brakes had been reduced to ashen twigs. Overhead, the sun hiked up a purple sky.

It was early evening before they reached the headlands. Panting, Kamahl and Ixidor clambered up the final rise. They stared out, amazed.

The river of fire cut across a hanging valley, and on the near side hovered a glorious figure. She seemed a living star, bright and beautiful. The air sang as if with love, and light was her

152

raiment. Around her in a spiral flew a choir of heavenly beings. They were meaty beasts, though they floated effortlessly on small and rapid wings. Below them, the ground was smooth and fertile and fragrant, smelling of richest chocolate. In the midst of that brown field stood two robed figures, lifting their feet from the sticky mess.

Ixidor fell to his knees, and tears brimmed in his wide-open eyes. "Mother!" he cried. He cradled his slender hand to his chest. "She's terrible and wonderful. I hate her and love her."

Kamahl peered down at his comrade, kneeling worshipfully, and remembered when he had done the same. Now he felt only sick horror.

"She's casting a spell," Ixidor said quietly.

The field of melted chocolate stiffened. Its surface grew dull, and tiny lines spread across it, crackling. The two priests pulled their feet from the sucking stuff and stepped out on top of it. Molten chocolate solidified like volcanic glass. Next moment, it *was* glass. Every ripple, every contour of the land shimmered, first translucent and then transparent. Under that thick sheet of glass was darkness, as if a canyon had opened beneath the valley.

"You were right about her power," Kamahl said, his teeth set on edge. "She grows only stronger. Perhaps we can't wait for your brothers. Can you kill her today?"

"No!" Ixidor spat. "How can you say that? How can you *stand* there?" He stared at Karona. "If Mother is here, there's no hope."

The spell deepened. A grid of slender white lines crisscrossed the glassy surface. Real land forms gave way to a topographic chart. On its lines, the two robed men balanced. They staggered to intersections and stooped, holding on. The hems of their robes dangled into oblivion below them.

"Do you see what she's done?" Kamahl asked. "She's removed the land. She's opened a bottomless pit, and this is only the start.

She's learning her powers, and if we don't destroy her, soon there'll be no escape."

Ixidor listened, though he shook his head. "You're right. No escape. We must embrace her and become her servants."

A terrible cry erupted from the far side of the valley. A motley mass of warriors flooded from between the two claw-shaped mountains. They rushed toward that terrible plunge into oblivion.

"Now you'll see," Kamahl whispered in dread. "Now you will see."

* * * * *

Most of the army slogged far behind, but for those who could run and not die, glory waited beyond the next rise.

Braids could do more than run. A quarter mile ahead of even the horsemen and avens, she hurled herself up the steep embankment. Feet touched down between creosote bushes, and Braids leaped into dementia space. Out again and in, she had stitched her way across grasslands and wastelands, foothills and hilltops. Now she rushed toward the Glorious One.

"Karona!" Braids cried. "Karona!"

How strange life had been. Braids had risen from street waif to dementia summoner, from lovesick servant of the First to shattered slave of Akroma. She had saved Phage only to bow before her, had murdered Phage's husband only to guard her son. In Braids, all things were in conflict. She was not covered by skin but by scars, and her soul was knitted together with pain.

"I'm coming, Karona!"

Braids leaped atop a ridge of stone, the pass between two peaks. She set her feet on the ground and saw the Perfect One.

Karona hung there, arms embracing the wind and eyes blazing with fire. Her body was perfect and smooth, quintessence bundled in skin.

Oh, to touch her, to cling to her and be unraveled.

Braids leaped again, feet leaving the rocky ridge and flying out above nothingness.

Below her opened a bottomless pit. Only a grid of rumpled white lines extended above the depths. Braids shifted her feet in air and glided into dementia space. She emerged again, rising higher. Out of reality she went then back in. She pieced together a path that rose obliquely toward the angel. With arms open wide, Braids soared through the air toward her heart's desire.

"Karona!"

At the sound of her name, the woman pivoted toward Braids.

Braids shot herself from dementia space across the final few feet to Karona and wrapped her arms around the woman's legs. She clung to that beaming presence and wept in joy.

"Save me, Karona! Save me!"

* * * * *

Waistcoat was sitting atop two topographic lines when the creature soared by overhead. It latched onto Karona's legs and hung there, wailing. Waistcoat stared at it and scratched his head.

"What is it?"

I DON'T KNOW.

Sash, sitting on a nearby intersection, squinted to make out the riling figure. "Can you get it off?"

HOW?

Sash counted on his fingers. "Well, there's lightning, fireball—"

"Chocolate," Waistcoat said.

Karona merely put her hand on the thing's head and shoved. It lost its hold and dropped away. It looked like a cross between a woman and a wolverine. The thing tipped backward, one leg hitting a line as it toppled through the grid. It plunged quickly, its cry echoing from the walls of that infinite pit.

"Nice work," Waistcoat said.

"Sometimes you don't need to use magic," Sash added.

The congratulations cut short as more creatures arrived— riders on horseback. They rushed over the ridge and hurtled out on the grid. Unlike that first thing, though, these creatures couldn't fly. Some horses plunged right through the squares. Others caught and broke a leg before plummeting into the pit. A few dropped onto lines and were nearly sliced in two. The riders fell from their backs, cascading into the pit. They tumbled like pepper from a mill.

"This is bad," Waistcoat said.

Hundreds more crossed the verge and plunged. Perhaps a dozen caught hold of a line and held on, but the rest all poured into oblivion.

Waistcoat gabbled, "We have to do something."

Sash looked to Karona. "*You* have to do something."

With horror, she gazed toward the rocky ridge, where the hundreds who fell were followed by roaring thousands.

WHAT SHOULD I DO?

"Well," Waistcoat shouted, "fix the ground!"

* * * * *

For the first few hundred feet of her fall, Braids could do nothing but mourn the loss of the lady. In these arms, Braids had held the Perfect One. Now she held only roaring air.

On either side of her, walls of ragged rock shot skyward. She was falling into a bottomless canyon. Already the light of Karona failed her. Braids couldn't fly, not truly, but she could fall *differently*. She fell into dementia space, her foot catching ground there and hurling her sideways. Back into reality she rushed, leveling in her plummet. Again into dementia space for another leap, and out. By increments, Braids rose slowly and edged nearer to one of the canyon walls. It was exhausting work, but if she could get a hand-hold on stone, she could climb to the top.

Overhead, something buzzed like a gnat. The sound swelled into a roar. Braids looked up to see a gutted horse fall past, rolling upside down. Its bellowing rider followed. He screamed as he plunged, rushed past, and dwindled into the dark depths.

Braids bounded higher, threading her way between worlds. The man's cries diminished, replaced by more shrieks above. Hundreds more rushed over the cliff and began their tormented tumble. It was a waterfall of bodies—folk hoping to grasp Karona but clutching nothing. Braids almost empathized, though she had no intention of falling.

With three more leaps in dementia space, she reached the rock wall and a ledge she could grasp. Clinging tightly, she clambered onto the shelf of stone and stood. Before her, creatures cascaded—elves, minotaurs, humans, centaurs. Their legs flailed, and their hands clutched the air. Braids watched them.

Poor fools. To die plunging away from the most beautiful light in the world.

Then all light and all screaming were gone.

The air had solidified. Rock and soil encased Braids. Silence and stillness and darkness. She couldn't even draw breath to scream. Only her heart thundered on in fast panic. Braids was buried alive. So was everyone who had plunged into the canyon.

It would be quick now, but even one minute was an unbearably long time when measured in heartbeats.

Withdrawing into her mind, Braids retreated into dementia space.

Instead of entombing ground, she suddenly stood on a twisted plain. To one side loomed a forest that shivered with the movements of monsters. To the other side stretched a sea of serpents. Braids had come on safari to this place many times, capturing the monsters of her own mind and bringing them into reality.

Now, she was here to stay, and the monsters had captured her.

For the last moments of her life, Braids walked among them. It was fitting. She was home, surrounded by a great crowd of beasts. They welcomed her with grinning fangs and open claws.

And she was simply dead.

* * * * *

When the grid solidified to soil and stone, Sash discovered that his feet were trapped. To the knee, rock encased his legs. He couldn't pull free. Rolling backward onto the now-solid ground, he dragged futilely at his knees.

The ground trembled and the air too, both pummeled by the approaching throng. Sash glanced their way, glad they weren't plunging into the pit.

Instead, they stampeded directly toward him.

Sash stood, his lower legs still gripped by the stone. He was as short as a dwarf and soon would be flattened. He raised his arms to his sides and ruffled his robe, doing everything he could to look big.

The running masses came all the faster, some on hooves and steel-soled boots. Nothing got their attention except the object of their love—Karona.

"Karona's prophet cries, 'Heed!' Heed Karona's prophet!"

They did not heed, but neither did they trample him. The crowd rushed around the robed midget the same way they would avoid a fire. The front ranks reached Karona and leaped for her, elves and centaurs near to grasping her legs.

"Rise, Karona!" Sash called. "Don't let them tear you down!"

She listened, at least, her feet gliding up and away from the reaching hands. She was beautiful there in the purple heavens, pigs flying circles around her. The crowd saw her beauty too. They bunched up yearningly beneath her.

Sash suddenly remembered the folk who had fallen. They were buried alive underfoot—but alive for how long?

"Clear away! In the name of Karona, leave! She must dissolve the ground! You cannot stand here! In the name of Karona, listen!"

They did not. Oblivious to the folk dying beneath them, the people lifted worshiping hands.

*   *   *   *   *

Ixidor still knelt at the edge of the plain, but he no longer looked to his glorious Mother. He watched the crowd. It grew by the second, packing tighter and tighter beneath her. Soon, those in the center would be crushed to death, and those on the outside would be trampled by new arrivals. All of them stood on the ground that entombed hundreds of others.

The avens arrived. They dived through the air and jealously ripped into the flying pigs. Talons and beaks tore away hunks of skin and muscle. Shoulders smashed wings. Screaming, the bloody pigs tumbled from the sky and crashed atop the crowd. No sooner had the avens dispatched these grotesque attendants than they attacked the woman at their center.

Ixidor doubled over, putting his face to the ground. He couldn't bear anymore. At first, his eyes had been flooded with beauty, but now he could see only terrors.

It was just like last time. The incarnation of magic had brought horror to the world. If she continued to grow in power, all Dominaria would be destroyed. If the numena of old came together against her, they could stop her, yes, but they too would be destroyed.

Who will I be this day? Ixidor the avatar or Lowallyn, lord of waters? Will I be a mortal or a god? Ixidor would flee from Dominaria and live. Lowallyn would fight for Dominaria and die. Will I sacrifice the world to save myself or sacrifice myself to save the world?

The chain on his wrist rattled. Kamahl was attached to the other end.

Turning, the wretched man stood. He stared, eye to eye, with the barbarian who had brought him here.

"I've seen enough. Let's go."

Kamahl's eyes smoldered. "You look at these things and turn your back?"

"We must get my brothers. Only then can we stop Karona."

The barbarian nodded. "You've seen what I've seen, and we agree." He reached to the shackles that bound them and worked the key. "You're free, Ixidor."

"I'm no longer Ixidor. Now and forever, I am Lowallyn."

* * * * *

Waistcoat had thought it was bad to have his lower half buried in rock. It was worse to have his upper half buried in people. Someone sat on his head. Soon, he would be dead.

"Karona! Save me!" Waistcoat shouted, though she couldn't possibly hear his cry amid all the others.

Couldn't possibly hear! If he believed she couldn't, of course she couldn't. "I'm an idiot." Mustering his most ardent faith, he cried, "Karona! Save me!"

Waistcoat was suddenly yanked from the ground like a fat carrot. Through a flurry of aven feathers, he flew up into Karona's arms. She can yank Sash too, he thought. There was a pernicious moment of doubt, but faith returned, and he soared upward.

"Together again," Sash shouted as Karona grasped him.

Kicking his legs to fend off an aven, Waistcoat said, "Let's be together—alone."

Karona launched skyward, leaving all the creatures behind. She and her prophets flew through the purple heavens above their burning river.

"I think we learned something today," Waistcoat said as they tripped among the stars.

"What?" snarled Sash. "Don't dump people down a bottomless pit and then fill it in?"

"No. We learned Karona can do anything, but she'd better not."

CHAPTER 17

KIN

Sash's legs were starting to get numb. It often happened when Karona hauled him around. Still, he loved to be held by her, power coursing through his veins and nerves. Achy legs were a small price to pay. He glanced down at the dangling things and below, where the people of the world converged.

The troops were no longer crushing and trampling each other but falling back to defensible positions. They lined up in rows and companies. Riders formed vanguards, with infantry behind and archers in the rear. This wasn't the way mobs fought, but armies. The riot was turning to war.

"Uh, Karona, things look bad down there."

Don't look.

From anyone else, that advice would have seemed cruelly cold. In her arms, though, all was kind and warm.

Peering past his purplish toes, Sash said, "It looks like they're about to start killing each other again."

They're always killing each other. The sooner we get away, the better.

"I don't think that'll stop them," Sash said. "They're not looking at us anymore. They're bent on war."

What's there to fight for in that desolate place?

162

"Who knows? They marched side by side to find you, but now that you're gone, they're squaring off."

"Idiots," Waistcoat observed.

Karona shook her head, and the energy pouring from her into Sash grew dark. *I USED TO THINK I WAS THE REASON THEY FOUGHT. WHEREVER I WENT, THERE WERE ATROCITIES. NOW I THINK THEY KILL EACH OTHER BECAUSE THEY LOVE TO. IT DOESN'T MATTER WHETHER I'M THERE OR NOT.*

"When you're with them, one believer fights another. When you're gone, nations fight nations."

IDIOTS.

Sash nodded. "Idiots or not, we can't just float away while they chop each other to pieces. You have to stop them, Karona."

I CAN'T STOP THEM.

"You *can* stop them. You can do anything." Sash pointed to a curved peak nearby, as sharp as a black claw. Its rocky summit overhung the battlefield. "Land there, and we'll stop this war."

Karona glided down out of the sky. The purple winds of evening fled past them. Below, a black summit rose. She set down on the barren knob of stone. On all sides, it sloped away to a sheer drop. No one in the world could reach them there. Even an aven would find the air too thin for its wings. On this perch in the middle of the sky, Karona released her two prophets.

On nerveless legs, they stumbled and fell. Sash twisted, clutching his tingling thighs. Waistcoat rolled like a sausage beetle.

SUGGEST SOMETHING. Karona folded her arms across her chest and peered down at the battlefield.

"How about opening the pit again?" Waistcoat asked.

"Shut up," said Sash. He rolled to his belly and peered out toward the armies below. "There has to be a better way."

Waistcoat stroked his chin. "How 'bout turning the ground to pudding?"

"No! They'll drown in pudding. You'll change it back to ground, and they'll be buried again." Sash said. He scratched his head. "Why not make them love each other?"

Karona pursed her lips. She extended her arms and drew the mana power of the mountains into her. The red heat of passion glimmered in her fingers and flooded her arms. It poured through her until every part glowed. She swung her hands forward and let the enchantment rush out. In an instant, it reached down from the claw-tipped summit, across the purple sky, and to the battlefield.

"What's happening?" Waistcoat said. "I can't see."

PASSION IS FILLING THEM. WARRIORS ARE RUSHING TOWARD EACH OTHER, ARMS OPEN.

Sash spread his hand below his chin and smiled in satisfaction. "I told you—"

THEY ARE TAKING OFF THEIR CLOTHES—

"Let me see!" Waistcoat shouted.

THEY'RE FALLING DOWN, ROLLING, CLAWING EACH OTHER TO PIECES.

"Try the pudding!" Sash gasped. "Just a foot deep!"

Blue sparks poured from Karona's hands in a wide shower.

IT HAS ONLY ENCOURAGED THEM.

Sash clutched his hair. "What else can we do? How do we stop them?"

I COULD ERASE THEIR MINDS.

"No! Certainly not!"

I COULD PUT THEM TO SLEEP.

"While they wallow in a foot of pudding? I don't think so."

Waistcoat said, "Change them to giant rabbits."

Karona irritably pressed her lips together and gave a careless wave of her arm. A veil of green magic trailed her fingertips. It spread like a cloak across the battlefield. The naked bodies bounded up one by one, transforming into great white puffs.

Sash stared down in horror, barely making out the huge beasts, their haunches and chests draped in pudding. They rutted and fought just as before. "Change them back."

With another indolent gesture, Karona withdrew the veil of green. The giant rabbits below reverted to their original forms: human, elf, dwarf, minotaur—killing, raping, dying. . . .

I'M FINISHED WITH MORTALS.

Sash gaped, his mouth like a wound in his face. "What about us? We're mortals, Waistcoat and I. Are you finished with us?"

YOU'RE NOT LIKE THE OTHERS. Karona peered distractedly past their hunched shoulders to the killing fields. *NEITHER AM I.* Her eyes widened, and a light kindled in them. *I WISH TO FIND OTHERS LIKE ME—GODS AND GODESSES. KIN.* She closed her eyes, reaching out on the wind. *I LONG TO MEET THEM.*

Sash said, "You can meet them right here, right now."

YES.

Karona strode to the center of the peak, the highest point in the Shadow Mountains. Pinnacles were places of power, where the mass of red mana locked in the rocks met the mass of blue mana swarming through the skies: old foes balanced on a pinpoint. She projected a circle on the stone, and it appeared—a line deeply etched as if by a hundred chisels and a thousand hours.

Upon that great circle, in every seventy-two degrees of arc, her mind hewed out more small circles, five in all.

The first glimmered. The stone within it faded to show a field of tall grass, waving in the wind. This was no mere painting, no reflection, but a window that had opened through stone to the grasslands of the far north.

Pivoting to her right, Karona focused on the next circle. It opened like a shutter from a window, and salt air poured through. Beyond, a swelling sea tossed whitecaps so lofty that they danced among the clouds.

Karona turned to the next circle, and it opened—a doorway to a wide, wet swamp, overhung with old-man's moss and filled with cypress. Scaly things shifted on the land, and dark things moved through the water.

She did not open the fourth circle, but only looked to the mountains around her. All the while, the stone grew smoother, brighter, as mica sifted to the surface. The spot became a metallic pool, reflecting the power of the mountains.

Karona turned to the final circle, which revealed a dense and ancient forest, trees reaching their shaggy heads skyward.

Karona stood amid the circles, embodying every color and none. From each spot, mana flowed in abundance. The power poured into her, igniting her like a lantern.

Sash stared in awe.

Karona faced the forest portal and called into it, "COME TO ME. I SUMMON YOU, GREAT SPIRIT. FROM ROOTS AND BRANCHES, COME! KARONA CALLS YOU, MAGIC CALLS YOU!"

Something in the forest-mind heard. A powerful impulse raced up the tree nearest the portal and took form from living boughs, vines, and leaves. Moss became a head, which balanced atop broad-beamed shoulders and a triangular torso. With arms and legs of twisted wood, the thing bounded above the treetop. It grasped hold of the portal. Flexing massive sinews, the god-thing pulled itself through.

It climbed onto the stone, towering above Karona and staring with mushroom eyes. After the briefest moment, the creature dropped to one knobby knee, bowed its head, and said, "I have come, Lady Magic. I will serve."

"WHAT IS YOUR NAME?"

"I am Multani," the wood-man said. "I am the spirit of Yavimaya. I was born after Argoth, was a foe then a friend to Urza Planeswalker, fought the war against Yawgmoth, and have lain in mana destitution for a century. You have awakened me from sleep, and I would serve you."

"YOU ARE A GOD, MULTANI?"

"No. I am only a spirit. I am the will of the wood, and I take my form from the living things around me. There are no true gods on Dominaria, Lady, except you—and Gaea."

"WHO IS GAEA?"

"She is the world, the life of it—and you are her opposite—"

"THE DEATH OF IT?"

"No, the magic of it."

Karona's eyes narrowed. "AT LEAST IF GAEA AND I ARE OPPOSITES, WE ARE EQUALS."

"No. Gaea is in all things, and all things are in her. She imbues the world with life. You are separate, and you draw mana and magic out of it."

Karona's face darkened. "THEN I *AM* THE DEATH OF IT."

"Those are your words, not mine."

"GAEA REJECTS ME. I SENSE IT."

The nature spirit seemed evasive. "I cannot speak for her, but all of her creatures crave you."

"YOU ARE A CREATURE, MULTANI. DO YOU CRAVE ME?"

He nodded, avarice blooming in his mushroom eyes. "I am the sum of a million million living things. Of course I crave you!" He reached suddenly toward her.

"BEGONE!" commanded Karona. Her hand swatted the air, and her radiance crashed fistlike into him.

Multani fell through the circle of stone. His twiggy fingers scrabbled to hold on but couldn't. He plunged into the forest.

Karona snapped her fingers, and the stone circle slammed shut.

"Didn't like the look of him, anyway," Sash said.

Waistcoat nodded. "He seemed pretty mossy."

GAEA REJECTS ME . . . SO I WILL REJECT HER.

Pivoting to her left, Karona faced the mica pool. Its crackling surface reflected the summit, and its depths reached into the heart of the mountain.

"POWER OF THE MOUNTAINS, I SUMMON YOU. I, KARONA, WHO HOLD ALL RED MANA IN MY GRASP. COMMUNE WITH ME, THAT I MAY KNOW THE GODS OF MY LANDS."

The mica glinted. Fractures reflected a stocky outline. It moved soundlessly along the folds of metal, hues widening and joining. A leathery face took form, and an iron-gray beard jutted from it. Fiery eyes smoldered beneath long, hemplike hair. The figure climbed up from the ragged mirror. A stiff reddish collar emerged, a leather coat beneath it. A white apron covered the creature's powerful chest and was tucked into a fat black belt. Rough-woven knickers ran to hairy calves, and they to broad, black boots. The dwarf stepped forth, dragging a smithing hammer that smoked from whatever it had been pounding.

He sized up Karona before going to one knee and bowing his head. "I am Fiers, smith lord of the Otarian dwarfs," the stocky fellow said. His beard and mustache wavered like tendrils of smoke. "I've heard your summons, and I come."

"ARE YOU A GOD?"

The dwarf blinked gravely. "I've been called such by my people. To them I am."

"BUT TO ME?"

He drew in a long breath. "In truth? I'm a planeswalker. I've made the mountains of Otaria my home, for these places welcome me."

Karona averted her awful gaze. "I'VE BEEN WELCOMED, TOO, BUT DEATH ALWAYS COMES WITH ME."

The dwarf spoke reluctantly. "Seems to me you haven't found your home."

Karoma nodded grimly. "RETURN." She held out a mana-blazing hand, and its aura drove the dwarf back down into the shimmering metal. A moment later, the circle went dark.

Sash said, "Again, not your type."

"Stumpy's the word," Waistcoat said.

Karona lifted her hand to silence the prophets. Clenching her jaw, she pivoted to face the swamp portal.

"POWERS OF DARKNESS, I CALL TO YOU—GODS THAT RULE DEATH AND DECAY. CLIMB FROM THE MUCK TO HAVE AUDIENCE WITH MAGIC!"

This time, all was still. Even the crocodilian shadows ceased their swimming. The trees stiffened as if frightened. Above their mossy tops, a volcano showed. A presence lurked there—a fell ghost as large as a mountain. It was not a true power, but once it had been. It spoke in a sepulchral whisper:

"I know you. We've been bosom companions, you and I. For nine thousand years, I was the keeper of artifice, and you the keeper of magic."

"YOU WERE. . . ."

"The world did not receive me. Those I chose turned from truth to perversions. I persisted. I built a whole world for them to inhabit, and when they would not, I built another world to bring my people to them. I came myself, embraced all of Dominaria, welcomed every last creature into my touch, but they reviled me. They called me, 'destroyer,' and Gaea cast me down. "

"I HAVE BEEN CALLED SUCH THINGS. I HAVE BEEN REJECTED BY GAEA. BUT WHY DID SHE REJECT YOU?"

"She is jealous of us; it is as simple as that."

"EMERGE, THEN, SO I MAY SEE YOU."

"You have called me, but I cannot leave the lands where my essence is gathering. Instead, come to me. We will be friends in an unfriendly world. We are the same, you and I."

"ARE YOU A GOD?"

"I was a god, truer than any. I will be a god again soon. Only come to me and help me, and you will have a companion forever."

"WHAT IS YOUR NAME?" asked Karona.

Only silence answered from the circle.

"I DEMAND TO KNOW."

"Names have power, Great Lady. Come to my lands, and I will tell you my name."

"NAMES DO HAVE POWER, AND MY NAME IS KARONA, AND I DEMAND TO KNOW YOUR NAME."

"I am Yawgmoth."

Sash clamped his hands to his ears, but he could not shut out the sound that came from Karona's mind. A billion billion shrieks— every dark enchantment, every horrid sorcery and deadly intention bore that name. Yawgmoth was indeed the destroyer, and he had nearly obliterated a whole world.

Karona held her hands flat before her and screamed.

"Come to me, Karona, and we'll divide the world between us, and you will never be alone again."

The stony circle slammed shut and fused with the rock. The sound reverberated through the heavens.

Sash reeled and gasped, his hands clutching his knees.

YAWGMOTH . . . DESTROYER . . . KIN. Karoma trembled. PERHAPS THE WORLD WILL BE RID OF ME, AS IT WAS RID OF HIM.

Waistcoat said, "You don't stink like him."

Karona slowly pivoted toward the blue circle. In a voice that shook, she said, "I CALL TO YOU, POWERS OF WATER AND SKY. ANSWER ME. COME TO ME, AND WE WILL SPEAK." The summons was quiet, almost apologetic. Still, a creature came.

A being rose from the changeable essence of blue magic. He was gaunt, his hair white and spiky as if from a great fright. Up from the hole he climbed, reluctant, his eyes guarded. He never fully stood as the others had but bowed as though he knew Karona. A single withered hand rested atop the stone.

"I come, Karona, as you have bidden."

"WHAT IS YOUR NAME?"

At last, he looked at her. His eyes were bright blue, robin's eggs. "All mortal folk call me Ixidor."

Sash cringed. He looked suddenly away, shading his eyes and

whistling nonchalantly. Beside him, Waistcoat still gaped at the man. Sash slapped his cheek, jutted a thumb over his shoulder, and said, "Ook-lay away-ay."

"Oh," said Waistcoat, "right!" He became very interested in his navel.

"AND YOU, IXIDOR—ARE YOU A GOD?"

The man dropped his gaze. "Many say so, but I'm not—only a long-dead sorcerer swallowed by a great wurm. While I was gone, I was great. Now that I've returned, I'm only . . . this." He raised his hand to indicate his ravaged figure.

"I SEEK A FRIEND, IXIDOR. YOU KNOW WHO I AM. COULD YOU BE HE?"

"Sadly, great lady, I cannot."

"WHY NOT?"

He breathed deeply. "I seek my brothers. I'm sworn to this quest. Until I am reconciled to them, I can be nothing to you. Once we are reunited, perhaps then you and I will speak."

"I WON'T KEEP YOU FROM YOUR TASK. GO, IXIDOR, AND WHEN YOU FIND YOUR BROTHERS, COME AGAIN TO ME."

"I will," he said solemnly, "if you haven't come to me first." The man crawled backward down the portal, and the stone sealed shut above him.

Sash sighed in deep relief. "Good riddance."

"That guy's nothing but trouble," Waistcoat agreed.

I HAVE FOUND NO OTHER GODS—

"There's one more portal," Sash said. "Maybe you'll find something there."

Karona grimly turned toward the last circle, plains white with harvest. She peered down through the hole.

A tall, regal man stood there. His robes were impeccably white against his black skin. Beneath his caftan, intense eyes peered out. His hair was braided and strung with colored beads. From his sandaled feet spread grasslands that were high and golden—*his* lands. He stood on them and stared up at the hole that had opened in his skies.

In a small voice, Karona said, "I CALL YOU FORTH, POWER OF PLAINS."

The man's feet lifted from ground. He slid up through the portal and set his sandals on the pinnacle of Shadow Mountain. He was imposing there on the mountaintop, though immediately he knelt and touched his head to the ground.

"Hello, Karona."

She studied him. "YOU KNOW ME?"

The man sat back on his heels, lifting his face. He smiled impishly. "All my life."

"WHAT IS YOUR NAME?"

"Teferi."

"ARE YOU A GOD?"

Teferi's smile only deepened, and it was dazzling. "As a child, I was convinced of it. Now I know I'm not."

Light faded from Karona's eyes. "WHAT ARE YOU?"

He shrugged. "Wizard. Planeswalker. Ruler of pocket planes—I'm godlike but not a god." His eyes pried at hers, which had turned downward. "I came from your world a century ago. Dominaria was in great peril, and I carved away a piece of it—Zhalfir is its name—to save it from Yawgmoth. I took part of Shiv too. I've kept them safe all this while, waiting to bring them back. Perhaps it's time."

"NO. THE WORLD IS STILL IN PERIL. THERE'S ANOTHER YAWGMOTH WHO THREATENS IT."

"Who?" Teferi asked.

"ME."

Karona waved her hand, and the man was swept up off his feet and sent back down through the portal. He landed on the grasslands below and stared up toward her. With another wave, Karona slammed the portal shut.

She shook her head sadly. *MULTANI WAS RIGHT. THERE ARE NO OTHER TRUE GODS ON DOMINARIA—ONLY GAEA, AND SHE HAS REJECTED ME.*

Waistcoat stepped up to her and slung his arm over her shoulder. "You're better off without her. You're better off without 'em all."

"Ixidor knows more than he's saying." Sash said.

"Yeah. I thought so too. The bastard!"

"*I'M GOING TO WATCH HIM AND SEE WHERE HE GOES.*"

CHAPTER 18

OLD DEBTS

*L*owallyn and Kamahl descended the suspension bridge that led
to Coliseum Island. They had become a team.

Few of the Cabal guards on the islands even thought to question
them. Those who did heard that these two men were brothers—and
believed it. Lowallyn's skin had grown smooth and tan during their
journey beneath the desert sun. His muscles had filled out again,
nourished by Kamahl's rations. Using a stick and hard-packed sand,
he had drawn a simple backpack with one arm-strap and brought it
into being. He also created more rations—a wheel of cheese, tubes
of dried beef, flatbread, and best of all, skins of wine. Lowallyn was
gaining power outside of Topos. Soon, he would be the great sorcerer he once was.

"She's watching us, you know," Lowallyn said casually, his
boots scuffing the planks of the bridge. He had fashioned the boots
as well—black and slender, with flared tops.

Kamahl scowled. He was red from sun and exertion, and the
prospect of confronting Kuberr unnerved him. "She'd be stupid
not to."

Lowallyn tilted his head. "She's naive but was never stupid.
When she called me before her, she sensed I was holding back."

"Shhh," Kamahl warned. "If she can watch us, she can listen too."

"Yes," Lowallyn said, "though such spells are harder. A glance every day tells her where we're headed, but she'd have to listen to every conversation."

"Even so . . ."

"Even so." Lowallyn stared at the great coliseum. Its huge curve swelled toward them, and its battlements looked like hippos' teeth. "Kuberr's quite a builder."

"So are you," Kamahl said.

Lowallyn's eyes grew wistful. "Yes, Locus is a beautiful palace. Did you notice the waterfalls? My springs aren't so hidden there." He shook his head. "It's hard to be away from it. If the world's doomed, it'd be nice to spend my last days there."

"The world isn't doomed. We're seeing to that."

"Yes," Lowallyn said, blinking away the vision. He studied the marketplace that spread around the coliseum. Canvas triangles flapped in the wind, and hawkers babbled beneath them. "You think they sell paints, brushes, canvas, and sculpting clay?"

"They say anything can be bought and sold in the shadow of the coliseum. I think they mean human flesh, but maybe you can find art supplies."

Side by side, the two men stepped from the suspension bridge and onto a brick path. It led up through the marketplace and to the coliseum. Stalls and tents crowded beside it. Wares filled bins and lay in wide array on cloths. Gladiatorial souvenirs, betting sheets, spy glasses, meat on sticks, skins of liquor, hallucinogenic scarves, tobacco for chewing or smoking, brass cuspidors and ash trays, holy relics of Ixidor, knives, walking sticks, gods-eyes, toys, pottery, jewelry . . .

Lowallyn approached a corner stall where a quick-sketch artist sat. Sheets of paper were pinned to an easel before her, and rows of chalk lay near her blackened fingers. She was thin and watchful, with faded ribbons braided in her auburn hair. She wore a mismatched vest and skirt, stitched together from rags.

"Hello," Lowallyn said.

The artist looked hopefully at him. Her eyes gathered the contours of his figure, the ravages of his face, the hollows in his eyes.

"Do you wish a portrait?"

Lowallyn said, "In barter for this skin of wine."

"Hold on," she said, lifting her hand. "Let me taste it."

Lowallyn pulled the skin from around his shoulder and handed it over. The artist took the skin, unstopped it, and drank. The deeply red wine darkened her lips, and she smiled. She stopped the skin and set it aside.

"Accepted. Sit, please."

She sorted among her pastels—most just little nubs—and gathered the colors for Lowallyn.

Without sitting, Lowallyn said, "There's one more condition— that after you draw me, I draw you."

The artist blushed, staring at him. "All right." She carefully laid the tiny chips of chalk on the edge of her much-battered easel. "As long as you don't use much chalk. Now, please, sit."

He perched on a rickety stool. Kamahl strode up behind him and crossed his arms, watching.

As the artist put the first lines on the canvas, she said, "What's your name?"

"Lowallyn, lord of hidden streams. What's yours?"

She blinked at him. "Verdanna." She returned to drawing. "What do you do, Lowallyn?"

"I'm an ancient sorcerer, one of the three numena of old who imprisoned the Primeval dragons and brought about the age of mortals. With my brothers, I ruled the world for a thousand years, and I've returned after twenty millennia to rule it again."

Verdanna's eyes and mouth formed three circles on her face, and she withdrew her hands to her lap. Trying to cover her shock, Verdanna laughed nervously, but her false humor quickly drained away. She became solemn.

"Good luck, Mister Lowallyn."

He stared levelly at her. "You don't believe me."

"I always believe my customers," she said uneasily. She tried a lighter tone. "Besides, we need a new ruler. The coliseum's turned crazy. I thought the First was bad, but Kuberr's ten times worse."

"Oh, I know. He's my brother."

She blinked in shock and grew very pale. "I'm not sure whether you're teasing me."

"I wish I were."

Verdanna hastily put the final strokes on her portrait. "Well, Mr. Lowallyn—" she set aside the scraps of chalk and removed the pins from the sheets of paper—"here's your portrait." She turned the sheet around.

Lowallyn gasped, and Kamahl was startled as well. She had rendered the numen in caricature, perfectly capturing his best and worst traits. His head was overlarge and bony, with regal lines beneath flesh that was scarred and leathery. His eyes were exaggerated pits, but somehow she had cast a childish twinkle on their surface. She had portrayed his mouth open, as if in oration, and his single hand was poised before him in a grand gesture. Around his fingers circled worlds and stars. His body was strong but drawn, with limbs like driftwood. One foot kicked the backside of a king, propelling him off the small ball of Dominaria.

Verdanna nervously studied his face. "I—I hope I got it right. . . ."

"Perfect," Lowallyn said. "Except that instead of a king, I should be kicking an angel. Still, I'm thrilled. Now it's my turn to draw you." Rolling the portrait, he stood up and gestured her into his spot.

Uncertain, Verdanna got up and shifted to the squeaky stool. Lowallyn slid past her and took her seat. He settled in that shabby spot, his fingers walking among the chalk nubs. He glanced toward Verdanna seeing her small figure before a watchful Kamahl.

"Tell me about yourself, Verdanna. What is an artist of your caliber doing drawing caricatures?"

A regretful smile crossed her face, and Lowallyn waited, evidently unwilling to capture that look.

"I was an artist in the courts of the Northern Order. I did frescos mostly, but also sculptures and altar paintings. Then came the Mirari, and there was nothing to draw except people going crazy and killing each other. I did draw them. . . ." She dropped her chin and went silent.

"I can't draw you if I can't see your face," Lowallyn said.

Taking a calming breath, Verdanna lifted her eyes. "Well, the Northern Order fell, and many people died. I was one of the fortunate ones. I wandered for a few years, looking for more commissions and doing odd jobs. I got my big chance when High Priest Aioue hired me to do the ceiling of the new Chapel of Ixidor in Topos, but when I showed up at the palace, the High Priest was gone, and Akroma, and everybody else."

"You were supposed to do a likeness of Ixidor?"

"Yes. Hundreds of them. Ixidors everywhere, but I didn't do a single one." She paused, staring at Lowallyn's vacant shoulder. "Well, I figured my trouble was worth something, and I took some easels and paints and pastels when I left. I came here, like everybody who's down and out. I've run through all my supplies, all my food and nerve." She shook her head. "People want pictures of gladiators killing each other, and I hate to draw them."

Lowallyn leaned back, examining the image he had made. Kamahl moved behind him where he could see it as well. It was a flawless rendering of this woman, accentuating her intelligence and beauty, her focus and good soul. The artist had de-emphasized her nervous worry and the hard lines around her eyes. Instead of a threadbare vest and skirt, she wore a fine suit of silk. Instead of a rickety stool, she sat on a grand throne. To one side were piled hundreds of rolled canvases, and to the other side jar upon jar of the finest pigments. Brushes in every shape and size jutted from a wide-mouthed container, and large slabs of clay were wrapped tightly in waxed paper. Between her feet sat a fat drawstring bag, its wide mouth open to reveal a gleaming mound of gold coins.

"Well?" prompted Verdanna. "Are you finished?"

Lowallyn nodded. He stared intently at the image, as if memorizing every detail and willing it into reality. Then, solemnly, he removed the pins from the corners of the paper and turned it around for her to see.

Verdanna's jaw dropped. The paper was blank. "What?"

Only then did she notice the silken touch of her clothes, the art supplies, and the bag of gold. She held her arms up, gaping at the rich fabric. One foot kicked the bag, and it jingled, spilling gold. Her eyes fluttered like wounded birds, and she fell backward, half swooning. If it had been a mere stool beneath her, she would have sprawled on the ground, but a cushioned throne caught her limp and trembling body.

In a delirious voice, she asked, "What's happening?"

Lowallyn shrugged. "I hope I got it right."

Verdanna panted. "How did you . . . ? What did you . . . ?"

"First hire a bodyguard; then buy a mule to carry your things. Sell the throne and anything you don't want, and leave this place," Lowallyn said. "I wish only one canvas, one brush, a set of paints, and a batch of clay."

"But, how . . . ?"

"I told you. I'm Lowallyn, lord of hidden waters, numen of old—no, don't bow to me."

She knelt, straddling the bag of gold. "But why?"

Lowallyn smiled sadly. "A dear friend of mine was an artist, and he and his girlfriend were stuck in the pits. They couldn't make enough money to leave, and staying killed her. It killed them both, really." He pursed his lips, considering. "This is just the repayment of an old debt."

She wept into her smile. "Thank you, Lowallyn. Thank you. I'm going away from here. Perhaps I'll even cross the sea. They're rebuilding Benalia City. Lots of new walls. Lots of frescoes." She shook her head in amazement. "You've saved me."

"An old debt," Lowallyn said simply. He stood and stepped past her. Bending, he lifted a single rolled canvas, a brush, and a few pots of paint. He ended up with a woman in his arm and a kiss on his cheek.

"Thank you, Lowallyn!"

"It's quite all right. When you get to Benalia City, you tell them that you have indeed done a portrait of Ixidor." He held up the caricature of the man with worlds at his hand and Dominaria at his feet. Instead of a king receiving Lowallyn's boot, though, there was an angel.

Verdanna stared at the image, her face flushed with embarrassment. She turned toward him to apologize, but Lowallyn was no longer there.

* * * * *

Kamahl and Lowallyn walked down a corridor beneath the coliseum. They approached Kuberr's luxury box.

Obsidian doors stood there, fronted by a squat and pallid guard, as if a mushroom had put on a black suit. Behind the glass waited two more thugs. Nothing would get past them.

Kamahl stopped before the guard. "We've come to see Kuberr."

"No appointment, no audience."

"I'm Kamahl, slayer of Chainer, champion of Krosan, his father's ally—"

"We know," the guard said. "We've known for a week you was coming, but who's this?"

Lowallyn stepped forward. "I'm Kuberr's brother, Lowallyn."

"He don't have a brother. He's an only child. Even his ma's dead."

"You're wrong," Lowallyn said easily. "His mother is Karona. You tell him that. Another son of Karona is here."

"It ain't my job to tell him nothing."

Kamahl growled, "How's he supposed to know we're here?"

"Kuberr knows all. Hears all. Kuberr's here. Kuberr's everywhere." The guard raised a pudgy hand and waved his fingers. "See ya later."

Kamahl stared in astonishment, but Lowallyn wore a knowing smile. "Yes, you will." He crooked a finger at Kamahl and said, "Let's go."

The lord of hidden waters led the fighter away from the luxury box. The two men headed back down the corridor.

Whispering, Lowallyn said, "He's the real Kuberr all right—wrapped up in his blood-sport empire. I'll get his attention."

They ascended a set of stairs to the stands and emerged into sunlight and a loud roar. Just below them, Kuberr's luxury box looked out on the coliseum sands, where a large melee took place.

A platoon of avens battled a mob of dementia creatures. Already, three of the bird folk lay dying, their feathers and blood dotting the sand. One dementia creature had fallen too, a great round thing with scaly flesh and red spikes at elbows and knees. Swords flashed, and a second monster went down. Its tentacles crawled away from the thing's porcine body. The crowd shrieked its approval.

Lowallyn led Kamahl to a landing nearby. There, the numen set down his pack. With his hand, he brushed clean a section of the stone floor and unrolled his canvas on it. He set out his paint pots and pulled out his brush. Rubbing another spot clear, Lowallyn began loading globs of paint on it, mixing them.

"It'll be a crude rendering, but enough to stop the match in its tracks and bring my brother out."

Kamahl shook his head but said nothing.

Lowallyn painted. A blue blur became the sky. Tan-colored pigment made concentric ovals below. With a few quick strokes, he had evoked the great coliseum. Mottled colors in black and gray created spectators, though Lowallyn was not focused on them. He rapidly laid in the sand, and the figures that even now battled on it. Those impressionistic strokes somehow seemed more real than real.

"Here is the way things stand," Lowallyn said. " But now . . ."

Mixing up a glob of pink, Lowallyn painted a huge circle like a great balloon. He added four round legs and a bewhiskered head worthy of a stuffed animal. Lowallyn leaned over, staring into the image. He closed his eyes and leaned back again. letting out a long breath.

"There it is."

Suddenly, it was. A pink creature sat in the center of the coliseum, its head rising halfway to the top. Its stupid face stared in confusion at the tiny figures that fought between its legs. It rolled forward, seeming almost weightless until its forelegs pounded the sand and shook the stadium. Avens and dementia horrors alike fled from the monster.

The crowd went from roaring to laughing.

Lowallyn smiled. "Kuberr has no sense of humor. It'll be just a matter of time."

The enormous beast lumbered forward on plump legs. It opened its toothless mouth and let out a sound halfway between a lamb's bleat and a frog's croak. The monster waddled after its prey, and laughter bore it forward.

The door to a certain luxury box swung open, smashing the face of the guard who stood there. He slumped as if bowing at the feet of the young man who stepped out. Kuberr wore a long black cape over a finely cut suit—a thirteen year old in a vampire costume. He stared imperiously at the spectacle and scanned the crowd. His eyes locked on Lowallyn and the barbarian. Kuberr marched up the stairs.

"You've made him mad," Kamahl whispered.

Lowallyn shrugged. "He's my little brother. I'll just hold my hand on his forehead while he takes his swings."

Snorting like a bull, Kuberr approached the two men. Behind him marched Cabal thugs, including the mushroomlike guard. All looked gravely serious, their hands on weapons in their cloaks.

Kuberr stalked up within swinging distance of Lowallyn and demanded, "What do you think you're doing?"

Lowallyn gave a winning smile. "Just a little painting."

"How dare you come to my realm and foul things up?"

"Interesting," said Lowallyn, stroking his chin. "I seem to remember something called the Nightmare Wars when you did the same to me."

"Well, that's what you've got here, now," Kuberr said. "A war."

"We all have a war on our hands. In case you haven't noticed, Mother's back."

"Of course I've noticed, but she hasn't come here. Until she does, she's not my problem."

Lowallyn clucked. "We're going to have to take care of her this time just like last time. We have to do it before she has full power. Come with me to Averru."

"No. I don't have to do a damned thing you say!"

"Ahem," Kamahl interrupted, gesturing beyond the giant pink monster. A brilliant light shone in the sky above it. "Whether or not you two are ready to face her, Karona's here."

CHAPTER 19

EPIPHANIES

I SOAR, DRAWN BY THE SMELL OF KIN. OVER THE CORIAN ESCARP-
MENT AND ABOVE THE FETID SWAMP, I HAVE FOLLOWED THIS SCENT
TRAIL. IT WILL LEAD ME TO CREATURES LIKE ME, TWO OF THEM: IXIDOR
AND ANOTHER. . . .

KUBERR.

HIS NAME OPENS A DOOR OF MEMORY, AND AMAZING THINGS
POUR OUT. KUBERR IS ONE OF THE NUMENA OF OLD. HE IMPRISONED
THE PRIMEVAL DRAGONS AND STOLE THEIR MAGIC. WITH IT, HE RULED
THE WORLD FOR A MILLENNIUM—AGES OF AGES AGO. NOW KUBERR
HAS RETURNED, AND HE WAITS WITHIN THE GREAT STONE COLISEUM.

I FLY TOWARD IT, A PROPHET CLUTCHED UNDER EITHER ARM.
BENEATH US, CYPRESSES SWAY, AND SWAMPS GLEAM WITH BEASTS.
ACROSS SUSPENSION BRIDGES RUN SENTIENT CREATURES. THEY CRY TO
ME, BUT I AM NOT INTERESTED IN MORTALS.

I SEEK NUMENA, KUBERR AND IXIDOR—BUT NO, HIS TRUE NAME
IS LOWALLYN.

THE NAME OPENS ANOTHER ROOM OF RECOLLECTION. LOWALLYN
WAS A SECOND NUMEN, THE LORD OF WATERS. HE AND HIS BROTHER
JOINED TO BRING INTO BEING SOMEONE GREATER THAN THEM BOTH.
THEY WORKED A MIGHTY SPELL THAT SUMMONED MAGIC AND GAVE
HER A BODY. THEY INCARNATED ME.

I FEEL SUDDENLY FAINT. THESE ARE NOT SIMPLY KIN. THESE ARE MY CREATORS. THEY INCARNATED ME . . . TWICE.

MY HEART LABORS UNDER THE WEIGHT OF THAT REALIZATION. I SLOW MY FLIGHT, TREMBLING. ALL THIS HAS HAPPENED BEFORE.

* * * * *

"What's wrong?" asked Waistcoat from under one of Karona's arms. NOTHING.

From under the other, Sash said, "Let's not go on to the coliseum. It's a brutal place—not fitting for such as you."

MY KIN ARE THERE. I LIVED WITH THEM ONCE, AND I'LL LIVE WITH THEM AGAIN.

"I don't like this place. Once the First shoved me full of ogres," Waistcoat said.

THE FIRST IS GONE. Karona stared past wide skies to the coliseum walls. KUBERR IS HIS SON. THE GAMES ARE HIS NOW. I'M GOING TO DWELL WITH HIM.

"You're going to live with that little monster?" Sash asked.

"He's your kin?"

HE IS MY CREATOR.

She flew faster. Ragged rafts of leaf rushed away beneath their feet. The swarms in the water and on the bridge could not keep pace. Karona's radiance deepened as she approached the coliseum. After long months of mobs and riots, of tribal wars and genocides, this was her first chance not to be alone.

Karona soared above the tents and stalls of the marketplace. Between folds of fabric, faces looked up in amazement, wonder, and love. Hands rose toward the one who flew overhead. She did not linger but flew up over the battlements of the coliseum.

"Whoa!" Waistcoat said.

Below them, the stone oval opened like an enormous mouth. Its seats were filled to capacity—row upon row of teeth poised to bite.

On the sands lolled an enormous pink creature, and as Karona flew out above it, a roar shook the heavens.

A hundred thousand souls beheld her and welcomed her. It was as if she were returning home. In waves that spread beneath her, the crowd stood, cried in wonder, and fell to its knees. Whatever battle had been taking place on the sands ceased. Even the great pink beast dropped to its belly and bowed its absurd head.

Karona flew above them, heading straight for the far side of the coliseum.

"Please," begged Waistcoat, "don't take us to Kuberr!"

Sash said, "Put us down somewhere."

Karona swooped toward the stands. Folk rose from their prostration and reached for her, their eyes glowing with green light.

"Not there!" Waistcoat cried.

"How about that pillar?" Sash pointed toward a stone column that rose in the center of the coliseum, thick cables radiating from its peak. Atop the massive column rested a huge capital, and around it ran an iron rail. "Please, Karona! For the love of life, put us up there!"

She flew out of the grasping hands of the mob and skated across the sky. The stands boiled as Karona floated over the column's rail and set the two men down.

"Be careful, Karona," Sash warned. "This creator of yours—he's a bad seed."

WHY WOULD HE CREATE ME ONLY TO HARM ME?

The prophets had no answer.

She turned, diving from the column and soaring out across the coliseum. Sash and Waistcoat stood and watched their Glorious Lady drift away, growing smaller against the sea of faces.

Ahead of her, people stared with hopeful eyes, their backs bent low. Behind her, riots began. The stands farthest back had cleared, as everyone scrambled over each other to reach the coliseum floor. Folk caught beneath this tide began to fight back. Accidental deaths led to intentional ones. Blood ran, and shouts of joy turned to screams of despair.

"Could it be true," Sash wondered aloud, "that she was created by the Cabal?"

Waistcoat pursed his lips. "She sure does their business."

Sash shook his head, the color running from his face. He steadied himself on the metal rail and realized just how high they were. His knees buckled, and he knelt. Waistcoat also knelt, and the two men clung desperately to the rail.

Sash said, "If it's true—if Kuberr created her—she truly is home now. She'll live here and fly from here to destroy whatever the Cabal wants her to destroy."

"That'd be just about everything," said Waistcoat.

"You and I will be back working for the Cabal," Sash said miserably.

Waistcoat's nostrils flared as if he smelled a stench. "Damn."

That eloquent word summed it up. Sash could think of no other explanation for their predicament. Why else would Karona destroy any city she approached, whip up war among any people she encountered? She was the Cabal's ultimate weapon, irresistible and inescapable. She was a bomb that people begged to be killed by.

"Look," Waistcoat said. "She's even destroying the coliseum."

Sash blinked tears from his eyes.

Karona's radiant nimbus enveloped the stands, and they began to shudder. Benches of solid stone bounced and cracked. The magic lanterns blazed with sudden light and popped. They spewed sparks and smoke.

"Not only do the people praise her, but the very stones worship her," Sash said.

The crowd made no attempt to flee. They were too busy with their reverence. Manifold cracks opened in the stone beneath them. Huge chunks fell, and people too. A large slab of seats dropped in atop the corridors underneath.

"They're not even trying to get out," Sash said.

"Look at that dumb thing." Waistcoat pointed at the huge pink monster.

It lulled ponderously on its stubby legs. Its toothless mouth gabbled after Karona as she passed overhead. It nipped again.

A cry of outrage came from the stands. Spectators dropped onto the coliseum floor and swarmed the pink monster. They tore away hunks of it, and the beast roared and thrashed. It killed dozens with each strike of its limbs, but hundreds more came.

"They're defending her," Waistcoat said.

"No," replied Sash. "They're killing it out of jealousy."

The pink monster bulled into the arena wall, shattering stone. Chunks dropped in a landslide before it. The monster rammed the spot again, intent on escape. The thing's flesh was freckled with assailants, and hunk by hunk, they flayed the monster. It pounded the wall, and its head slipped through the broken stones. With freedom in sight, it could go no farther. Its head was lodged as if in stocks. The monster could only crouch there while others tormented it to death.

"I hate this," Waistcoat said. "If this is what she's meant to do— make everybody go crazy and kill each other—I quit."

"Me, too."

The pink monster ignited. In moments, all the people that clung to it were fried to black corpses, and fire spread to anything that would burn.

Waistcoat shook his head. "I hope Kuberr didn't make her."

"Me, too."

* * * * *

Amid a rioting throng, a man crawled toward freedom. The stones under his fingers moaned, each block resonating with a different pitch. They began to shake. The mortar between them cracked, and dust jetted into his eyes.

"Help! I can't see!"

Someone fell across his back, and then someone else. The man collapsed to his face, pinned under a mound of flesh.

"Get up! You're killing me."

None of them did. In moments, none could. The south wall of the coliseum fell on them all.

* * * * *

A child stood at the height of the stands and screamed, "Mother!"

She charged through the brawl that separated them, using her elbows like machetes to clear the way. One man whirled on her and smashed her in the jaw. She staggered to her knees.

"Mother!"

"I'm coming!" she screamed, clawing toward her child.

The stands gave way beneath her. Rioters, stones, mother, and son all dropped in a giddy rush. They hung for a moment together and struck ground as one.

The rocks were like molars, grinding them to pulp.

* * * * *

Another section collapsed, though it was full of avens. They plunged down, their wings pounding the air. Some could not escape the sucking pit and fell to their deaths. Others labored up from the darkness.

Their eyes broke through the dust cloud and glimpsed the sun above, but then terrible things rose beneath them. This section had rested above the dementia pits, and the collapsed ceiling had freed a legion of monsters. They bit and clawed, dragging every last birdman down.

* * * * *

Pale and black-haired, young Kuberr stood beside Lowallyn and Kamahl. All three stared, aghast.

The whole coliseum was falling to pieces. The monster did some of it, but Karona did most. She sucked mana from the stones, making them dead and brittle. Her power shook the grains until they separated and tumbled. The greatest structure ever built by mortal hands was crumbling like a sand castle. The people in the stands fell amid the stones and were crushed to red mortar.

"Mother . . ." Kuberr whispered, disbelieving.

In the midst of the apocalypse hung Karona—Mother Magic— beautiful and terrible. Her arms were spread as she approached her sons. In less than a minute, she would arrive, and the numena would fall to worship. Once she had power over them, no one could stop her.

Someone shook Kuberr's shoulder. He wheeled angrily. It was that water-brained Lowallyn and his blow-hard friend, Kamahl. They were saying something—

". . . Out of here! There has to be!"

"What?" asked Kuberr.

"There has to be some way out of here!" Kamahl roared. "When your father built this, he had to have planned an emergency escape!"

"Of course! I got a million of them!"

Kamahl's eyes swelled. "Let's *use* one!"

Kuberr managed a nod and bolted back down the stairs. His Cabal guard eagerly went with him, and Kamahl and Lowallyn ran behind.

Kuberr rushed through the open door of his luxury suite. The black-marble walls had cracked, and the fissures were widening. His father's statuary lay in pieces on the floor. The chunks shook and danced with each jolt. The whole place would crack open when Karona landed.

Kuberr ran down a narrow hallway to a tapestry. He pulled it aside, felt along the wall for the door trigger, and engaged it. A stone panel swung inward, revealing a spiral stair. Kuberr turned to his guards and said, "Wait here. Defend the escape." A profound boom sounded, and Kuberr flicked his eyes toward the ceiling. He laughed at the panic on the guards' faces.

Turning, Kuberr descended the spiral. The walls trembled and cracked. Down a secret hall, Kuberr reached a plain, cubic room with a reed mat on the floor and stony walls. He tromped to the center of the room and faced the one wall made of metal.

Holding his hands out, he said, "In the name of me, open!"

Kamahl and Lowallyn staggered in just as a golden line appeared in the center of the metal wall. Two steel doors separated and swung inward. They were like floodgates, releasing a tide of gold coins. The slippery metal roared as it poured into the room, flooding to their knees.

Kamahl said, "What good is gold at a time like this?"

"Plenty good," Kuberr snapped. "Gold is mine. This gold and all gold. It listens to me." He lifted his hands. "We can swim through it to safety. Just stay close, or you'll get stuck and crushed alive."

"What are you talking about?"

"Explain it, Brother," Kuberr said. He dived.

The coins greeted him like water, splashing and glad. Kuberr plunged through the trove and dragged great armfuls of gold down to his side. He held his breath as he swam. Though the coins obeyed his every whim, he couldn't breathe the stuff. He stroked again and wondered how long it would take Lowallyn to explain that the doors were portals to Kuberr's infinite trove—a pocket plane full of gold. All they had to do was swim into the plane and back out another portal. It was simple, but it might take Lowallyn awhile to explain, and it would be too late. Kuberr *had* asked them to stay close.

Two crashes came behind. They must have dived and would be stroking now—if they were inside Kuberr's radius of control. With a nod of his head, Kuberr willed the trove to gather itself again into the doors. He could hear the rush of metal as coins poured back in, and a profound boom followed. The vault had slammed shut. Then even the doors disappeared, for Kuberr would never again need that portal.

He wondered if his poor brother and the barbarian were within or without.

A hand tugged at Kuberr's heel. Lowallyn was a great swimmer. Kuberr tried to kick it loose, but Lowallyn's grip was strong. No doubt Kamahl hung onto him as well. These two were going to be no fun.

Kuberr stroked for the nearest sluice gate. His hangers-on came along like lampreys on a shark. The coins here were packed tightly, reluctant to make way. Kuberr could sense a pair of doors ahead and willed it open. The coin stack shifted, and Kuberr washed out in a huge flood of gold. On that deafening tide rode Lowallyn and a gasping Kamahl as well.

They gushed through a pair of doors that opened behind an opulent throne. No one sat on that gilded chair—of course not, since it was Kuberr's own, in his estate in Aphetto. He slid to a halt beside a nude statue. Lowallyn and Kamahl fetched up sloppily on either side of the throne.

"Get back," Kuberr commanded the gold. It did, coins tumbling over each other to roar back through the open doors. The vault slammed shut.

Kamahl twisted a finger in his ringing ear. "Where in the Nine Hells are we?"

"Aphetto," Kuberr said quietly. "Don't you recognize it? Oh, yeah. You've never seen the good side of it. You know just the pits and the hospital ward. Lucky you don't know the morgue."

Lowallyn stood and held out his hand. "Enough, Brother. We've no time to waste. If this is Aphetto, we're farther from Averru City than Mother is. We must hurry."

The young lord of greed shook his head. "Why?"

"You saw what she did to the coliseum."

"I'll build another one."

"She'll come here," Kamahl said.

"It's a big multiverse. I'll find some other place."

"In the meantime, she'll find your gold, and it'll be yours no longer."

Kuberr went very pale.

"The only way for your wealth to be safe is if Karona is gone. The only way for her to be gone is for us to join with Averru to defeat her," Lowallyn said.

Kuberr scowled. "That's what you said last time. We got killed, and it took us twenty thousand years to come back. I've been back, what—a year? I've just hit puberty, man, and there's a couple hundred million women on Dominaria—"

"Oh, grow up!" Lowallyn spat. "It's always this way with you. More. More. More. Greed and debasement—everything low and debauched and grotesque."

"Yeah?" Kuberr shoved his brother, delighting in the fact that the older man had only one arm to defend with. "Yeah? Yeah? Easy for you to say, prissy little painter, frolicking in your smock!"

"I don't frolic!" growled Lowallyn.

"You and your unmen friends—you don't know what it's like to burn for a woman."

"You truculent imbecile! You don't know the difference between a woman and a hole in the ground!"

"A woman *is* a hole in the ground."

The two men lunged at each other, their fingers like claws. They never came together, though, a wall of muscle rising between them.

"Enough!" Kamahl growled, grasping them. "Enough! I can't believe you'd let a little sibling spat destroy the world!" Kamahl's breath caught, and he went on in subdued tones. "No. I *can* believe it. Jeska and I did the same. We started a war—dragged the whole continent into it. I wish I could take it back, take back all of it." He stared levelly at the two men. "I can't, but you can. You can take it back and save the world." He glared significantly at each man. "Do it."

Kuberr stared at the barbarian, who still clutched his shoulder in a viselike grip. "He's the guide, isn't he?"

Lowallyn only nodded grimly, clenched in the man's other hand.

"Well," Kuberr snorted. "What's the use? If the guide's here, we've got to go."

"Come on, Brother. It's off to the City of Averru," Lowallyn said. With a sly smile, he added, "Besides, doesn't Averru owe you ten gold?"

Kuberr's reluctance transformed into indignation. "Yeah, that's right. Bastard owes me ten gold! At twenty percent interest, compounded hourly, over twenty thousand years. . . ." Only half mockingly, he blurted, "Averru owes me his whole city!"

Releasing the two men, Kamahl shook his head. "Averru *is* the city."

"Ha! He owes me *himself*," Kuberr cried exultantly. "He'll be my slave!"

Lowallyn laughed. "You'll have to take that up with him when you get there."

"Yeah, I will."

CHAPTER 20

COMING OF AGE

I DESCEND OUT OF THE SKY, AND THE COLISEUM DEVOLVES. HALF THE PEOPLE RIOT TO REACH ME. THE OTHER HALF WORSHIP AS ROCK CRUMBLES TO SAND. WITH FINAL CRIES, THEY PLUNGE INTO THE FOUNDATIONS AND ARE BURIED ALIVE.

I DON'T INTENDED ANY OF THIS. I HAVE GROWN GREATLY IN POWER SINCE EROSHIA. NOW EVEN STONES FAINT BEFORE ME.

BUT NOT NUMENA. THEIR SCENT GROWS STRONGER AS I APPROACH THE SIDE OF THE COLISEUM. I SPOT THEM.

LOWALLYN'S WATERY CLOAK WAVES LIKE A FLAG AS HE RUSHES DOWN A SET OF STAIRS. IN FRONT OF HIM LOPES THE LONG-HAIRED DRUID, KAMAHL, AND AT THE HEAD OF THE GROUP, A MERE BOY: KUBERR. THEY ARE MY KIN, AND THEY SEEM TO BE RUNNING TO GREET ME.

I OPEN MY ARMS.

THEY DUCK AWAY INTO A PRIVATE BOX. THE DOOR BEHIND THEM SWINGS CLOSED.

I LIGHT ON THE ROOF OF THE BOX. POWER RADIATES FROM MY FEET, EATING THE STONE. I FLING MY HANDS DOWN, AND LIGHTNING ROLLS FROM MY FINGERS. IT JABS INTO CRACKS AND EXPLODES THEM. CHUNKS OF STONE LEAP UP, TUMBLE, AND ARE PULVERIZED.

A THICK CLOUD OF SAND RUSHES INTO THE ROOMS BELOW, BURYING EVERYTHING IN A FOOT OF DUST. CHAIRS AND TABLES ARE

MIRED IN THE STUFF, PAINTINGS INDISTINGUISHABLE ON THE WALLS. STILL, THERE IS NO SIGN OF LOWALLYN OR KUBERR OR EVEN THE SHAGGY KAMAHL.

TWO GUARDS STRUGGLE UP FROM THE DUST. I WILL QUESTION THEM.

* * * * *

Joaj and Knuckles coughed gustily, and dirt made gray smudges under their noses. They looked up to see that radiant woman sweep down on them. Gladly, they buried their faces in the suffocating dust.

"We praise you, Gracious Lady," Joaj said.

"WHERE HAVE THEY GONE?"

Knuckles asked, "Who, milady?"

"KUBERR AND LOWALLYN."

"On pain of death, we cannot tell," Joaj replied, his meaty fingers grasping and releasing the silt.

"TELL ME."

"We cannot, Great Lady—" Joaj's breath failed as a knife plunged through his lungs. The poisoned dagger did its work in moments.

Knuckles used the blade like a piton and dragged himself up on the dead man. "Forgive my partner's stupidity. Kuberr went that way, beyond the tapestry, where a secret stair descends. He goes to his treasure vault. I'll show the way." Drawing the knife, Knuckles scuttled like a black crab to the tapestry. He yanked on it until the end pulled free, revealing a dark stair. He descended into darkness. "Come on. No time to waste."

Karona ducked beneath the tapestry and strode down the stairs. All around them, walls crackled as stone disintegrated. She would bring the whole building down.

The stairs ended in a dark hallway, and Knuckles ran down it to a door. He yanked on it but couldn't drag it open.

"STEP ASIDE."

Knuckles dropped to his face.

Karona reached the steel door, set her hands on it, and ignited the metal. It sloughed like hot wax, pouring onto the floor. She stepped over it and into a room with plain black walls and a reed mat on the floor. The mat greened under her feet, and then began to grow. Overhead, the ceiling shuddered and cracked.

"WHERE ARE THEY?"

Knuckles moaned. "They're gone?" He scrambled up, forgetting to jump over the molten puddle and stepping right in it. With a shriek, he fell on the floor of the room, his foot mantled in hardening steel. He kicked and thrashed, flesh baking inside its metal shell.

"WHERE HAVE THEY GONE?"

"Try . . . the . . . vault. . . ." Knuckles managed to gag out. "There." He gestured toward a stony wall. It showed no seams. "It *was* . . . there."

Karona only stood, glancing about as hunks of stone dropped around her. One piece struck her head, but it bounded away. "COME NEAR ME. MY AURA WILL PROTECT YOU."

Knuckles did not. His own poisoned knife jutted from his heart. He lay dead, unable to bear that he had failed Karona.

* * * * *

I CANNOT ENDURE THESE FRAGILE MORTALS. THEY CAN ONLY WOR-SHIP AND MURDER. GRIT SHOWERS ME, AND ROCKS HAIL DOWN, BUT I DON'T CARE. I SIT ON THE FLOWERING MAT AND LET THE COLISEUM COME TO PIECES.

THE WORLD IS TOO WEAK. ITS PEOPLE ARE TOO STUPID, TOO VICIOUS. EVEN MY OWN KIN DESPISE AND REJECT ME. THEY BROUGHT ME INTO BEING BY ACCIDENT AND HATE ME NOW, AND WHY NOT? I WILL BE THE DEATH OF THEM.

THEY ARE PLANNING THE DEATH OF ME, JUST AS THEY DID BEFORE:

THEY CALLED ME, AND I CAME, THESE LOVELY BOYS—ALL *THREE*. LOWALLYN AND KUBERR AND . . . AVERRU, MY CHAMPIONS AND SONS. THEY BROUGHT ME TO THE WORLD AND CALLED ME TO THEMSELVES. WHAT BLESSED RELIEF IT HAD BEEN TO FIND OTHERS SUCH AS I IN THIS STRANGE, WILD DOMINARIA.

THEY STOOD AT THE HEIGHT OF A GREAT CITY, ITS RED TOWERS CURVING LIKE ROSE PETALS TOWARD THE SUN. THE CITY WAS BRIGHT AND FRAGRANT. AT ITS CENTER WAS A GREAT PLAZA AND A DOMED TEMPLE. MY CHILDREN HELD THEIR ARMS WIDE AND STREAMED MAGIC INTO ME. THEY COULD GIVE NO GREATER GIFT. THE SPELLS ENLIVENED ME. SUCH A WELCOME!

THEN I SENSED IT—THE DARKNESS IN THESE SORCERIES. THEY WERE NOT SIMPLY POURING MAGIC INTO ME BUT SUBTLY CHANGING ME. THEY USED MY OWN POWER AGAINST ME. THIS WAS HOW THEY IMPRISONED THE PRIMEVALS OF OLD AND HOW THEY IMPRISONED ME.

I TRIED TO SOAR AWAY, BUT ALREADY THEIR SPELLS HAD THEIR HOOKS IN ME. I COULD NOT ESCAPE, BUT ONE HOPE REMAINED. TURNING MY BROW ON THEM, I DIVED. I WAS DONE WITH MYSELF AND THEM IN A SINGLE MOMENT.

NOW I SIT IN AN ASH FIELD WHERE ONCE THERE HAD BEEN A COLISEUM. MY SONS HAVE SLIPPED AWAY FROM ME, BUT I KNOW WHAT THEY PLAN, AND I WILL BE READY.

* * * * *

Waistcoat and Sash might have been the only two creatures who remained alive in the ruined coliseum. The parts of the structure that still stood were littered with bodies, and the parts that had dissolved were mass graves. Some few thousand survivors even now fled across the rope bridges like rats across mooring lines. Coliseum Island was becoming again what it once had been—a desolate mound in the midst of an endless swamp.

"At least the pillar didn't fall," Waistcoat said.

Sash shook his head, peering down at the frightful drop on all sides. "We've got no way down."

"Well, there's one way. A real quick way."

Sash knelt beside the rail and reached down to touch a metal loop jutting from it. A fat cable descended from the loop. Once the cable had run to the outer coliseum, but now it hung straight down to the sands. "We could try rappelling."

"Repelling?" Waistcoat asked, sniffing under his arms.

"Going down this cable."

"Why not wait for Karona?" Waistcoat asked.

Sash sat back on his heels and held his arms out. "Look around you, moron. She's destroyed the place. She's killed thousands."

"So, what're you saying? We slide down the rope and hike out of here and it's just, so long, good luck, Karona?"

Sash stared blankly at the ruination below. "I don't know."

Waistcoat pursed his lips and nodded sadly. "Well, we got about half a minute to figure this out. Here she comes."

Out of a deep hole in the settling sand, the beautiful woman ascended. Even at this distance, Karona was stunning. Her brilliance lit the underbelly of the clouds and cast lovely shadows across the coliseum's wreckage. In that light, anyone could believe anything. Karona drifted up the skies straight toward her prophets. Her eyes were sad, and her jaw set. Something had changed forever.

Waistcoat held his hand out to her. "What's wrong? What happened?"

Karona reached the height of the column, her feet drifting above the rail. *I CANNOT LIVE WITH MORTALS.*

Sash nodded shallowly and shot a sidelong glance toward Waistcoat.

The fat prophet laughed. "Come on, that's not true. Me and Sash're mortals."

IF IT WEREN'T FOR YOU, I'D BE ALONE IN THE WORLD.

Waistcoat smiled reassuringly. "Me and Sash were saying just the same. Let's fly off someplace where nobody is. Maybe an island, with lots of sand and sea and palms. Someplace beautiful. . . ."

Karona's feet turned the top of the column to sand. *THE NUMENA WOULD ONLY TRACK US DOWN. THEY WANT TO ENSLAVE OR KILL ME. THEY WANT MY POWER.*

"Who are the numena?"

THE THREE TYRANTS OF OLD. The column began to pour a sandy cascade down its edges. *ONE OF THEM IS YOUR CREATOR, IXIDOR.*

Sash was suddenly sitting, the breath pounded from his lungs. "Ixidor? We're shadows of the world's oldest tyrant?"

Karona merely nodded.

Waistcoat clucked. "No wonder I got such a bad self-image."

WE WON'T BE SAFE UNTIL THEY'RE GONE.

Waistcoat struggled to stay on top of the shifting sand. "Well, Ixidor's got a groin, and I got a knee. I figure I could take him. As to Sash, he was feeling repellant before you came—"

"So, if we get rid of the numena, then we can go seek our perfect place?"

YES.

He shrugged. "I guess I'm in, too."

Karona held her arms out to them. Her prophets stepped into the embrace. She wrapped them tightly and soared from the pinnacle even as it crumbled. Much of the dust and debris went airborne, and the rest scoured the tower all the way to its base.

"So, where are we headed?" Waistcoat asked.

AVERRU.

"What's in Averru?"

MY THIRD SON. HE'S CALLED THE OTHER CREATORS. WE'LL FIND THEM THERE, AND WE'LL KILL THEM.

CHAPTER 21

THE PERFECT REFLECTION

W̲e have to assume she knows everything," Lowallyn said grimly. He set his hand on the windowsill of Kuberr's palace in Aphetto. Beyond the glass, the gray city huddled on the wet slopes of the canyon. "She remembers what happened last time. We have to get to Averru. We have no time for this . . . extravagance."

Kuberr laughed, his feet propped on the feast table. He held the rib of some beast in his hand and gnawed on it, the sauce making a red stain around his mouth.

"Every condemned man gets a last meal—right, Kamahl?" He grinned, meat dangling between his teeth.

Kamahl looked up like a guilty dog from the cheese and bread he was eating. "What? I'm hungry. We need to eat—"

"Can't kill a goddess on an empty stomach," Kuberr quipped, taking another bite.

Lowallyn shook his head and turned from the window. "Whatever we know, she knows. Whatever we can do, she can do. She might be there already."

"Fine, fine, whatever!" Kuberr waggled sticky fingers beside his ear. "Since you're not going to eat, *you* do the spell."

It was what Lowallyn was waiting to hear. He turned to a wet sink nearby, draped a towel over his arm, lifted the pitcher into the basin, and carried the basin to the table. He shoved aside a platter with a roast pheasant, positioning the basin before Kuberr. "Clean up, both of you. Do you want Averru to see you like that?"

Kamahl and Kuberr reached their hands over the basin. The lord of hidden waters lifted the pitcher and poured.

Water gushed forth, bright and vital. It splashed from hand to hand and into the basin, cleansing as it went. A minnow plunged with the water, slipping past both sets of fingers and into the sink, where it swam in circles.

"I've diverted the flow of the Deepwash," explained Lowallyn, "to pass through this pitcher. Water carries all things, and this water will carry us to Averru."

"Blah blah blah," Kuberr sneered. "Just tell us what to do."

Lowallyn's jaw flexed in irritation. "Normally, I'd invite the traveler to step into the sink, but in this case—"

Lowallyn tossed the pitcher of water into Kuberr's face and brought his knee down on the edge of the basin, hurling its contents on Kamahl.

The floor and table vanished. Water flooded everything. No longer were they in a great hall but a dark river.

Kamahl thrashed, his dreadlocks streaming like tentacles. Kuberr dogpaddled. Both rose to break the surface, gulping breaths. Between them, water solidified into Lowallyn, and he shoved his comrades onto the rocky bank.

Amid river-smoothed stones, the men lay like drowned rats. Kamahl jetted water from his nostrils as Kuberr said, "Nice! Really nice! Where are we?"

"This is the Deepwash River, running through Sanctum Valley." Lowallyn glanced along the bank. "There's the ford and the arched gate before it and—" a huge beast bounded over the bank and clomped to a halt above them "—a giant centaur!"

"Stonebrow," Kamahl gasped.

Massive hooves, shaggy fetlocks, muscular shoulders, a thick-thewed upper torso, and a huge, simian face—Stonebrow held a great lance in his upraised arm as he stared at the three intruders.

"Stonebrow!" Kamahl said again, louder. "I should have known I would find you here."

The giant centaur stared at the wet tangle of hair. "Kamahl? You've come at last!" He dropped the spear, grasped Kamahl's hand, and yanked him into a massive embrace. Stonebrow held the hug only a moment before he released his old friend and stepped backward. "Forgive me, Commander. We've been waiting for you. Averru said you'd bring his two greatest weapons, which will win the war. Where are they?"

"May I introduce the brothers of Averru—Lowallyn and Kuberr?" Kamahl said, gesturing to the two men. "Our hope for salvation."

Stonebrow blinked at Kuberr, but his gaze caught on Lowallyn—that famous face, the hair that should have been black, the missing right arm. "Y-you—you look like . . . like Ixidor?"

Lowallyn nodded grimly. "I once was he but am no more."

The centaur nodded nervously. "So Ixidor is . . . or was . . . well . . . *real?*"

"Of course—"

"I mean, well . . . a real god?"

Lowallyn's eyes narrowed in consideration. "I take it you once believed in me?"

Stonebrow shifted his forehooves as if preparing to kneel but kept his feet. "I believed in your Vision . . . but the world would not . . . and too many people died in the wars to make them believe. . . ."

"You lost faith. . . ."

Stonebrow only nodded.

"So did I. You chose well. Ixidor is gone, and even I am not what I once was. Believe in yourself, Stonebrow, and I will believe in me. It's better that way."

"*Now* who's wasting time?" Kuberr complained. "This mule man doesn't look like Averru to me." He reached out and knocked on Stonebrow's nearest hoof. "Averru! Hello? Are you in there?"

Stonebrow retreated a step. "Of course not. Averru is in the city above. He *is* the city." He swung a powerful hand out to gesture across the river.

Averru City hulked there, blooming from nearby rocks. Its towers looked like the curved stalks of an agave. A thousand feet tall and wide and deep, the city straddled the Corian Escarpment. It eclipsed half the sky with its endless windows. On the streets of the city moved men of red crystal.

"I helped to found Sanctum, I witnessed its growth, I fought in the war that killed Akroma and Phage. . . ." Stonebrow trailed off. "I was here when the city began, and I'll be here when it finishes."

"You serve Averru?" Kamahl asked.

"Voluntarily, yes."

"Blah blah blah!" said Kuberr. "Let's get moving!"

"Averru is expecting us," Lowallyn said. "Take us to him."

Stonebrow reached down his huge hand, grasped Lowallyn, and hoisted him onto his back. The numen hadn't time to protest. A moment later, an indignant Kuberr was lifted up beside him then Kamahl as well. They looked like children on the back of a plow horse.

"Hang on!" Stonebrow commanded.

He wheeled and bounded down the bank. Reaching full gallop, Stonebrow clattered along the river, heading for the stone arch. Its now-famous inscription came into view—runes that meant, "Battlefield of the Numena." Stonebrow dashed across the ford, rooster tails spraying around him. He climbed the far bank and crossed beneath the arch. The road led among river-bottom farms, abandoned in the shadow of the city. Stonebrow charged up a slope of scree and curved along the main way toward the first of the great red towers.

Though the heat of day had been oppressive in the valley, cold winds blew along the shadowed streets. Stonebrow galloped up the steep slopes. He passed great hanging gardens where no one lingered, multileveled restaurants where no one ate, aerial bridges that held only Glyphs, flying buttresses and inverted domes, mosaics and fountains and every monumental work of art and architecture. The buildings seemed vibrant and utterly alive, though the streets were nearly deserted.

Averru was a ghost city, abandoned by all but the numen who built it.

"Brother," whispered Lowallyn as he rode through another canyon of towers, "it has been too long. We are so much alike, you and I, yet . . . different."

Stonebrow charged up the final course to the headlands of the escarpment. He galloped through a broad courtyard and out onto a wide, paved plaza. At its center stood a domed temple surrounded by arched entryways. Hooves sparking, Stonebrow thundered across the plaza. On his back, Lowallyn smiled. He was the only one. Kuberr clung on miserably, and Kamahl jolted with each bound. The temple grew larger without seeming any nearer. It was wrapped in enchantments, layer upon layer, the spiritual focus of the whole city. Averru waited within.

"Too long, Brother."

Stonebrow approached the great dome and skidded to a halt. He nodded toward the nearest archway. "The temple is the eye of Averru. He sees all within, and you will too."

Reaching back, Stonebrow grasped Lowallyn and lowered him to the paving stones. Next, he set down Kuberr. Kamahl couldn't wait, sliding down the centaur's haunch.

Stonebrow nodded to him. "Commander, it's good to be fighting side by side again."

Kamahl gave him a grim smile. "Yes, General. It is."

"Averru waits," Stonebrow said. "You may enter."

Lowallyn squared his jaw and strode toward the archway. Kamahl joined him, and Kuberr sullenly followed. They passed beneath the broad arch and into the cool darkness beyond. It took a moment for their eyes to adjust. A great spherical space resolved itself, with concentric seats descending to a hole in the center of the floor. From that wide gap protruded a giant ruby sculpture in the shape of the City of Averru. The sculpture gleamed with an inner light, and red beams shot from its facets to shine upon the dome above. The whole space seemed a great jewel, and it was unutterably beautiful.

Only the three men—Lowallyn, Kuberr, and Kamahl—stood there, but each sensed a fourth presence.

Kamahl fell to his knees.

Lowallyn said, "We are here, Brother-Sorcerer."

Polygons of light shifted, skating across the ceiling. The shapes joined, making larger, brighter beams. Three rays glided downward until they rested on the men. The radiance was alive, and it studied them, reflecting and refracting. It beamed their likenesses back into the great ruby, which blazed with light. It cast the faces and figures of Lowallyn, Kuberr, and Kamahl across its inner dome, pieces of a puzzle it was assembling.

Kuberr narrowed his eyes, and the face above him did likewise. "Enough games. I know what I look like."

Yes, but do you know what I look like?

The projections grew angular, breaking into countless planes. They reoriented themselves in new forms: floor plans and elevations of the buildings all around; schematics and diagrams of Glyph biology; runes and symbols in complex sorceries.

"Yes, yes," Kuberr said. "We've seen your city, Brother. We saw it once before. You're the one who brought Karona here, this time and last. You'll just have to get rid of her. I hope you're up to it."

I'm no mere man this time. I'm a whole city. I can make words live.

"All of us are stronger," Lowallyn said. "I can make images real."

Kuberr growled, "And I can make live men dead. What good is any of it? Karona is stronger too, and she knows what we're up to. She can strip our powers with a thought. How are we supposed to capture her?"

Fragments of light swarmed kaleidoscopically across the vault. They amalgamated into a single figure—tall, slender, and beautiful. It was Karona. Lowallyn went to his knees, and Kuberr as well. Kamahl slumped to the floor, overcome

If no one can stand against Karona, we'll make her fight herself. We'll set up a mirror and lure her in. She wishes a comrade, so we'll give her one. She'll stare herself in the face, mesmerized as we all are, and then we'll spring the trap.

Kuberr laughed wickedly. "Oh, Averru, you're a cruel bastard."

Lowallyn was less impressed. He struggled to his feet and descended the stairs. "We were fooled into bowing, but she won't be. Karona's no parakeet. How will we ever convince her that the creature she sees is real?"

First, we'll all build the illusion. What you see is created from words—art in sequence. To it, we must add your image magic. You will paint her, Lowallyn.

The man reached to his pack, still wet from their journey through the water. He set it on the ground and opened it. "I can't paint on wet canvas," he said, pulling out the roll and watching water run from it. He reached deeper and drew out a clay bundle wrapped in waxed paper. Holding it high, he said, "This, though, will be unharmed." Dexterous fingers unwrapped the bundle and worked the clay to warm it.

Kuberr watched, a delighted smile on his face. "What do I do?"

You have the power of death over life, and unlife over death. You'll infest our illusion with the smell of flesh. You'll take the word and image and make them seem real.

Lowallyn set the clay on a bench and began to sculpt. It ceased looking like a lump and became the miniature of a living thing. He wasn't trying to capture Karona's body, but her soul—hopeful, curious, insatiable, and ingrown—too powerful to sustain itself. She was like a very tall person amid midgets, stooping so as not to seem a monster. Lowallyn sculpted her that way. Her face was gorgeous and yet downturned to hide its radiance. Her arms were powerful but tucked shyly against her body. Her body was perfectly formed, muscular in the limbs but soft and smooth everywhere else.

At last, the image was complete. Lowallyn gently pried it up from the bench and lifted it in his hand.

"Here it is, the soul of Karona."

Give it to Kuberr, and he'll add his touch—but Kuberr, be subtle.

Lowallyn walked to Kuberr and reluctantly handed him the sculpture. "Don't ruin it."

Waving him off, Kuberr took the image. He stared lasciviously at it. "I'm just going to do two things to make it more believable. First, unless our Glorious Lady is a lesbian, it'll be easier to trick her if this is a male." With one thumb, he flattened the breasts and added a lump lower down.

"You reprobate," Lowallyn growled.

"If you liked that trick, you'll love this one." He reached into his pocket, produced a coin, flashed it between his fingers, and rammed the thing into the backside of the figurine. "Everyone's got something up his ass, and usually it's money. There, now you've got a true image."

Lowallyn tried to protest, but his cries were drowned out by the mind of Averru.

Throw the figure into the vision of Karona at the center of the temple. Aim well. It will combine only if it passes right through the matrix of her image.

"Not to worry," Kuberr said. "I can break a window from a block away." He reared back, cocked his arm, and let fly. The clay figurine soared through the air and struck the Karona vision square in the face.

Light flared as word and image combined into something new. No longer could it be mistaken for Karona but for a man much like her. His shoulders were powerful, his face strong and handsome, but most convincing were his eyes. They gleamed like gold, as if reflecting his soul.

Kamahl could not even drag himself off his face.

Kuberr giggled in delight.

Lowallyn's breath was taken away, but he felt vaguely sickened. "Now that we've created our bait, what do we do?"

Set the rest of the trap. The moment she touches him, the entrapment spell will be triggered, and she will be ours, as were the Primevals of old.

* * * * *

Kamahl lay there and panted. Only in that moment did he realize what they intended. They would replace one tyrant with three. They would steal Karona's power and make it their own.

Now, Kamahl, we need your sword. It will carve new Glyphs in the walls of my temple, the words of a great spell.

Kamahl rose. He sat on his heels, steadied himself, and then climbed to his feet. Keeping his face averted from the glorious figure that hovered above them all, Kamahl said quietly, "I won't do it."

Kuberr and Lowallyn turned amazed eyes on him, and Averru's shock filled the chamber. Kuberr spoke for them all: "What in the Nine Hells are you talking about?"

Sweat poured down Kamahl's face, and his heart pounded. He spoke quietly, "You aren't trying to rid the world of a destroyer but to gain her power yourselves. You'll become the destroyers." His voice grew stronger. "You orchestrated this confrontation so that you could claim Karona's power. This is just another stage of transformation, isn't it? You want to become gods, and this is your way of doing it."

Lowallyn approached, concern written on his face. He clasped Kamahl's shoulder. "Are you all right?"

"Of course," Kamahl snarled, shrugging off the man's touch. "I'm only just beginning to see the way things are."

Lowallyn shook his head sadly. "Kamahl, if we had planned this, why were *you* the one who gathered us? Why did *you* cajole *us* into confronting Karona? We wanted to flee to other worlds. You convinced us to come here and battle her—perhaps to our deaths."

Kamahl nodded, trembling. "Yes . . . that's true—"

"Look, you massive moron! She's on her way," Kuberr broke in, flinging his hand up toward the glowing man. "The bait's made sure of it. Now, either you help us, or she'll kills us all!"

There is no other way, Kamahl. We must trap her and contain her or allow her to destroy the world.

"No," Kamahl said firmly. "There is another way. Banish her. If you can bind her, you can banish her."

Lowallyn lifted his brows in consideration. He glanced to Kuberr, and then said, "Is it possible?" His voice echoed away to silence, and Averru did not answer for a long while.

Yes. It is possible. We can place wards on her that will keep her away, but a being more powerful than us could remove the wards, and she could return. Banishment is possible, but it is much less certain.

"Swear to it," Kamahl said. "Swear that you will banish her instead of binding her. All of you swear to it. Otherwise, I will not help you."

Lowallyn shook his head. "I can't believe you killed a death-wurm, dragged me out, drove me across a desert, and forced me into this confrontation only to make me swear anything at all—" He laughed lightly "—but I'll swear it."

Kuberr spoke a sentence constructed entirely of expletives, and finished by saying, "which means I swear it, too, you stupid f—"

I swear it as well.

Kamahl sighed and nodded. "Good. Let's get to work."

CHAPTER 22

SPRINGING THE TRAP

*A*bove Kamahl hovered a strong, lithe, handsome man. How like Karona he was. Curiosity filled his eyes as the four men did their work below.

"Let's get on with this spell," Kamahl said.

Red light lanced from the great ruby sculpture. It struck the walls of the temple, forming runes as tall as a man. Averru shaped and ordered those runes into a powerful sorcery. When at last the forms were perfect, the light intensified and the hue deepened. The rock on which those words were cast grew as soft as wax. It was time for the words to be carved in stone.

Up stepped Kamahl, the Mirari sword glinting in his hand. He trained his eyes on the red figures and summoned strength. With teeth locked in a grimace, Kamahl set the sword tip on the stone. He drove it in along the line projected there. The sword slid in the contours. Stone drooped from the form and fell to the floor. Even as Kamahl finished the figure, it began to fill with rubious crystal, as if the rock bled. In time, these forms would emerge as new Glyphs, living words in a great spell.

On another portion of wall, Lowallyn worked with brushes and paints. He created images to dance with the words, amplifying and modifying them. He was the illuminator of this great manuscript, and from his brushes emerged gold-gilded traceries. These lines would tangle Karona. He deepened the lines into mazes and four-dimensional labyrinths. Once she had gone that deep, she would never escape. To ease her isolation, Lowallyn filled the tangled world with gardens and fountains, leaping hinds and huntsmen with bows on their shoulders, trumpeters and fife players, knights, ladies, and kings. So vivid were these visions that they began to peel away from the wall.

Lines wove through the air, all around the perimeter of the temple. Among the lines moved Glyphs in an intricate dance. Streamers reached up from them to the creature that floated in the midst of the temple. The spell was taking form. One more component would make it complete.

Kuberr worked at that component, though he seemed to work at nothing. The young man wandered the temple. His head was downcast, his fists clenching and releasing. A haunted look filled his eyes. He was tapping the powers of death in Averru City—powers that reached back over twenty thousand years. A cold wind riffled his cloak, and suddenly the spirits arrived. Gray specters drifted through the arched gates of the temple. They sifted among Glyphs and traceries, coiled about Kuberr, and waltzed in a macabre circle around the glowing man. The powers of death and of life joined.

Panting, the two men and the great city watched their spell swirl—a maelstrom of power. At its center was the great lure, a man like Karona. The three numena called him Arien.

When Kamahl asked why, Lowallyn replied, "He is made of air."

The circle was complete. The spell vortex would banish Karona and save Dominaria.

Now, Kamahl, it is time. You must go meet her and guide her here.

Kamahl nodded, hair dangling in a curtain around his head. "I will go, but if she is omniscient, she will know."

Pray she is not yet omniscient.

* * * * *

With Sash and Waistcoat in her arms, Karona stepped across the sky. One moment, they hung above the ruined coliseum, and the next, they reached Averru City.

It opened below, as beautiful as a red rose. Its petals were tall towers, which lifted their curving spires to the sky. Between them ran roads filled with creatures—crystal men and beasts from all nations. They were the ants and aphids of this great bloom. Its fragrance was magic itself, for the whole city breathed power. The center of that energy, the source of it all, was a great stone dome.

Karona swooped down to it, her robes whistling as they shed air. The dome was huge and white, suffused with power, and a lone figure stood atop it. He looked to her, eyes intent within a dark mass of dreadlocks and beard.

"KAMAHL."

As she approached, Kamahl went to his knees then to his face. Karona swept down to light on the dome. She set her prophets down beside her, and the three of them stared at the prostrate figure.

"RISE, KAMAHL. WE ARE FRIENDS, OR ONCE WE WERE. I HAVEN'T COME TO BATTLE YOU."

The man lay a moment more on his face, shoulders trembling. Then he looked up to her radiance, and tears rolled from his eyes.

"DO NOT WEEP. THIS IS AN IMMORTAL WAR. YOU NEEDN'T GET CAUGHT IN IT."

Kamahl wiped his eyes on his cloak and climbed to his feet. "You mistake me, Glorious Lady. I'm not sad. How could I be sad in your presence? These are tears of joy—"

"I KNOW WHAT THEY PLAN FOR ME. ENTRAPMENT OR DEATH. IT'S THE SAME AS LAST TIME."

"You have learned not to trust them, but they have learned not to cross you."

"POWER BLEEDS FROM THIS DOME. THEY'VE DEVISED A MASSIVE SPELL—"

"Yes, they have, Great One, but it's a different sort of spell. We're paper dolls to you. Even the numena aren't your equals. You need someone greater, a true companion."

The light from her eyes wavered. "YES."

"Think back on the deaths—the riots and tribal wars, the catastrophe in the mountains and the atrocity at the coliseum. All you sought was to be in communion with other souls—someone like you."

"YES."

"But there's never been anyone like you. That was why they destroyed you before—because you needed something the world could not give, and your need destroyed the world. Now they can give it to you."

Karona stared numbly at the man.

Waistcoat butted in. "What are you saying?"

"The spell that has brought you into being—Averru's great spell, which is the city itself and the Glyphs that dwell here—has created another creature like you. He is made of magic. He'll be everything to you."

Sash pulled at Karona's arm. "Don't believe him. If they're so afraid of you, they'd never make another creature like you. Don't go into the temple. It's a trap."

Kamahl's eyes never left Karona's. "You needn't go into the temple. Your counterpart—Arien is his name—will come out to you." He reached over his shoulder and drew the huge Mirari sword.

Lifting her prophets, Karona lunged out of reach of the blade.

Kamahl didn't pursue her. Instead, he swept the sword through a vertical arc. Its tip struck the dome and cleft it as if it were cheese. He made another swing, perpendicular to the first, and cut a second stroke in the peak of the temple. A third and fourth, and he had carved an eight-pointed star. Four more, and it was a sunburst that trembled with barely concealed power.

Kamahl retreated, and the stone began to peel back. Points lifted and curved away from the center. Cleft lines lengthened. The whole dome began to open like a bud to flower. Power rushed skyward from the space within.

Karona lifted off of the stone dome. Clutching Sash and Waistcoat, she watched the temple bloom.

Triangular sections of stone parted, widening the column of energy that erupted skyward. It whirled in a vortex of gold, red, and black. The storm stretched to the clouds and sucked them in. It widened, fists of power spinning farther out.

Karona hovered out of their reach, poised in case the spell erupted.

In one arm, Sash murmured, "Good. Stay back. It's a trap."

I KNOW.

The dark vortex spun through one more angry revolution then transformed. Within the temple, its base shone brilliantly. The light rose up the throat of the cyclone, bleaching the shadows from it. The glowing object balmed the storm. Turbid winds softened to playful breezes. The vortex's wall turned gossamer, revealing the beautiful figure within.

He was young, as was she—tall and slender, with strong shoulders. His arms reached gently forward, palms upraised in welcome. Lightning-bright robes draped his body, and a handsome face peered levelly through the dissipating magic. His eyes were like hers, still bright from the heavens whence he came.

"Karona," he whispered, and the soft sound carried through the roaring tube. "I am Arien."

"He's an illusion," hissed Sash.

HIS FLESH SEEMS REAL.

"He's a gigolo," said Waistcoat.

NO, HE IS LIKE ME.

* * * * *

In his first moments of consciousness, Arien had watched his makers at work. He had learned his own name and how to speak. Now he learned what he wanted: Karona.

She hung there before him, beyond the envelope of air. She too had been fashioned of spells by these same hands. She was first and he last, she female and he male—counterparts.

Something niggled at him. These men had done more than just fashion him.

Arien drifted forward. "Karona! You are beautiful. Come to me!"

"IF YOU'RE LIKE ME, YOU CAN DO ANYTHING. TURN THE SKY PURPLE."

Arien's brow furrowed. Turn the sky purple? "I have no idea how to do so."

"YOU NEED ONLY WILL IT IN THE PRESENCE OF A BELIEVING MORTAL, AND IT WILL BE DONE."

"Where's he gonna get a believing mortal?" scoffed her pudgy prophet.

The thin one also shook his head dubiously.

Kamahl stood within one crevice of the open dome. "I'll be his believing mortal. I know he can turn the sky purple."

Arien turned his eyes toward the heavens, bright blue above him. He lifted his hands, fingers spreading as if to hold up the firmament. He closed his eyes, summoning up whatever power lay within him, and wished for the sky to turn purple.

Energy fountained through him. It jetted from his fingers and palms. Even his mouth dropped open, and his eyes could no longer remain clenched. Red power shot from him and vaulted in a fierce column into the belly of the sky. At the height of its ascent, the pillar spread. The stain moved in irregular waves until half the heavens were purple.

Arien dropped his arms, letting the power bleed away. Red tears ran from his eyes, but his smile was glad. It was no trick. He had turned the sky purple and had proven himself.

Karona smiled.

"Come to me," he beckoned.

She glided forward across the air, smooth and serene, though the men in her arms kicked.

One said, "What about the flying pigs? Try that!"

The other said, "Don't cross into the spell area!"

She listened to neither of them. They had no idea what it felt like to be alone, but Karona knew—and Arien also.

"Thank you," he whispered to his creators as the woman crossed the purple sky to reach him. It was not good to be alone.

He reached to her, clasped her hands, and felt her warm flesh in his fingers.

Instantly, he knew they had been betrayed. They both knew. Arien had flesh, yes, but not like hers. His was cold and silicate— false. He was an artificial intellect, and even his power was a sham. The spell that had transformed the sky was not his own but the sorcerous concoction of the three numena. It all had been a trick. Arien was no more than bait, his hands the magical hooks that had snagged Karona.

"Forgive me," he said, even as his flesh adhered to hers, encasing it. Arien began to dissolve. His body boiled, turning to mana energy.

"I didn't know . . ."

He wept then melted into ropy lines of power that wrapped around her. Every tissue of his being unraveled, and magic sinews spun rapidly around Karona and her prophets. They could not escape. They would be captive to the numena forever.

Arien spoke on the wind. *Forgive* . . .

* * * * *

Kamahl stood, feet wedged in a crevice of the open dome, and he gaped at the terrors above. "Not the two men!" he shouted. "They were never part of the agreement!"

The numena did not reply. They had their hands full. Lowallyn's labyrinth peeled off the wall faster than he could paint it. The lines spooled upward, borne on the red sparks of Averru's magic and the gray souls that Kuberr raised to life. All whirled around Karona, encasing her.

The goddess struggled. She punched through three layers of the conundrum but could not break free. The lines of power dragged her down toward the riven temple.

"Now, banish her!" Kamahl shouted. Still, Karona and her prophets sank inexorably toward the temple. "You swore to send her away! To banish her. Not this!"

No one listened. The numena drew down the goddess of Magic, bound in their spells. Soon she would be bound by their will.

So, he had been right all along. He would be trading one tyrant for three. Yes, they had ruled the world for a thousand years without destroying it, but their rule would be absolute.

"I almost hope she gets out," Kamahl muttered. "It'd serve them right. At least she is a true goddess."

Heart pounding, Kamahl suddenly realized he had the power to save her. She could do anything if she had a believing mortal. Sash and Waistcoat were apparently too terrified to believe . . . but not Kamahl. A momentary certainty would be enough.

He gazed at the struggling figure. Visions of atrocities returned— in the desert, in the mountains, in the coliseum. . . . Were she loosed on the world, they would only repeat, and worse. But if the three numena held her power, what atrocities then? Kuberr and Averru had already shown themselves capable of terrible things, and Lowallyn had, just two years before, touched off a world war. Such power should be held by no one on Dominaria.

He remembered her—sad and sweet on the desert. THE WORLD IS COMING, she had said, and it sounded as if she were saying it again. WHO IS KARONA? WHO IS KAMAHL? THE WORLD IS COMING, AND THE ANSWER LIES IN WHAT THEY WILL DO.

Such power belongs nowhere on Dominaria.

Kamahl bowed his head and closed out the awful sight of her, bound in magic. She couldn't escape to Dominaria, but she *could* escape to some other plane. . . .

* * * * *

Go, Karona, whispered Arien on the torrid wind. *A mortal believes. Banishment is better than oblivion. Go!*

* * * * *

"The spell fabric is weakening!" Lowallyn shouted. "She's going to get loose!"

Not if she's dead, Averru responded.

Kuberr gesticulated skyward, and hundreds of specters whirled from his fingers and up through the riven dome. "Give me a moment, and she will be."

* * * * *

I LATCH ONTO KAMAHL'S FAITH AND BID DOMINARIA GOOD-BYE.

CHAPTER 23

THE BLIND ETERNITIES

I CLING TO SASH AND WAISTCOAT AS WE ARE CATAPULTED FROM THE WORLD.

DOMINARIA RUSHES AWAY. SKY AND GROUND DISSOLVE INTO CHAOS, AND WE ARE IN A NEW PLACE: THE BLIND ETERNITIES.

A MOMENT AGO, I DID NOT KNOW THAT NAME, BUT IT SHOUTS TO ME FROM THE BOILING AIR. OTHER NAMES RING OUT, TRAVELERS WHO SAILED THIS CHAOS SEA: THE MAGE MASTER BARRIN, THE LEVIATHAN *WEATHERLIGHT,* THE REBORN PRIMEVAL RHAMMIDARIGAAZ, AKROMA OF THE NIGHTMARE LANDS . . . THEY HAD PLIED THIS CRADLE OF WORLDS ON THEIR WAY FROM ONE PLANE TO ANOTHER.

COLORS FAN OUT AROUND ME. IMAGES SOLIDIFY FROM THE TUMBLING ENERGIES—A TREE, A FISH, A CLOCK, A CLIFF—AND DISSOLVE. ENERGY SEEKS FORM AND FINDS IT IN OUR MINDS—A BARN, A CYST, A COIN, A TIGER. ALL ARE SOLID FOR BUT A MOMENT BEFORE SHREDDING INTO PURE POWER. PLASMIC CURRENTS COURSE OVER US AND STICK TO OUR SKIN. THEY TAKE THE FORM OF OUR FLESH.

POWER CONGEALS ON WAISTCOAT AND SASH. THEY FLAIL WILDLY, LEGS AND ARMS DRAGGING LONG VEILS OF THE HALF-FORMED STUFF. THEIR FACES ARE ENCASED, AND THEY ARE SUFFOCATING.

I MUST CARRY THEM FROM THIS NOWHERE PLACE. MY MIND REACHES AMONG THE STRANDS OF ENERGY AND DRAGS ON ONE OF

THEM. THE CORD SOLIDIFIES. THERE IS A NAME IMBEDDED IN IT: GERRARD CAPASHEN. I RUSH DOWN THE WIDENING BAND.

* * * * *

Beneath Karona's feet, ground solidified—hot cobbles with grit in their seams. The stones extended to a curb, above which other things took shape. Out of the air precipitated brick buildings. One shop displayed plucked geese and chickens; another had brass vessels arrayed down its front steps; a third breathed the scent of yeast and sugar. Folk took shape in the buildings and in the lane between them. Most wore yellowish cloaks in many layers, their faces painted with makeup and clouds of perfume enveloping them.

Karona set Sash and Waistcoat on the cobbles, and her fingers flung the last clinging plasma from their faces. They grasped their knees and coughed.

"Is this Otaria?" Sash asked.

A stout man with a cane strode right toward them. His eyes flew open, and he swerved. His ample paunch tipped over a peddler's tray, and the toothless old man launched into a tirade.

"What?" Waistcoat asked as the peddler hopped before him, ranting. "I just got here!"

A crowd gathered, paunchy and dingy in their yellow cloaks. They gaped at the newcomers, and a few traded odds on the coming fight.

"ENOUGH!"

The crowd recoiled as if they had not noticed Karona before. Their piggish eyes fastened on her, and they paused. Even the peddler backed up, trampling his notions. He knelt and spoke a single word—Magic.

It was her name in their tongue, and it broke the code for her.

WE SEEK SHELTER.

More of the folk went to their knees, and more mouths whispered the name of Karona: "Magic . . . Magic . . . Magic . . ." The stones, too, responded, beginning their faint trembling beneath her.

WHERE ARE WE?

Only the peddler could muster the courage to reply. "This is Mercadia, fair one."

WE NEED A PLACE TO REST, AWAY FROM THE CROWDS.

The street shook, and folk melted away from the center of the road. Something massive approached. People whispered, "Masters," and bowed prostrate before the new creatures.

Around a corner came a great metallic talon. It spread its toes and stomped on the ground. The crowd quailed. A gear-work leg carried the beast into view. Its body was toadlike, a fusion of gray flesh and gray metal. The creature's other leg pounded the ground, and it halted before Karona. Where the toad's eyes should have been, wires emerged in fat bundles. They ran up into the severed legs of a smaller creature that sat on the back of the toad. It had once been a goblin, but it too was shot through with mechanisms. Its spine prickled with metal spikes, which ran from the goblin down into the frog. The two creatures had been wired together into one.

The goblin opened its mouth and bleated, "Who are you?"

I AM KARONA.

Webbed fingers fiddled with a necklace of gears. "You've come without permission. No one may come to Mercadia without the permission of the Masters."

ARE YOU ONE OF THE MASTERS?

"I am."

WE COME IN THE NAME OF GERRARD CAPASHEN.

The metallic eyes of the goblin-toad lit with fury, and a scandalized murmur rushed through the prostrate crowd.

"The name of the saboteur is forbidden!" shrieked the master. "You are Cho-Arrim! Cho-Arrim beyond the forest are sentenced to death!" It leaped toward Karona, its metal talons swinging foremost to pounce.

She swept her arms out to grab Sash and Waistcoat, and her eyes flared. Raw mana gushed from her pupils and sprayed across the airborne creature. Where power struck, metal vaporized. Gray flesh burst open. The lunging monster imploded, but momentum carried its husk to crash into Karona—except that she leaped into the air.

As the ruined master tumbled across the cobbled street, Karona, Sash, and Waistcoat lifted above the crooked chimneys of the city. Tile roofs dropped away, with the streets in their twisting labyrinth. The people who crowded them shouted in anger.

Above, perverse flying machines filled the skies. On the decks of those ships were more goblin mechanisms.

MERCADIA IS NOT THE WORLD FOR US.

Waistcoat's eyes fluttered like a pair of butterflies as he gazed at her. "It can't be all bad. Couldn't we find somewhere away from the masters? Anything but that horrid nowhere place!"

Karona pressed her lips together. Already, Mercadia was unraveling around them. The magical skein they clung to thinned, devolving into chaos.

OUR JOURNEY WILL BE QUICK.

The yellow-tinged sky and its flocks of vicious warships disintegrated into swirling motes of power. Sash and Waistcoat gasped last breaths as the air dismantled itself and all became flux.

* * * * *

THROUGH THE RIPTIDE WE SWIM. I CLUTCH MY FRIENDS TO MY SIDES AND SEEK ANOTHER NAME THAT WILL BEAR US FROM THE BLIND ETERNITIES.

THE STORM WHISPERS, *"WEATHERLIGHT,"* AND I GLIMPSE THE SPECTER OF THAT GREAT LEVIATHAN, SWIMMING THROUGH THE ENERGY

TIDES. SHE HAS AN ENORMOUS HEART OF CRYSTAL, A DARK AND COLD HEART. I FOLLOW *WEATHERLIGHT*'S WAKE AS SHE DIVES TOWARD A DEEP PLACE. I PLUNGE THROUGH CURRENTS OF POWER AND RUSH OUT INTO A GLORIOUS WORLD.

THE ENERGY STORM PARTS BEFORE A BRILLIANT BLUE SKY. IT STRETCHES IN ALL DIRECTIONS, WITH NO GROUND BELOW, NO HORIZON AROUND, NO STARS ABOVE. THE SKYSCAPE IS PEOPLED BY GREAT CONTINENTS OF CLOUD. AMONG THEM FLOAT ISLANDS OF ROCK AND GRASS. SOME ARE FORESTED. SOME GLITTER WITH WIDE LAKES OR DAPPLED MEADOWS. OTHERS HOLD GREAT CASTLES, MAJESTIC CITIES, GRAND CATHEDRALS. AMONG THEM FLIT GRIFFINS AND ZEPHYRS, PHOENIXES AND ANGELS.

* * * * *

PERHAPS WE MIGHT REST HERE.

Sash's chest heaved. "What's happened to us, anyway? What was that spell?"

"Where's the land?" Waistcoat whimpered, legs kicking above an infinite drop.

Karona glided toward a garden that hung in the nearby air. Trees gathered around a grassy glade, and a spring burbled up amid time-smoothed stones. A fawn stood on a nearby burl of rock.

Warm winds caressed them as Karona angled down to touch ground. She paced across a berm of grass. Well away from the fatal plunge, Karona eased her hold on the two prophets. They still clung to her.

"I don't want to fall," Waistcoat said.

Sash let his fingers slip free. "Well, at least there'd be nothing to hit. You'd just fall forever. Of course, your skin would be flayed one layer at a time. You'd die from the outside in."

Karona walked down the green slope and came to the bank of the spring. The water chortled in its channel. This was a beautiful place, drifting in illimitable heavens. There was no sun, only the ubiquitous light of the blue skies. Karona walked to a quiet pool where the waters gathered. A long flat stone reclined there, and she sat down. Her fingers trailed through the pool, but her eyes were sad.

On quiet feet, Waistcoat and Sash approached. They came up beside her and sat too, their toes in the water.

Sash ventured, "So, we've been banished from Dominaria?"

Karona only dropped her head and stared at her hands.

"Damned world." Waistcoat put in. "Damned stupid world."

IT WAS OUR HOME.

Sash lifted a stone and hurled it sidearm. The rock skipped across the pool, bounded over a small verge of rock, and fell off the edge of the island. "Some home. Sure, we were created there, but it never welcomed us. We've been on the run all our lives, and now we've just run a little farther than before."

The three sat in silence, and only the spring spoke.

"Why not here? This could be our new home," said Waistcoat.

The air shifted as if his words had caused some offense. Across the stream, light thickened and coalesced into a tall shape. It might have seemed Karona herself, this statuesque woman in white robes, though she had the wings of a great eagle. Her face was beautiful, her eyes very wise and very sad.

"No Karona," she said. "You cannot remain here. This is my realm."

Waistcoat furrowed his brow. "Who are you?"

"I am Serra," the angel said.

"SURELY YOUR WORLD IS LARGE ENOUGH TO GIVE US REFUGE."

"No," Serra replied flatly. "Not one such as you. You're like Urza—you drain my plane of its power. For a thousand years, my world was imprisoned in the power core of Urza's ship, *Weatherlight*. Only when the stone exploded was my realm released. I've labored for a century to rebuild it, and I'll not allow one such as you to destroy it."

Waistcoat snarled. "One such as her? Criminy! *You* are one such as her!"

Both women looked at him, anger in their eyes. In unison, they turned to stare into each other's faces. They moved with the symmetry of reflections in a mirror.

"After all," Sash put in nervously, "Karona's just sitting here."

Serra stared levelly at her counterpart. "Just sitting here? Look." The angel pointed to the pool. The waters were troubled. They trembled, and the shallow basin of stone that held them began to tip. Waves crowded back toward the stream, and the tide slowly reversed. Water spilled across the stony banks and ran in long trails through the grass.

"What's happening?" Sash asked.

"The island is tilting," Serra said. "Your lady drains it of power. Her aura will consume every island in my floating paradise. You cannot remain. You must go."

"I'M BANISHED FROM MY HOME WORLD. I SEEK ANOTHER PLACE TO LIVE."

"There's no home for you, Karona, not outside of Dominaria. You are her magic. You cannot live anywhere else," Serra said. The trees behind her creaked as the island listed. "You must go now."

Karona stood. The stones beneath her feet hissed as their magic was drawn away. She gathered Sash and Waistcoat, took one step, a second, and floated into the sky. The island shrank beneath them, its near edge lolling upward.

Serra remained beside the now-empty pool. Her shimmering figure poured magical energy back into the ground, and her wings stroked as if she could hold the island aloft by herself.

IS THERE A WORLD FOR ME?

"Try to get back to Dominaria," Sash said, filling his lungs.

Waistcoat plugged his nose. "Eroshia, if you've got a choice."

Karona closed her eyes, and her mind reached out to the broad coil that had brought her here, the path of *Weatherlight*. She clung to it.

The sky dissolved. Clear blue became a torrent of colors. Karona and her prophets had one final glimpse of heaven before chaos swallowed them.

* * * * *

MY MIND IS DARK AS I FLY THROUGH THE RAVENOUS WIND. I HEAR A HUNDRED NAMES—WAYFARERS AMONG THE WORLDS. WERE THEY BANISHED? DID THEY FIND HOMES?

ONE NAME SHOUTS ABOVE ALL THE OTHERS. "YAWGMOTH."

THE TRACE OF HIS PASSAGE TO DOMINARIA LINGERS IN THE CHAOS WINDS. PERHAPS I CAN FOLLOW IT BACK HOME, THOUGH I FEAR TO FOLLOW IT THE WRONG WAY. . . .

I LATCH ONTO THE NAME OF YAWGMOTH AND RIDE IT DOWN OUT OF THE BLIND ETERNITIES.

* * * * *

The panoply of color peeled back, and a strange site opened before Karona and her prophets.

They hovered above a gutted world. Perhaps once it had been a globe, a set of nested spheres, but three quarters of that world had been ripped away. What remained was a crescent-shaped wedge like a slice of onion with a hollow center. Concentric layers of metal radiated from the core toward the outer skin. All around it floated the shattered remains of a blasted world.

Sash and Waistcoat kicked furiously, their faces red and bulging. They couldn't breathe—there was nothing to breathe.

Karona soared down toward the riven place. Wind billowed around her and tore at her. Still, the atmosphere was thin. She plunged farther, and her prophets gasped in the rarefied air.

Beneath them, great machines moved across the land. Behemoths grazed among rusted hulks of metal or marched behind—what were those? Living things? On each level, creatures moved. Karona cut across the layers. Enormous furnaces belched flame, great piles of scrap rose into mountains, vast pipes twisted like metal guts.

Karona rose above the outer layer, and everything changed.

Wide fields opened below, stretching to tall mountains, trees, and lakes. It was as if all the grit and ugliness below existed only to create this lush land above.

Karona glided above a tossing forest. Beyond, a hill in bronze heather rolled down toward a rippling lake. She descended, her feet touching on an outcrop of gray stone. Relaxing her arms, she let Sash and Waistcoat find their own feet.

All of them stood there, side by side, and breathed the faintly metallic air. Perhaps, at last, they had found a refuge.

Sash stared out at the rumpled horizon, shorn off abruptly only a half mile away. "Where are we?"

THE NAME THAT LED ME HERE WAS YAWGMOTH.

Waistcoat breathlessly echoed her words.

"If the stories are true about him," Sash said, "we'd better get going."

YES—A DESTROYER BANISHED FROM DOMINARIA . . . THE SAME STORIES TOLD ABOUT ME.

Sash and Waistcoat glanced fearfully about, as if a predator waited in the weeds.

"You're not like . . . him," Waistcoat said. "No one would say that."

I MIGHT. THEY CALL HIM THE DEMON YAWGMOTH. PERHAPS THEY WILL CALL ME THE DEMON KARONA.

Welcome, said a dark, insatiable presence. *Remain.*

I THINK WE'VE FOUND A NEW HOME.

Waistcoat shook his head violently. "No. We have to leave this place. It's evil."

Stay, Karona. You need shelter, and I need magic.

A breeze ran through the heather, passed beneath the trees, and tore itself across the edge of the world.

Rest here, Karona. I'll rebuild you, and you'll rebuild me, and together we'll return to Dominaria. Come to me. My arms are open.

"Just like the arms of Arien! It's a trap!"

Karona's eyes grew dark. *JUST LIKE THE ARMS OF ARIEN.*

She lifted her friends and soared away. Metallic heather slipped by beneath their feet, and they floated above a tin tree. A dragon beyond it raised its metallic neck and watched as she departed.

The presence remained, beckoning: *Return to Phyrexia. Return. . . .*

Once again, the world atomized around them, metal dissolving into chaos whorls.

CHAPTER 24

RIDDANCE

Kamahl clung within a crevice of the riven dome. His ears still rang, though the magic vortex had dissipated, and his fingers still tingled from the raw power that had flashed past him. Lines of force had etched themselves across his eyes.

"I'm alive," he told himself uncertainly. "I *am* alive."

It was a wonder. He had cut open the dome and stood at those floodgates as continental magic poured forth. The sorcerous might of all Dominaria had channeled through this single spot.

Kamahl peered down into the riven temple. Its circular seats formed a vortex around the ruby statue. It seemed inert, its inner light gone. Karona was not within it.

To one side sat Lowallyn, lean and tan. Not one of his elaborate illuminations remained on the wall. He slumped in the posture of defeat, his face cradled in his hand. On the other side of the temple, Kuberr lay on his back. Blood trickled from his nose, and he draped an arm across his forehead. He breathed ever so slightly but otherwise looked dead.

"What's the word?" Kamahl called down to them.

Kuberr drew his hand from his face and looked up. Utterly weary, he said, "You know what the word is: Betrayal."

Kamahl canted an eyebrow. "Yes."

"You believed in her. You let her go."

"I merely did what you swore to do."

Kuberr sat up and clutched the hem of his shirt beneath his nose. "Nope. She's not even warded. She'll be back."

Gritting his teeth, Kamahl pivoted in the crevice. He worked his way to the outside edge of the ruptured dome. The stone was smooth and hot beneath the staring sun. Kamahl climbed out onto the sloped surface. Taking handholds, he lowered himself from the crack. On his belly, he slid down to the sandstone plaza. Glyphs stood in knots all through the plaza, but there was not another living thing under the sun.

Kamahl strode into the temple

On opposite sides, the two numena lifted their eyes and stared levelly at him. Kuberr's nose had stopped bleeding, but his black shirt was wet with blood.

"Traitor."

"She's gone," Kamahl responded. "That's what we wanted, to rid Dominaria of the Scourge."

Kuberr's golden eyes flared. He got up and strode toward the druid. "You don't know what you've done, do you?"

Lowallyn approached the two of them. He looked drawn, his eyes haunted. He gestured out the nearest archway and across the sandstone plaza.

"Tell me what you see out there."

"The city," Kamahl said, shrugging. "The Glyphs, the plaza— what of it?"

"Are the Glyphs moving?" Lowallyn asked.

Kamahl stared at the ruby men. They had not moved since he had first glimpsed them. "She froze them?"

"It's worse than that," Lowallyn said. He pointed inward, to the crystalline matrix that once had cast images out across the dome. Now, the sculpture was dark and still. "Averru is gone."

Kamahl gaped at the dark crystal. It was the very eye of a god, and that eye was lifeless. "What?"

"You killed him," spat Kuberr.

Lowallyn went on more gently. "Averru had taken this city as his body, those Glyphs as his hands. His very life was a great spell, but Karona was Magic herself. When she escaped from Dominaria, she took magic with her—she took Averru."

Kamahl couldn't wrap his mind around this catastrophe. "She drained all the magic out of the city?"

"Yes," Lowallyn said quietly, "and Averru is gone, perhaps dead."

Kamahl felt as if he had been struck in the chest. He bent over, catching his knees in his hands and breathing awhile.

Kuberr placed a bloody hand on his back and said, "You're lucky, Kamahl. If we still had our magic, you'd be dead too."

* * * * *

Stonebrow marched up the switchback road that led to the summit of Averru. He led what was left of his guard garrison: a pair of dwarfs, five elves, a barbarian, a mantis druid, and three avens. All the Glyphs were frozen, and Stonebrow wanted to know why.

"Draw swords. Bows out; arrows nocked. Be ready," he rumbled. His eyes darted along the silent street, up the towers that curved above the road. "If Karona rules the heights, we'll have to strike quickly."

Behind him, steel skirled from scabbards, and gut strings whined as they drew taut.

If you see her, attack before her aura overtakes you. A moment's hesitation—"

"Look out!" cried one of the elves, pointing overhead.

Stonebrow looked skyward. A balcony of one of the curving towers cracked loose. Hunks of stone shot from the crevice, and then the balcony itself rushed down toward them. It swelled in the interstices between buildings and cast a black shadow across Stonebrow's contingent.

"Forward!" he roared and charged out from beneath the stone. The rest of the contingent followed, their feet slapping the cobbles.

Overhead, the balcony shrieked as it fell.

Bounding out of its shadow, Stonebrow rounded the corner of a building. His troops piled in after him, the last dwarf diving to slide on his belly. Just behind them, the balcony struck ground. The road bucked, and a boom reverberated among the soaring towers. Hunks of stone hurled from the impact and slammed into walls, ricocheting. Stonebrow and his contingent crouched in the lee of the building and shielded their faces from shrapnel. A cloud of dust billowed around the corner and engulfed them.

Silence fell. Stonebrow waited a moment, breathing into his palm. Scree crackled beneath his hoof. He stepped forward and peered around the corner.

The balcony was no more than a long mound of rubble. The impact had pulverized it, and pieces littered the street. The walls of nearby towers were pitted from the shrapnel, and high above, other balconies shivered as if to crack loose as well.

"What was that?" Stonebrow chuffed, rock dust in his breath.

A nearby elf said, "Its magic failed."

"Magic?" Stonebrow mused. "What magic?"

"The magic that held the balconies. All these buildings are magical constructs. Those that couldn't stand without magic will begin to fall," the elf said.

"What are you talking about? What's wrong with the magic?"

The elf lifted an arrow and pointed to its steely tip. "This shaft is supposed to bear guidance magic that makes it unerring, but the magic is gone."

Stonebrow snatched up the arrow and bow, nocked, aimed toward a keyhole across the street, and shot. The arrow leaped out across the road, glanced off the side of a building, and tumbled end over end. The giant centaur watched it go.

"Magic is gone."

He turned to look toward the summit. "Something terrible has happened up there."

The elf stared into the distance. "It's not just up there. It's throughout Otaria. It's throughout the world."

* * * * *

A troop of goblins picked over the ravaged coliseum. Sure, most of it was rocks rocks rocks or sand sand sand, but sometimes you found a piece of something you could sell or a piece of somebody you could eat. There'd been elephants in the waiting pens when they'd gone down, and the goblins had just had to dig down ten feet to find a smorgasbord. Now, they were after gold. The betting booths had been robbed already, but there had to've been vaults below that nobody'd gotten to.

"C'mon, dig, you scabs!" roared the goblin captain as his troops hurled chunks of stone from the hole they had dug. It already delved through fifteen feet of rubble, and the crew had nearly cleared an intact corridor. "Holler as soon as somebody can worm through."

"I can make it, Cap!" called the youngest goblin. "Just a little wiggle!"

"Wiggle, then, boy! Wiggle and find me some gold." The captain peered down the black throat. Ears of skin spread wide on the wind, picking up the grunts and wheezes of struggle below. Then came a moment's jubilation, and a great splash. "What's happening? What's going on down there?"

"He's gone. The hallway's flooded."

"Flooded!" growled the captain. "How could it be flooded? We're a hundred feet above the swamp." Even so, he could hear the water—gurgling, rushing, bubbling all around. The captain scrambled up a slope of stone. He reached the peak and stood, gaping at the swamps.

Black waters lapped halfway up the rubble piles. The footbridges from adjacent land extended down into the wetlands and vanished. Coliseum Island was sinking.

Behind him, other goblins scrambled up the rubble field. They yammered like little dogs. "The water's rising, Cap! The hole's flooding! What do we do?"

"What do we do?" repeated the goblin captain. He watched the black tide inch up toward them. Among the ripples of the rising tide were the rugged backs of crocodiles. "We swim."

* * * * *

The great palace of Locus—a vision in the midst of a dream—began to dissolve. White walls of marble disintegrated. Each particle lost hold of its neighbors, and all sifted down as sand and silt. The palace poured into the lake at its base, filling it in.

Near the lake, Greenglades Forest withered. Three separate canopies and millions of tons of foliage desiccated. The barest breeze flaked them to ash. Even the beasts that laired there—monkeys and jaguars, birds of every plume—fell apart as if they had been made of nothing.

The Purity River dried and disappeared.

The Shadow Mountain fell in upon itself.

Even the original oasis was gone.

All of Topos returned to the sands that had spawned it. Even the Nightmare Lands, with their portals into the Blind Eternities—even they were only dunes of sand. The creations of Ixidor vanished like a dream.

* * * * *

They had all been so very kind. This room was the nicest, especially when the sun rose over the eastern sea and all of Eroshia glimmered like a geode. Lots of the inmates had no windows at all, let alone a window with such a glorious view. If it hadn't been for the bars, Dereg might've even felt he was still governor.

"Oh, the tea is hot this afternoon," he said to no one, whistling in and out to cool his seared lip. He put the cup down on the tray. It *was* hot. Lots of inmates never got tea or got it late or cold, but Dereg's tea always arrived on time and piping. It really was a luxury since the asylum was so full. Dereg wasn't the only one afflicted with "magic mania," the popular term for delusional psychosis. There were hundreds of others left in the wake of Karona.

Karona. He ached for her. He stared out the bars at a city bright with afternoon. The sky trams were running again, and workers crowded the rails. They had re-erected the great arch and the sea colossus, improving the spell work so that they would never fall again. Every last lantern had been replaced, and by night they made the city into a jewel. Yes, Eroshia was getting over its magic mania. If only Dereg could.

He lifted the teacup again, drew steam into his lungs, and took another tentative sip. The tea was just hot now, not scalding. The bitter liquid lolled on his tongue, and he swallowed it. She had been gone from Eroshia for nearly a year. Maybe soon he would be done with her.

Dereg shifted the cup back toward the tray. It was above his knee when a sudden and terrible tremor rushed through him. His hand convulsed, and the tea splashed on his leg.

"She's gone," he said quietly. "She's left the world."

Another psychotic episode. How could he know whether she was in the world or not? Instead of setting the cup down, he lifted it again and took another sip.

Beyond the window, people were screaming. They clung to the sky tram as it fell toward the street. It couldn't be true. Even if she were gone, how would that make trams fail? Another roar came. The great arch was tumbling, or the sea colossus.

"No, no. They can't be falling," Dereg said quietly to himself. "Even she doesn't wield *all* magic."

Still, as tea seeped through his pant leg, he couldn't stop the tears. He sat there until the sun set, until the lights in that great jewel would not twinkle. There was darkness over the sea and everywhere throughout Eroshia.

"She is gone from the world."

* * * * *

In the center of Urborg's Outer Isle stood the Heroes' Obelisk. Its five sides were inscribed with the names of those who had died in the Phyrexian War. Atop the obelisk were two stone faces, the bearded young hero Gerrard looking east and the queer-eyed sage Urza looking west. By day, the sun shone on this great monument, and by night it was lit by an array of power stones.

For the first few generations after the war, this island had been a place of spiritual pilgrimage. Folk came here to be moved by the lingering ghosts of those who had saved their world. Now, though, the island was a resort, with sandy beaches, seaside bungalows, tropical forests, and even the glowing and other-worldly obelisk.

No one sat in the black-marble benches anymore. No one said prayers, sang songs, or wept. Young people trooped in from the beaches to the great, glowing monument because they believed it granted virility.

Even now, in the moonless midnight, visitors gathered around the huge stone. Half-clad in swimwear, they gravitated toward one of the five sides. They traced the names inscribed there, which glowed with one of the five colors of magic, and leaned their lovers against the stone or retreated to the overgrown benches for more intense encounters.

The monument that had once honored the heroes of a world now was a deep-jungle liason spot. The dangers of the nighttime forest only accentuated the encounters.

Until the obelisk went dark. The names that had saved the world were gone. The champions of Dominaria—Urza and Gerrard—hid their faces in the black sky.

A generation who had never thought the world would need saving suddenly found themselves naked and stranded in the pitch-black heart of Urborg.

* * * * *

Amid the glaciers of Keld stood a strange and magical forest—the Skyshroud. For a century, it had been there, inviolate and warm despite the permafrost all around. No longer.

Fat white flakes tumbled among steaming vines. A cold wind stole through an arboreal village, silencing the laughter there. Elves emerged on their railed paths. They wrinkled their noses, smelling ice in the air. Their hands reached out, and flakes lit on their fingertips. The tiny works of art broke and melted to cold drops of water.

Not since Yawgmoth had there been so ominous a sign. That time, though, they had had Freyalise. This time, she was gone.

"What's happening?" asked an elf girl, too young to remember the war.

Her father knelt beside her. "The world is changing."

The platform where they stood suddenly gave way, and they fell. The man cried out the words of a levitation spell, but still they plunged. He was shouting more spells even when they struck the ground below.

* * * * *

Atop the crumbling city of Averru stood a handful of desolated souls. Kuberr, Lowallyn, Stonebrow, and a contingent of guards watched as their world fell to utter ruin. Magic had abandoned them all.

Kamahl stood apart from the others. Guilt set him apart. He had let Karona flee, taking with her the very life of Dominaria. Magic had fled from everything—except the Mirari sword. It glimmered in its scabbard on his back. The power of the Mirari must have come from another world.

If there was any hope for Dominaria, it resided in that wondrous sword.

CHAPTER 25

THE MIRROR WORLD

Amid the tangled skeins of the Blind Eternities, I find nothing worth clinging to.

My prophets are dying. They scrape at the plasma that encases them.

For their sake, I must grasp another line and ride it down. Will this be our fate, to flit world to world to world?

Something new enters my mind—a strong silver thread. It is the sort of string that links astral travelers to their bodies. I touch the line and sense the tensile strength of the mind. I latch on.

The silvery current drags us into the depths of the Chaos Sea. Energy boils away, and the silver road widens into a new world.

* * * * *

Karona stood on the mirror way, setting Sash and Waistcoat beside her. The prophets gasped a breath, and in sympathy Karona breathed too. The air was fresh and sharp, faintly metallic, but with none of the oily grime of Yawgmoth's realm.

A beautiful world unfolded before them—a looking-glass land beneath a sky crowded with faint stars. Every point of light in the heavens reflected in the plane below. Chaos swept back like stage curtains. To the right, a forest of geometrically perfect trees took form. Each had a straight and elegant trunk rising to branches at precise angles. There were fractal copies in twig, leaf, and stomata. All of it was silver, and each leaf was like a glass ornament. They shivered in metallic winds. To the left, the plane dropped away in a series of swooping plateaus, which at last delved into a great glassy canyon. Rugged walls gleamed above deep valleys where rivers of mercury ran. Mesas lifted their striated heads in the midst of the mazy waters.

"It's not a world," Sash said in awe, "it's an equation."

A BEAUTIFUL EQUATION.

"I hate math," Waistcoat added.

The curtains of chaos withdrew altogether, revealing a slightly curved horizon that separated the stars from their reflections. Directly before them, the road rose into a mighty pinnacle in silver. All around its perimeter stood rocky columns, as if this peak had been extruded volcanically from the underworld. At the height of that towering mesa stood a palace. It was larger even than Locus, its walls more sheer, its pediments more fanciful. Minarets twisted skyward all around, each in its own complex pattern. Flying buttresses linked keep to basilica to hall, as slender as they were strong. Silver and glass mixed in wall and window and brought the stars down to dance.

"Whoa! It's Locus all over!" Waistcoat said.

"No," Sash replied, his mouth hanging in awe. "Locus was a mad place. This place is all reason."

THE SILVER THREAD LED US HERE. THIS MUST BE THE PALACE OF THE RULER.

Waistcoat turned toward her, worry wringing his face. "Let's just rest awhile and move on. We don't fit in this world either."

Next to him, Sash looked similarly exhausted, but he kept his lips clamped.

WE DON'T KNOW YET ABOUT THIS WORLD. PERHAPS WE'LL BELONG HERE.

"What will we eat? An ingot?" asked Sash. "What will we drink? A glass full of glass?" He crossed arms over his chest. "We'd've fit in fine here when we were just living holes, but now we've got bodies, and bodies need food and water."

"And other bodies," Waistcoat put in. "Am I s'posed to make it with a mirror?"

"It won't have been the first time."

I MUST MEET THE MIND THAT MADE THIS PLACE. ITS MAJESTY OVERWHELMS ME. COME.

She gathered her prophets in a double-armed embrace, rose from the silvery ground, and soared up the cliff.

As natural as this outcrop had seemed, close up, its convolutions followed a precise calculus. These were not rough planes of fracture, but facets chiseled by a ceaseless mind. Whoever had made this place had designed every leaf, every contour. Here was a mind like Ixidor's, vastly creative, though with none of the torment.

Karona topped the great cliff and floated above a turreted wall. No one walked the parapets or manned the bartizans, though silvery flags flew in lofty breezes. Beyond the wall stretched a garden in florid symmetry, with paths leading to the gate to the palace. Karona swooped beneath the wide-open arch and into the palace bailey. There, she set down on a flagstone walk.

Her prophets sighed as she placed them on their feet.

The palace was so near now, they had to crane their necks to see its upper reaches. High up, windows abounded, but lower down the walls were solid metal.

"How do we call the master of the palace?" Sash said. "We can't just wander around and shout."

Karona's eyes swept along one wall, where a pair of double doors stood. Beside it was a small guardhouse, and within it, a figure slumped in sleep. She drifted toward it.

The prophets shrugged and followed Karona toward the guard station.

It was a simple structure, tall and pointed, though its materials made it seem fine. Within sat a sleeping man, bald and barefooted. His flesh was a lusterless gray, though the robe he wore gleamed with silver threads. Nothing else in this world had the tarnished cast of his skin, rough with age and grime.

Karona stopped at the doorway and peered down at the man. Even her radiance did not illumine him. He didn't stir.

"He's dead," Sash said. "Did you catch that whiff of rot?"

"That was me," Waistcoat confessed.

"WAKE UP. WE WANT TO MEET YOUR MASTER."

The man shifted. He woke like a lizard, his eyes slitting with cold-blooded patience. Beneath those crusted lids were orbs like great bearings—steely and inscrutable. The man looked neither young nor old, good nor evil. He had a nose and mouth like other men but didn't seem to breathe. Beneath the silvery cloak he wore, the man's chest was still. He lifted his head and peered at the three figures.

"Who are you?"

"YOU SPEAK OUR LANGUAGE."

Nodding his gray head, the man said, "I heard you speak. I know the tongue. I speak your language. Now, who are you?"

"I AM KARONA OF DOMINARIA. THESE ARE MY FRIENDS, SASH AND WAISTCOAT."

The gray man quietly considered. "You're the one called 'Scourge.' "

"I AM."

A bleak smile filled his lips, and his teeth looked like shiny nail heads. "Dominaria seems to have many scourges."

There was nothing to say to that.

The gray man rose, taller and broader than he had seemed when asleep. He filled the box, his shoulders brushing the walls and his head touching the ceiling. "I'll take you to the master of this place, though he may not grant you an audience."

"WE WILL SEE."

He blinked enigmatically at them. "Yes, we will. Follow me."

He emerged from the guardhouse and walked to the double doors. With a touch of his hand, the doors swung inward, opening on a grand entryway. Its floor was done in black glass, and from it rose a broad stairway with frosted spindles and a long, curved rail. It meandered up through four stories of empty space.

"I'd love to ride that banister," Waistcoat said.

The silvery walls contained etched-glass windows, opening on a courtyard garden. Overhead hung three chandeliers, their sconces empty. The metal provided illumination enough.

"WHAT'S THE NAME OF THIS PLACE?"

The gray man stepped out across the floor. "This world is Argentum. This palace is Galdroon." He spread his hand across his chest. "I am the Warden."

"Like, as in, a prison warden?" Waistcoat asked.

"No, moron," Sash snapped. "Like as in a protector, right?"

The Warden didn't respond, only headed toward the stair. "The master of this place is Lord Macht." As the other three climbed behind him, he said, "Lord Macht is familiar with your world. While he was building Argentum, he sent probes to many other planes. He sought to learn of their ecologies, flora, and fauna. Most of the probes worked well, and the beauties of Argentum are fashioned after them. The probe to Dominaria, though—well, Lord Macht has darkened his eye to that probe."

Sash sniffed. "What's so bad about Dominaria?"

"What's good about it?" Waistcoat asked. "After all, they threw us out—"

"Shut up!" Sash hissed.

"That's what's wrong," said the Warden. "Everyone fights. The probe made them fight only more. It was meant to see and learn, but the people of Dominaria thought it was a prize to win. They flocked to it and killed each other over it. They saw in it whatever they most wanted, and there is no more dangerous thing in any world than desire."

"I KNOW. I'VE BEEN ITS OBJECT."

"Lord Macht has closed his eye to Dominaria. His probe proved to be among the great destroyers of that world." The Warden's mouth hitched ironically. "So have you."

"Hey," Waistcoat said. "Watch who you're talking to. Karona's basically a goddess. You're just, well, a warden."

"*The* Warden," the gray man corrected, the crooked smile still on his teeth.

He led them to the top of the stairs and out into a grand ballroom. A vast mosaic filled the floor amid fluted columns and mirror walls. Above it all hung a great glass ceiling. Every panel gleamed with starlight, and the shifting firmament cast waltzing lines through the room. The space felt infinite, as though Lord Macht had boxed a corner of the universe and set it within his palace, but it also felt cold and desolate until Karona entered it. Faint starlight could not compare to her native radiance. The light from her being spread through those angled facets and lit every pewter seam of the floor.

"Whoa! Look at the picture in the floor!" Waistcoat said.

Each piece of tile in the mosaic had been hand-cut and placed to depict gears and cogs, flywheels, ratchets, springs, and levers. Close up, it seemed merely an assortment of odd mechanisms. As the three travelers wandered out across the floor, though, they perceived within the general gloom a pair of eyes and a pair of massive hands. Fingers of metal reached up from the dark well, a prisoner yearning for starlight above his cell. The image was poignant, a man trapped in mechanism.

"WHO IS THIS?"

The Warden studied Karona then glanced down at the image.

"Just some mythic figure. You'll have to ask Lord Macht—if he grants you an audience."

Karona walked on the mosaic, her feet tracing along one giant hand. She strode from the hand toward the eyes.

"THIS *IS* LORD MACHT. HERE IS THE SORT OF MAN WHO WOULD BUILD A WORLD LIKE ARGENTUM—A MECHANICAL MAN. MACHINES AND MATHEMATICS ARE LIFE TO HIM, BUT HE IS IMPRISONED BY THEM. HE LOOKS TO THE STARS, REACHES HANDS AND EYES TO OTHER WORLDS, HOPING TO FIND SOMETHING BEYOND HIS SILVERY CELL."

"You presume too much," the Warden said. "You've not even met Lord Macht, and you make up these stories. There's no sense in seeking an audience with him. You must go, now, back to Dominaria."

Karona stared piercingly at the gray man.

"YOU EXERCISE MORE POWER THAN A WARDEN—EVEN *THE* WARDEN. YOU ARE WARDEN IN BOTH SENSES OF THE TERM, KEEPER OF THE PRISON AND RULER OF THE LAND."

"You have been asked to leave. You will incur the wrath of Lord Macht—"

"MACHT MEANS MAKER, AND THE MAKER OF THIS SILVER WORLD IS ALSO ITS PRISONER—A PLANESWALKER AT HOME NOWHERE ELSE."

"You are wrong," the Warden said, fear in his gray face. "If you said such things to Lord Macht—"

"*YOU* ARE LORD MACHT. YOU SENT THE PROBE TO DOMINARIA, AND I FOLLOWED ITS SILVER LINE HERE. DOMINARIA CALLED YOUR GREAT PRIZE THE MIRARI, THE DESIRE OF NATIONS. THEIR DESIRE MADE IT A DESTROYER, BUT YOUR DESIRE CREATED IT IN THE FIRST PLACE."

Karona's nimbus grew brighter, and she gestured to the mosaic.

"THOSE ARE YOUR HANDS AND EYES REACHING OUT INTO THE MULTIVERSE. THOSE ARE THE PROBES YOU SENT TO LEARN OF OTHER WORLDS. YOU SEEK REDEMPTION FOR THIS MECHANISTIC PRISON."

"I do not," said the gray man. He averted his gaze, knowing he had given himself away. "Argentum is a perfect world. I have let no flaw enter it."

"YOU'VE TAKEN THE FLAWS OF DOMINARIA INTO YOU. THE MIRARI DARKENED MORE THAN YOUR EYES. YOUR WHOLE BEING HAS TURNED GRAY. YOU NO LONGER REACH WITH EYES AND HANDS TOWARD THE MULTIVERSE BUT SIT, COLLAPSED AND SLEEPING, OUTSIDE YOUR OWN PALACE."

Lord Macht's voice was low. "Truly you are a destroyer."

"WE ARE ALIKE, YOU AND I. OUR POWER IS DESIRE. THE BEST PART OF DESIRE IS CREATION, AND THE WORST PART IS DESTRUCTION. FOR FEAR OF DESTRUCTION, YOU'VE GIVEN UP YOUR POWER, YOUR DESIRE."

"You must leave! You cannot remain!" he said, though he lifted his hands before him and backed away.

"WHAT WILL YOU DO, GO BACK TO SLEEPING IN THE GUARD-HOUSE? THIS IS YOUR WORLD. YOU CREATED IT. DON'T LIVE IN IT LIKE A PRISONER. ONCE YOU SHONE WITH DESIRE. YOU CAN SHINE AGAIN. I CAN SCOUR THE DARKNESS FROM YOU AND REAWAKEN THE BEAMING BEING YOU ARE."

She advance, but he no longer retreated.

"ONLY LET ME."

The gray man stared into her face, radiance sinking into his dull skin. "Yes, Karona. I want to shine again."

Karona reached out her arms and wrapped the gray man in her embrace. Few creatures had ever borne that touch without going mad, and perhaps Lord Macht wouldn't either. He trembled, light pouring into him.

At first his gray flesh only drank in the radiance, sending none back, but soon the luminosity welled up in every tissue. It bled from his pores in bright pinpoints and curled from his ears and nose in hot wafts. The gray could not contain the power. It blazed like coals, red then white, and consumed even the silvery garment he wore. Lord Macht shone like a lantern's wick.

Waistcoat and Sash winced away, shielding their eyes from the spectacle. In that place of silvered glass, the transformation was amplified a hundredfold. He seemed a being made of lightning.

Still, Karona clung to him. The power of desire flashed both ways along the conduit. They fed upon each other, the goddess and the planeswalker. She too blazed.

The great chamber caught their light and sent it skyward, as if these two could cut new stars.

When at last they parted, both were changed. Lord Macht had a body like quicksilver, mercurial and utterly reflective. He shone like the Mirari itself, as if the thing had been drawn from his own flesh. All vestige of gray was gone. He was once again the color of his world. Karona's change was inward but no less profound. The weary woundedness of her eyes was gone. In its place was a new certainty.

Lord Macht went to his knees before her. "Karona! This world can be yours as well as mine. Yes, I am the one reaching out of a mechanistic prison, and you are the one I was reaching for. Remain here with me!"

Karona looked down into his eyes, gleaming with white purity.

"I CANNOT REMAIN. YOU KNOW THAT. YOU HAVE FOUND YOUR DESIRE AGAIN AND ARE EMPOWERED BY IT. SO TOO HAVE I."

She gazed up through the windows at the starry host.

"DOMINARIA IS MY WORLD, MY HOME. I WAS BORN THERE AND BELONG IN IT. OVER THE LAST YEAR I HAVE LEARNED WHO I AM, WHAT I CAN DO, AND WHAT I SHOULD DO, BUT NOT UNTIL NOW HAVE I HAD THE WILL TO PUT IT ALL INTO ACTION. YOU'VE COMPLETED ME, LORD MACHT. NOW I GO TAKE WHAT I MOST DESIRE."

The planeswalker wore an agonized expression. "What could you desire?"

"DOMINARIA. THEY CANNOT BANISH ME FROM MY WORLD. I'M GOING BACK. I'LL TAKE IT, AND I'LL RULE IT."

Bowing his head in what might have been resignation, Lord

Macht said, "I will send you back. For me, it is a simple thing. Where do you wish to go to begin your conquest?"

"EROSHIA."

CHAPTER 26

ARISE, SHINE

Above a benighted city, Karona and her prophets appeared. They had selected the highest spot, the grand cupola of the Eroshian Temple. It had once been the center of worship for the twin gods, Lomius and Lor. From this night on, it would be the Mount of Karona.

She shone atop its stone dome, but the rest of the great building was dark, as were the massive foundations and the mount on which it stood and the city all around. Karona's banishment had stripped all magic from Eroshia, and the people had already burned through every candle. This was their dark night of the soul.

SOON THEY'LL SEE ME.

Her prophets nodded, their shadows falling sharply away, like dead men lying on the dome.

DON'T SPEAK UNTIL MY POWER HAS STRETCHED TO THE HORIZONS. I'M REINING IT IN SO THAT IT DOES NOT DISSOLVE STONE OR WOOD, AND I'LL KEEP IT FROM EXTENDING BEYOND MY LINE OF SIGHT. THOSE WHO RECEIVE ME WILL HAVE MAGIC IN ABUNDANCE. THOSE WHO DO NOT WILL HAVE NOTHING.

Waistcoat and Sash nodded and sulked.

The dome flared as a ring of magical lanterns awakened in the presence of their mistress. Her nimbus was expanding. She had returned to Dominaria and brought its magic back with her. Gears shifted in the cupola, and the temple's great bell began to toll. Its peals rushed out into the night, advancing with the wall of magic. Chandeliers blazed within the temple, and its arched windows hurled wedges of light down on the city. At the base of the temple hill, streetlights ignited. In all directions, the radiance raced out through the city.

The shattered windows of a mansion blared with spell-alarms.

The forges of a blacksmith ignited and shot fire against the walls.

A hurdy-gurdy in a ditch cranked brokenly and filled the air with twisted music.

Aerial trams dragged across rooftops, and cables sparked in whirring wheels.

Carriages lurched down the streets, crashing into houses.

Horses shied as their enchanted mangers spewed hay.

Every window of every home lit, and shouts followed as folk startled up from bed. They came rushing out into avenues aflame with magic. Their neighbors pointed toward the tolling cupola.

THEY SEE ME BUT DON'T SPEAK YET. MY POWER ISN'T COMPLETE.

The advancing tide of light swept along the shore and out over the boats in their moorings. Animated oars drove boats up from the water and sent them scuttling ashore.

THIS IS MY WORLD. I WON'T LIVE IN IT LIKE A SLAVE. I'LL RULE IT. THE CREATURES HAVE TO LEARN TO LIVE WITH ME AND I TO LIVE WITH THEM. I'LL NOT BE BANISHED AGAIN.

Karona gazed out to sea, where the last boats lit, many miles out.

I'LL SEND MY MAGIC NO FARTHER. ALL THOSE IT TOUCHES CAN SEE ME. IT IS TIME.

Placing her hands on the backs of the prophets, Karona conveyed to them a spell that tuned their voices to the city. When they spoke, even the wind and waves would carry their words. She spoke through them.

Sash stepped out along the dome and lifted his hands. "Behold Eroshia, Behold Otaria—the day of wrath is upon you." His voice echoed down the city streets, bulling past the folk who stood there.

On Karona's other side, Waistcoat lifted his arms. "When last Karona came to you, you launched a tribal war to gain her. One worshiper slew another. All was madness."

"Now again she comes to you, and there will be no war," went on Sash. "In Karona, you are one. All who bow to her, to Magic incarnate, will live and inherit the world. All who resist . . ." He glanced back over his shoulder, his eyes pleading.

Karona nodded sternly.

"All who resist will die."

Waistcoat continued, "The darkness you have endured is a world without Karona. Without her, you will die. Those who bow to Karona subject themselves to life, and those who refuse subject themselves to death."

Sash visibly trembled as he finished. "It comes down to this: Karona was born of Dominaria, and Dominaria cannot live without her. Any of you who cannot live *with* her cannot live at all."

Beyond the beaming pinnacle of the temple, the city gleamed with magic. In every street, citizens stood, their faces round and dim. Still, no one bowed.

Waistcoat cried out, "The day of wrath is upon you! Fall to your faces! Kneel before her, or die. Now!"

In every avenue, road, and path, knees kissed the ground then bellies and faces . . . but not all. Hundreds did not bow before Karona. They had heard; they knew the penalty of resistance. They left her no choice.

* * * * *

I DO NOT WISH THAT EVEN ONE OF THEM WOULD DIE, BUT THESE HUNDREDS ARE INCORRIGIBLE. THEY WOULD BANISH ME. THEY WOULD

BATTLE THEIR NEIGHBORS. IN THEIR REBELLION, THESE HUNDRED WOULD KILL THOUSANDS. IT IS NOT HATRED THAT LIFTS MY HANDS TOWARD THEM BUT LOVE.

THE CLOSEST APOSTATE IS A BURLY BLACKSMITH WHO WEARS ONLY BREECHES. FROM ARMS AND CHEST AND SHOULDERS RISE GRAY HAIRS LIKE SO MANY CURLS OF SMOKE. HE TRUSTS IN HIS OWN ARMS, IN FIRE AND STEEL, AND IN NOTHING ELSE. HE DOES NOT TRUST IN MAGIC, BUT MAGIC WILL UNDO HIM.

POWER LEAPS FROM MY EYES AND JABS INTO HIM. HE SHAKES LIKE A MAN STRUCK BY LIGHTNING. BOLTS ARC BETWEEN HIS FINGERS, AND HIS HAIR FLASHES AWAY.

HE BURNS, A LIVING FLAME. THE FAT IN HIS BODY HAS IGNITED, AND HIS SKELETON IS VISIBLE FOR A MOMENT BEFORE HE FLARES ALMOST AS BRIGHT AS I. HIS LIGHT FAILS, LEAVING A DEEPER DARKNESS THAN BEFORE.

MY LIGHT SHINES. I TURNED FROM THE DARK SPOT WHERE HE HAD BEEN. I SCAN THE CITY STREETS. MANY HAVE SEEN THE MAN'S DEMISE AND FALL TO THEIR FACES. LET EACH NECESSARY DEATH PREVENT MANY UNNECESSARY ONES.

* * * * *

"Behold, Eroshia! Behold, Otaria!" cried out Sash, tears in his eyes. "The day of wrath is upon you. Bow before Karona!"

"Please!" Waistcoat shouted, and both Sash and Karona looked toward him in surprise. These were not Karona's words, but his own. "Please! Don't you see? She'll kill you if you don't! Get down! Everybody, please! Lie down and don't move, and nobody'll get hurt!"

His pleas reverberated among the doors and windows of Eroshia and knocked a few more to their knees but not all of them.

* * * * *

HERE ARE MY TRUE FOES—DEMONIACS. THEY ARE THE SCOURGES, NOT I.

POWER POURS FROM MY EYES, REACHING DOWN AMONG CHIMNEYS TO STRIKE A POXY WOMAN. MAGIC FLOODS THROUGH HER, IMMOLATING HER FLESH.

THIS IS NOT MURDER. THIS IS A CLEANSING.

WITHOUT EVIL FOLK SUCH AS THESE, THERE WILL BE NO WAR, NO HATRED, NO SUFFERING, NO PAIN. I WILL RULE A NEW PARADISE.

* * * * *

When at last the thrashing was done and the woman was gone and the last jags of power slipped to silence, there came another terrible sound. Glass shattered on a nearby prominence. Screams, once muffled by the glass, burst forth, punctuated by the thud of fists on metal.

"This is how much I love you!" cried a voice, so high and manic that it could have been male or female. "Here, Karona! Here, I have waited for you! Here is how much I love you!" There came a brutal clang—flesh and bone on iron, and another scream.

WHAT IS THAT PLACE?

Sash stared at it, thick-walled and spike-gated. "The asylum," he said, forgetting that the spell flung his words out to the multitude. "You toured it once, healing everyone, remember?"

"Looks full now," observed Waistcoat.

I'LL HEAL THEM AGAIN.

Another clang, and mortar failed. Bars fell from the highest window of the asylum, taking a large chunk of wall with them. A man tumbled out onto the ground ten feet below his cell. The fall might have maimed a sane man, but this inmate scrambled up from the rubble and stood, eyes peeled and mouth gaping gladly at Karona. He was whip-thin and wiry, his hair standing in strange tangles from his head.

"Bow down!" Waistcoat shouted. "For the love of life, bow down!"

"Oh, I'll do better than bow, Karona!" he vowed, his voice nearly singing. "I love you so much, I'll bow to death for you!"

"It's the governor."

DEREG.

"No, Governor," cried Sash. "Bow to live! Stand to die!"

Dereg released a long, tortured laugh. "I can't stand life or death. I can never be near enough to you nor far enough from you. My love for you is unbearable, so I'll bow to death, for love, my lady!" He ran to the cliff nearby and dived.

No!

He hung there in the air, and it seemed as if he might fly to her. Then the jealous world grabbed him and dragged him down. He plummeted between buildings and was gone but for the terrible crack of impact.

GOVERNOR DEREG IS DEAD—MY FIRST HOST, MY MOST ARDENT WORSHIPER.

"Poor, tormented wretch," Sash said. "First his home, then his mind, then his life."

HE DESTROYED HIMSELF, THOUGH. I AM BLAMELESS.

"Bow, damn you!" shouted Waistcoat. "Bow, or die!"

* * * * *

DESPITE IT ALL, WHEN I LIFT MY EYES, OTHER FACES STILL MEET MINE. THEY LEAVE ME NO CHOICE. I WILL FILL THEM WITH MY PRESENCE UNTIL THEY BURST.

* * * * *

He moved swiftly, shadow to shadow, keeping himself behind the buildings. The people lying in the streets made the way treacherous, but the middle-aged elf merely leaped over them. He was more worried about the other citizens who stood and gazed on Karona. They could betray him.

Elionoway would not look up to Karona's face. He knew too well the power of her eyes. Tonight was a night of ultimatums, bow or die, but there was one other possibility: flee.

Elionoway had run from the library where he had worked near the city center, through a score of blocks, and now here, within sight of the gates. Karona had lashed out a dozen times while he fled, but so far, her victims had been others. If he could just skirt past this final block of pie-faced folk, he could slip through the gates and down the Vonian ravine, and beyond, to life.

He fetched up beneath a thatched eave and gazed out along the path to the gate. The geography was merciful. For much of the way, row houses would shield him from the eyes of Karona. Moving slowly, he shifted along the shop fronts.

In the street before him stood four people, defiantly refusing to bow but unable to look away. They were doomed.

Elionoway's eye caught on the nearest figure—a leathery dwarf with a scowl that belied his good nature. It was his old friend Brunk. A frisson of guilt moved through Elionoway. He couldn't leave Brunk to die tonight.

"Hey!" he hissed. "Brunk! Idiot! Just look away! Look away!"

Brunk twitched but couldn't draw his eyes from the Glorious One.

Elionoway crouched, lifted a pebble, and tossed it. The stone sailed out to crack against the dwarf's forehead. It bounded off, leaving a small indentation but otherwise not changing his expression. Snorting, Elionoway resorted to an old standby.

"Hey, Brunk, free beer!"

"What?" asked the dwarf, though he didn't even glance from Karona.

"Free beer! Just come here, and I'll give you a free beer."

"It's a trick," groused Brunk, though his eyes did flit to the shadows a moment before returning to Karona. "There's no such thing as free beer."

"Damned dwarf," Elionoway muttered. Aloud, he said, "Look, you'll never know unless you come here. If you stand there, you'll die, and never have another beer, free or not."

That got through. Brunk stared into the shadows. "The lady said, 'bow or die.' "

"And I say, 'free beer.' "

Brunk seemed to consider. "That's a gospel I can understand." He turned from the light and strode purposefully into the shadows. Stalking up before Elionoway, he said, "Well?"

"It's me, Elionoway," the elf replied. "I just saved your life, Brunk."

"Where's the beer?" Brunk asked.

Elionoway almost told him that "free beer" was a metaphor for choosing life in all its bitter intoxicating loveliness, but Brunk was, after all, a dwarf.

"It's hid in the ravine. We've just got to sidle along this street and through the gate to get it."

"What's the catch?" the dwarf said suspiciously.

Heaving a great sigh, Elionoway said, "The catch is that you've got to help me tell others about the free beer."

Even in the darkness, the dwarf's rumpled brow showed clearly. "Less for us."

"No. This is enchanted beer. The more who drink of it, the more there is."

"Oh." Brunk sniffed. Then, cupping hands around his mouth, he bellowed, "Free beer!"

* * * * *

When morning dawned, Eroshia slept. Fifty thousand faithful souls rested in their beds. Three hundred faithless ones rested in their graves.

Sash and Waistcoat sat on the cupola dome, their faces turned down toward the burned and battered city. The streets were marred with black scorches where citizens once stood.

Karona sat in the center of the dome and greeted the sun.

IN ONE NIGHT WE'VE CAPTURED A CITY AND GAINED AN ARMY.

"And we've killed three hundred unarmed civilians," Sash said.

THREE HUNDRED DEATHS TO CAPTURE A CITY OF FIFTY THOUSAND. THAT IS VIRTUALLY A BLOODLESS VICTORY.

Waistcoat chewed on his lip. "What're you gonna do with 'em, I mean the fifty thousand?"

THEY ARE MY ARMY. THEY WILL MARCH WITH ME TO THE OTHER CITIES. WE WILL MAKE WAR ACROSS OTARIA UNTIL THE WHOLE CONTINENT BOWS. THEN, WE WILL SHIP TO KELD AND PARMA, BENALIA AND LLANOWAR, YAVIMAYA AND SHIV.

"A world war."

YES. IT IS THE WORLD'S WAR. I WOULD HAVE LIVED AT PEACE WITH EVERYONE, BUT THEY SWARMED ME AND KILLED EACH OTHER AND THREW ME OUT. BUT I WILL REMAIN. THE WORLD IS MINE.

She levitated slowly, her legs unfolding until she hovered above the Mount of Karona. Extending her hands to her sides, she reached out toward the horizons. Her fingers crooked inward, as if she were gathering a cloth.

NOW, I DRAW IN MY MAGIC. EROSHIA HAS SEEN AND CHOSEN, AND MY POWER REMAINS WITH THEM, BUT THE REST OF THE WORLD CAN STARVE FOR IT UNTIL IT SEES ME COMING IN GLORY.

The ocean waves lost some of their sparkle, the distant fields their buzzing glow. The very spark of magic retreated from the world into the woman who held it all.

* * * * *

Elionoway had led nearly seventy refugees out of the doomed city and into the Vonian Hills. Now they bedded down in a secret glen. Despite the snoring and incessant complaints about the lack of beer, these folk would survive.

The Tyrant would not find them.

Elionoway guarded them from his post in a nearby tree. He watched the walls of Eroshia and only wished he could save the rest of the people.

The air changed. Life went out of everything, and the world felt dead. Karona had withdrawn her magic, and without her, the hillsides were desolate. It was a bitter pill.

Karona was the Tyrant, yes, but she was also beautiful, powerful, and necessary.

"I know I made the right choice," Elionoway told himself. Still, he could not stop the tears.

CHAPTER 27

MIRARI VISIONS

Dawn stretched avid fingers across the City of Averru but found only desolation. The Glyphs had turned to statues, the towers were falling, and Averru himself had vanished. Lowallyn and Kuberr, stripped of magic and immortality, had retreated from the high, holy place. They had gone with Stonebrow and his platoon to find what might remain of the Gilded Mage Pub and the beer of a certain dwarf brewer.

Only one person lingered beside the shattered temple. Kamahl kicked a shard of rock, which scudded across the red sandstone and crashed against other remnants, sending them out. One solid kick could make twenty stones slide and spin. One simple act could rock a whole world.

Kamahl gritted his teeth. He'd been chewing on that thought for a whole week. He had set this cataclysm in motion with a single stroke—across the belly of his sister. If he had not wounded her and betrayed her to death, there would have been no Phage, no Akroma, no Karona. If not for Kamahl and his sword, Dominaria would still have its magic. He kicked another stone and watched it ricochet.

The Mirari sword had begun the evil, and it would end it.

Kamahl reached up over his shoulder. His hand tightened around the Mirari, which tingled with power. Ever since Karona's banishment, the Mirari had grown stronger. Its tarnish had steamed away, and it had reverted to its former self. Luckily, Kamahl was no longer his former self. He could resist the sword's seductions. It promised great power to any who could grasp and wield it and great destruction to any who tried but failed.

"Try me," Kamahl rumbled, drawing the sword from his shoulder sheath. It leaped into the air above him, glad to be free. The morning sun shone golden on that naked blade, and the Mirari gleamed like molten silver. It tried to speak to Kamahl, an inhuman voice, but he would not listen.

"Remember the desert. I tamed you there. I'll tame you again, today."

With that, Kamahl began his formal exercises. Man and blade both knew these ritual kata. They mapped out the perilous passage toward union between sword and wielder. Perfectly executed, they brought alliance. Botched, they brought destruction.

The sword scribed a long, slow line, its pommel resting against Kamahl's heart and its tip tracing the horizon. It snapped heavenward, a lightning rod inviting the powers of air into it, and down toward the ground, evoking the strength of stone. East in the place of beginnings and new growth, west in the place of endings and death, north where there is law and south where there is desire. In each cardinal direction, the blade took into it a different form of Dominaria's vitality, but its core strength came from beyond the world.

You know nothing, Kamahl, the sword said. *I'll show you what I've seen.*

An aven stands crucified. His head and feet are tied to the axis mundi. His wings are nailed to beams that point north and east, his hands to beams that point west and south. His people swarm about him, sculpting his dead form—a feather here, a tendon there, that he might be their perfect expiation.

Kamahl turned away from that stark image, swinging the sword through a series of lateral arcs.

A fat man in robes of black leather eats and eats. He rams food down as quickly as he can, hardly tasting it. In truth, his insatiable appetite is due to the maggots that eat his fat even as he creates more. He is consuming above and consumed below.

"I've seen such things," Kamahl hissed as he swung the great blade from his face and around his back, "the sins of the Cabal and the Northern Order."

You haven't seen all of them.

A cephalid's tentacles spread through waters charged with its own ink. Though it cannot see or comprehend, it apprehends, and the things it grabs it twists to its own ends. It turns over a stone to find the food that hides beneath; shifts another to make a barrier against the current; topples a third to plug the shaft that holds a foe. What it turns are not stones, but the grasping tentacles of others cephalids.

"Yes, the Mirari has seen our greatest faults—"

But you have not. Not yet.

A brass-fleshed barbarian climbs a heap of his dead folk. He wishes to ascend the heights of his tribe and does so by slaying them one by one and piling them at his feet.

"I'm not that man."

The same barbarian sits in a deep forest, his fingers become roots and his mind become the rot that slays it.

"I am not that man!"

There was silence from the sword. The blade had tried him, and he had indeed transcended his past. Now it would show him his future:

The goddess of Magic tumbles forever through the Blind Eternities, and her world dies for want of her . . . or she returns to conquer the world that had rejected her and becomes its immortal tyrant . . . or she is captured, and those who hold her crush the world in their iron fists. . . . All are doomsdays for Dominaria.

"Unless I kill her."

Are you that man, Kamahl?

He was surrounded by a storm of metal. His every swing of the sword was vicious, as if he wished to cut himself away from the world. In place of blue sky and red stone, Kamahl saw only the glint of edges and the sparkle of steel. A cocoon of light formed around him.

He had killed her once and twice and thrice. Could he bear to kill her again?

The nimbus of metal solidified around him. His whirling arms and whirring blade merged into utter stillness. A silvery plane spread before him, with a starry sky above. Every heavenly body shone back from within the admiring ground. A pinnacle with a great palace soared before him. Though he no longer held the Mirari sword, he sense that it was all around him. He had entered it, and through it he had entered another world.

In the palace of silver and glass, a light dawned. It didn't beam like a star, in all directions, but shone down on him with intent. The figure grew, enlarging as it emerged from walls of silver. It drifted down the shaft of light that pooled at Kamahl's feet.

Shielding his eyes with one hand, Kamahl squinted.

Within the light was a human shape—a muscular man. He seemed a statue of polished metal, every contour shining brilliantly. His silvery body did not just reflect light but shed it. The silver man touched down before Kamahl. He was tall and muscular, physically similar to Kamahl, though without a hair on his head or body. His eyes were intense, his face focused and serious. He stood for a long while in front of Kamahl before he spoke.

"Hello, Kamahl. Welcome to Argentum. I am Lord Macht."

Kamahl slowly nodded, though the words only jumbled in his mind. "What is this place? How do you know me?"

"I know all about you," replied Lord Macht. "The Mirari is my eye. I've seen through it and been with you through these five terrible years."

Blinking, Kamahl said simply, "Why?"

"I once walked your world as you do, understanding only in part. Even in my ignorance, I helped save Dominaria—as you will. Terrible things remain in your world, things that darkened my eye and darkened me. Only Karona could set me free."

A bitter smile spread across Kamahl's face. "Ah, now I see your seduction. Always you offer the heart's desire—that which will destroy. You're going to tell me that Karona must live, that she must be given the world as her footstool."

Sadness came into that gleaming face. "No. Though she saved me, though I worship her, I've seen how she is a destroyer in your world. Dominaria cannot survive without her magic, but nor can it bear her presence. There is but one salvation for Dominaria, and it is a difficult one."

"What is it? I will do whatever must be done."

"You must kill Karona. I will instruct you how."

Kamahl gritted his teeth. "You betray her lightly."

"No. There is nothing light about this," replied Lord Macht. "And though it may seem a betrayal, better that Karona die than that she become a monster."

* * * * *

No more motley assortment of creatures had ever gone in search of a pub.

In the lead were two former gods, incarnate but divested of all power—hungry and thirsty. Behind them trooped General Stonebrow, expatriated from Krosan (most recently). His wandering ways had been a vain attempt to undo the doom of the gods, but now he strode straight for beer.

Behind him were others with checkered pasts—elves, dwarfs, humans, avens, mantis-folk—witnesses of the apocalypse who presided over the disenchanting last days of Dominaria.

They all needed a pub.

Golden-eyed Kuberr shoved hands into his black overcoat and stared at the building that towered at the end of the road. "This is your pub?"

Stonebrow stomped to a halt behind them. "Ah, the Mage. I haven't been here for a year. It has . . . grown."

They all gazed at the Gilded Mage. It had become an enormous tower, reaching high into the sky, even after having lost its curved top. A wide, flat tree was imbedded in the front wall. It rose twenty stories and extended leafy boughs out into the air. A few of the branches had snapped off when great chunks of stone had fallen, and wood and rock lay before the building.

With a tanned hand, Lowallyn rubbed his week-old beard. "Surely Averru would've preserved at least this one pub."

"I'd've kept all of 'em," Kuberr replied. His stomach chose that moment to let out a voracious growl. "It's easy for you guys. Your bodies are old. I'm a teenager. I'm supposed to be eating twice my weight every day."

"That still wouldn't be as much as I need," Stonebrow said.

Kuberr snarled, "Oh, go graze."

Lowallyn laughed. "I'd forgotten how funny life is. Twenty thousand years of oblivion makes a fellow too serious. Life's a joke. If you don't laugh, the joke's on you."

"Oh, shut up," Kuberr said. "I'm still hungry."

"Hey, Kuberr?" Lowallyn said.

"What?"

"What's the sound of one hand clapping?"

"See, that's the kind of stupid—" he stopped short as Lowallyn made a clapping motion with his one hand.

Stonebrow guffawed. The sound was infectious; anyone within half a block was already shaking from it. The whole crew laughed, then, and the ancient numena traded shoulder punches.

Stonebrow stomped up the rubble pile and set his fingers in a tall vertical crack in the tree. "These used to be doors. They used to open." He kicked aside a great bough and set his hooves. With massive fingers, he pulled at the crack.

The rest of the group approached over the rubble and struggled to pull open the doors. They wouldn't budge, grown shut.

"Clear out," Stonebrow said. He pivoted around, bringing his hind legs up beside the bole of the tree. "I wish Chester were here. Still—" He raised his back legs and lashed out. The hooves struck solidly on the wood, denting it and producing a hollow boom. Eyebrows went up all around, and Stonebrow kicked again. The wood splintered in two long sections. A third kick crashed through. Stonebrow hopped away from the opening even as the rest of the crew surged forward.

They looked in, and their silence did not bode well. Then, Kuberr began to giggle, and Lowallyn released a long whistle.

"What is it?" asked Stonebrow breathlessly.

Lowallyn wore a crooked smile as he pulled his head back from the hole. "You were right. He grew everything: tables, chairs, the bar—even smoked sausage behind the bar and beer tuns all around the room."

"Told you," said Stonebrow.

Kuberr crowed delightedly. "How much beer is in a tun that's ten stories high?"

The others took handholds of the splintered wood and pulled it away, enlarging the hole. One by one they clambered in. Lowallyn hung back, waiting for Stonebrow.

The giant centaur said, "I'll have to break this bigger before I'll get in."

"I know," replied Lowallyn. "I can wait. Anticipation makes the reward all the sweeter." He hitched his head. "That's the strange thing about desire. It makes everything more wonderful."

"Sure," said Stonebrow as he spun about. "Now, clear aside."

* * * * *

"You're sure this will work?" asked Kamahl, not for the first time. The beaming creature before him only nodded deeply.

"It's a heavy burden," Kamahl said, "but I can bear it."

"Go, then," said Lord Macht. "Bear it." Suddenly, he shot away, a star leaping to his palace in the sky.

As he went, Kamahl became aware of the whirling of his own arms and the flashing of the Mirari sword. Argentum faded, and the horizon became a gray blur. Kamahl was once again in his cocoon of steel.

It began to unravel. His arms slowed, and the kata eased into their final few motions. Instead of a silver world, Kamahl saw the high, holy place in the City of Averru. Instead of the palace, he saw the ruptured dome of the temple.

He completed the final kata, lifted the Mirari sword overhead, and sheathed it on his back. Sweat ran down his body, and it made a dark ring on the stone. Once again, he had battled the Mirari sword, and once again he had mastered it. This time, though, it had taught him what he must do.

"When she comes," Kamahl vowed breathlessly, "I'll be ready." He turned and began to walk across the crackling sandstone. "Until then, I'll join the others. I hope they've found some beer."

CHAPTER 28

THE FALL OF APHETTO

Karona floated ahead of her Army of Right as they crossed the arid planes above Aphetto. It was a nowhere place, and Aphetto was less than nothing—a deep canyon filled with unbelievers.

Karona drifted down between her prophets. They rode in the vanguard of her cavalry—a thousand mounted troops, with a thousand archers behind them, and ten thousand foot soldiers at the rear.

THIS WON'T BE LIKE EROSHIA.

"We know," answered Sash and Waistcoat.

MANY OF THE FOLK WON'T BE ABLE TO SEE ME OR WON'T TRY. THEY'LL BURROW AWAY FROM MY LIGHT. UNLESS WE CAN FORCE A SURRENDER, THIS WILL BE A MASSACRE.

Sash said, "You think the Cabal will surrender?"

I DO. SASH, YOU'LL LEAD HALF THE CAVALRY AND HALF THE ARCHERS ALONG THE EASTERN WALL OF THE CANYON. WAISTCOAT, YOU'LL TAKE THE OTHER HALF TO THE FALLS ABOVE, FORD THE STREAM, AND TAKE THE WESTERN WALL OF THE CANYON.

Waistcoat clucked happily. "Sure! Least we don't have to go in there."

THEN YOU AND SASH WILL ENTER THE CITY TO NEGOTIATE THEIR SURRENDER.

Sash's eyes dropped wide. "Who're we suppose to talk to? The First is dead. Phage is gone. Who's in charge?"

EVERY NEST HAS A LEAD RAT. TELL THE GUARDS YOU'RE MY PROPHETS. IF YOU'RE HARMED, THE CANYON WILL BE DESTROYED AND ALL THOSE WITHIN WILL DIE.

"Oh, good," groused Waistcoat.

THE LIVES OF EVERYONE IN THAT PIT HANG ON YOUR MISSION. IF YOU CAN'T FULFILL IT, I'LL FIND OTHER PROPHETS WHO CAN.

Sash and Waistcoat considered the threat. "We'll do it," Sash said, dragging his reins to one side. He shouted over his shoulder, "Companies One, Two, Five, and Six, come with me."

Waistcoat watched him go. "Uh, yeah. We'll do it." He lifted his hand high and called out, "Companies Three, Four, Seven, and Eight, let's go."

The Army of Right split on the plains above Aphetto. Two companies of cavalry and two companies of infantry followed each of the prophets. They peeled away, leaving the main column of infantry to follow the goddess.

Karona headed straight for the fortified arch. No gate garrison could hold back a whole army, let alone Magic herself. She flew on ahead of the troops, faster than foot soldiers.

Ahead, the soldiers stiffened behind their portcullis. They had watched the army all morning and readied their arrows and spears. They were still far enough away that they could resist Karona's overwhelming aura. Of course, if the gate itself fell, they could always cut the rope bridges that extended down into the gorge.

Karona would not allow that to happen.

From the battlements, arrows leaped into the air. Dozens of shafts arced, black against the bright sky, toward Karona. She idly looked up, and her mere attention was enough to send some of the shafts spinning end over end and falling away. Others caught fire and flared to ash.

Two, though, soared past the rays of her mind. The first struck her chest, tearing through skin and sinew to pulverize bone. It was a wicked arrowhead. Fashioned of cold steel, the head had front spikes to punch through the muscle wall but stop among the organs. Poison in three chambers of the head burst out within the torso to bring certain death. A second such missile struck her belly and ripped through her intestines.

The guards on the wall cheered the end of their foe.

They cheered too soon. Karona floated onward, the arrows jutting loosely from gaping wounds. Poison ran down their shafts and dripped on the ground. The arrows flared as had the others. In a puff of smoke, they disintegrated to ash, and the steel of their heads drooled in molten lines from the wounds. The flesh rebuilt itself, and the gouges closed. Karona's gaze did not waver from the guards.

"Vipers. Irredeemable."

More bowstrings hummed above the wall, and more arrows streaked into the sky.

Karona lifted one hand before her and made a single wiping motion.

The arrows reversed their courses, shrieking down to strike the warriors who had loosed them. Eyes that had sighted along the shafts now sprouted shafts. Spikes dug through soft orbits to the brains beneath.

That gesture killed perhaps a third of the garrison. Karona had to convert or slay the other two thirds before they cut the bridges. She could simply have soared down in their midst, and they would have to convert, but she wanted their decision to be voluntary.

"I am Karona! I am Magic. Lie down before me or die!"

Of course they did not. Soldiers are not trained to surrender, even in the face of truth. It was too bad for them. Karona brought her hands crashing together. The concussion doubled and redoubled as it rushed across the plains. By the time it reached the stone arch, the noise was an aural fist.

The archway shattered. Ten-ton stones burst into gravel. The storm of it caught and killed the rest of the garrison. Hunks of stone pattered down atop the cliff, and the way lay clear to the bridges.

Karona smiled and soared up to hover there. She turned, watching her army of ten thousand converge. "APHETTO WILL BE CLEANSED TODAY."

* * * * *

It was late afternoon before the two prophets made their reluctant way down the suspension bridge. The expanse was long and taut, with scorch marks at its far end where Karona had incinerated soldiers who had tried to cut it. Sash and Waistcoat hung in open air above a great wet canyon. Below, the spires and markets of Aphetto promised death should they fall.

"Behold, the prophets of Karona!" shouted Waistcoat as he'd been instructed. "Any who harm us will be slain by our lady! Hear us, damn it!"

"The 'damn it' adds a nice punch," Sash muttered through the side of his mouth. He listened to make sure the words hadn't been amplified to fill the canyon. "Really, Waistcoat, you sound terrified."

"I *am*. Aren't you?"

Sash's nostrils flared as he continued his descent. "Of course I am. More mortified, though. That means scared to death."

Waistcoat cast him an exasperated look. "Well, la-de-frickin'-da! I guess that tops me. I'm just scared enough to wet myself."

"As usual, Mr. Puddle, you miss the subtlety of my point," Sash began. A Cabal guard approached the bridgehead below, and Sash yelled, "Get back, you bastard, unless you want to burn!"

"You scream like a girl," Waistcoat said.

Still, it worked. The black-caped man lifted his hands and backed away from the bridgehead. Clearing his throat, Sash continued in low tones, "When I say I'm mortified, I don't mean I'm afraid of dying, I mean I'm already dead. Don't you see what's happened here? The trauma, the tribal wars, the banishment, the unspeakable power—it's all made her crazy. We're agents of genocide."

Waistcoat replied, "She *does* give them a choice," but his voice quavered.

"Worship or die isn't a choice. That's not what a goddess says. That's what a thug says. We're the mouthpieces of a thug."

Waistcoat began to tremble. "Oh, great! Now you've morterfied me as well!" He bellowed down the bridge. "You get that, Jack? She'll kill you! She's vicious!"

"Why do I ever tell you things?" Sash wondered aloud. To cover up his partner's error, Sash yelled, "Bring us your ruler, your chief, whoever's in charge. We wish to negotiate your surrender."

Sash's words echoed among the noble estates, high on their plateaus in the midst of the city. The shout rolled into all those vacant windows and reached ears hiding within, but no one emerged.

"Does it matter if she's right or wrong?" whispered Waistcoat. "Once everybody worships her, there'll be peace."

"Yeah," Sash said, "and if you slaughtered every living thing, there'd be peace too. Peace isn't everything. It can be a tyranny just like any other."

"What's the use of all this talk? We still got to do this thing. She'd burn us as soon as any other."

At last, they had voiced it, the fear they both had. Karona no longer cared for them. No one and nothing were special to her anymore. She would conquer the world and rule it, but not a speck of it would matter to her.

A little man stepped regally from the door of a noble estate and walked toward the bridgehead below. Two hulking guards in Cabal black walked behind him. The little man's head hardly broke the plane of the windowsills, and the way he swung his arms importantly as he walked made him seem a child.

"What's this?" Sash wondered quietly.

"A dwarf," Waistcoat said. "Hey! Shorty! Get away from those ropes!"

The little man strode up to the bridge and stood there, his hands on his hips and his feet spread wide. His pallid face stared straight up the bridge toward the prophets.

"That's no dwarf. That's a kid," Sash said. He quickened his pace. "Hey, boy, better run home and get your dad."

"You summoned me," cried the child. "I'm the ruler of Aphetto." Pale flesh stretched over his angular skull, with a shock of black hair above and a tailored leather suit below. He seemed a boyish version of the late, great First of the Cabal. "I am the First."

Waistcoat's nose rumpled. "You're not the First. You look more like the Half."

"I'm the First," said the boy, his voice deepening. "The child channels me. I yet rule the Cabal!"

The two prophets reached the bridgehead, and they pushed their way onto solid ground. The boy stood before them, half their height.

"You can't be the First. He was killed by Phage."

The boy laughed, the pitch slowly rising. He shifted his legs together and folded his arms. "Sash and Waistcoat. You've come a long way from the cockroaches I knew."

"What?" they chorused.

"Don't act so surprised. You were in different bodies, but I still recognize you." He flung his hands out to his sides and cocked his hips. "It's me. Phage. Old death-fingers."

The prophets flinched. "No."

"Yes—well, I don't rot anybody anymore. This child can speak for me, but he hasn't got my special touch."

Waistcoat hitched his lip. "They both rule—Phage and the First?"

Sash looked past the boy to the two guards. "Is this some kind of joke?"

Neither of the Cabal thugs moved, though from under one broad-brimmed hat came the response: "Speak to the Boy. He channels our ancestors."

"Ancestors?" Sash said. "Next thing you know, it'll be Braids—"

The Boy released a maniacal whoop and turned a back flip. "You rang? Wait a minute! I know you two—dragged me halfway across Otaria in a sack!"

The prophets could only stand, mouths gaping, and stare. Sash leaned to Waistcoat and whispered, "They're following a lunatic."

One of the enforcers said, "The Boy brings our great rulers back to advise us."

Waistcoat blurted, "Can he do Kuberr?"

Again, the boy's stance changed, shucking its girlish posture. "Sure, Gash and Waistcan. The Boy speaks for me as well."

Through his smile, Sash said, "Well, Mr. Boy, it's good to know I address all the great leaders of the Cabal, past and present. You all must listen to what I am about to say."

"Shoot."

"We speak for Karona, who is Magic incarnate and rightful ruler of all Dominaria. Her cavalry and archers surround your canyon, so no one will escape. Her infantry wait to invade your city and go room to room, rooting out every person and beast. The greatest terror of all is Karona herself. A month ago, she conquered Eroshia in one night. She will do the same to you." Sash spoke very deliberately. "Here's the point: Bow to her and live. Refuse and die." He crossed his arms over his chest. "Well, BoyFirstPhageBraids-KuberrWhosits, what's your answer?"

Blinking thoughtfully, the Boy shrugged. "Seize them."

The Cabal thugs lunged past him, grabbing the two prophets in brutal headlocks. Their arms, as broad as most men's legs, cinched like vices.

"Hey!" Waistcoat shouted as they wrestled him toward the noble estate. "We're her prophets . . . touch us . . . and die. . . ."

The man growled something inarticulate and yanked Waistcoat toward a doorway. The pudgy prophet dug in his heels. Beside him, Sash bounced like a leaf-spring. Both played tug of war with their heads, and both were losing.

A sudden flash and a whiff of burning wool, and the guards let go.

Clutching their heads, Sash and Waistcoat crouched on the ground and panted thankfully.

The brutes meanwhile convulsed as twin beams of power roared through them. Smoke whistled from every pore, and skin contracted around vanishing muscles. In moments, only leather-encased skeletons remained, then nothing.

Sash and Waistcoat had the grace to retch. Doubled over, they heard their lady's voice resound in the air:

"Behold what my prophets do. This is the true response to my presence. It's what all of you must do to be saved—bow and receive me!"

Wiping his mouth on a priestly sleeve, Sash said, "She thinks we're bowing."

"Yes. Yes! I see you. Come to me!"

Sash and Waistcoat lifted their heads. In a cave mouth on the far side of the canyon, a man had thrown himself to his face in worship.

Karona flew out above the canyon. She gestured toward the man, and he levitated off the ground. At first he kicked in panic, but as he soared out of the cave to meet his lady in the air, he laughed with delight. Others emerged—a rich woman on her balcony, a slave girl from the muck, a boy with a fishing rod, an old man in his nightcap. All bowed to their faces and moments later soared from the ground. The company swarmed toward Karona. Their cries of rapture brought more and more from the hovels.

"Maybe we were wrong," Waistcoat said. "Maybe she is all good."

The hand of Magic reached down to snatch them up. The prophets were whisked off their hands and knees. They rushed up into the air, leaving behind the Boy, who stood scowling at the sky.

All around him, many others emerged and went prostrate. From plateaus and trails, cave mouths and market stalls, they soared to join the great cloud of worshipers. Hundreds circled Karona, planets around a glorious sun.

All along the cliff tops, cavalry watched in awe. Infantry chanted a hymn to Karona. Who could doubt such signs? Clearly she was Magic incarnate, and clearly Magic loved her people. What more could one wish for? Anyone who rejected her in this moment was surely a craven monster.

One by one, the last of the believers floated aloft. Karona had harvested perhaps five hundred souls out of a pit of ten thousand.

Her eyes scoured the canyon. No one else emerged. The hymn on the cliff top ended, and wet winds moaned in the cave mouths.

"It is finished."

She brought her hands together.

As soon as flesh met flesh, the canyon was gone. Soil, deep and black, filled the basin, a great scar on that arid plain.

Ten thousand throats screamed silently into dirt.

Karona descended, easing her five hundred new souls down to the ground. She lighted among them, and her worshipers dropped to their knees in a great circle.

Sash and Waistcoat doubled over in nauseated praise.

CHAPTER 29

THE GODS LAUGHED

APHETTO IS DESTROYED. EROSHIA IS CONQUERED. THE COLISEUM HAS BEEN RAZED, AND LOCUS HAS SUNK BACK INTO THE DREAMS THAT SPAWNED IT. ONLY ONE POWER REMAINS IN CENTRAL OTARIA. ONCE IT IS BROUGHT TO HEEL, I WILL RULE THE HEART OF THE CONTINENT.

I HOVER ABOVE THE CORIAN BADLANDS AND GAZE GLADLY AT MY GREAT ARMY, TWO LEGIONS SURROUNDING THE CITY OF AVERRU.

THE CITY WILL FALL, BUT NOT AS EROSHIA OR APHETTO. THIS CITY IS A SLUMBERING GOD. I WITHHOLD MY MAGIC FROM AVERRU, LEST I AWAKEN HIM. I CANNOT ENTER THE CITY UNTIL MY ARMIES HAVE DESTROYED ANY CHANCE OF HIS RISING. INSTEAD, I SEND MY PROPHETS.

THEY DESCEND THE DEEPWASH VALLEY AND HEAD FOR THE FORD AND THE GREAT STONE ARCHWAY THAT PROCLAIMS, "BATTLEFIELD OF THE NUMENA."

MY MEMORIES REACH BACK TWENTY THOUSAND YEARS, TO THE FIRST TIME THE NUMENA INCARNATED ME. AVERRU HAD MEANT TO GIVE HIMSELF A NEW BODY, AND LOWALLYN AND KUBERR HAD MEANT TO STEAL HIS SPELL. IN THE END, THEY ACCIDENTALLY GAVE FLESH TO MAGIC, TO ME. I LIVED THIRTEEN MONTHS ONLY TO CONFRONT THEM HERE AND DIE, DISPERSED TO THE WINDS.

THAT TIME, MY POWER WAS INCOMPLETE. THIS TIME, ALL MAGIC IS MINE. NUMENA WITHOUT MAGIC ARE ONLY PULING MEN.

SASH AND WAISTCOAT ARE TOO. THEY DOUBT ME, DISAPPROVE OF EVERY DEATH. WHAT WAR HAS NO DEATHS? I SHOULDN'T TRUST THEM, BUT I LOVE THEM. TWENTY THOUSAND YEARS AGO, I WAS ALONE, BUT THIS TIME I HAVE FRIENDS.

THE ROBES OF MY PROPHETS SOAK UP WATER AS THEY CROSS THE FORD.

FARE WELL, FRIENDS.

* * * * *

"Know what I'm doing?" asked Waistcoat.

Sash glanced over at him as water dragged at the hem of his cloak. "Getting soaked?"

"Praying," Waistcoat said proudly. "Do you know who I'm praying to?"

"Is there a god for morons?"

"Karona." He smiled. "See, she's not really our friend anymore. She does things friends don't do."

"Like genocide."

"Right, but gods do that stuff all the time. If I can't talk to her like a friend, maybe I can talk to her like a god—so I'm praying."

Sash rolled his eyes as he stepped into the shadow of the archway. "If it hasn't occurred to you, we're about to run face to face into our original god—Ixidor. Have you ever prayed to him?"

Waistcoat blinked. "Well, if you want a one-armed god, go ahead."

"Idiot."

"Moron."

The prophets halted, water pouring past their legs. A familiar figure stood in the arch—massive and shadowed and scowling.

"Uh, hi, Stonebrow," Waistcoat said. "I thought you were a boulder."

The centaur looked down at the two men in their sodden robes. "You look familiar, but I can't place you."

"We used to be a couple of nobodies," Sash said. "Empty out-lines. Friends of Phage. Remember? Sash and Waistcoat?"

A brief smile came to the centaur's face. "Where's Umbra?"

"Gone," said Waistcoat wistfully. "In the bargain we got these bodies. His choice, you see. We've been trying to make good on his sacrifice."

The giant centaur shook his head. "*This* is how you make good? March with Karona? Help her massacre a continent?"

Sash said, "Yeah, well . . . we're, ah—"

"It's not like we're friends or anything," interrupted Waistcoat. "She's just our god. Gods're all a bunch of rascals, but what can you do?"

"We're here to negotiate your surrender," Sash said. "We've got two legions and a goddess. You've got a city of falling-down towers, a bunch of red-glass statues, and about ten defenders."

"We have three numena."

"Two, really," Sash said, "and our scouts say you can't count Kuberr and Ixidor either."

"Ixidor?—oh, you mean Lowallyn . . ." Stonebrow paused. "That's why you look familiar. You've got the same face. One tall and skinny, the other short and fat, but you're him, all right—except for having two arms."

"Listen, Stonebrow, we've got a pretty easy mission—just a couple sentences for whoever's in charge. Are you in charge?"

"Come with me," Stonebrow said, an inscrutable smile on his face. He turned to march up the farm road toward the city.

Sash and Waistcoat shrugged and followed.

* * * * *

The numena had needed an epic pub, and the Gilded Mage fit the bill. Ten-story-tall tuns of beer, three-story-tall chairs, knives the size of ironing boards, foil-covered cards with life-sized illustrations. These last had been taken by Kuberr and Ixidor and lined up along the walls to create a gallery of art. The two circulated among them, clutching boots filled with beer (the steins were too large to lift).

"Do you see, here?" asked Lowallyn. He pointed at the painting of an angel, her wings in the shape of a butterfly. "A brilliant use of light and shadow. The upper half of her face is dark, and the tips of her wings, but the rest—"

"You always had a soft spot for angels," Kuberr said.

"I guess so. Transcendence was the point. A creature who could rip from the covetous ground and climb to illimitable heavens—"

" 'Covetous ground,' " mocked Kuberr, slapping Lowallyn's back, " 'Illimitable heavens.' You know what this means?"

Lowallyn stared sadly at the foamy boot. "Too much beer?"

"Too little." Kuberr shoved the boot up into the man's face. Foam mantled his beard and ran like tears from his eyes, but both men laughed.

Someone entered the big hole in the side of the tree-doors. It was Stonebrow, as dour as ever. He could drink a tun of beer himself, but always he was busy "defending the gate" or "watching for scouts." The great ungulate! Just the sight of him made the numena howl with laughter.

Behind him came two other figures—a tall gaunt fellow and a short stout one. They stumbled through the door and blinked stupidly as their eyes adjusted. Again, the gods laughed. The two men strode purposefully toward Kuberr and Lowallyn. As they neared, it became clear that they had the same face, though one was gaunt and the other fat, and that their face was Lowallyn's own.

Kuberr cried out, "Hilarity ensues!"

Lowallyn was not amused. "Who are you? What're you doing with those masks?" He lunged, dropping his boot so that it gushed beer across the floor. He grabbed the fat one's cheek and tried to rip off the mask.

The little man fought back with slapping hands and broke away, spluttering. "Get away!"

"Ahem," interrupted the tall one. "We are the prophets of Karona, on official business. We have a message for the ruler of Averru City."

Behind him, Stonebrow cleared his throat. "These are Lords Kuberr and Lowallyn, brother numena to Averru, whose city this is. Lords, these are the prophets Sash and Waistcoat, companions of Karona."

Lines of anger creased Lowallyn's smile. "And why would Karona send out two prophets with *MY FACE!*"

The tall one took a step forward and said haughtily. "If you must know, Lord Lowallyn, it is because we are your sons." His eyes flashed. "Oh, you may not remember us. We came from that time when you called yourself Ixidor, when you were making things—real, amazing things. That was before you were a god and . . . a drunk."

Lowallyn clenched his hand into a fist, beer dripping from it. "I know you. You're the nothings that betrayed me."

"Yeah," replied Sash. "When you made us, we were nothing. Look what we've made of ourselves. Meanwhile . . . look what you've made of yourself."

"You see only the shell of me. Before your mistress stole my power, I was greater than you could ever be."

Sash nodded. "Your power came from Karona. Now she demands your fealty. Receive Karona, worship her, and you will be saved. Refuse her, and you will die."

Lowallyn shrugged, and Kuberr laughed.

Sash's face flushed. "Is that your answer? The most powerful being in the world comes before you, and you snicker?"

"Tell someone who cares," Kuberr said. "We're not the rulers of this place. We're the town drunks. Go find Kamahl. Go tell him."

The fat prophet stuck out his tongue, turned in a huff, and said, "Maybe we will."

Sash and Waistcoat retreated from the Gilded Mage. Stonebrow followed them out the shattered door and into the streets.

When they were beyond earshot, Lowallyn turned toward his brother numen and said, "If they think we'll lie down before her, they must be out of their minds. When she gets near enough, we'll have all our power back. Then we strike as one—you, me, and Averru. And this time, we strike to kill."

* * * * *

"—And so, Mr. Kamahl," Waistcoat finished, "either bow or die. That's all we came to say." He brushed off his hands and tucked them under very nervous armpits.

Kamahl didn't respond. He was an imposing figure, tall and powerfully built, with gray and black dreadlocks all about his intense face. He struck a noble silhouette here beneath the ruptured dome of Averru.

"Well," Waistcoat said, "what's your answer?"

The great druid barbarian looked down, and his eyes sparked merrily. "If this is Karona's ultimatum, I'll give my answer to her." He took a deep breath and looked around at the devastation. "I've got to tell you, and this is between us human beings—my inclination is to fight her with everything in me."

The prophets exchanged amazed expressions.

"I know. I don't have much of a chance. I can't stand against Magic herself, but the question is whether it's better to die free or to live a slave."

Waistcoat nodded shallowly, catching himself too late. Sash looked thoughtfully away.

Kamahl shrugged. "We're not supposed to live forever, after all. If we have to die, we might as well die for something rather than for nothing."

"You're suggesting we abandon Karona, the most powerful

creature in Dominaria, to stand with you in a doomed fight?" Sash asked.

Kamahl gave a crooked smile and said, "When you put it that way, it sounds bad." He reached up over his shoulder, gripped the gleaming hilt of his great sword, and yanked it out before him. The sword was massive, as tall as a man, with a blade as wide. It shone eagerly beneath the sky. Its pommel morphed like quicksilver.

"I have a secret weapon," Kamahl continued, "and you can decide whether to tell your lady about it. There's no magic left in Dominaria except this sword. That's because its power comes from another world. With this sword, I can kill her, and if she enters this city, I will."

"If only you could," Sash muttered feverishly. He winced and glanced around. "She'll just send her army ahead to kill you before she even comes near."

"She's welcome to try." Admiring the blade a moment more, Kamahl lifted it and sheathed it in the shoulder harness. "I'll answer her ultimatum when she comes to face me. Until then, our business together is done."

With a grim nod, Sash turned away and motioned Waistcoat to follow.

Coming up alongside him, Waistcoat said, "Did you notice? I held my tongue. I didn't say a single word about Lord Macht and Argentum."

"Shut up, idiot."

"Fair enough."

* * * * *

NO ONE GUARDS THE GATES THIS EVENING—NOT STONEBROW NOR HIS NIGGLING TROOPS, NOT THE DRUNKEN NUMENA NOR KAMAHL AND HIS MAGIC SWORD. A HANDFUL OF SOLDIERS COULDN'T HOLD A WHOLE CITY.

TONIGHT, AVERRU IS MINE. I CIRCLE ABOVE IT, TRACKING EVERY GLYPH. A FEW THOUSAND CRYSTAL STATUES FILL THE STREETS AND THE TEMPLE PLAZA. THE ONLY OTHER DEFENDERS HOLE UP IN THE SHATTERED TEMPLE.

KAMAHL HOPES TO DRAW ME IN, TO SHUNT MY POWER TO THE GLYPHS, AWAKEN AVERRU, AND EMPOWER KUBERR AND LOWALLYN. THE STRATEGY MIGHT HAVE WORKED, BUT SASH AND WAISTCOAT TOLD ME OF IT.

I CLIMB HIGH, WHERE ALL MY TROOPS CAN SEE ME. THE LEGIONS SURROUND THE CITY, POISED TO FORD THE RIVER OR CLIMB THE WALLS. ONCE INSIDE, THEY WILL RUSH THROUGH THE STREETS AND SECURE THEM. BY MIDNIGHT, THEY WILL HAVE CAPTURED ALL BUT THE TEMPLE PLAZA. THAT IS MY JOB.

AT THE TOP OF THE SKY, I EXTEND MY HANDS, AND BRILLIANT LIGHT FLASHES.

MY TROOPS SEE THOSE TWIN LIGHTS, AND THE SIEGE TURNS TO STORM.

IN A BLACK RING FAR BELOW, THE ARMY OF RIGHT RUSHES THE GREAT CITY. HUNDREDS FLOOD THROUGH THE UNDEFENDED GATES IN THE NORTH AND SOUTH. THOUSANDS SWIM THE RIVER AND PELT TOWARD THE CITY'S LOWER REACHES, OR CLIMB THE WALLS AND POUR INTO THE STREETS.

A SWORD STRIKES, A GLYPH SHATTERS, AND A SMALL RED SPARK OF LIFE FLEES AWAY. TEN MORE WEAPONS HIT AND TEN MORE SOULS FLY. THE SOUND REACHES ME: ANGRY VOICES AND THE CRASH OF GLASS. MY ARMY ROARS HUNGRILY, ALMOST GLEEFULLY, AS ALL THAT CRYSTAL TUMBLES TO THE GROUND.

I MATCH EACH DEATH AGAINST THE CATALOG OF GLYPHS IN MY MIND. ONCE THEY ARE GONE, I WILL ATTACK. WITHOUT THE GLYPHS, AVERRU CANNOT RISE, AND KAMAHL CANNOT HOLD THE CITY.

UNTIL THEN, I LISTEN AS GLYPHS DIE LIKE JANGLING BELLS.

CHAPTER 30

BATTLING MAGIC

*I*t's a terrible sound," Kamahl said. He lifted his ear toward the ruined dome overhead. The others listened as well.

An eerie racket converged from all around the temple. Karona's army had begun an all-out charge up the city streets, and they roared like a mob. Beneath their feet, they shattered the Glyphs of Averru. Without the spark of magic to sustain them, all those crystal men died forever.

"A horrible sound," agreed Lowallyn. The torn dome overhead only amplified the noise. "Without those Glyphs, Averru may not be able to rise."

"Forget Averru," Kuberr said. "Without the Glyphs, it's us against an army."

Kamahl nodded grimly. He couldn't deny any of it. He studied the black sky, looking for a sign of Karona, but saw only the stars in their watches. She was there too, waiting for her moment.

Kamahl began to pace. "It's crucial that all of you stay undercover. She could kill you with a mere look. Anyone in line of sight is in danger. I'll go out and draw her down. Lowallyn, you and Kuberr hole up as near to me as possible. She'll try to kill me, but she won't get past the Mirari sword. I'll use it to deflect her spells toward you. Absorb what you can. Don't emerge to fight until you've regained enough power to keep her close. If she escapes before I kill her, our chance is lost and her armies will bury us."

He turned toward Stonebrow, who stood with the elves and dwarfs and humans who had been his troops. "As to the rest of you, wait for your chance. Immortal wars are sometimes won by mortal hands." He patted the giant centaur's shoulder. "Take no needless risks, General, but take every needful one."

"Yes, Commander." Stonebrow bowed.

The roar of the army welled up outside.

Clenching his jaw, Kamahl reached over his shoulder and drew the Mirari sword. The mercurial pommel gleamed like a crystal ball. Without another word, he strode through the temple arch and out into the night.

He sensed Karona overhead, watching. It was as if the fire from her eyes already etched its path in the air. Kamahl didn't search the sky for her or listen to the army's keen. He had to fight his own fight—on his own terms and in his own time.

The sword circled in a great wide ring, passing through each compass point and receiving its strength. It jabbed skyward, calling down the powers above, and then groundward to draw the energies below. So began the training kata, preparing sword and wielder for the fight of their lives.

Kamahl reached inward to tap the serene vitality of the perfect forest. He reached back in time to tap the spontaneous fury of his barbarism. Green mana and red flooded through him and into the sword. The blade answered with its own mana powers—visions of Pianna of the Northern Order, seascapes with Laquatus and the cephalids, the Pits and dementia space and Chainer's torment. White, blue, and black mana completed the circle.

With a final, all-encompassing swing, the Mirari sword and its wielder were one. They were empowered by internal magic, and they would need every last color.

Karona had arrived. Just beyond reach of his whirling sword, she stood. She wore an elegant stole above gleaming armor. Her magic was drawn up tightly within her; she spared not even the wafting power that would hold her aloft. Her mana was the crux of this battle, and her enemies were starving for it.

"BOW TO ME. I AM MAGIC, THE POWER OF DOMINARIA. WHO ARE YOU? WHO IS KAMAHL?"

The question tore his breath away. Kamahl stood, sword at the ready.

"I am the Guide: defender of Averru, mentor of Kuberr, savior of Lowallyn. I am the bane of deathwurms, champion of Krosan, brother of Phage, slayer of Laquatus and Chainer, the Pardic gladiator—and I wield this sword." Kamahl kept the Mirari sword before him, ready to deflect her magic. "The power in you should be everywhere in Dominaria, not hoarded in one person."

"I AM KARONA! I AM GREATER THAN YOU AND ALL THE WORLD!"

She rose from the ground, the first whisper of a magic that was about to roar. Her eyes beamed. Jets of red power hurled out of them, stabbing down toward Kamahl.

Mirror-bright, the Mirari sword swung before the beams. It cut through them and hurled the power aside. Red plasma lashed the side of the temple dome, spattering before being absorbed.

Kamahl grinned fiercely and turned the blade to catch the next onslaught. He had resumed his kata, and sword and man moved in synchrony.

Power splashed off the Mirari's edge, much of it bounding down to lave the plaza stones. Some, though, rushed into the blade. It sparked with life, crazing the orb as if it were a bloodshot eye.

Karona's shriek joined the horrible chorus of her armies. Power mounted through her torso and stabbed from eyes and mouth and fingertips, thirteen blood-red beams converging on Kamahl.

Before he could respond, the Mirari sword leaped of its own accord. It swept out before him, deflecting the lower beams into the upper ones and hurling all of them toward the temple. Power struck and liquefied a stone wall before it was drawn away.

The sword did not catch it all. A stray ember fell on Kamahl's leg and burned deep into the muscle. He lurched off balance and began to fall.

Karona's eyes lit.

Kamahl toppled sideways but jabbed his sword toward Karona. A blast of energy emerged from its tip. Silver and crimson, the beam hurtled through the air and engulfed the floating woman. She thrashed but did not fall or retreat. The mana sank into her veins like lifeblood. Untouched in the conflagration, she gathered the power and flung it back down on Kamahl.

He couldn't defend himself, lying on his side with one hand on the deep-burned scar. A red wave of force rushed over him. It mantled his flesh. Kamahl gripped the Mirari sword and drew healing power from it, but it wouldn't be enough. Magic sizzled him, and he roared.

He was a dead man.

The plasma suddenly thinned and was gone like blood down a drain. Two drains—Lowallyn and Kuberr, standing on either side of him. They had emerged to absorb the cloud, stoking their power.

Karona shot up and away.

"Keep her here!" Kamahl cried, flames licking between his teeth.

Already, the numena cast spells.

Lowallyn produced a small mirror from within his robes and hurled it skyward. The silvered glass spun into the air and grew. It passed Karona, stretching into a great wide membrane. She soared through it, vanished, and emerged again, plunging instead of rising. The spatial membrane had reflected her flight groundward.

Kuberr's spell waited there, a black net that wrapped around her. Lines of mana burned into Karona as she tumbled.

Between the two numena, Kamahl staggered to his feet. His skin was burned and his thigh deeply wounded, but still he stood. "How long before Averru awakens?"

As Karona fell, Kuberr said, "A few more big spells."

"Here's the first," Lowallyn warned, dragging the men back toward the temple.

An explosion rocked the sky. The black-mana net around Karona detonated, blowing away from her. Hunks of burning cord flung out across the plaza. They pitted rock and burned long scars across the ground. Where they hit, the ground absorbed the mana and the force that had hurled them. Averru was rousing.

Lowallyn shoved Kamahl through an arch of the temple and turned. He and Kuberr caught the mana blast. Wounds opened across their bodies, but next moment those wounds were mouths that swallowed the mana and closed again.

Karona pulled out of her dive and hovered, hands spread to her sides and eyes blazing. She considered the two numena and the druid barbarian who struggled to his feet behind them.

From all around, a huge roar mounded up. The Army of Right flooded out from between the city towers. Thousands of warriors rose, fresh from the massacre of Glyphs. Reaching the temple plaza, they converged at a steady march.

"Behold my people, the people of Otaria. Their belief makes me omnipotent. Enough of the execution. On to the burial."

Karona's hands cut quickly through the air, and it solidified into a small cube.

"Back!" Lowallyn shouted, shoving Kamahl once again into the temple. It was all he had time to do. The air around Lowallyn and Kuberr turned to stone, encasing them.

Kamahl staggered back, a wall of solid rock closing off the archway. The only light now came from the Mirari. Kamahl held it up and saw that every archway was closed off by stone. Even the ruptured dome had been sealed. Karona had encased the whole temple in a great cube of rock.

"Kamahl!" bellowed someone behind him. Stonebrow's hooves clattered on the temple stairs as he rushed out of the murk. "Look up!"

A network of cracks raced up the temple dome. The structure was failing beneath that horrible weight.

"There's no escape, Commander," the giant centaur said, panting. His troops arrived behind him, their faces fearful in the silvery light. "She's buried us beneath a mountain."

Kamahl stared fiercely at the giant centaur. "At least we have air. Lowallyn and Kuberr are buried alive in the stone. Kick here!" He slapped his hand where Lowallyn had been a moment before and shifted aside to give Stonebrow room.

The giant centaur pivoted to bring his massive hind legs in range and kicked the wall. Rock cracked but did not fall away. Again he kicked. Chunks of stone flew. A third kick and a fourth spread cracks across the spot. Larger shards toppled. Two more kicks, and a hunk dropped free to reveal Lowallyn's side.

"Wait," Kamahl said. He knelt and clawed rocks away from the numena. They fell from a narrow channel in the wall. With a great heave, Kamahl pulled loose the slab that covered Lowallyn's face. The man was dusty and blue, but as soon as air spanked his skin, he began to breathe in short, rapid gulps.

"Kuberr!" Lowallyn gasped, his body still pinned within its stone sheath. "He's deeper!"

"We know," Kamahl said. "Hold tight!"

"There's . . . no other way . . . I can hold."

"We've got to get Kuberr out! Stonebrow . . ." Kamahl prompted, slapping the stone where Kuberr had been.

The giant centaur shifted and kicked again. The stone in this spot was much harder—thicker. Ten kicks brought only the narrowest crack. Kamahl shoved the Mirari sword into the gap, trying to widen it. The orb at the end of the sword sparked, but still the fissure wouldn't open.

"Damn it! He's dying."

Another volley of kicks cracked loose more of Lowallyn's sepulcher but still left Kuberr in solid stone. Lowallyn took the opportunity to pry himself loose. Jagged edges of rock cut him as he emerged, and hair tore away where it had been trapped. Bleeding and blue, he fell to the ground.

Hooves and sword pounded that rock until Stonebrow bled at his heels and Kamahl's sweat made the floor slick. With agonizing slowness, the stone broke away. At last, a hunk dropped to reveal Kuberr's back. More kicks, and they could yank rocks away from his hips to his head. He faced away, into the heart of the stone. Kamahl dragged at the body, clutched in the suction of a perfect fit. Air slowly tricked in around the man's ears, and they pulled his face out.

Kuberr's skin was blue, and his eyes were like gold coins staring out of his face. He was dead.

"She's gotten one of us!" Kamahl whispered. He trembled from exhaustion, from the sudden realization of loss, and from terrors yet to come.

It took three of them pulling on the man's upper body to free his legs from their stone sheaths. They dragged Kuberr out and laid him on the floor. Already, his blood had begun gathering in his legs, turning them livid.

Lowallyn knelt above his brother and looked into his eyes. "Yes, she's gotten one of us." He closed the lids over those golden orbs.

Exhausted and bleeding, Kamahl dropped down beside him. He clasped the numen's shoulder. "At least she didn't get you both."

Stonebrow gazed down at the three men—one lying, one sitting, and one kneeling. He shifted uneasily, his hooves leaving half-circles of red on the stone floor. "Forgive me, great lords."

Kamahl looked up, "Forgive you, General? You did everything you could."

"No. Forgive me for not kneeling," Stonebrow replied. "I'm not sure I could get back up."

Lowallyn studied the massive centaur. "You needn't kneel to any of us."

Stonebrow shook his head. "I'm a mortal in the presence of gods." He held his hand out toward Kuberr. "Here is a numen who died fighting the Scourge. He deserves homage." His hand shifted toward Lowallyn. "Here is a numen who once was my god and my Vision. He deserves worship." Last, his gaze came to rest on Kamahl. "Here is my creator. He deserves my life."

Kamahl rose slowly, eyes fixed on the giant centaur's. "I'm not your creator, Stonebrow, not anymore. I made you once, but you've remade yourself a hundred times since then. You're your own god now."

The dome overhead began to shudder, and the maze of cracks extended farther.

Lowallyn watched it. "The mortals have become gods and the gods have become mortals. If she can kill one of us, she can kill any of us."

Kamahl shielded his eyes from a shower of stone dust. "It shouldn't give way—"

"Unless the rock itself is shifting," Lowallyn interrupted.

It was. The stone that once had held Lowallyn and Kuberr in its suffocating grip now smoked with heat and oozed like wax. Glowing rock ran down to pool on the floor and slide through the cracks. Red globs of lava fell through the ruptured peak of the dome and coated the dark crystal statue of Averru. The whole huge mass of rock atop the temple shifted and slid.

"She's sure you and Kuberr are dead, and now she coming after the rest of us," Stonebrow said.

"No," Lowallyn replied, rising. "Karona isn't doing this. Averru is." He pointed down to the crystal statue of the city. Lava sank away between the seams. "That stone spell held enough mana power to awaken him. Now, he's drinking it in. He'll fight for us."

Kamahl nodded. "She kills one of us, and another rises."

"It's not a bad idea," Lowallyn said. He walked to the smoking wall, rammed his hand into the hot substratum, and drew the power in. "We'll be fully charged by the time we're out of this."

Kamahl grinned ruefully. "If only I could get this leg fixed—"

Pulling his hand out, Lowallyn set it on the deep-scarred spot. His touch was like a branding iron. A flash of mana power came, and Kamahl was healed. Lowallyn turned back to absorbing Karona's spell. The wall of stone shifted downward, as if it were being sucked away into the very mountain.

Kamahl glanced at the glowing statue of Averru. "We might just win this thing."

Lowallyn nodded hesitantly. "We'll have to see what the army's been up to while we've been trapped."

The wall before them sloughed, and the first glimpse of night sky showed above the stone. The stars seemed brilliant after the darkness of the temple, and they showed Karona's Army of Right marching in their masses. They swarmed the temple plaza, their eyes fixed on the melting mound.

"We might just lose this thing," Lowallyn said. He scooped up a great wad of the red rock, set it on the ground, and sculpted it with expert fingers. "Karona has the military and magical superiority—but maybe I can turn her spells against her." A few quick jabs, and the blob had a humanlike form. Another sweep of his fingers, and its legs and arms were separate.

"No time for subtlety."

He wrote a word on the brow of the crude statue, snatched it up, and hurled it into the melting stone.

Stonebrow watched, his forehead knotted in disbelief.

The statue seemed to swim a moment, its arms and legs working against the lava. Then it sank away, but its swimming motion translated throughout the mound. Beyond the archway, the amorphous stuff took on the shape of the homunculus. Molten rock compacted around the thing. Soon the pile congealed, becoming a forty-foot-tall man of magma. The word of life shone on its forehead.

The soldiers of Karona fell back from that awful man.

It raised its arms and began to run across the plaza. Many soldiers fell beneath its pounding feet or were scooped up in its blazing hands and burned to nothing. The army that once had filled the plaza now ran for cover.

Lowallyn looked grimly satisfied. "Let's go. We'll strike while her believers disbelieve."

Kamahl nodded. He and Lowallyn set out from the temple, with Stonebrow and his contingent behind.

While her army fled the field, Karona watched with what might have been fury or fear. The molten man thundered across the plaza, driving away her troops. It reached the first towers, turned, and loped slowly back toward its master.

Lowallyn smiled. "I've always been saved by my artwork."

"AND DAMNED BY IT."

Lowallyn had time only to gasp in realization.

The molten man who had been his own creation, his own servant, jogged up and brought is burning heel down. Red rock gushed down over the numen, trapping him.

Kamahl staggered back in shock.

Broken and burning, Lowallyn struggled within the magma monster's heel.

Kamahl lifted his sword high and charged the beast. He rammed the blade into its fiery flesh. Even the Mirari sword could not cut its way to Lowallyn.

Stonebrow turned and kicked his bleeding hooves against the monster. They were cauterized immediately, and the fetlocks flared.

Roaring, the magma man swatted Stonebrow, hurling him away. It lunged for Kamahl.

He rolled. Even as he did, Kamahl looked to the smoldering heel and saw Lowallyn burn to ash. Molten rock closed over the place where he had been.

CHAPTER 31

THE FINAL DEFENDER
OF DOMINARIA

Kamahl leaped up and ran, keeping the Mirari sword tucked beside him.

The monster didn't pursue him. Its foot seemed stuck to the plaza stones as if rooted in place by the death of its master. The creature roared, but its body diminished. The core of the thing was being sucked away. Lowallyn must have enacted a final spell, shunting his life-force and that of the magma beast down into Averru.

The city was Kamahl's final ally against Karona and her Army of Right.

Kamahl halted, whirled, and lifted the Mirari sword. He searched the skies for Karona but instead saw the wonders of Averru.

The towers around the high holy place suddenly grew. They seemed enormous red claws that converged toward the center of the sky. The tips touched and united, forming a gigantic cage around Karona, her armies, and Kamahl. Inexorably, the towers widened. Their walls came together to merge into a great dome. The dome shrank inward, clenching like a giant fist. The foundations of the towers tore up the plaza as they cinched together. Many of Karona's troops were ground to grist, and all the rest were trapped in the fist of Averru.

Karona darted beneath the dome and rammed futilely against it, but this was more than stone. It was the flesh of a god.

Averru's voice came, omnipresent and ancient. "Now, Karona, your power is mine. You cannot escape me. I will crush you and possess your mana. Then we will see who rules Dominaria."

Karona hurled arcs of lightning and bursts of flame at the dome, but it only drank them in and became more powerful. She couldn't escape. Averru had her, and he would crush her. Instead of the tyrant Karona, there would be the tyrant Averru.

"Take comfort, dear mother," Averru said. "I had planned this from the beginning. Of course you would kill Kuberr and Lowallyn, and of course I would absorb their souls and the power you spent to destroy them. Not only would I have the strength to defeat you, but I also would rule alone. You cannot win, Mother."

A spell storm erupted from Karona, but it only drained her and fed the constricting dome. She could not break through physically or metaphysically, and below, her army was being ground to pieces. She was doomed.

Even as troops ran screaming around him, Kamahl knew it was a lie. Karona could do anything that a mortal mind could conceive. She could even slay Averru.

The thought was out before he could stop it, and Karona seized it from the air. She ceased her hopeless battles against the sphere. "If you want my Magic, take it. Take it all."

She dived straight into the crystalline eye of Averru.

"Get down! Everyone!" Kamahl shouted. He threw himself behind one of the temple walls.

Karona blazed as she struck the nexus of Averru's power.

A world's worth of magic exploded from her. It scoured the interior of the temple. Bolts demolished the walls, and stones flew in a massive hailstorm. Chunks impacted the cage of towers and punched right through. Ravening rays of magic followed. They riddled the fist of Averru and blasted it away entirely.

The temple evaporated, gone but for a few standing stones. Energy ripped across the plaza, leaving but a ragged hundred or so warriors alive. Beyond them, the mountain opened to the sky. Not a single tower remained. Every last structure was pulverized and hurled out across the badlands. Great boulders tumbled among the hunks of stone thrown there twenty thousand years before. The city was razed to its foundations. The only buildings that escaped the blast were those sheltered by the northern overhang—the very ruins where Sanctum had begun.

Thousands died in the rush of magic. Most were Karona's own troops, torn apart by hurtling debris. A number of Averru's defenders were vaporized by the blast, too, but the greatest casualty of all was Averru.

The city was destroyed, and with it the god. Gone was the last of the numena.

A dread silence fell across the black mountaintop.

In the lee of one monolith, Kamahl rolled over. His whole body ached, and his head rang from the horrible explosion. He coughed dust, struggled to his feet, and stared out across the wreckage.

"It's over," he told himself. Surely a blast that could kill Averru would have killed Karona too—

Kamahl whirled, the Mirari sword before him. Beyond the blade, beyond the standing stone, Karona floated in the midst of the decimated temple. Her arms were held out to her sides, drawing in the power she had expended. She floated serenely and seemed even to smile. Her eyes blazed.

"You, Kamahl, are the final defender of Dominaria."

She nodded toward the scoriated plaza, and her ragged hundred or so warriors rose from the rubble.

"There've been enough deaths tonight. Bow to me, and I will withdraw my wrath from you."

Wearily, Kamahl stepped away from the stone. He backed up slowly, the Mirari sword slicing through the first of the practice kata. All the while, he kept his eyes on Karona. "Look at yourself, Karona. You're the destroyer of millions."

"I DESTROY NO ONE WHO WORSHIPS AND OBEYS."

Kamahl smiled bitterly. "As I said. There are millions who can't live that way." The Mirari sword sped up its path. It hummed angrily in his hand, eager for battle. The voice within it spoke to him, reminding him what he must do to save the world. Kamahl nodded, drew a deep breath, and said, "The final defender of Dominaria calls you out, Karona. One last duel. Know that I bear the one weapon in all Dominaria that can kill you."

The woman rose above the temple. Light streamed into her, and her power compounded.

"MY SERVANTS TOLD ME YOUR PLAN. ONCE YOU ARE DESTROYED, I WILL VISIT LORD MACHT AND REPAY HIM FOR HIS TREACHERY. YOU WERE MY FIRST FRIEND, KAMAHL, BUT NOW WE END LIKE THIS."

"Yes," he said. "Come down and fight me."

"YOU KNOW I DON'T HAVE TO. I CAN DO ANYTHING YOU CONCEIVE. YOU KNOW I CAN DESTROY YOU WITH A SINGLE GESTURE."

She swept her hand to one side.

Kamahl swung his blade out to block the spell. Magic latched onto the blade and yanked. Kamahl roared, feeling the fingers of both hands break. The handle ripped from his grip, and the Mirari sword spun away across the plaza. It clattered to the ground.

In agony, Kamahl clutched his ruined hands to his stomach. Still, he staggered toward the blade.

Karona came down to bar his path. A pulse from her open palm struck Kamahl and flung him back on his elbows. She stared at the fallen hero and shook her head slowly.

"IT DOESN'T MATTER IF THE SWORD HAS THE POWER TO KILL ME IF THE MAN DOESN'T HAVE THE SWORD."

Kamahl rolled to his knees, hands cradled in his lap. He stared into her eyes. "You are so beautiful, Karona."

"ARE YOU BOWING TO ME?"

He looked just beyond her, regret in his gaze. "No. I am not."

"THEN YOU MUST DIE."

Karona lifted her hands. Bolts of lightning arced between her fingers. She brought her hands down to unleash the power.

A great silver sword sprouted from her midsection. Gasping, Karona grabbed it. Power sparked from her hands into the blade.

"Forgive us!" cried her prophets, Sash and Waistcoat. They stood behind her, clutching the hilt of the Mirari sword. They had driven it like a battering ram through her.

"WHY . . . ? WHY . . . ?" Karona shivered and began to fall.

The prophets released the sword and stepped up to catch her. One on either side, they cradled their lady.

"Forgive us!" Sash said. "We snatched up the sword, planning to kill him, but Lord Macht spoke to us. He told us how to fix everything—"

"HE . . . CORRUPTED YOU." Blood limned Karona's lips and poured across the stone. "YOU'VE . . . KILLED ME. . . ."

"Karona," Waistcoat blurted, "we love you."

"MACHT WANTED . . . MY POWER. . . . YOU GAVE IT TO HIM. . . ."

Sash shook his head. "No. Your power is the one thing he didn't want. He's giving it back to the whole world."

Even as blood poured from her back and spread across the mountain, power geysered from her stomach and spread across the sky. This was no explosion but an effusion of magic. It emerged brighter every moment. On beams of light it leaped out among the stars.

"Do you see it go, Karona," Sash asked, "magic for everyone everywhere?"

Karona's head lashed back and forth. "MY MAGIC . . . MY LIFE . . ." She clutched the wound in her belly, but it was a dam burst. It gushed skyward and ripped wider. The rush of it was blinding and beautiful. "I'M DYING."

Crouching in that flood of power, Kamahl said, "Yes, but the world will live."

* * * * *

Her power came to Eroshia. It had been her first home on Dominaria, the site of the first tribal war. This city had suffered with her and languished without her, had received her back from banishment and sacrificed its citizens to her ambition. She came again to them, this time as gentle as a summer rain.

Across the early-morning skies spread a magic cloud. It rushed, high and fleecy, from west to east. In an eye blink it crossed a hundred miles of ocean. No corner of the sky remained uncovered, and from that white blanket fell motes of power. They cascaded in a soft shower. Where particles of magic lighted, a new sheen came to old things. Shingles and thatch thickened, cobbles glowed, and magic items hummed to life.

The folk left in that ravaged place hobbled from their cottages and stood beneath the enchanted rain. Eyes that had seen Karona's atrocities filled now with the glimmer of hope.

* * * * *

For three months, the Skyshroud Forest had lain frozen beneath the boreal blue. Icicles hung thick from every branch, and frost added white bark to every tree. Those bugs and beasts that could go to ground had, and those that couldn't died. Elves shivered in their trees and, at the suggestion of their Keldon neighbors, had even resorted to lighting fires.

All that was changing. White clouds covered the piercing blue, and flakes fell—but not of snow. Where these particles settled, ice melted. Wood thawed. Warmth came. Elves who at first had stared in grim grief at yet another blizzard now peered in wonder from their windows. Vines shucked their icicles, and new life surged through them. The trees shivered, their leaves drying in strange winds.

For three months, the elves had had no reason to smile. Now their warm homelands were returning, and they had reason to dance.

* * * * *

No one remained by the Heroes' Obelisk, not since the massacres. Only panthers came to the spot, sunning themselves on the black-marble benches where pilgrims were supposed to sit. They had eaten the last folk who had gathered here, trapped in lurid embraces when the magic failed.

Only panthers remained to see the whirling mist that descended through the thick canopy. Magic ran caressing fingers across the obelisk. From black and forgetful stone, names rose and shone. The heroes who had saved the world from the last great tyrant were remembered once more. And above all those names, the powerstone eyes of Urza Planeswalker and Gerrard Capashen gleamed.

* * * * *

Rapid and silent, the magic of Karona rushed around the world. Plain and forest, wetland, mountain, and island drank in the rejuvenating downpour. Dominaria slowly awakened from its disenchantment.

Gaea groaned and shuddered and began to breathe again.

* * * * *

Within a blinding storm of magic, Sash and Waistcoat clung to their goddess. Power roared out of her into the world.

Lord Macht had promised that if they stabbed her, they would save Dominaria, but no promise could ease their grief.

"Forgive us!" they shouted, though they couldn't hear their own voices. Mana had turned the air to cement. "Forgive us!"

Someone new came. He emerged out of the sword. Gales of magic whipped around him, but he was unaffected. His flesh was the same stuff as that magic—quintessence, the element of stars.

The stellar man stepped from the sword and knelt beside Karona. He wrapped his arms around her and seemed to be weeping silver tears. All three men held her, this star man and the two ex-prophets, ex-roaches, ex-unmen—two who had once been nothing at all.

"Lord Macht," Sash shouted, his words nearly torn away by the storm. "What do we do now?"

Somehow he heard. He lifted mirror eyes to Sash and Waistcoat and said, "Let go."

They did. After a final tight embrace, they released her.

Lord Macht lifted Karona, lifeless in his arms. The sorcerous flood from her belly began to taper, and Lord Macht took a single step. With a clap like thunder, the air closed over the spot where they had been.

The star man, the Mirari sword, and the mother of magic were gone.

Sash and Waistcoat stared at the spot. The lights were still emblazoned on their eyes. It all seemed a dream, a nightmare from which they were only now awakening.

For a time, neither man could do anything but breathe. Finally, Sash said, "Well, Mr. Puddle. Look at us. Created in the image of a god, but god-murderers."

"We saved the world," Waistcoat said, smiling feebly. "That's got to count for something."

Sash shook his head and peered into the dust. "What's the good of saving a world that's filled with people like us? I mean, really? Without gods, nothing's true, nothing's beautiful, nothing's . . . magical."

"No, Mr. Stick," replied Waistcoat. "Just because Karona's gone doesn't mean magic's gone. Without her, magic's everywhere."

Light dawned in Sash's eyes. "You know, Duke Waistcoat, I think we've finally done it."

"Done what?"

"Become human."

They sat for a moment while that thought sank in. Waistcoat said, "I'm hungry."

"I could use a drink."

"What about the Gilded Mage? I mean, sure, it got leveled, but there was lots of beer in the basement."

Sash slapped him on the back. "Even if it's just a big puddle, I'd get down on my knees."

Wearily, the two men stood and staggered across the desolate plaza, on their way to the Gilded Mage.

* * * * *

Kamahl watched them go. He shook his head in amazement. Lord Macht had said this was the only way, that the prophets would be man enough to do the job. They had been.

Someone groaned. Kamahl turned toward a section of stone wall that had blasted from the temple. The rock seemed to be breathing. A moan came from whatever beast was trapped beneath it.

Kamahl steeled himself with a breath and reached up to draw the Mirari sword. It was gone, of course, vanished from the world forever. "Good riddance." He still had his hands, despite broken fingers.

Kamahl marched across the temple plaza to the stone, which leaned up against another pile of rubble. He glimpsed a pair of hooves jutting out one side of the rock. The vision took him back to the Krosan Forest, to the tree where Seton's desiccated body had lain.

Reaching the rock, Kamahl peered beneath it, "How are you, Stonebrow, old friend?"

"Been better," came the rumbling reply.

Kamahl set his palms on the edges of the stone but did not shift it yet. "Anything broken?"

Stonebrow snorted. "Probably. I've almost gotten this slab off me twice, but it keeps rocking back and crushing a little more."

"All right then," Kamahl said, setting his teeth. "On three. One, two, three—"

They both shoved the stone. Massive and slow, the boulder shifted. It inched up away from the trapped centaur, rose onto its tip, and began to lean backward again.

"Push! Push!" Stonebrow roared.

Man and beast drove against the block, and it edged upward. The slab teetered then dropped, striking the plaza with a profound boom. The stone cracked in large wedges and fell apart.

Stonebrow kicked one. "Take that." He clambered to stand and swayed alarmingly.

"Whoa, there. Are you all right?"

Stomping, the giant centaur riffled his coat. "Of course I'm—" The words ended in a coughing fit.

Kamahl shook his head. "I bet you wish we'd never met, Bron of the Cailgreth centaurs."

"Hmmph." He looked around at the scoured mountaintop. "I could have been happy there in the woods, yes, but I'm a different creature now. There's no turning back."

Kamahl also stared at the desolation. "So, what next?"

Shrugging, Stonebrow said, "There's more folks to rescue, and I like the sound of the Gilded Mage. After that, it's the jagging way."

"The jagging way?"

Stonebrow placed a massive hand on the shoulder of his creator. "Come on, I'll show you. You walk where your eyes lead, and your feet, and your heart."

"Sounds erratic—"

"Jagging."

"—and kind of meaningless."

"No," Stonebrow said. "Meaning is like magic. When the gods are gone, it's everywhere."

THE HEALED WOUND

*I*n a mirror-world beneath a star-cluttered sky, there stood a castle of silver and glass. Within its highest courtyard, among its whitest lilies, Lord Macht appeared. He cradled a woman in his arms—a woman and a sword.

"Oh, Karona," he said tenderly, holding her against his gleaming breast. "You don't even begin to understand what's happened to you."

He knelt among the lilies, laid her on her side, and grasped the sword that jutted from her back. Closing his eyes, the silvery man gave a sudden, swift yank. The massive blade slid from her as from its own scabbard. Blood and magic mingled on it. He pivoted the blade down and rammed it deep into the garden path. It skirled on glassy stones then lodged in the ground, its hilt jutting waist-high.

Lord Macht stooped, looking at the silvery pommel. It glinted at him like a great eye. "So much trouble, just to understand . . . but now I do."

He turned to Karona, lying amid white flowers. She had been nearly cut in half by the sword, and blood and magic still streamed from her. She was beautiful, even dying.

Lord Macht knelt. He reached into his quicksilver breast and pulled out a hunk of flesh. With his other hand, he dragged another from the other side. The silvery man leaned over Karona and laid one gobbet on the wound in her back and the other on the wound in her front.

Closing his eyes, he whispered, "Be healed."

The silver flesh fused with her skin and transformed to take on its color and texture. The wounds knitted together. A wave of life radiated from the spot, sweeping across her. Flesh that had been bereft of blood received it again. She was subtly transforming, not just from death to life but from false life to true.

"There is a single reason that all of this has happened," the silver man said. He watched feverishly as the wave reached her shoulders. "The first stroke of the Mirari sword should have killed you, but it didn't. The touch of the First should have slain you, but it didn't. The Soul Reaper that unmade Akroma and Zagorka should have unmade you, but it didn't."

Her eyes opened slowly. Like a woman awakening from a sweet dream, she turned her head toward him. Her face was changed, the face not of Karona but of Jeska.

"You became the conduit for all magic on Dominaria, rose to become a goddess, and even survived the Mirari sword again . . . all for one reason."

"Macht," she said wearily. "I'm not a goddess, not anymore."

"No. You're a planeswalker."

Jeska blinked, and her eyes cascaded with memories. She clasped the silver man's fingers and clung tight. "I am truly like you, then."

"Yes," he replied gently. "I knew you would be. I knew that the Mirari sword would save Dominaria and save you."

Jeska searched his gleaming face, filled with her own reflection. "There's something more."

"Yes. It's time you knew: Lord Macht is not my true name."

"Then, who are you?"

"My name is Karn."

*   *   *   *   *

It would take awhile to learn. She had walked the Blind Eternities, of course, but she had never simply stepped world to world to world.

"Are you sure Argentum will be safe?" Jeska asked. She glanced fondly around the courtyard, elegant in silver and glass. "This place has become my home."

Karn gently took her hand. "We won't be gone long. Even if we were, the guardian will keep everything in order." He nodded toward a metal man who sat within the guardhouse.

Jeska smiled. "He's an ingenious creation, Karn, but he's only a machine."

"So was I, once. And he's more than a machine. The Mirari has suffused him. He's living metal, now." Karn cupped his hand beside his mouth and whispered. "He needs a chance to prove himself, and this is it. You need a chance, too."

"Is this the way?" Jeska asked tentatively, clutching Karn's hand and thinking of other worlds.

Karn nodded his encouragement. "Take me out there."

Jeska stepped from the mirror planes of Argentum, taking Karn with her.

They crossed the multiverse as easily as children stepping across stones.

Tales of Dominaria

LEGIONS
Onslaught Cycle, Book II
J. Robert King

In the blood and sand of the arena,
two foes clash in a titanic battle.

January 2003

EMPEROR'S FIST
Magic Legends Cycle Two, Book II
Scott McGough

War looms above the Edemi Islands, casting the deep
and dread shadow of the Emperor's Fist.

March 2003

SCOURGE
Onslaught Cycle, Book III
J. Robert King

From the fiery battles of the Cabal, a new god has arisen,
one whose presence drives her worshipers to madness.

May 2003

THE MONSTERS OF MAGIC
An anthology edited by J. Robert King

From Dominaria to Phyrexia, monsters fill the multiverse,
and tales of the most popular ones fill these pages.

August 2003

CHAMPION'S TRIAL
Magic Legends Cycle Two, Book III
Scott McGough

To restore his honor, the onetime champion of Madara must
battle his own corrupt empire and the monster on the throne.

November 2003

Legend of the Five Rings

The Four Winds Saga

Only one can claim the Throne of Rokugan.

WIND OF JUSTICE
Third Scroll
Rich Wulf

Naseru, the most cold-hearted and scheming of the royal heirs, will stop at nothing to sit upon the Throne of Rokugan. But when dark forces in the City of Night threaten his beloved Empire, Naseru must learn to wield the most unlikely weapon of all — justice.

June 2003

WIND OF TRUTH
Fourth Scroll
Ree Soesbee

Sezaru, one of the most powerful wielders of magic in all Rokugan, has never desired his father's throne, but destiny calls to the son of Toturi. Here, in the final volume of the Four Winds Saga, all will be decided.

December 2003

Now available:

THE STEEL THRONE
Prelude
Edward Bolme

WIND OF HONOR
First Scroll
Ree Soesbee

WIND OF WAR
Second Scroll
Jess Lebow

Capture the thrill of D&D® adventuring!

These six new titles from T.H. Lain put you
in the midst of the heroic party as it encounters
deadly magic, sinister plots, and fearsome creatures.
Join the adventure!

THE BLOODY EYE
January 2003

TREACHERY'S WAKE
March 2003

PLAGUE OF ICE
May 2003

THE SUNDERED ARMS
July 2003

RETURN OF THE DAMNED
October 2003

THE DEATH RAY
December 2003

The Minotaur Wars

From *New York Times* best-selling author Richard A. Knaak comes a powerful new chapter in the DRAGONLANCE® saga.

The continent of Ansalon, reeling from the destruction of the War of Souls, slowly crawls from beneath the rubble to rebuild – but the fires of war, once stirred, are difficult to quench. Another war comes to Ansalon, one that will change the balance of power throughout Krynn.

NIGHT OF BLOOD
Volume I

Change comes violently to the land of the minotaurs. Usurpers overthrow the emperor, murder all rivals, and dishonor minotaur tradition. The new emperor's wife presides over a cult of the dead, while the new government makes a secret pact with a deadly enemy. But betrayal is never easy, and rebellion lurks in the shadows.

The Minotaur Wars begin June 2003.